THE NOVELS OF GERALD WARNER BRACE

The Islands (1936)
The Wayward Pilgrims (1938)
Light on a Mountain (1941)
The Garretson Chronicle (1947)
A Summer's Tale (1949)
The Spire (1952)
Bell's Landing (1955)
The World of Carrick's Cove (1957)
Winter Solstice (1960)

Winter Solstice

A NOVEL

BY GERALD WARNER BRACE

W · W · NORTON & COMPANY · INC · New York

Darkness and light divide the course of time, and oblivion shares with memory a great part even of our living beings; we slightly remember our felicities, and the smartest strokes of affliction leave but a short smart upon us.

—*Thomas Browne*

⊸ş CHAPTER 1 ş⊷

No DAWN in East Compton. Night and morning the same.

Lights shone from windows, early cars and trucks rattled chains along glazed streets, suburban life moved and breathed, but darkness prevailed.

Longest night of the year.

A time of drizzle and freeze. Hard drops against the glass like whiffs of birdshot. At quarter of seven the mill whistle blew two notes of doom. At ten minutes of seven Mary Kyle Eustace reached a white hand and pressed the switch of her alarm. At nine minutes of seven she heard the slap of her father's straight razor, then a splash of water, then the gurgle and retch of the drain.

Time.

She was out on the cold floor, turning on the radiator, slamming down the window, staring for a grim moment at the outside dark, the gleaming black road, the lonesome yellow light above the intersection two hundred yards down. Hell frozen over, she thought. She stood on an oval braided rug and touched her toes eighteen times—a tall strong girl with prominent hips and long feet. "*Ein, zwei, drei—nicky, nocky, nye; nicky, nocky, nuss—duss, bis, druss. Ein, zwei, drei—what a damn fool am I.* Keeps you limber, keeps you young. Jesus."

Mary Kyle, who swore a good deal to herself, snatched up her underclothes and headed for the bathroom just as her father came out. "Happy winter solstice, Father," she muttered. "Or whatever they call it." He said nothing. He wore dark serge trousers and a shirt with no collar and a gold collar-button. In

7

the light from the open bathroom door his face looked like a mask of tragedy.

Four rooms on that floor, square bare rooms with the kind of furniture the Morgan Memorial deals in. In the southeast room Mary Kyle's father, Edwin Goodman Eustace, put on his semi-starched collar and tie and his dark vest and suit-coat. He wound his heavy gold Waltham watch and noted that it was eight minutes after seven: his face expressed satisfaction and even courage at the sight, and no longer suggested the mask of tragedy.

The southwest room was closed and silent, and would remain so until after ten: Patience Starrett Eustace slept there and since this was the first Monday of her vacation she felt a duty to indulge herself. She was a junior at the University.

The northwest room stood open and vacant—and of course still dark in this murky dawn: its tenant should have been Mortimer Crabb Eustace, but his college basketball team was playing in a tournament in North Carolina and he had decided to drive down and spend Christmas there with some of his team-mates. He had last been home at Thanksgiving.

As for the northeast room, that belonged to Mary Kyle Eustace, who was in the bathroom getting herself ready for the day's work at Allston Associates on Federal Street in Boston. The freezing rain still rattled against her windows.

Seven-fourteen. Mary Kyle descended the stairs, not lightly or quietly, but very fast, like an avalanche, bouncing at the bottom, then turning left through the dark living room to the lighted dining room where Edwin Goodman Eustace sat at the end of a white-clothed oval table with fried eggs, toast, and coffee before him. He had already finished his stewed prunes.

"Morning, Father. Morning, Mother." She poured coffee from the percolator and put two slices of bread in the toaster.

"You want eggs?" came her mother's voice through the passage from the kitchen.

"Fried? My God."

"I've got water boiling." A strong, explicit voice, full of anxiety.

"No, no eggs. Who could eat eggs on a day like this?"

"Well, cereal. You can have cream—" She appeared in the doorway, Josephine Starrett Eustace, tall and gaunt and terrible, holding a long spatula like a weapon in her right hand. Her mouth had a fierce twist to it as though she were about to shriek. "How about a slice of ham?"

Mary Kyle jumped up and slapped herself below the hips. "See that? That's me. That's good meat." She flipped open the toaster, turned her bread, and flipped it shut. The table rattled.

"Creamed potatoes," Edwin said, his voice sharply nasal and accented to mimic country dialect. "Three hundred and sixty-five mornings a year—creamed potatoes. And pork and beans and ham and chops—"

"And pie."

"Sure—pie!"

"And hot biscuits."

"Twice a day, hot biscuits—"

"And pounds of butter and quarts of cream."

"We needed it, I tell you. Work? Why, no young feller nowadays knows what work is. Seven hours a day just pushing buttons— that's what they call work. Sitting on their rumps on a spring cushion. Why, when I was twelve years old—"

"I plowed and harrowed and planted twelves acres of corn—" Her voice mimicked his and managed to sound like a well-known radio comedian's.

"Funny as hell," he muttered. "But it's a fact just the same." His face had strongly modeled bones, sunken cheeks, deep lines round the mouth.

Mary Kyle buttered her toast.

Josephine glared at them from the doorway. "Grandfather Starrett insisted on kippered herring. The old fish, he called it." Her voice was emphatic and loud. She pointed her spatula at the portrait over the oak sideboard.

"Old kippered Starrett," Mary Kyle said. "I bet he never plowed any acres."

"No, of course he didn't. He sat in his bank and admired his bags of money. But *his* father—"

"Mortimer," Mary Kyle said as though she applied a refrain to a ballad.

"Mortimer—he was a drover. He drove cattle over the roads from Greenfield to Boston—"

"Over the hill to the slaughterhouse."

"He was a wrestler too," Josephine went on relentlessly. "Six foot two, and the best wrestler in Hampshire County—"

"You going with me?" Edwin folded his napkin and stood up.

"Coming, Father." Mary Kyle gulped the last of her second cup and started for the door. "Save the next installment, Mother. How Mortimer rescued the beautiful heiress, how the grateful Squire Lawrence made him his trusted agent, how he married the lady and grew rich and respected." Her voice at the last came from the hall closet under the stairs where she rummaged for overshoes. The hall light hung so as to throw the closet in impenetrable darkness and she fumbled among boots and old roller skates.

They made ready with coats, mufflers, hats, mittens boots— and Edwin waited while Mary Kyle pounded up to her room in all her storm clothes to fetch her bag and throw the bed together and bundle her night things into the closet.

"You'd suppose," he said in his strong, nasal, up-country voice, "that a woman could figger this problem out—after a few years, that is. She gets herself rigged out like Tweedledum for the battle and then goes and makes her bed." No one was there to hear him but when Mary Kyle clumped down she gave him a quick grin.

"Patience, Father." She dove into the closet again and after a rattle of bats and rackets came out with an umbrella. "Remember, no tension, no anxiety, no ulcers. 'Bye, Mother. Stay home, keep the fires burning."

Josephine looked at them from the end of the hall.

"The shrieking of the mindless wind," she intoned, pronouncing the long i's with emphasis:

> The moaning tree-boughs swaying blind,
> And on the glass the unmeaning beat
> Of ghostly finger-tips of sleet.

Edwin raised a buckskin-mittened hand.

> There are strange things done in the midnight sun
> By the men who moil for gold:
> The Arctic trails have their secret tales . . .

"Not now, Father. My God, let's go. Let's break our necks quietly."

He stepped to the door with a glittery smile as though he could do much more if he tried, then bethought himself, took off a mitten and unbuttoned the layers of his coats and groped for the Waltham watch. "Seven forty-one *and* a half. Get out the skates, damn it all. We can't make it walking." He nodded with compressed satisfaction and rebuttoned himself. "What'll you bet they'll be all fouled up as usual. Whenever the wind blows north of east the whole goddam railroad breaks down."

"Beyond the circle of our hearth," Josephine continued from the end of the hall, "No welcome sound of toil or mirth . . ."

Out they went into the storm. Front steps like black glass, path and street glare except where car chains had crunched. They shuffled and slid along, leaning leftward into the wind, turning faces away from the blowing ice.

"For thirty-five years," he pronounced bitterly, "she's been getting mileage out of that damned poem." His nasal voice seemed to rise and fall in the gusts. "It's got so I can quote it myself. I never know what part goes where, but damned if I don't wake up in the middle of the night spouting some of those lines. 'All night long the storm roared on'—if I don't say it she will."

Mary Kyle made a loud derisive sound.

"Hey? What you say?"

"I say you better not talk about damned poems. You've been inflicting Sam McGee on us for at least thirty-five years—I'd a good sight rather wake up spouting *Snowbound* than that stuff."

"That stuff, she says. Honest-to-God drama with whiskers on it: none of your dear old aunt-with-a-smile-of-cheer. And thirty-five years—why you weren't even an idea then! You don't know a thing about thirty-five years."

"I know you first declaimed it at a college party—must be at least forty years—and you admired yourself so much you've been doing it ever since."

He hunched into his collar and spoke theatrically: "Talk of your cold! through the parka's fold it stabbed like a driven nail."

The morning had turned gray. Cars and trucks forced them to walk on the slippery edges. The sleet was half rain and a film of wet lay on the ice underfoot.

Three-quarters of a mile to the station, and a half-hour wait for a late train. Edwin crowded in among the ones standing inside, all patiently motionless, reading folded newspapers under yellow light, peering through cloudy windows and watching the empty track curving away into the murk.

Mary Kyle backed under the overhang on the lee side among the outdoor waiters, standing the way sheep stand in the shelter of a barn wall.

Winter dark and cold can be borne, she thought. All things endure.

The whistle came against the wind and the company stirred. Men with briefcases moved out and stood waiting. She didn't join her father again—he sat in the smoker with two or three friends who condemned the government, the taxes, the foreign policy, and all crackpots. She took a volume of Proust from her bag and read until they reached Boston.

Then the long morning march up the platform, the steady shuffle of booted and rubbered feet, the grim facing forward to the city, the queer silence of separate people moving shoulder to shoulder in a kind of daily oblivion. It seemed like night still under the platform roof, and yellow lights made whirls in the misty air. Sprays of rain blew in from the side. Diesels hummed or roared aloud. No one seemed to speak or show human feeling. They marched intently with closed faces.

Mary Kyle knew that her suitor was one step back of her left shoulder. She arranged her face—a cool smile. He always mentioned the day—good, bad, cold, hot—

"Kind of a dismal morning, eh? Did it freeze out your way?"

CHAPTER 2

EDWIN PUSHED ALONG step by step out of the car, nodded without expression to his cronies, and saw them no more. He marched in the silence, a slightly old-fashioned figure, tall but a little stooped, with a fusty dark-gray overcoat and a shapeless felt hat and bulky country rubbers on his feet. His leather mittens bulged from the side pockets of his coat. He carried a small satchel that contained chiefly a sandwich and a thermos bottle of coffee and the morning *Herald*.

In the station concourse he unbuttoned his coats, pulled out the gold Waltham and checked it with the clock on the end wall. He nodded once, put it away, and headed for the stairs to the elevated railway. They never built a better watch, he thought. The pieces of junk they put out now—they were just decorations. Bangles. His uncle Gordon had used it for forty years on the railroad—best watch on the line, he said.

Twenty-five minutes through the city and out to the university, standing in the packed car, swaying and pitching, roaring underground. Mostly he didn't think about it—no one thought about it. They hung and clutched and staggered through the stops and starts. But sometimes bitterness attacked him. He reckoned the hours, three a day, fifteen a week, seven hundred and fifty—damn near, at least—a year given up to fighting your way into the city and fighting your way home again. And thousands, millions, spent their lives at it. Civilization, it was called. Jesus.

Edwin Eustace was a positive man. He spoke with clenched fist or pointed finger; his cultivated up-country twang made a sound of finality. "I'm an old-fashioned bastard and proud of it," he said. He had a long jaw, sunken cheeks, a nose with a slight beaklike curve to it, pale grayish eyes that seemed usually blood-shot. He looked like a dour Uncle Sam, without whiskers. He made a symbol of his people in Starkville, Vermont—of his father, deacon, selectman, dairy farmer, who in old age fell from a hay-rick and broke his neck. He remembered his grandfather in the state legislature at Montpelier. He often remarked that the best advice he ever had was from Hez Applegate, who ran the store at Starkville Four Corners. Hez always said that there was no opportunity for a man up there in Vermont, unless all he wanted was to be free and honest; the smart ones naturally went away where they could hire out to somebody else and do work they didn't give a damn about. Hez was a hard-cider man, and full of funny stories, so naturally no one took him seriously; he stam-mered too—the more he stammered the funnier he was.

After the age of eighteen, Edwin Eustace had done no farming, and had quarreled irrevocably with his father and mother and sisters. He came to town first as a freshman at Tufts College, failed, tried again and passed, worked at a dozen jobs, graduated with a bachelor of science degree in engineering, took to drink, went to war as a second lieutenant, came back a captain, married Josephine Starrett, prospered in the Twenties, lost everything in the Thirties, took to drink again, prospered again during the war in the Forties, settled down afterward as supervisor of production in the Higgins Ball-Bearing Company, was abruptly fired when the company merged with a big corporation. At fifty-five he looked for a new job. He serviced and repaired washing machines. For three years he had been on the staff of Commonwealth University as assistant to the Superintendent of Buildings and Grounds. "Just a plain goddamned janitor is what it is. I better be thankful, I suppose. Nice cultural surroundings, doctors, deans, professors, student bodies. The damnedest fool thing I ever did was not to listen to Hez Applegate forty years ago."

At nine-five he left the car, dodged across the traffic to his build-ing, descended into the basement and unlocked the door of his office. No sense in being here today—the place was mostly closed and empty and as dismal as some sort of modernistic hell. He stared at the cement, the pipes overhead, the ranks of steel lockers diminishing down the shadowy corridors. The world, he told himself, is just about four-fifths hell—at a fair and conservative estimate.

The telephone rang. The dean's office was cold, someone said. Could he do something.

He opened the big drawer of his metal desk, took out the bottle and drank.

ᦞᦉ CHAPTER 3 ᦲᦞ

BACK HOME in East Compton Josephine Starrett Eustace sat on a hard rocking-chair in the southwest corner of the kitchen and read a book called *Mr. Scarborough's Family.* She was wholly absorbed in it and the frantic anxiety of her face had settled to an expression of judicious concentration. She looked like a scholar at work. Her thoughtful frown, steady eyes behind the formidable horn spectacles, her slightly pursed-up mouth, her wrinkled age and untidy white hair with streaks of rust, all gave her a severe intellectual aspect. In the gray light from the window near which she sat she looked like a Flemish painting. She sat for two hours with hardly a motion.

The breakfast dishes remained untouched on the dining room table, the butter, the cream, the remnants of egg and toast, the coffee cold in its pot. The cluster of light-bulbs still shone from above. The dim hall light also cut across the darkness of the open closet door, and in the kitchen a naked bulb shone down on the tall black gas range. A table in the center of the kitchen was stacked to the edges with dishes and pans. The sink counter along the south wall was also stacked. Except for the electric refrigerator in the corner near where Josephine was sitting, everything in the kitchen dated from the first twenty years of the century.

In the half light Josephine's face had a look of patrician wisdom and even beauty. All her features were austere and finely-cut. The net of settled wrinkles suggested years of trustworthy thinking. As it was now, in repose, contemplating Trollope, it was a face one would turn to for truth and understanding. Even the threads of rust in the pulled-back white hair implied a kind of authenticity.

You could see that she had once been young, had grown, aged, weathered, suffered, but in all essentials was the same person, unconcealed and unashamed.

She had been born and bred in the proudest tradition of plain living and high thinking. Her grandfather was in his time a Boston banker with a ten-acre estate on Warren Street in Brookline. Her Uncle Timothy Starrett had been president of Bedford College in Pennsylvania; her Aunt Martha had married Dr. Theodore Harvey, the authority on the brain. Her father, Charles Crabb Starrett, had collected valuable books, written a life of Lady Hester Stanhope, gone into debt, speculated on the stock market, lost everything. She was his only child, and had inherited nothing but the debts and legal confusions. But before the wreck she had graduated from Mount Holyoke with the highest praise and might have gone on to graduate school if the first World War had not involved her in what at that time was called canteen work. She went to France, met Lieutenant—later Captain—Eustace, resolved not to marry him or anyone, but did so as soon as they came home. By then her father's property had all gone—it actually went before the war started, but she had hardly noticed—and she possessed nothing.

But she remembered everything. Her family to the third and fourth generation were all present in her mind; she discussed the Starretts and Crabbs and Lawrences as though she had known them all, and even the branches and collaterals, the Fullers, Livermores, Cowleses, on and on without end. She knew that Mortimer Starrett was left-handed, that his favorite oath was "Great Jehovah," that he fell dead of a heart attack in his Batterymarch office (his "Chambers") on the last day of January in 1849. She kept in touch—chiefly by Christmas cards—with her cousins and second cousins, though she almost never saw them. She could recite pages of Whittier, partly because she considered him one of the family by reason of her great-uncle's marriage to the poet's cousin. She knew all about Harriet Livermore, another remote cousin, and how she proclaimed the Second Advent and was accepted as a prophetess among the nomads of Arabia—and of course it was her connection with Lady Hester Stanhope, a prophetess similarly mad, that led to Charles Crabb Starrett's biography.

Now, on this shortest day of the year, in the perfect silence of the storm-bound house, she read Trollope. She loved Trollope more than anything in the world, and had read him intensively, but there were volumes that she had never been able to get hold of. Whenever she scanned the long list of his titles the unknown ones beckoned like promised lands. Most of the time she lived in sorrow and desperation and those unread Trollopes were like the last little reserves of hope: *Ayala's Angel, Dr. Wortle's School, The American Senator*—some day she'd discover them and beguile herself in their world of humor and order and security. It seemed to her that no biographer or critic had ever spoken wisely enough about Trollope; in her mind as she read him she composed papers, she gave talks, on his wisdom, compassion, tolerance, candor, humor—on his clairvoyant understanding of the claims of convention on the one hand and revolt on the other, the social necessities and the individual rights. No other English writer, she told her audiences, not Fielding or Jane Austen or Thackeray—certainly no modern—could create a character like Mr. Scarborough, that shrewd, unscrupulous, cynical, altogether human country gentleman: a Russian might have done it—old Karamazov was such a one—but except for Trollope the English were all too self-righteous. She had the greatest respect for Jane Austen—since the age of fourteen she had been a devoted reader, she was in fact a lifelong Janeite, but nothing annoyed her more than the priggish critics who praised Jane at the expense of Trollope, as though he were an inferior imitation. The fact was that with all her skill Jane was actually a provincial snob with the narrowest of human sympathies; whereas Trollope . . .

A small thump and shuffle right over her head announced the rise of Patience. Ten-fifteen. Josephine looked round at the choked and cluttered kitchen without seeing any of it, read two more paragraphs, then folded her spectacles into the book, put it on top of the pile of canned goods on top of the refrigerator near her chair, and went to fetch the coffee-pot in the dining room. As she returned with the pot and some of the dishes her mouth twisted and crookedly opened again as though it tried to conceal a chronic pain. There was hardly room for the dishes anywhere in the kitchen but she managed to balance them on a pile in the sink; then she struck a match and lighted a gas burner and turned it as low as possible under the coffee.

Patience, aged twenty-one, was lighter and less muscular than her sister Mary Kyle, and somewhat prettier in the fashion of modern girls, but made the same kind of noise coming down stairs—even though she wore sneakers. It was a family habit to thump up and down stairs. "No mail?" she cried.

She had on blue wool slacks and a blue jersey, and her blonde hair waved prettily round her neck—both girls described their hair as dirty blonde, but Mary Kyle's had some reddish tones and Patience's was caramel.

"Why, it's like perpetual night," she chattered. "I thought my clock was crazy—why, it's hardly light yet, and fog, rain, ice— I've simply got to get my shopping done—Beth's awful party is tomorrow and Wednesday's the play—"

"You can't shop in trousers," Josephine said.

"Well—I looked out and saw all that sleet and stuff. I don't know—maybe it won't look so bad when I put some coffee in me. I mean, if I don't get to town today—it'll probably all turn to rain anyway: did anyone listen to the weather? It's always snow changing to rain except in the interior suburbs. Are we an interior suburb? In a real storm it's all right to wear slacks—everybody does. But what's happened to Mike this morning—do you think he broke his neck?"

"Oh, Christmas mail," Josephine said. "They come round in trucks—"

"Christmas! I haven't done a thing. What do people all want, anyway? I must say, it gets to be more of a panic every year— why, the city will be an inferno—I mean the mobs."

She had her coffee, two cups, and toast, and a doughnut Josephine had specially saved and toasted for her, but she hardly noticed what she had. She talked lightly and nervously, without seeming to listen to the banalities of her own chatter.

Josephine had poured out the last of the coffee for herself and was sitting rigidly erect and sipping it. "I used to think," she finally said, "that you learned all this cynicism from your father. Goodness knows, he's bad enough." Her voice had an explicit emphasis. As she spoke, she recognized the quality of each word. "But it's the way everyone goes on—it's like a virus you've all caught. Be cynical, be ironic, talk in wisecracks—"

"Mother—for heaven's sake!"

"Oh, I can't do anything about it, any more than I can about the popular music or the television shows or any of the horrors we have to endure. Vulgarity is a disease I have no control over—except that I can try to keep out of sight and hearing of some of it."

Patience, hardly listening, glanced at her wrist watch.

"But so much of the vulgarity is simply the face of hypocrisy," Josephine went on, not in anger or disgust, but with the careful speech of reflection. "All the people who advertise, they are calculating liars and deceivers—and what you young people watch and listen to is the product of the same commerce of deception."

The last somewhat oratorical phrase seemed to get through to Patience. She looked up with a faint flush. "Mother, what *are* you griping about?"

"I've given up on the world, goodness knows," Josephine went on. "But I still hope my own family will learn some honest values. It's what we inherited and it's what I've tried to keep alive—" The articulate voice suddenly stopped.

Patience made a small theatrical gesture of hopelessness. "I can't think what in the world I could have said to start this—this lecture. I know you don't ever approve of anything I do or say but I really don't see why you have to pick this godawful dismal morning to jump on me."

Josephine sat up straighter and took a sustaining breath. When she spoke her tone was strongly rational. "You mustn't take things so personally, child. I'm not thinking as much about you as an individual as I am about the world you live in. All I want you to do is to see it and think about it for what it is—I mean the organized hypocrisy and ugliness that we are supposed to accept and admire. I wasn't brought up to believe in the devil, but if I did I'd have not the slightest doubt that he personally writes and produces the cigarette ads. Of all the utterly diabolic—"

Patience clutched her hair with both hands. "Mother! For Pete's sake—I don't write the cigarette ads. I don't give a damn about them—in fact I think they are perfectly foul. I don't know why you go on saying I accept and admire or whatever it is—"

"I don't—and I wish you'd listen to me instead of jumping to conclusions. But actually I can't tell what you do admire. You and that university crowd of yours—what do you believe in? Your only idea of humor is to be cynical about everything—you do as little work as possible—you talk about how they cheat on papers as though it was the smart thing to do. And the parties and drinks and wild affairs—"

Patience groaned again. "I still don't see why we have to go into all this on the first Monday of my vacation—but I'll tell you one thing: you don't really know anything about it. You sit home here in this dismal house day and night, you never see anyone, you read Trollope—you haven't the faintest idea what it is to have to live in the world. It's easy to talk about hypocrisy and all that, but if you were eighteen or twenty-one and out there in the middle of it you wouldn't go on that way." Her voice had taken on some of the explicit tone of her mother's. They stared at each other with similar expressions.

"Well, I'd just like to know," Josephine said very quietly, "what you do believe in—what you think is worth living for."

Patience carefully marked the white cloth with the edge of a spoon. "I'll tell you—if you really want to know. I believe in survival."

A silence followed in which they took note of what she had said.

Josephine spoke first. "That's what apes and tigers believe in."

"So do bugs." It was an effort for Patience to say it lightly and her voice almost cracked.

"Do you learn that in college? Is that what they teach?"

"Oh, God no. I mean, it all depends. They teach everything. Physiology, psychology—instincts, reflexes, habits of rats—sure. But they pour on the ideals too—stuff like social responsibility, duty, the nature of virtue, even God. This philosophy I'm taking is nothing but what is God and as far as I'm concerned the whole thing is twaddle. All you do is tell him what he tells you and you get a B. If you smile sweetly and make like an angel you get an A."

A twist of pain seized Josephine's face and she looked for an instant like a caricature of misery. Then she drew a deliberate breath and spoke out. "I don't believe you mean just survival—just that, like a toad buried in stone for centuries. You're only talking—it's part of your act . . ."

Patience shrugged as though she preferred not to argue.

"You have feelings and hopes," Josephine went on, "just like anyone, but I think you're afraid to say so—you're afraid you'll be disappointed. Nothing counts, you say—nobody wins, nobody loses, nobody cares. I believe it's just plain cowardice—or it would be if you were older. I suppose I shouldn't get so impatient with youngsters—but my goodness, you're twenty-one already. At eighteen my great aunt Margaret Crabb married James Murdock and they went west in a covered wagon and a week after she gave birth to her son in the Wasatch Mountains Murdock was killed by the Indians—but she made it to California and she ran a hotel in San Francisco and that boy, that Jim Murdock born in a covered wagon, he got to be governor of the state of Oregon."

"Cheers for cousin Jim," Patience muttered in a tone of half-suppressed insolence.

"And Grandfather Cowles," Josephine went on. "Thirty years in Nigeria—if his letters were ever published, as they should be, he'd be recognized as the Albert Schweitzer of his time—"

Patience stood up so abruptly that her chair almost tipped over. "Will you please stop ramming your damned old family down my throat!" Her voice shook and the color flamed in patches on her face. "I just can't stand it. I'm so fed up with all these pioneers and missionaries and pious stuffed shirts I could scream. I don't *care* about them. They may have been as godly and noble as all get-out, but they aren't me and I'm not they. Why don't *you* get out and do something noble, for heaven's sake—why do you keep nagging at me about it?" Her voice failed for a moment. "I realize I'm a terrible disappointment to you—we all are, apparently. But I honestly think if you didn't coop yourself up here and *brood* all the time you'd be better off—you might understand us a little better. Why, my heavens, you aren't even realistic, you don't know any more about the facts of modern life than Alice in Wonderland—all you do is act like we were all going to hell—" She broke off, choked, stood for a moment in silence. "I'm sorry," she whispered. "I—I—" She turned away with a rush of tears and went upstairs.

When she came down a half-hour later Josephine was still sitting at the table with a cup of cold coffee before her. She took a swallow of it.

Patience had on a woolen dress, outer coat, overshoes. "I thought

I'd better go in town," she said quietly. "I won't have time later. Anything you want?"

"Haven't you got a hat, child?"

"Oh, I'll take an umbrella. It's just raining now. Anything I can do?"

"Well—" Josephine got up and rummaged among some newspapers piled on the radiator. "There's this. What do you think?" She pointed to an advertisement of a corduroy smoking jacket, $16.95. "I haven't a thing for your father except those wool socks, and I thought maybe if he had this he'd wear it instead of that terrible old sweater—"

"Father—in that?" Patience's voice rose sharply, then checked itself. "Well, golly—I don't know. Maybe he would. But not *lilac*, for heaven's sake. Gray and dark blue—shall I get one?"

Josephine had gone to the kitchen cabinet and returned with two ten-dollar bills. "Size forty long," she said. "Gray, do you think?"

"Well, a good dark blue would be nice on him. Why don't I wait and see which is prettier—okay?"

"And the change is for you—do something with it; get a good lunch at least."

Patience turned away, fumbling in her purse. "See you around six. I—I didn't mean to make all that fuss. I'm sorry—I—maybe it's this awful weather. And *please* let us do up the dishes—I mean Kyle and I can perfectly well do them tonight."

In the silence she went out.

Josephine carried some things into the kitchen. She picked up her Trollope and held it for a minute. Then she looked round, taking stock. She had once had a system about dishes: they were rinsed and stacked after each meal, and washed twice a week, but after a time it seemed simpler to wait until no more clean ones were available. Usually it was possible to wash a few as they were needed, leaving the basic stockpile stacked on tables and counters, and for most of the time she was not aware of them at all.

But now she saw them. She felt the hot-water tank, relighted the gas heater under it, and began burrowing into the sink. Four hours later she was still at it. Her face was crossed with lines of fatigue and her mouth was partly open in a crooked twist. She looked more than ever like a caricature of desperation.

⤐ CHAPTER 4 ⤏

MORTIMER CRABB EUSTACE had always been called Buzz by family and local friends, though in his newer life at Wyndham College he was known as Mort. He had been a large, strong baby, and the Buzz was a modification of Buster, a detail that he concealed when he went to college. He also concealed his middle name—the whole thing embarrassed him, in fact; he wished they had called him John.

But it was a matter he hardly dared speak of to his parents. All the fancy middle names meant too much to them, and then of course the death of his two brothers was something they had never got over. Buzz understood almost subconsciously that the illusion of family continuity meant more to them than anything: his mother specially was sustained by her dream of the passing-on of virtue and love from generation to generation like the apostolic succession. Her oldest child had been Charles Lawrence, and the name was the emblem of all her hope. When he was twelve he broke through the ice of Powderhouse Pond and drowned. Buzz was barely five at the time and remembered it like a dream. He had tumbled down the cellar stairs and cut his forehead and when they dressed him in his best clothes and took him to the funeral service he thought it had something to do with his fall down the stairs and his injured head. He knew that something terrible had happened, and felt that he must be guilty. His other brother, Edwin Goodman, had died earlier, when Buzz was too young to understand, but Mary Kyle remembered all about it and had told him that it was during a polio epidemic. The two names, Charles and Edwin, were spoken frequently enough in the house—specially

Charles, who at twelve had had a memorable character: Josephine talked of him quite explicitly, and assumed that he embodied all the inheritance of integrity and competence from both sides of the family. Without intending to, she held him up to the others as the ideal of Starrett and Eustace virtue. But of course the circumstances of his death were not spoken of directly: only, in the skating season a palpable anguish made itself felt in the house, and they tried to keep news of other accidents from Josephine.

It was partly because of all this that Buzz played basketball. He also grew tall, had big hands, and devoted more effort and time to it than to anything else he had ever done. In the summers he had worked as a stockroom boy in a big department store, where he could toss things about as though they were basketballs—at least he pretended to; sometimes he was reprimanded for it. But everyone referred to him as a good kid. When he grinned his mouth almost touched his ears; he was homely in a picturesque fashion, with sandy hair cut very short and bony features and the overgrown look of a setter puppy.

That he had gone to Wyndham College was mostly due to Josephine's ambition, and the fact that her second cousin Albert Livermore was an assistant director of admissions. She assumed that her family had claims on Wyndham; she made it known that her Uncle Timothy Starrett was one of the celebrated class of '88. What she didn't recognize was the fact that Wyndham needed better basketball players, though naturally they never said so, and when Buzz was named for his league's all-star team, Wyndham admitted him on the basis of his character and all-round abilities. No claims were made for his excellence as a scholar, but he passed his courses. "He can throw the bull," his father said. "He takes after me—he hates to work, he'd rather fool round with a basketball any day than read a book, but he can bluff it through. He gets by just the way I did. The trouble is you can't live just by fooling with a basketball. He's never learned one damn thing that'll do him any good making a living."

Actually Buzz was the only one of the family who didn't visibly worry. His life seemed to be the easiest sort of self-indulgence. As long as he played his game he sustained himself in health and pride and the esteem of his fellows. He slept soundly and his appetite was enormous. He had simple tastes, cared nothing about clothes or social display, drove a sixteen-year-old car, was willing to work at any job that turned up, looked upon all the functions of life prosaically and unimaginatively. He was infinitely good-natured.

The family knew that he had a girl to whom he was more or less faithful, a Carol Rosen, whom they all referred to as Lollipop. "What they both are is normal," Mary Kyle said—it was she who first applied the name of Lollipop. "Whatever Norman Rockwell paints, that's Buzz and Lollipop. Any *Reader's Digest* piece about the state of American Youth—that's Buzz and Lollipop. What ails modern youth? Nothing. Look at Buzz and Lollipop. Normal. Healthy. Uncomplicated. Devoted to sports, comic-books, hot dogs. Not a brain in their two heads."

It was Josephine's belief that Buzz was actually a latent intellectual, and that as soon as he found himself he would go on to graduate school and become a scholar. She scolded Mary Kyle for her arrogance, and pointed out that Buzz was getting a B in at least two courses. "The trouble with you girls is you think you're too smart—you don't realize that a boy takes longer to grow up. Look at the size of him." When he finished playing basketball, she said, and outgrew Lollipop, then he'd really come into his own.

But the fact of his being away at Christmas troubled her. It had never happened before. He'd be lonesome and homesick, she thought. She and the girls had sent off a box of presents and fruitcake.

"I expect he'll have the time of his life," Mary Kyle said. "Southern hospitality and all."

Josephine spoke sharply. "I wish you didn't have to be so *cynical*. A girl of twenty-eight, my goodness—it's time you outgrew it."

"Twenty-nine, Mother. Let's face the facts."

ᴗᔰ CHAPTER 5 ᔰᵇ

Mᴀʀʏ Kʏʟᴇ's sᴜɪᴛᴏʀ was Harold Chivers, and in the afternoon he lay in wait at the station. She saw his tall figure by the gate, the stiff hat in a horizontal position on his head, the gray tweed coat with a half belt in back, the green wool scarf showing above the collar, the gloves, the briefcase. She saw the twinkle of his thick spectacles. His face seemed perfectly white and as thin as if it had been cut out of cardboard, with sharp angles at the nose and chin. His smile made a V, like a line drawing for a cartoon.

He raised his hat and bowed slightly from the waist.

"Well, Miss Eustace," she said, "and how are *we* this darkest evening of the year?"

His face expressed polite inquiry for a moment, then responded with zeal. "In the best of health, thank you—quite blooming, in fact; quite—er—beautiful, if we may say so."

"Oh, Harold—how reckless you are!" Her smile was actually beautiful. Her rather austere face was transformed into brightness and sweetness.

He gazed at her with intense pleasure. "Oh, not at all—not in the least; I'm the very model of cautious conservatism, as you so frequently tell me. I have a most literal mathematical mind."

His eagerness before her was childlike. She could see that he was quite happy.

Her face sobered at once. He was a problem. He seemed to live in a state of dedicated innocence. He operated as simply and transparently as a big doll, with perfectly rational intelligence and all the small virtues. There was something absolute about him— his cleanness, tidiness, preciseness, his devotion to duty, to good

27

manners, to the routines of respectable living. She mocked him and scorned him, but every now and then his whole formidable character astonished her. The stiff horizontal hat was a deliberate statement of principle. Come the deluge, the revolution, the holocaust, she would expect Harold Chivers to remain faithful to his code. But she couldn't stand his shirts and ties, the white starchy collars and cuffs with gold links, the silk ties with patterns —all selected by his mother: even on Saturdays and holidays he dressed like something in a clothing-store window. The thought of his socks and underwear made her shudder.

Would she allow him to sit with her, he modestly asked as they walked to the train. There were many shoppers as well as commuters but he hoped they'd find a seat together . . . perhaps the bad weather—the rain—though it seemed to be clearing and turning colder—they couldn't count on a real white Christmas, of course, but it would be nice—

"I wish you wouldn't keep saying things like *real white*," she said viciously.

"Oh? Why not?" He smiled again as though she had been playful.

"It's illiterate, that's why not. Didn't they teach you better in college?"

"Well, of course, I didn't take much English—"

"English! It isn't English, it's just common decency. It's elementary manners."

He laughed as though he relished her wit but an expression of resolute logic came over his sharp features. "I seem to remember that the chief purpose of language is to transmit thought clearly and accurately. Now—"

"Stuff! Academic twaddle! It's the sort of huffing and puffing professors do to earn a living. Maybe the purpose of your mathematics is to be accurate—but language, my God! Is a girl's dress meant to protect her from the weather? What's music being accurate about? Do you mean to tell me that the only thing Shakespeare does is to transmit accurate thought?"

"Well, surely he—"

"Will you kindly tell me what the hell Blake meant when he said the stars threw down their spears and watered heaven with their tears? Accurate thought my foot!"

"Well, perhaps—"

"And don't tell me it isn't good. I can't explain what it means, but it's the best damn poem in the English language."

His V smile was as wide as it could be; he moved his head with great appreciation. "Of course you know I don't understand poetry very well—not advanced poetry, that is. As you point out, mathematics is my field—"

"Well that's just too bad, because when you talk about your *real white* Christmas you're simply making incompetent poetry. It's what I'm trying to tell you."

"Oh, of course we can't all be as artistic as you are."

She seethed. "Harold, for God's sake—do you have to be such a fish?"

In the last car there were seats.

"Forgive me," she said. "I have a mean streak in me. All the Eustaces do. It comes out specially in bad weather."

He nodded with pleasure at her wit. "I wanted to ask you if you and perhaps some of your family would care to hear the *Messiah* at our church this Wednesday evening. We have a very capable director, you know, and they are getting professional soloists. I'm sure you would enjoy it—I mean, I presume you approve of the *Messiah*; I understand it is regarded as one of the great masterpieces—"

Mary Kyle laughed. "I'd better approve, hey? If I said I thought it was a bore you'd think I was kidding you anyway."

"Oh, I appreciate how much you enjoy irony," he said approvingly.

She was silenced for a minute. She stared at the lights going by in the gloom outside. There was at least something reliable about his obtuseness, she thought; you could always count on him to mean well, like an unusually upright child. There might, of course, be hidden darkness—the modern view of character was entirely based on the premise of the hidden darknesses, and the fact that Harold at the age of thirty-five still lived with his parents in South Compton implied the worst about him. They all three seemed to exist in a state of changeless and literal virtue, without experience of sin, and she had been taught that nothing could be more deadly. She eyed his profile and imagined him in the black vestments and steeple-crowned hat of the puritans. Young Goodman

Chivers.

He smiled boyishly and she laughed—at her fancies. He had asked her to his house to a meal now and then, and they all behaved like good children with party manners. The food. The weather. The seasons. The basement bargains at Filene's. The new cars. The bad train service. Harold held her chair. His father mumbled grace. His mother deprecated the plain fare: she seemed just like him—kindly and simple-minded and literal and quite happy. His father taught mathematics at Compton High, and had the same angular profile. In the summer he grew roses.

"It's at seven-thirty," Harold said, "but unless the weather is very bad we should be there by seven. People come from all over —it is considered very fine, really." He glanced to see if she laughed; he was all ready to smile. She seemed to be brooding. "Perhaps your folks would enjoy going too. I'll come in my car, of course, and there'll be plenty of room."

The old four-door Chevrolet, always in the best of condition. The cautious and reliable progress from house to church and church to house.

"Father wouldn't be hired to sit through the *Messiah*," she said. "I wouldn't dare mention it to him."

"Well, I'm sure your mother—"

"Oh, Mother—she hasn't been anywhere in ten years. If I could just throw her out of the house, I would—but she won't budge. All she does is read Trollope."

He took it to be a jest and smiled appropriately. "How about your sister?"

"Patience? My lord—we won't lay eyes on Patience from now to Christmas morning, or more likely noon. Not that we don't all appreciate being asked, but I'm afraid we just aren't *Messiah*-minded. My brother Buzz, incidentally, enjoys singing, but he's off in North Carolina."

"Well, but you," he said eagerly. "After all, it was you that I specially had in mind."

"I know."

"Oh, I'm certain you'd find it very rewarding."

"I know."

His church was the Walnut Avenue Baptist in Waltham, where his parents had been married, a yellow brick byzantine structure with complicated oak-beamed vaulting over the main crossing. She thought of herself there among the well-dressed Christmas folk, and the spruce boughs and the ropes of ivy and the candles, and the vested choir massed in the chancel, the pink cheeks and open mouths giving forth endless allelulias. She'd need a hat, of course—the dreadful little mustard one, inevitably, unless she could snitch one of Patience's; and gloves rather than mittens. Miss Eustace, she said to herself, tasteful in a brown wool from Filene's basement, with mustard accessories. And Mr. Chivers in pin stripes attending studiously to the endless allelulias, and all of them obediently rising at the last chorus and acknowledging the glory of God.

"Yes," she said, gathering her bag and mittens and umbrella, "I'll come. Thank you very much. I'll ask Mother but she won't budge."

As she walked away she felt him still bowing and smiling behind her.

She nodded to several who got off. No sign of Father. Darkness prevailed but the platform and streets glistened with wet. Colder. Crystals of ice in the puddles—she tried an experimental slip on a smooth surface. Taxis and cars roared off, footsteps faded in other directions, she was alone in the outskirts of East Compton walking northward uphill on a black road, being careful not to slip.

Three-quarters of a mile, day or night, rain or shine, forever. First a cluster of stores: Narragansett Ale, Seal-Test, Holsum Vita-Bread. Then a straggle of houses each with a splash of Christmas lights—an occasional outdoor tree in a blaze of red and green and blue. Taverns, drugstores, and Christmas trees. Far off to her left, toward the center of East Compton, the sky glowed as though the town were afire. A sober and worshipful *Messiah* was what she needed.

The road cut away from town into darkness—or seemed to. Actually there were lights here and there, but the town dwindled to vacant lots and small gardens where tomatoes and celery and rhubarb were grown in summer for the market. In the cold and dark it was a waste land of broken fences, withered vines, sheds, abandoned cars, mean houses. Italians lived there, and produced enormous quantities of tomatoes in a small space. In spring and fall, in the afternoon light, with leaves and grass covering all, in the sweet and temperate air, the way often seemed pleasant. But now it was more like a frozen purgatory with ice underfoot and wind pressing down from the north and rustling in the dead vines and burdocks. It was one of the times when she thought, day after day, day after day, and week after week without end. They all made jokes about the grind, the weary round, the treadmill to oblivion, but the truth of it sometimes came over her like a suffocation. You trained, you prepared, you took care of body and soul—all for what? For commuting daily to Boston and working for a bunch of money-making charlatans?

There was some little pleasure in being dutiful. What she earned sent Buzz to Wyndham—though he didn't know it. Maybe he would find life's secret—at least he would involve himself in wife and children. He had simple instincts—which is all anyone needs, she had always thought. The normal animal seldom bothers himself with questions. That's why she tried to touch her toes eighteen times every morning—why she slept and ate and preserved herself from colds in the head. Life had to be lived.

To be candid, though, she had some illusions still about her looks. She saw herself as fair—and even queenly: she was tall and fine, on occasion she could carry herself splendidly, and her face had the strong bones and fine modeling that could be called striking—or distinguished—or even regal. She would look well on platforms, in reception lines, opening a grand ball. She would wear expensive gowns to conceal her hips and display her wide-apart breasts, and her hair would curl and shine like red gold. And of course he would be at her side—not as a king, because after all the whole regal illusion was silly, but simply as her opposite self, her complement and other half. He was a celebrated character, he would speak and be applauded.

No one in the course of a day's living was more rigorously practical than Mary Kyle. She terrorized her office mates, male and female, by her competence and her scorn of folly and human weakness. She seemed to be always on the far side of experience, ahead of the others, full of the knowledge they should have had all along. She entertained them with candor. She discouraged sentiment and kept all males well away from her. The illusions of sex amused her, not grimly or self-righteously, but as evidence of the hilarious childishness of mankind. But she was in love.

A part of her was, at least—the part that brooded as she walked in the dark, tired after a day's fruitless work, questioning the predicament of being alive. He was John Rossiter, not yet celebrated or applauded, nor expecting to be, but in her view of him deserving of much honor. No one in the world knew how she felt; she hardly permitted herself to know, and satirized her own schoolgirl dreams. But some part of her responded to him as though he were a magnet: the sound of his voice, the shape of his hat, even his dusty old car, pulled at her vitals, made her aware of tears behind her eyes.

⚜ CHAPTER 6 ⚜

HE LIVED a couple of blocks nearer the center of town in a house even shabbier than theirs. His wife was known in the neighborhood as a competent practical nurse, though she was criticized for not taking enough care of her house and children. She was plain, even crude and tactless, and took a somber view of life.

Mary Kyle used to see them at church, where John Rossiter played the organ and directed the choir; sometimes they met for special rehearsals at his house, which were the only times she had been there. For a good many years she had been the one reliable contralto. It was the sort of church that scraped along on small income and not much religion; the social amenities were unpretentious and pleasant. The choir consisted of anyone who cared to join it—but few did, partly because John Rossiter was very fierce.

He intended to be tactful, he respected the sensibilities of sopranos and contraltos, he was almost ludicrously humorous and diplomatic, he talked always with such a metaphorical flourish that no one could clearly follow him, but he rehearsed his amateur singers as though every performance were a celebrated musical event. "It's all very well to make joyful noises unto the Lord, but whoever said it let us in for a good deal of sound and fury. It's a good thing, no doubt—in its place—but it isn't Bach, not as I understand it, anyway, and what we have here is Bach, or so it says on the printed sheets. Not that being joyful isn't a whole lot nicer than being doleful—that isn't the point, I suppose. The *point* is that you've got two things to control here—tempo and tone. Now . . ."

Those who could stand him at all got along well, but they had to be patient. "If he'd only say what he means and be done with it—but half the time you don't know what he's talking about." He kept at them and kept at them, smiling, tactful, allusive, always unsatisfied. "A man who won't compromise will get snapped off at the base—I believe that's one of the themes in Sophocles, is it not? It isn't so much a matter of accepting imperfection as it is of being aware that two perfections can't tolerate each other—they are simply incompatible, like a virtuous husband and wife who can't stand one another. But even so—even if compromise is the last resort of wisdom—you keep in your mind the ideal and the vision—"

"My God," Letty Hirsch used to whisper. "The man is too deep for me. He just doesn't make sense—he sounds like a professor." She carried the sopranos, not by musical skill but a loud voice.

But he persisted, Sunday after Sunday, with smiles, philosophical jokes, and infinite good will. Mary Kyle was in a way hypnotized by him, the eager leaps of his mind into metaphorical space, the absurd adventurousness of his imagination. He was like a small boy cavorting on a ridgepole. "Here we are with an awareness of the most exalted austerity on the one hand—was it Browning who said three notes make a star?" He grinned. He waved his left hand. "And here we have our beloved public, our friends and relations, who desire nothing so much as a continued diet of chocolate marshmallow. Do we choose between the highest and lowest manifestations of Sunday?" His grin made him seem like a boy because of the gaps in his teeth. "My own feeling is that if we do it at all we'd better do what in other circumstances would be called our damnedest: here no doubt it is our blessedest. God knows we can't do it very well but even if we get a B for effort we'll feel better about it. I mean . . ." Actually he never stopped. He simply went on. He wasted time. He defined great visions and achieved very small results. The choir always sounded like a group of eager amateurs in a small suburban church, which is what they were.

The cause of love is seldom known. It may not have been his talk that won her heart, any more than the spaces between his teeth when he smiled. She was emotionally aware of his shabby, rumpled clothes, the frayed edges, the shirt collar that never seemed to have been ironed, the button showing above the knot of the tie. She admired the theory of his clothes, their strength and comfort and even their style, and his indifference to them both pleased and annoyed her. His ties seemed to her beautiful in color and pattern, but badly tied. His shoes always suggested vigor and much walking in the open, but they were never shined and never new. In his rough and shabby carelessness he was the exact opposite of her friend Harold Chivers, but even the thought of his socks and underwear gave her pleasure. The main thing was that in her view of him, at least, he was a genuine man: it didn't much matter what he wore or didn't wear.

It was perfectly futile to think these thoughts, it was the sort of stupidity she mocked. That the one emotional pull of her life should be to a shabby little married man who played the organ in church was one of those fatal dirty tricks that life arranged for the knowing ones. "You," she said, "*you* have the nerve to laugh at the damned fools you have to associate with. Jesus!" Mary Kyle was not given to looking at herself in mirrors, but at these times she examined her image with contempt. Here is a practically middle-aged biddy with a hellish disposition, she said, eating her heart out, pining away, mooning and weeping and dithering—my God!

But of course he wasn't just a shabby little man or even a Sunday organ player. She defended him. She knew he was a hero, a fighter, a preposterous martyr, with the strength and courage of a heraldic lion. In the flow of his poetic talk he had let out a good deal about himself and his life. He had a Ph.D. in psychology— which he kept implying was four-fifths an academic racket: "Laboratory science my foot! You remember Sherlock Holmes thought he was a lot smarter than other folks because he had counted the steps up to his place and they hadn't, but what in the name of Jehovah is the sense of wasting your wits counting steps? But compared to a lot of graduate students I used to know, Sherlock was as profound as Socrates. They'll write two-hundred-page theses, with graphs and charts, on the correlation of eye-blinks and heartbeats with due allowance for age, sex, environment, and color of hair. Why I wrote a thesis myself—well, I won't tell you what it was, but I consider it exactly as useful to mankind as last year's telephone book. I took it pretty damn seriously, too—I had every intention of being a respectable scholar and all, but one day I woke up and said the hell with it."

What he did was to work as executive secretary, as they called it, for the Children's Aid Association. His pay was low, his hours of work continued day and night. He dealt, sometimes physically, with human evil in every form, in and out of tenements, schools, police courts, jails, alleys, taverns, and, as he often noted to point a moral, behind the façades of respectability. He never spoke of any of it in plain detail, but used allusions and illustrations. "I swear the boy had a blade down his pants legs *that* long and he swore if it was the last thing he did he'd get his old man—well, you can't argue morally at that point, specially when you have a pretty good hunch that's what the old man deserved. I tell you this, if I didn't get in a little pious anthem music on a Sunday morning I'd probably go and murder someone myself."

She knew just where his offices were in Haymarket Square; she could walk within sight of them to and from the station, though he came and went so irregularly she never expected to see him. As like as not he'd be driving an orphan boy off to Vermont or Maine, or he'd be in a police court somewhere. "Judges," she could hear him say, "seem to retain occasional seeds of humanity, but God preserve us from prosecutors and lawyers and all the minor officials in the house of justice." Whenever she did see him on other days than Sunday he was in motion. He scurried with clothes not quite buttoned and hat on the back of his bushy head; in good weather no hat at all. Nearly always a pipe, used theatrically or argumentatively or as a baton.

Once on a spring morning when she had been late and running for a train he stopped in his car—a dust-covered and noisy Ford. "I won't apologize for it," he said at once, opening the door for her. "I consider it the most miraculous heap of junk ever assembled. Sixty-five thousand miles in three years; nor snow nor sleet nor anything—just push over all this stuff on the seat and rest your bones easy, as my grandmother used to say. Will Haymarket suit you, or do you insist on making the train?"

She sat there staring at his strong brown hands on the wheel. She was suddenly inside his environment. She felt the energy of the car, the rush of it, the turns and darts, the certainty; it was

like being in a taxi, except that his own stuff was scattered about
—books, maps, bag, hat, pipe. She smiled prettily and heard herself
say it was a lovely morning, but for all she could tell he paid no
attention to her charm. He talked metaphorically about politics,
taxation, and mechanical inventions. He speculated about city
life, prosperity, and depravity. He hoped she hadn't missed the
Verdi Requiem—he had missed it himself but he had a talent for
neglecting opportunity. The only thing he insisted on going to
conscientiously was baseball—how did she feel about baseball?
The human animal was fallible, he pointed out, not waiting for an
answer, more obviously fallible than the natural animal—if she
would allow such a term—but in baseball you had glimpses of in-
fallibility: a good third baseman playing a bunt, for example—
every now and then—

"You mean someone like Frank Malzone?"

His smile showed all his separated teeth.

She felt a physical clutch at her heart. It was outrageous of
her, she told herself: behaving like the meanest sort of female. All
her instincts at concert pitch. If she had done it all ten years
earlier and got it over with . . . her answering smile was warm
and gentle and appreciative. Nothing could be more purely delightful than baseball. Of course working girls didn't have many
chances to go to the actual games—she broke off as though someone had poked her. But the idea of really being at a game was
so magnetic that her eyes sparkled and her mouth softened. What
delight it would be, in the air, in the sun, in pure freedom, with
peanuts, with a hot dog, with him grinning like a clown. Tears
stung her eyes.

He shot into the Cambridge Street traffic, weaving and dodging.
The really great thing about his kind of job, he said, was its scope.
No office work if he could help it. They had to keep records, of
course—reports, files, all that—but mostly he was on the go:
juvenile court today—a boy seventeen had been printing ten-
dollar bills in his bedroom—said he learned how in vocational
school; clever as hell—a young prodigy—what do you do with such
a one? Take him to a game? Be a pal to him? Appeal to his finer
nature?

"Is that how you conscientiously go to the games?"

"I do it to save souls—mainly my own. It is a nice problem in ethics, I can tell you. Should I charge it to the Association or pay for it myself? If I pay, is it deductible as a business expense? The income tax has made us a nation of ethical delinquents—or I should say, it simply encourages us in our natural depravity."

He fought his way into a jammed parking lot in an alley near Haymarket. Maybe, he said, he could deputize her for a game some Saturday. He often needed a strong girl. But his smile was so metaphorical she couldn't tell what he meant. He was exchanging intimacies with the attendant, whom he introduced by name as a valued friend—a man with a depraved unshaven face and shifty eyes.

For the rest of the day Mary Kyle was full of an irresponsible humor, and took special delight in satiric attacks on Joe Bass in the office. The man without a soul, she called him. The satanic bachelor. Get-thee-behind-me Joe. Every month he invited her to spend a week end in New York with him.

"I'm tempted," she said. "It's the only way I'll ever find out how you manage your special equipment."

"My—which?"

"Oh, the horns, cloven hoofs, tail—"

He shook his head, smiling darkly. "You're very old-fashioned, Mary."

CHAPTER 7

EDWIN EUSTACE might have slipped out early that dark day, but at four—or maybe later—Grogan stopped in to see him. The Superintendent, everyone called him, but he was nothing but a retired cop, a tough Irishman with a foul temper and no brains. What especially annoyed Edwin was his car, a new black Cadillac like the governor's; he came in it every day, though he lived in Somerville and could have come quicker by subway, and he parked it in the special area reserved for presidents and deans.

They'd have to move his office, Grogan said. They needed more locker space—in fact, they needed space for everything, and what they'd do he couldn't tell. They had this new man called a provost —he was supposed to show them how to handle twice as many students in half the space, and doubtless no one's job was safe any more. They'd have to cut down somewhere, that was certain.

The sight of Grogan always made him angry. A flabby man with bad teeth, wearing an expensive suit, usually holding an unlighted cigar, talking down to his underlings, buttering up his superiors, losing his temper at every crisis. One day Edwin came upon him scolding a shabby old man in a shabby old car, a full-dress traffic-cop performance, and before he knew it he had intervened. His own temper was as bad as Grogan's and the two had shoved their chins together and cursed. The shabby old man, who was the most celebrated physicist on the faculty, observed them curiously and then went about his business. It was a story Edwin told again and again—to illustrate Grogan's savagery and his own foolish virtue.

But it sounded now as though he might be paying for it. If Grogan could get him out of there, he would. He talked about cutting down—no one's job was safe. If this new provost was any damn good he'd get rid of Grogan, but you couldn't expect the administration to use ordinary common sense about anything. All they seemed to care about was jamming in more students, stuffing the classrooms, filling up the corridors. As for a shabby old physicist whose name was known round the world—the hell with him. Edwin made a profession of bitterness. It gave him what amounted to his chief pleasure. If they fired him—and kept Grogan—it would be a kind of satisfaction to him to know that his view of human stupidity was sound. He took a last swallow of his late afternoon whisky and nodded complacently. He rather hoped they would fire him—he'd enjoy telling them candidly what he thought of them: not in anger or petulance but in sober man-to-man truth. He was still a free man. His folks were free Vermonters. He didn't have to take anything from anybody if he didn't want to.

It was after five when he bundled himself for the trip home, a somewhat incongruous arrangement of city and country clothes, serge suit, white collar, mittens and bulky rubbers, rough overcoat —an anomalous figure with the aspect of a farmer, a mechanic, a clerk, and a minor executive all in one. The drink insulated him against the traffic, the windy corner, the crush and racket of the car: he went through the routines in a sort of weary trance; in the train he half dozed and was roused at East Compton by a neighborly hand and voice.

But then the dark road and the wind, the frozen purgatory of the winter gardens and the rural slums. He pushed along too slowly to keep warm. His rubbers shuffled on the icy surface. He took the wind head-on. Bitterness gave him no satisfaction, and he was too weary even to curse his fate.

✍ CHAPTER 8 ✎

THAT HOUSE in East Compton—on the outskirts, among the plots of tomatoes and rhubarb—was what Josephine had bought with the only money that ever came to her. In 1925 it had a sort of rural respectability, even though it was nothing but a box on end, with an oddly gabled third floor. Only a small lot came with it— barely enough to allow a driveway back to a garage—but there were acres round about. They could build up a country estate, she thought, with gardens. They could change the iron gray to white. They could paint the interior varnished oak a charming ivory. Josephine had dreams; she was modern at that time, and read Dreiser and Lewis—she was aware of the low state of American culture, and she was determined to live with the beautiful simplicity she attributed to her ancestors. In the great transcendental days of Compton, a century earlier, the Crabbs had played a part —especially her grandmother's uncle Alexander Crabb, who had published a translation of the *Lusiad*.

The house was all they could afford. It had been built during the first world war, was ugly, flimsy, drab, ornate in the wrong places, and spiritually barren. The rooms were square. When the girls were growing up, and Mary Kyle was majoring in art at college and dabbling in water colors, they discussed what to do about it; they sketched and measured and argued, and Josephine took part, and for a while there was a feeling of good hope among them. The living room and dining room could be thrown to- gether; the foolish little ornamental fireplace would have to be somehow rebuilt further along the wall with honest bricks— otherwise all they'd need was some good paint and paper, and

42

they could do that themselves. But the kitchen was the worst problem. It was Mary Kyle's plan to cut a wide door into what they always called Father's study and make a dining alcove out of it: with a big south-facing window it would be a pleasant spot, and of course as a study it was a waste, a junk-room and catch-all, full of dusty relics of college and army, with a sagging cot where Father snoozed.

But nothing was ever done. Josephine read Trollope. Edwin continued to snooze. Mary Kyle talked. To most of them the house was invisible—except when Mary Kyle pointed to it. Their symbol, she called it. A kind of neutral residual, a spiritual slum, a visible confession of defeat—she fumed and fussed and crackled, and she brought home color charts and scraps of wallpaper and catalogues. She painted her bedroom in tones of turquoise and gold, and did the furniture in black enamel which she rubbed and touched up with gold. She hung yellow curtains. She fixed a reading lamp above the refinished Morris chair, and another over the head of the bed; she built a bookcase of boards and bricks. She framed and hung some Matisse and Van Gogh and a Picasso. But the enterprise never went further and even her own room, her private retreat and sanctum, gradually reverted to type. The paint faded, and there were cracks. The iron bed looked like an iron bed. The pretty rug she had paid so little for seemed to be made partly of paper. Her habits were hasty and cluttery, and before her grand design had ever been carried out through the many fits of week-end activity it had lost its impetus. But the lamps worked well and she read in solitude, often with the door closed or a few inches ajar as a symbol of her semi-detachment from the family.

Edwin, who took no interest at all in decorative or aesthetic appearances, kept things in working order. He cleaned out gutters and spouts. He replaced window cords and puttied and painted the sashes. He had an oil burner installed in the old furnace. But his major devotion was to the automobile he almost never drove, the polished Chrysler in the little wooden garage, a fair-weather, Saturday-and-Sunday car. "I'm willing to confess that a good car appeals to me—in fact, I'm nuts about it. I'd be the same way about a horse—or I would be if we still used them; it's one of the things I remember about my old man—the way he felt about the pair of carriage bays he had. They were without doubt the sweetest team in the township—why, they'd coast along over a packed dirt road like flying. He didn't need 'em any more than I need this Chrysler: it's just a damned extravagance, but I love it." He washed and polished it on fair Saturdays, and drove it to his chosen garage for small clinical consultations.

Behind the gray house was a patch of grass with clothes-posts and lines, and behind that was a square of weedy earth they called the garden. Each spring since they had lived there they had looked on it with hope. Edwin spaded it with a ritualistic—almost a pious—pronouncement of principle. A man has to get close to earth, he said. A man has to bend his back and sweat. If any of the family appeared in range, he lectured. "I honestly don't know what life is for—" He said this with slow and heavy emphasis. "Why in God's name we are supposed to suffer the stupidities of modern life I don't know. Day after day batting our way to town and then batting our way home again, wasting ten hours or so in smoke and exhaust and the stench of humanity—all for only one purpose: money—pay. Why, Jesus—there's no sense to it. As a matter of honest fact, there's not much sense to anything—but by God, we came from earth, and if there's any meaning anywhere we'll find it in the earth." The nasal, back-country quality of voice came out strongly, with overtones of cracker-barrel humor. "That's where we've all got to go anyway —back into the cold ground." He seemed more gaunt and prophetic when he spaded. Sweat glistened in the shadowy hollows of his face.

But he seldom achieved more than a plot of tomato plants. He spoke of peas, the delicacy of young, new-picked peas such as they had grown back on the farm; he discussed the varieties of beans and the pleasures of corn in August; he pointed out that store-bought vegetables were old and tasteless, and he pitied the city-bred multitudes who never knew what a fresh ear of corn tasted like—he generally went on to remind his hearers of the milk, the cream, the butter, and the native produce he had thrived on in the time of his youth. But then he pointed out the economic folly of growing vegetables, the preposterous cost of fertilizer, seeds, tools, water, time—he said he wasn't a rich enough man to raise enough peas for a couple of meals.

There were tomatoes, though. They sprawled in a natural tangle among the jungles of weeds. But in August and September the neighborhood was laden with tomatoes—they seemed almost too plentiful to have value.

Josephine seldom went out of the house. In her youth she had walked and observed birds and flowers; when she first came there to live she had a vision of gardens. But now she read books. She seemed not to notice the house or the place, inside or out. When she hung clothes she spoke of the air, the season, the quality of sky, but she paid no attention to the matted weeds and the dried vines—nor did she see the weathered back steps and peeling gray paint and the whole ugly blank wall of the house. As for the kitchen, as long as the gas and water flowed she had nothing to say about it. The girls argued and conspired and brought pictures of new equipment, but Josephine might have been blind for all the notice she took. The only sign of her feelings was the strange desperation of her face, the droop and twist of her mouth and the glazed look of her eyes.

❦ CHAPTER 9 ❧

AT TEN O'CLOCK in the evening of the winter solstice Mary Kyle
Eustace came downstairs to look for some white embroidery thread
she had seen earlier in her mother's work basket. She sewed badly
and impatiently, but it was her duty, she felt, to make presents
by hand; her project for her mother this year was six bath-towels
and six washcloths with embroidered initials, and by now she had
regretted it. She had begun with a fancy monogram of three initials
and then decided that one large E was all she could achieve, and
even that was almost too much for her. She cursed and muttered
to herself and used up her thread and mislaid her needle and
begrudged the time spent, though she did admire each finished
towel, the white E against the rich blue. Her mother would doubtless put them away and keep on with the ragged odds and ends
they were used to.

Downstairs her mother snoozed in the kitchen rocker with
Mr. Scarborough in her lap. No use telling her to go to bed. She
did most of her sleeping there in the rocker with her face tipped
back like death. In the night silences the sound of her breathing
filled the halls. Now she was quiet—she had not fallen into the
heavy sleep of midnight. The dim light was on in the lower hall
and one shone from the study door where she heard her father
stir and faintly clink a glass. Patience was still out—she had called
from town to say she'd be late.

She turned on a light in the living room, rummaged for the
thread in the market basket where the family sewing was kept,
then tried the television to see what was on. It was warmer down
here and she lingered. The living room was not much used, even

46

with its television—it seemed more like a passageway than a room; but tonight with a cold north wind whining through the cracks of the upstairs windows she stayed a while.

"A little snort?" Edwin said at the door. He held a glass half full and a bottle. "My Old Swanee River—cheap but good. Not that any of the stuff is cheap, but what they soak you for the so-called best bonded is nothing but piracy. It's mostly damn superstition—the notion that some whisky is a rare collector's fluid worth six-fifty a fifth—why, damn it to hell, you could fill those bottles with this Old Swanee and not one in a hundred would know the difference. Specially with ice in it—I mean to say, the only reason they use ice in liquor is to take away the taste of it. You get something cold enough, you can't taste it—and yet they'll buy that high-priced stuff and fill it up with cracked ice: there's no damn sense in it." He lifted his glass with a gesture of anger. "You take a martini, now—you take gin: it isn't fit to drink; it is vile—why you might as well swallow hair tonic. But get it cold enough and you don't really taste it—you just kind of feel a little tingle as it goes down, and then you wait for the kick. It isn't a drink, it's a medicine."

His anger made her laugh. He glowered down at her, his face dark with hollows and shadows. He set down his bottle and glass, went to the kitchen—where he tiptoed with bearlike motion—and came back with two tumblers, one full of water. "You think I'm nuts, but let me ask you this: did you ever try to drink a warm martini?" He poured out an inch of Old Swanee and added about half an inch of water. "I wouldn't inflict a warm martini on my worst enemy. But you get a decent bourbon, it's just as good warm as cold—a damn sight better, in my personal judgment. Try it now. Here's to a short life and a quiet grave, as old Hez Applegate used to say."

He lowered himself into a stuffed chair and squirmed a little as the springs creaked and twanged. Mary Kyle sipped and swallowed with no comment and suddenly he pointed at her with his extended arm and glass. "You drink like a damned lady—all you're doing is trying to humor the old man. You think if you just play along you can do me good—you can appeal to my affections and conscience, remind me of my duty as a father. You think maybe I can still be saved."

She laughed, but uneasily. "You don't know much about me, do you, Father?"

"I know about good women. My family has always been full of good women. About all they can do is suffer."

"That's me, you think?"

The hand extended itself, the voice came out in a blast of self-assertion: "I think—" Then it stopped. He drank. He changed his tone, though the accent remained. "Your cheapest bargain-basement wise guys always take it out on virtue. Matter of fact, I love those old girls; my heart aches for them. Aunt Margaret Kyle, the nicest, the goodest, the most saintly human creature, married to that real-estate son of a bitch there in Rutland: to the day of her death she never would admit she suffered the tortures of hell. She bore it—she was a good girl first, last, and always. I have infinite respect and pity for Aunt Margaret. But the grim fact of the matter is that that bastard, that Herman Elder, he had a pretty good time in life. He made a lot of dishonest money and spent it on himself, and so far as anyone could tell he did a good deal better than the rest of us—and I *doubt*—" again the extended arm and glass and the blast of self-assertion—"I *doubt* if he ever paid any piper. By all Christian logic, he ought to be frying in hell, but if I had to bet on it I'd say they were both nothing but dust and humus in the local cemetery."

He finished his glass.

"Do you know I'm sixty-two? I'm not any sorrier for myself than I am for anyone else, understand. In fact I ought to consider myself statistically fortunate to be alive at all—and I gather that what most folks primarily want is life—life in any shape or form. Survive, brothers, survive! Preserve the self. Live till tomorrow and tomorrow." He poured some whisky and a little water into his glass.

Mary Kyle watched him with sorrow in her eyes.

"You don't have to argue with me," he said strongly. "I know the theory of love, and it's a pretty good one. I admit I haven't done well at it. But with love you get loss—somebody loses out—" He paused in the familiar gesture of hand and glass extended like a threat. "Who suffers more than a bereaved lover? Heaven and then hell—on earth, that is. I don't know about any other kind." He looked at Mary Kyle with a discovering eye as though he hadn't seen her clearly before. "You don't go for love."

"No love, no loss," she said.

It stopped him for a moment. "I don't know, girl—I don't know. I guess we just whistle a little in the dark. Anything to forget what actually is. The trouble with me is that I've never done a single damn thing I can be proud of—there's nothing I can even *pretend* about."

"Well, you've got the Chrysler."

"Hell, yes. I've got the Chrysler." His mouth made a sardonic twist. "You think that'll fool me? I've got this too." He lifted the glass. Then he roused and stirred as though he were shaking off a mood. "No use bellyaching. We either take it or we don't take it. We sleep and eat and function. We have fun—sometimes. We give out—we work—we make moves like a checker player trying to win. We do what we can't help doing." He brooded and there was silence. The television had been on, with no sound: the pictures had flashed on in meaningless sequences. She switched it off.

"What gets me," he said, "what *astounds* me is the blind, insane ambition of the human creature—I mean the Hitler-like instinct that drives for power. You keep seeing it in the damnedest places—drive, drive, drive. The same thing that makes beetles destroy elm trees. Primitive urge. But in people it is both terrible and stupid." He tried to shrug it off. "Damn cracker-box philosopher, that's all I am. I remember the old boys in the back of Hez Applegate's store in Starkville Four Corners—playing checkers and spitting into the pot-belly stove." He drank again and looked at her. "Why don't you at least get yourself out of this damn birdcage—I mean, you could find some sort of male critter that would take you off: maybe not that cold-water chap who hangs round, but *someone*. Or you could just light out on your own. I mean to say, you might as well have some fun in life, and I doubt very much if you have any here."

"Fun," she said. "Like what?"

"Well—hell, you know you can't talk about it. It's a mistake to even think about it. That's what I do—I think, I talk. You know the centipede who tried to think which leg to move first— he never budged; he didn't have fun. Just motion is fun, for God's sake—here to there and there to here—" His voice had grown a little fuzzy; he made an effort to speak more precisely. "That's elementary fun—that's the first principle. Theory of the merry-go-round. As for love, that's advanced fun—or so we are instructed. I don't mean just sex, I mean friends and family and all—and I'd like you to note that I can be pretty damned high-minded when I drink whisky. It shows character—a sort of character. I can understand the theory, anyway, even if my practice is bad. And of course, it is more complicated than this—all I'm doing is sketching a few outlines. God, for instance—a lot of folk have that dream: you don't, I presume. And drink—you don't seem to have that. But good work—I presume that's one of the best: *doing* something, like making mousetraps. What do we *do*, for God's sake? What do I do—what have I ever done? There's the rub, my girl. As you rightly point out, what I have done is to acquire a shiny black Chrysler—and I can tell you that when I'm sober I'm damned proud of it. But you'll admit it ain't much to live on, as the parson said when they paid him in turnips and pickled pork."

After another drink he shook his head in a gesture of dismissal and despair. "What it comes down to—in the end—for me—is nothing, zero. As far as I personally am concerned, the struggle availeth exactly naught. I say it, with a little help from Old Swanee." He made a prophetic and theatrical gesture in her direction. "Go, love, do. Delude yourself with dreams. Enjoy the merry-go-round. Do your damnedest. Never ask why or what for."

Josephine's breathing from the kitchen was louder and more regular.

CHAPTER 10

In January snows piled up, and melted, and piled up again. Mary Kyle had a cold in the head, but went to work every day. Edwin coughed. Josephine had headaches, attributed to bad light, lack of proper sleep, and escaping gas in the kitchen. Patience seemed to be full of health and vigor and was in love. Buzz came home when his team played in Boston; he looked pale and thin, and said he was probably overtrained, but his appetite was huge and he slept late.

On a Friday evening during dinner, about the middle of the month, Edwin remarked that he was being fired. "They try to do it genteel," he said. "As of next July one—end of fiscal year. They thank me for my service to the university. They explain that they have had to reorganize the whole maintenance system in the interests of economy and efficient management."

He made a kind of death's-head grin. His voice was lightly sardonic, but theatrical. "What I am looking forward to is the letter I shall write—or rather *compose*. I intend to produce a masterpiece. It will be temperate, exact, thorough, and candid. 'Dear Mr. President: My Vermont grandmother used to speak of the plain burlap truth. My intention in this letter . . .' "

"Don't do it," Josephine said with a fierce twist to her mouth. "You'll be angry, you'll be intemperate, you'll say terrible things."

"Six months—if I stay that long. All I need to do is to tell him the simple truth, for God's sake. With a copy for the chairman of the trustees—they'd like to know the facts too. They don't—none of those birds up there in their offices know what really goes on: they haven't the dimmest idea what that bastard Grogan does. But don't you worry—I'll put a little sugar on it, I'll be diplomatic. I won't send it without reading it in the morning when I'm cold sober."

"Well, you'd better let me write it," she said. "I don't trust you."

It was a good feeling to be fired, he said: you didn't have to take anything from anybody; you could tell them all to go to hell. And maybe he could retire from commuting. Get an honest job mowing lawns. Live a little, as they said—it was time he tried it. How life began for me at sixty-two.

Josephine spoke suddenly. "You'll have to sell that car." Her tone was explicit and final.

"Be damned if I will," he whispered.

"You've got two children still in college," she said.

"Well, be damned to them." His mouth twisted and he winked at Patience. "They're of age, I take it." He made a left-handed gesture that included the house. "What we ought to sell is this parrot-cage. I used to think property was security—you had a roof, a bed, a place to hole in like a woodchuck in a burrow; but all it is, is a way of existing. I don't see any sense in a woodchuck."

"He survives," Patience said.

"He eats and sleeps. In the course of time he dies. I can do that too. But what he doesn't do is see the world—go places in a Chrysler—"

"Like going to buy a Sunday paper," Mary Kyle said.

"Well, I had Florida in mind. That's where the smart folks go. They bowl—they roll balls on the green grass. Like Joe Myers and his wife—all they can talk about is that damned bowling league of theirs, the sixty-fivers, he calls it. I guess that's what I live for—to go to Florida and be a sixty-fiver. Two and a half years and I'm in." He glanced at Josephine but she was paying no attention. "Your mother is too young to take any interest in that, but she'll appreciate the palm trees and alligators."

"Maybe she'd get some sleep for a change," Mary Kyle said.

"How about it, old girl? Do we sell the house and go?"

"We don't sell the house. We don't go anywhere."

They were all silent under the finality of her voice. She spoke distinctly, as though she were instructing children.

"I believe," Edwin said, "if there was a fire and the house burned down, she'd stay right in it like a horse in a stall."

"It's my house," she said. "As long as it's my house I'll stay in it."

"I don't seem to get a damn bit of appreciation from anybody," Edwin said. "I lose my job—who cares? I aspire to go off and have a time for myself, the way other folks do, but no—it can't be done. Maybe some day I'll just go anyway, by myself." He glanced about to see if they'd come back at him. "You think I'll need money, no doubt. But they tell me there are ways of getting along without it—what with unemployment benefits and social security and all. If a man had a trailer, for example, he could move round pretty much as he damn pleased."

Josephine advised them to read Anthony Trollope's book about his travels in North America during the Civil War.

"She reads about travels," Edwin said, "but she won't go around the block herself." His tone was as petulant as a boy's. "I'll be damned if I see any sense in it. If we had some sort of function— sure: I mean land to cultivate and cattle to tend. But what do we do that is worth doing?" His voice had dwindled to a mutter. He got up and buttoned his brown sweater. "We go shopping in the bargain basements. We wash the car. In summer we mow the lawn. Thank God we can still drink a little whisky in the evening." He went off into the hall, then came back. "If any of you are figgering on me being the breadwinner of this family, you'd better begin to change your mind. As of July one, I quit. I retire. I take no more responsibility. Starve, go naked, freeze—it's up to you." He turned away, then looked in again. "I admit, freely and frankly, that I have been a damned failure. There are times, like now, in the presence of my family, when I regret it." He glowered at them a moment as though he waited for a response, then disappeared.

✎§ CHAPTER 11 ৡ৯

ON FEBRUARY FIFTEENTH the weather bureau predicted a cloudy cold day with a chance of light snow. At noon the wind blew from the east and small flakes whirled in the air and whitened the ground. The weather bureau predicted an accumulation of two or three inches and advised drivers to be cautious.

At three o'clock the fine flakes swirled and blew like flour. Traffic moved slower, in muffled and shrouded silence. The weather bureau predicted five or six inches and advised motorists to go home early.

At four, Edwin took his dose of Old Swanee, put on rubbers, scarf, coat, hat, and mittens, and butted his way across the avenue to the trolley stop. He felt comfortable and careless inside his clothes, and admired the storm. Wind northeast, he noted. Dry fine snow blowing horizontally right up the avenue. As an old Vermonter he could appreciate a blizzard; he had standards, he didn't talk foolishly about weather the way city folks did. This one seemed like the real thing, though you couldn't tell how much snow had fallen.

Cold—really cold, and wind in gusts. A knot of people waited, backs hunched against the blast. No trolley. Then three together, all crowded. Then a fourth, also crowded, but it stopped and they squeezed in. Edwin had begun to shiver.

The station already choked with waiting people, trains delayed, schedules abandoned. He stood for an hour, then boarded a car and stood in the aisle. Eight inches, some said. Ten inches. A foot.

Edwin's hollow face looked sardonic. He grinned to himself. The poor bastards, huddling like cattle. The human race on its daily round. They swayed and jerked as the car started and stopped, they peered helplessly at the black glass of the windows. Women wearing open slippers with spike heels and hats like cupcakes. The car was cold, breath showed. He shivered again. He used to be tough—way back, in his army days, and before that, plowing the cornfield in Starkville; used to walk three miles to high school, blizzards and all. Now he felt his legs trembling—these city girls with their heels and slippers and silk panties probably had more stamina than he did. But what a welter, a mass of human desires—all these people pushing and pushing toward self-satisfaction, existing mostly to achieve sensual pleasure: what a miserable and terrible thing humanity was. He always felt it when he saw people massed together, each one carrying separately the primal urge like a charge of nuclear power.

The train hesitated, felt its way along, waited at stations, got to East Compton where Edwin and others descended into the blizzard. It was after seven. The streets were partly bare where the wind scoured them, and partly deep in flour-like snow. He leaned diagonally to his right and pushed up the deserted hill into the darkness. Cold like needles through his clothes. Fine snow inside his shoe-tops. Right ear nipped. He mushed along, wading against drifts, lifting his knees over ridges and blowing cornices.

"It's a corker," he said. "It's a doozer." The whole damned city would be paralyzed. People caught in their cars, sleeping in stations and lobbies. Shovels and plows would be out all night. Old men would die. Kids would stay home from school.

He hoped it would snow and snow, would pile up bigger than anything ever known. He hoped the wind would blow from due north, the cold would be everlasting. He began to quote Whittier. "All night long the storm roared on." It revolved in his mind like a chanted tune. All night long . . .

The last hundred yards went very slowly. He couldn't hold a straight course in the wind and dark. He stepped into the foot-deep ditch at the edge of the road and found himself crumpled down in a wallow of snow with his face covered. He swore bitterly and then grinned at the power of the storm. A doozer, he thought. Let her rip, by God. Blow, damn it all—blow; pour it on, pile it on, keep it coming. He stood up, wavering, making motions of brushing himself. I hope it buries everything, he prayed; ten feet

৶ঽ CHAPTER 12 ৡ৯

MARY KYLE came out into the storm about four-thirty, noting the clock in the main lobby of the office building and figuring to herself on making the four-fifty-seven. It usually took sixteen minutes to walk to the train—maybe a couple of minutes more in the snow, though she didn't pay much attention to it. It was nice of them to dismiss everybody early—evidently there had been a broadcast warning by the mayor: but she recollected the morning weather prediction of a chance of light snow. She hadn't even worn overshoes—it was easier to walk in her regular rubber-soled oxfords. She had considered the problem of dressing like the other office girls, with heels and sheer nylons, and decided if they didn't like her the way she was they could go to hell. She wasn't just an office girl anyway—she was a layout editor.

So she walked strongly through the storm, tramping on the churned-up white stuff. Thousands of others tramped, or shuffled or hopped or slipped. Cars were already jammed at the crossings. Horns and police whistles blew.

Because of the extra ten minutes she took the route through Haymarket, and there, right across the sidewalk, with engine running and wipers slapping, sat John Rossiter's car. He nudged it toward the street, not seeing her. But the glass was down on his side and he had his bare head out. She walked up and said hello.

"If you want to risk it, get in," he said. "Do it quick, though— I see an opening right here and I intend to jump for it. I've been blocking this sidewalk for ten minutes."

She tumbled in the rear door on his side, the car started and stopped several times, and they were out among the trucks and taxis. He looked back with his small-boy grin. "If you care about getting home you'd better walk. I'm supposed to go to Worcester tomorrow, but the way it looks I don't expect to get anywhere at all. I believe she's a lulu—the storm, I mean. I didn't pay a damn bit of attention to it till I tried to drive out of the lot there—I haven't got my chains on—I don't usually use them till I get hopelessly stuck, but I have a feeling that's going to occur any minute now." He rushed at another opening, skidded left and then right, and came to rest a few inches from a ten-wheel van. "But once you start, you're a goner—it's like going over Niagara in a barrel—you can't decide you'd rather quit. I mean—there's the station, and I presume they'll still run a few trains before the whole system expires. But once we get out on the parkway we're over the edge—we're out in space, survive or perish, hell or high water." He darted ahead and slewed round the van.

"Is it warm up there?" she said.

"Warm?"

"I mean where you are."

"Oh—you mean the heater here. It's what I'd call temperate. It prevents ice in the blood. If you plan to stay for the duration you'd better climb over. You understand that if I stop here on this imperceptible grade I won't be at all popular with the folks behind us."

She studied the high seatback, then removed her hat. She stood, lifted her right leg, lowered it, pulled up her skirts, then sat down.

"Did you ever try this?"

"Try what?"

"Climbing over."

"Oh—well, just give a plunge."

"You mean head first?"

"It might work. But I'd think a sort of high-jumper's roll would do it. I suppose you never did any high-jumping."

"No."

"I did. I did everything, from putting the shot to pole vaulting. I was no damn good at any of it."

"Well, what's this high-jumper's roll?"

"Oh, you just kind of go over sidewise—you get yourself horizontal, if you follow me."

"I see."

The car moved along slowly.

"Just step right over," he said. "You've got long enough legs."

"That's the trouble—they're too long. Maybe if I was a neat little thing I could roll over the way you say. But not with this build." She pulled up her skirts, flung her right leg over the back of the seat, snatched up her left leg with graceful speed—and failed to make it. It didn't come.

She arranged her skirt as best she could. "At least my right leg is warmer," she said. "But as far as I can see, I'm stuck."

"Now is the time to roll," he said. He glanced politely at the long legs on each side of the seatback.

She laughed nervously and checked herself. "This is no time for hysterics, my girl," she said. "You'll have to bear some of the brunt of this—whatever the brunt may be." She spilled herself over the seat in a dead weight of body and limbs, part of her on top of him. "If I had the instincts of a lady I'd have shivered quietly in the back seat. Are we still on the road?"

"We seem to be on a road—or street or thoroughfare of some sort. I can't really see anything except the car in front."

She gradually pulled herself together. "I'm sorry. I feel like a giraffe in an upper berth." She subdued her giggle. "How come you aren't laughing? Was I appalling, perhaps?"

"Well—" His smile glowed with benevolence. "You weren't any worse than a human being has to be sometimes. I take it we have delusions of pure grace and dignity as though we were kings and queens on display, but sooner or later we get upended by fate or gravity—"

"Upended," she said. This time she laughed abruptly. "No doubt of that—"

"Why, I believe you're a little bit embarrassed by all this—or should I say upset." His grin suggested long friendship. "The thing is, when you ride in my car you just have to abandon your dignity."

"Oh—I know—I have. It's nothing, really—except when a girl has to stand on her head it always makes her a bit hysterical. You get so used to being right-side up. But I'm fine—and it is much warmer here and I'm glad I didn't send you into the ditch while I was having convulsions."

The car crawled along through dusky space. The windows were iced, the wipers labored against the piling snow, the heater hummed: it seemed snug inside, and safely isolated, as though city and storm hardly existed—except when he lowered the window to peer out, and a whirl of flakes and icy wind filled the interior. The parkway was jammed with slow-moving cars. Presently they stopped—there were minutes of waiting.

"You are always sure the drivers ahead of you are incompetent," he said. "Someone gets stuck in the bottleneck—someone skids and blocks the road. You can't do a thing about it. No use cussing and fuming."

The car rocked in the gusts; snow rattled on the metal.

They crawled through crossings, over bridges, in and out of choked-up rotaries, and came to rest at the foot of a hill. Seven o'clock. No movement for a long time. He got out and walked ahead, and she was aware of the full blasts of the storm. The motor was off, the air icy; above the rattle of driving snow was the deep roar of wind. The blowing drifts made a seething noise.

She curled on the seat, holding in warmth, not thinking about anything. She seemed to be in space, going with the elements; she had no concern for time or destination. The storm went on like a dramatic performance.

When he came back, slipped into the seat, brushed snow, slammed the door, she smiled with lazy sweetness. "Are we lost in the storm? Are we abandoned, buried, cast away?"

"Exactly," he said decisively. "Abandoned. Almost buried."

"It's a superb storm, isn't it?"

There they were, wrapped in the little space, held by the same force.

"We are stuck," he said. "The cars are tangled hopelessly all the way up the hill."

"No cloud above, no earth below—a universe of sky and snow!"

"Eh?"

"It's what my mother taught me to say at a time like this." She felt the cold seeping in through her clothes and gave a luxurious shiver.

"Yes—a superb storm; there's no doubt of that." He started the motor again. "But the elemental fact is that if we stay here long enough we'll freeze to death."

"I won't mind—not very much, that is. It would be comfortable, wouldn't it?"

"I doubt it." His voice was sharp with disapproval. She looked at him curiously.

"No joke, you think?"

"Oh, as for a joke—all right, if you like it."

She curled up tighter, still watching him. "I was being a little funny, maybe—I mean, it's what you try to make jokes about. My dad drinks toasts to a short life and a quiet grave. But in a way he means it. I guess I do too—in a way."

"I don't think I believe you," he said.

"No, you wouldn't." It gave her pleasure to say it.

"I understand you, all right—at least I understand the theory, if that's what it is. The instinct of staying alive is basic, but it is weaker in some than others. They get tired, they half give up—"

"Half in love with easeful death," she said.

"Okay—but it isn't you."

"Me," she said eagerly. "What do you know about me?"

He drew back a little—she could almost feel him move.

"I presume you aren't one to give up." His tone made light of it. "I've even thought of you as one who enjoys a fight—in other words, pugnacious." He chuckled to ward off the issue.

"That's your image, you see—not mine. But even so, even if I fight—or squabble or whatever—that isn't quite the point. I don't doubt I'll stay alive as long as I can, even tonight, but I can't really say I see any sense in it—not if I think reasonably, that is. Life is a sort of compulsion—I agree to that, all right. But the mind can't make any sense out of it—all it can do is invent illusions."

"I don't believe it—"

"Don't believe what?"

"That you are as cynical as you pretend."

His anxiety pleased and annoyed her. She smiled impatiently. "Cynicism—for heaven's sake, whenever I try to speak the truth they all call it cynicism. You think I'm putting on an act or playing a game: that's what you mean when you say cynical. It's got so I don't dare speak truth—nobody does, actually—"

"Truth," he said, rousing as though he had heard a bugle call. "You mean death, I suppose. You mean we're doomed anyway, so what the hell. You mean—"

"Yes—yes, I mean just that. I mean logically, rationally, actually, that all we do is walk the plank like the victims of Blackbeard." She said it with a kind of exaggeration that startled her. She drew back from her own vehemence.

But he laughed—it was pleasant to hear him chuckle. "My dear girl—" The wind boomed and seethed and the car rocked. He waved a gloved hand. "The truth that really counts is right there on the plank. All you have is that short walk to oblivion—that's your allotment, your freedom or fun or success or failure; I tell you, you'd better not waste it in lamentations—"

"But I—"

"You simply make the most of what's given—"

"But you don't—"

"It isn't necessarily rosebuds—"

"Will you please—"

"Or eating and drinking, though there's much to be said—"

"There's certainly much to be said—"

"You have, say, one week to live—the judgment is given by medical authority: do you make the least or the most of it—that's the whole thing."

"I know, I *know!* My God, you aren't human. This one-week-to-live gambit—there's no sense in it. Living under sentence of death —if that's the best you can say for existence I don't think much of it. It might do for saints and martyrs, but—"

"Well, let me tell you—"

"That's what I've been doing—but I'd like to tell one or two things myself—"

"Anyone who has the courage to think has to be a saint and martyr—or has to try to be. There's nothing else for it. The end of any train of honest thought is pure terror."

She opened her mouth, then closed it. "Did I hear you right? Is that what you said?"

"That's what I said, or tried to. It's not wise for people to think —unless they are strong enough to stand the consequences."

She was silenced.

"I supposed you were," he went on.

She shook her head a little. "There's something wrong somewhere along the line. We're brought up on virtue and rainbows; we learn in college that life is merely a by-product of electronics—"

"Luckily we don't believe it. We go back to rainbows. But there are disasters, there are those who are frightened to death—"

"Like me, you think?"

"You? You're probably frightened about being a spinster. Here you are, twenty-five or six, and no husband—you've been absorbing all this modern hokum about frustration, you think life doesn't count until you have a lover and a child, though I don't expect you for a moment to admit it: but let me tell you right now, the whole thing is mostly a racket designed to promote movies and magazines and soap operas. Love and motherhood are all very well, though they achieve as much misery as they avoid—maybe more. If I had to pick the ten all-round best women I ever knew, six of them would be virgins—but try to tell Hollywood, or try to tell the department of psychology at that university of yours: they are all professionally committed to the dogma of sexual frustration and are thereby doing incalculable harm to half the gullible women in the nation."

Mary Kyle looked at him. "I don't know that I'm quite keeping up with you. I mean, my sex life—"

"The thing is, this modern education is every bit as dangerous as a nuclear explosion. So far, out of the millions exposed to it, only a few actually realize what it means—and an appreciable number of those few end up in the state hospitals for the insane. The rest all go on dreaming the same old dreams—"

"And you? What do you do?"

"Oh, I keep moving. I learn from the ant. He goes from here to there and there to here—he never stops to rest or think or use any intelligence about anything."

The storm rushed over them, beating and rocking the car.

"The tragedy is," he said, "the universal tragedy of humanity is that people learn to think just enough to recognize their misery. If they learned nothing they would retain all their natural illusions. If they learned everything, they would achieve sainthood and martyrdom, just as you say. But Lord help the ones in between— which nowadays means almost everyone. Universal education is just a way of insuring universal misery—"

"Ha! Talk about cynics."

He sucked on his empty pipe. "Oh, I'll own up to—well, not

cynicism, but call it theoretical pessimism. I'm not bellyaching, though—don't accuse me—"

Voices went by the window. He put his head out; she saw people moving, a policeman's uniform. "We won't be clear for an hour," he said. "I better get the chains on."

CHAPTER 13

By TEN O'CLOCK he had called his wife and told her to call Mary Kyle's house: they'd be home some time next day, he said. They were in a store somewhere. They had coffee and a box of crackers. The car was a half-mile or so away, buried and lost. They were fine . . .

Side by side in a corner, sitting on the floor, shoulders touching, isolated among twenty people.

"Best thing in the world," he said. "A little hunger, a little weariness, a little fear. A glimpse of greatness, a touch of catastrophe—"

"And comes the dawn?"

The place was charged with life. It became a theatrical school where actors stamped on and off the stage with loud utterances of complaint or humor or rueful irony. Rumors flew: the plows were coming through, the plows were stuck, Route 60 was still open—or not open; someone was found dead, a woman had a baby in her car, an old couple were frozen or nearly frozen; the police wouldn't let a car move without chains; a foot of snow had fallen— two feet—drifts six feet deep. At the counter a shouted argument on the definition of a blizzard, in one booth a quartet rendering "Smiles," in another a game of bridge. Everyone watched the entrances, the door flung open with a gust of wind and fine flakes, the hunched white figure pitching in, stamping and flailing and blowing and calling out to Jesus Christ. "Shut the door!"—a chorus. But then time wore on; they sprawled and drooped and slept at awkward angles.

Never again, Mary Kyle thought, will we be like this, alone

and apart, together all night, sleeping together sitting in a corner. She could smell his pipe and the damp wool of his clothes; she felt his warmth and heard his breath. He talked, a steady, subdued, affectionate talk as though no separation of soul existed between them: he talked about the puritans—his people and her people. He had outlined a book—it was one of his innumerable projects: not a defense or a special plea, but what he called a recognition of a civilization. No one had done it, he said. Not merely the New England phase of it, but the whole thing from Cromwell to Gladstone—

"You ought to talk to Mother," she said.

"The modern attack on puritanism is nothing more than an adolescent's attack on his parents. The child's dream of pure freedom and unlimited indulgence, with no end to the ice cream, the toys, the pleasure, the love—that's what we come to as a world. We hate any word like duty or discipline—we everlastingly talk freedom, freedom, freedom, as though the law of gravity didn't count any more."

She drowsed and yawned and kept her head from falling on his shoulder. His voice seemed delightful to her. "Didn't you ever hate your parents?" she murmured. It was like being on the deck of a ship in a storm on a far sea.

". . . Shouldn't boast," he said, "but I was known as the last wild oat—I mean I thought I was a sort of welterweight hellion. But hate is a strong word, my girl—"

"So's love, they say."

"The thing is, they were not vulnerable—they were immaculate, like a couple of elves. I tried hard enough to hurt them—I grew up without acquiring any sense whatever."

It was easy to keep him talking. His father was a doctor in Connecticut, eighty-two, still practicing; his mother—he plunged into a complicated and metaphorical tale of a wreck on the highway, of juvenile demons, and bodies hurled through the air, of his mother spending ten years on crutches with no more flesh on her broken bones than a grasshopper. It all had something to do with his own career—before he realized what had happened he had abandoned theoretical psychology and become a caseworker for the Boston Children's Aid. He had once been a hot-rodder himself—way back when a car that did ninety was a prize: he had been one of the demons of his day. But as for his mother, all it did was to purify her as though she had been tried in a furnace: she still used a cane, was no more than a bundle of crooked bones, but she seemed to live without any of the burdens of flesh. They both had gone beyond selfhood, he said—at least it seemed so to him: you had to call it pure spirit, there was no other word. They looked like a couple of little nuts that had come to the end of all visible change. "Mind you, it isn't piety, it isn't even doctrine or profession. I believe piety is a sign of troubled self, it is the drama of the ego: I abase myself, I make myself holy, I appeal to God, I resist evil, I demonstrate my goodness, I hope for reward. And as for doctrine . . ."

His voice hovered in a timeless void. A midnight quiet settled on the drab bright variety store, and the waiting people slumped against each other and drowsed and snored. The card game went on. The gale boomed like a distant sound of bass strings and a little whining rose and fell in the crack of the door. Pressures built up with the gusts, as though the outer wall were squeezed like one side of a bellows. Flakes rattled and seethed on the windows.

"It is the everlasting desire to avoid the issue." His mouth was eight inches from her ear. "Generation upon generation looking for ways to fool themselves. Learned Thebans, learned Thomists, learned apologists of all sects, trying to convince themselves that God plays hide and seek or blindman's buff. Those five blind scholars trying to figure out what an elephant was—that's a reasonable human predicament: it's what we are all up against. But twenty or thirty centuries of theological argument about what God is, with numberless volumes and libraries, all leading to nothing, arriving at nothing, yet covering up the simple fact in mountains of solemn rhetoric—it is a vast intellectual catacomb. They call it apologetics, without irony. Apologetics! Onward Christian soldiers, marching as to war—"

She laughed suddenly; she shook, trying not to make any noise. He glanced at her with sudden fierce suspicion. "Funny, you think?"

"Oh, *it* isn't funny—at least—"

"I am, though."

"No."

"Let me tell you, Miss Eustace, that I spent most of my

adolescence fighting the ones who thought I was funny—I mean damn near everybody. When I said I was a welterweight hellion I meant just that. I was a runt, an undersized package of vanity. If I had more natural ability I'd turn into a gangster—"

"I was watching Gus over there—he's trying to sleep with one eye and keep the other on the customers to see that they don't steal anything, and just watching him and listening to you at the same time made me laugh. His face has no more expression than a bag of flour."

"Gus, eh? You know him already. But I expect he's a man at least, not an apologist. Mind you, I'm not against philosophy as such: if a man has a brain, let him exercise it—muscles ought to be used. But one has obligations to truth."

"I'm not arguing with you, Mr. Rossiter."

"No, but you are laughing."

"Oh, well—I'm light-headed. Aren't you? Aren't you even hungry?"

He grinned, he showed his widely spaced teeth. She felt the impulse to reach out and touch him. "My habits don't allow for much eating, but I'm not opposed to it." He roused and peered energetically round the store. "Any choice? He's out of coffee and ice cream and bread and butter—" He sprang up. She watched him approach Gus—they chatted a long time, they nodded and gestured for minutes, for a quarter of an hour. She thought he had forgotten about food, but at last there were motions. Others clustered round the counter. There was laughter; she heard his voice, saw his hand on Gus's shoulder, saw his grin. He held up a can of Spam; he gestured. He seemed like an emblem of life.

At home, she thought, they lived like prisoners. Under sentence. Waiting and waiting. Mother in the kitchen with Trollope. Father in the study with Old Swanee. Maybe in some secret way they communed with God; maybe without ever mentioning it they took comfort—she hoped they did, but the thought was suddenly poignant and she felt the sting of tears behind her eyes. She could never think clearly about it: she went along in a vaguely hopeful, vaguely skeptical state of mind; when she listened to the *Messiah* she was carried aloft on wings of piety, but it was nothing she could think about seriously. The pronouncements of great men about God and the soul seemed as remote as the voice heard by Moses; when the president of Harvard attacked secularism she felt personally a little guilty but unable to do anything about it. She supposed the president of Harvard had some advanced knowledge about God that she obviously didn't have; he was in on the secret—as others seemed to be. T. S. Eliot, for example, was said to know all about it, and she kept intending to read him seriously —after the Proust, perhaps. But she was secular, no doubt of it— as far as she knew what it meant. Worldly. Getting and spending, eating and sleeping, staying alive. No communing with God. Her father was certainly secular too, with his bottle: he was exactly what they disapproved of—he was the exhibit, the example, though there was a devout Catholic named Callahan in the next house beyond theirs who drank more and suffered more than even her father did—they had bleeding hearts and wounded Christs all over the house. As for her mother, what would the president and Mr. Eliot say about her? Too worldly? Not enough prayer? No soul? Would God make her happy? But the godly ones never seemed to be interested in happiness; they aimed rather at suffering, the right sort of suffering, the prescribed agonies of initiation permitted only to the chosen. The notion flitted across her brain even that a certain social position—or perhaps a sort of cultural eminence—was necessary for the best kind of salvation. But the whole business seemed to require special knowledge, like nuclear science or horoscopes.

She wondered how seriously he scoffed at it. His laugh rang out like a fanfare from the group by the counter: not a scoffing laugh, rather a jovial enthusiasm for the ceremonial carving of a hunk of Spam. A secular pleasure. Not that any of it troubled her at all: the speculation made a pleasant light-headed montage in her consciousness. He led the choir in Bach. He went to ball games. He rescued the perishing delinquents. He honored his father and mother, the two little nuts—she saw them like hickory nuts, faces carved and fixed by time: spirit—courage, not so much faith as faithfulness. Country doctor and wife doing their duty, regardless of doctrine or the prescriptions of the godly. Did they think about their souls? Were they secular? How did they fit in Mr. Eliot's scheme—if it really was a scheme? How did he, John Rossiter, fit? How would presidents and archbishops regard him? She wondered suddenly if he had gone to Harvard—there was much about him she must find out: the war—he flew in bombers, over Germany in the great raids; some of his metaphorical discourse had to do with flight. She remembered how he said "apologetics," the timbre of his voice: the theologians, she knew, had to include bombing raids in their explanation of God. Onward Christian soldiers. Where did the bad secular business end and the good divine part begin? She had a notion that St. Thomas proved that it was the duty of good men to exterminate heretics—or if not St. Thomas it was some other master of sacred wisdom. She remembered how they talked about God in the war—all through her college years: God in the foxholes, God on life rafts, God at the controls, God on our side. But she never figured it out clearly, she had no systematic theology; the enemy was merely the enemy, and war the black death that had to be endured.

He came toward her, grinning, holding a tray higher than necessary. She hadn't moved from the corner they had claimed, tucked partly behind a counter; she still felt detached from ordinary reality, as though the mottled gray linoleum under her were the deck of a ship of souls voyaging to another world. He made gestures like a steward as he lowered the tray: our special midnight collation, he said. There were sandwiches built of crackers, thin-sliced Spam, and pickles. Tall glasses of chocolate milk, beaten to a froth—his own recipe, he said, a careful blend of canned milk and cold water. If they were on a honeymoon, she thought, they could play like this, and feed on nectar and the milk of paradise. She tried to see what it meant to him; she knew he was a friend to all, an adventurer in the amenities, with the characteristics of a yearling puppy; she knew well that the illusion was all on her side, but the pleasure of it was too great to resist. She saw her hand tremble as it reached for a cracker sandwich; she hardly dared lift the foaming glass.

✍§ CHAPTER 14 ౾✍

THE LIGHTS went out a little before one and the card players cried out in protest. But the dark subdued them. The storm sounded louder; a dim whiteness shone through the glass, and a ghostlike stir of the snow on the panes.

"No power, no heat," Gus said without accent. He poked and rattled and lighted matches and set up a single candle in a bottle on the counter. For a time the only noise was the boom and seethe of wind; then, faintly, the mutter of distant plows on the highways, the diesel engines coming closer, the clash of steel blades on pavement. The awful voices of progress, John Rossiter said, the armored divisions of civilization coming to the rescue. They sounded pretty fearsome.

She tried to curl up under her coat. He lighted his pipe. The cold came over them imperceptibly. "When you think about it candidly," he said, "do you feel that you lead a life of quiet desperation?"

It was rhetorical, she figured. He was poised for a speculative plunge.

"No amount of thinking could put it more candidly. It is the Eustace way of life. Why do you ask?"

"Well, it's one of those excursion trains of thought. You begin with a blizzard, you think of Whittier and how it was then, you think there were more natural harmonies a century ago when men and nature were supposed to go hand in hand, when there were fewer causes of frustration—and then you remember that this is also the centennial of Thoreau's remark that most people lead lives of quiet desperation. And of course you wonder if the condition of man isn't inevitably desperate. I mean, discontent—"

"Divine discontent?"

He saw her watching him. He missed very little, she realized.

"Oh—divine. Yes, if you like. There's mystery enough for any amount of divinity. But as long as we are men we are destined for trouble. That's what the 'p of m' people—"

"The who?"

"The peace-of-minders. They don't face it. They don't admire suffering as they should. They aim at painlessness, as though you were to subsist on aspirin. But of course suffering is God's greatest gift to man—it is why men are men."

She hardly listened seriously. The talk went on. He improvised; he rendered his phrases with all varieties of accent, with pseudo-seriousness, irony, laughter, indignation, ostentation, humility. "You hear a lot about Gresham's Law," he said, sucking at the cold pipe. "A great boon to debaters and amateur oracles—but I am introducing a new law that I hope will be equally useful. Rossiter's Law. It has to do with truth, and I must state it in classic terms so it will look well on the books of time. How would it sound if I said, *Truth is self-corrupting*"? He stared at the flickering candle across the room. "All right, that's Rossiter's Law. Truth is self-corrupting. Sounds pretty good if I do say so. You take the vision of peace on earth—it is the kingdom of God, the ideal, the very truth of man's hope, but it is false to man's nature. Or take the opposite, the strife, the suffering, the crucifying, at exactly what point along the line does the truth begin to go bad?"

Suddenly he fixed her with a direct and personal look. "It all comes down to how much. How much peace, how much strife. Too much is always wrong. You spoke—I think you spoke bitterly about desperation, as though you . . ." He grinned. "No one is ever reconciled." He meant to be kind to her; she could see it occurring to him and taking hold of his imagination. "It's a foolish thing to say, but I'm a professional consultant for desperate characters. It's what I do. Mostly I just have to listen—" He gave a sudden yelp of mirth. "I want you to know I can listen. My wife calls me a compulsive talker—she only says it when she reaches a saturation point, but that word *compulsive* is a sandbag: any time you want to put somebody out of business, just hit him with 'compulsive' . . ."

His wife was German, she suddenly remembered. No frivolity, no grace, but great strength and competence. She sang with them sometimes. She always wore blue—her eyes were pale blue, her hair brown and tied in a bun; on Sundays when she came to church with her small girl and boy she was dressed and decorated beyond her usual functional minimum, and the flush in her fair skin made her seem attractive—or at least pleasantly feminine. But at home she looked like a practical nurse, which is what she professionally was. She probably got him when he was sick, Mary Kyle thought—it was a trap no man could escape. She did everything as though it were a business—at least, it seemed so: she married, conceived and gave birth, kept house, went to church, sang anthems, carried on her profession, all with practical intent, much as an ant or squirrel seems to go through its destined motions. The two children seemed like practical results, subdued and obedient: the girl, about seven, with blonde pigtails and pink skin, always speechless and dutiful, the boy of four very stout and red like a miniature traffic cop. They were his too, of course, but she had never seen him with them—she separated them in her mind, she thought of his life at home as only a minor duty. It could be that his children shared some of his own wondrous qualities, even though they were outwardly hers. They would inevitably grow up and be extraordinary, but in what way no one could tell.

He was talking of her family. He knew about Buzz playing basketball. He knew Patience, who sometimes sang in the choir: the Misses Eustace, he said expansively, were great additions to the choir, both musically and ornamentally.

"If you are trying to say that Patience is pretty, I agree. You don't have to be so elaborately tactful." As soon as she said it she felt foolish, but something made her go on. "She can't sing worth a darn—but on the other hand no one ever referred to me as ornamental."

In the silence she felt more foolish, not knowing whether he was amused or critical or indifferent. "Mother was the beauty," she rushed on. "It is frightening to realize—I mean, she looks like doom, she looks worse than that, worse than anything, but once she was celebrated—in a modest local way, that is. She had natural golden hair and classic features, but they never made much of it—they cultivated her mind and character . . ."

She talked on more securely, with increasing intensity. She half realized that it was a sort of confessional that she couldn't prevent. He didn't draw it out of her; she went on and on. The cold intensified; she curled tighter against herself, and her damp feet grew icy. He smoked. The tale of her family unrolled in her mind like fiction, but not so much drama as a case, a brooding query into their failings and failures. "I sometimes think it's just the house there, like a dead end of hope. There seems to be no point in living under those conditions—I mean, it isn't only ugliness, it is abandon all hope, ye who enter. There's no way of escaping—outside is as bad as inside. But then I know it isn't the house. It's us—the house only reflects what we are—"

When they listened they realized that the wind no longer blew so violently; in the lulls the mutter of the plows came from far distances. A few of the waiting people stirred; one opened the door and went off into the darkness. "A blizzard," someone earnestly said, "is when you get a north wind like this, with a foot or more of dry snow—but the big thing about it is the cold. It can't be more than ten above out there and it'll get colder—"

"Ten above in here, I bet," a sharp voice said. "I feel like a froze mackerel."

"Fifty-two," Gus said. "I got thermometers, anybody wants to buy 'em."

"No good if that's all they say. You musta read 'em wrong."

She turned again toward John Rossiter. "You aren't trapped that way. You live in a dismal house, goodness knows, but you—you seem to—at least, you aren't sorry for yourself. Of course I don't intend to be either, but—it isn't only me I'm sorry for, its actually everyone. Those people on the train every day. I see Father going up the platform looking worn and drab, marching like a conscript to a day's job that means nothing to him, and then suddenly I see all of them marching the same way morning and night, morning and night and winter and summer—it comes over me that none of it has *meaning* any more than the rising and falling of the tide, less than that, probably: I can accept the universe, I suppose—I mean the stars in their courses and the moon and all that—there must be some point to the way they work: but people—you think of them as aiming, achieving, getting somewhere. Am I just having delusions? Am I still suffering from romantic adolescence?"

"You want me to try to tell you or are you just saying it?"

"Well, what you said about advising desperate characters—"

"Why don't you leave home?"

"That's no answer."

"Not philosophical, no—but my business is mostly with what's expedient."

"You mean rent a room in Boston?"

"You going to marry? Have a family?"

"Am I—? Well, how should I know? You were just telling me it didn't matter—you told me not to be silly about it."

"Well, it's what some people do. I was just trying to see it your way. You say aiming and achieving, and that's one method. But you could achieve a lot of other things if you tried hard. You could go into foreign service, you could be a scholar, or an artist, or go off to New Zealand and raise sheep—they like strong girls in New Zealand, I'm told. Or I could give you a job in the Children's Aid caring for orphans and bastards—"

"Me? You'd give me a job?"

"Sure thing. I know a good woman when I get caught in a storm with her."

"Romantic delusions and all?"

"Oh—that. You haven't paid enough attention to Rossiter's Law. You try to push your truth a little too far. Aiming and achieving is a good idea, all right—I'm strongly in favor of it, but there's a big part of human nature that doesn't much care about it. I believe if you offered people a choice—on the one hand a chance to achieve, with all the hazards and hardships to go with it, on the other hand six thousand a year with no strings at all— you *know* what would happen. A good many would take the free money with the best of intentions to achieve something—they'd write or paint or do research, and one in a thousand might succeed. But the strongest desire of most people is to stay alive comfortably —and that's all."

She let herself shiver. "C-comfort, he says. All those miserable c-commuters—"

"Nothing you can say about mankind is wholly true—that's another version of Rossiter's Law. But what you idealists always forget is that the main business of mortal creation is simply existence. It's all very well to consider the lilies, but most of us are basically devoted to sleeping and eating and buying raiment—and I'd add that drinking and buying cars is part of the same intention to overcome time, to get from here to tomorrow as securely and painlessly as possible."

"Do you hear how quiet it is?"

He seemed to hold his breath for a moment. No wind anywhere, no shakings and rattlings on windows and door. "It would be well," he said, "if I talked less and listened more."

John, she thought. John Rossiter. Her head swam with sleep and weariness. The young people at the church all called him Mister Ross; they said it quick and sharp. *Mister Ross*—like that. "Do they call you that everywhere?" she murmured.

"Call me what?"

"I'm sorry. My mind wanders. The kids all call you Mister Ross."

"Oh, half the delinquents of Boston do that."

"Well—" Her head tipped and she tried to keep from snuggling against him. "I think I like John better." It goes better with Mary, she almost said. John and Mary. It sounded like a soap opera. John's Other Wife. She dimly wondered if she had said it aloud, or mumbled it in her half-sleep.

ᥤᥥ CHAPTER 15 ᥬᥨ

THEIR HOUSE seemed to be a small pure-white palace on a mountaintop, a sort of Taj-Mahal without any domes, but with delicate carvings in alabaster and many terraces and pools. He pointed to the lovely blue ice of the pools: it was a winter palace, he said, and the walls were really made of snow and were very solid and wind-proof. After a while you didn't mind the cold—you had to learn to like it. It was the most beautiful place ever seen and they were there together, apart from the world, as far as possible from Boston and the North Station, and soon, very soon, when they stopped shaking, their happiness would begin.

She snuggled her head closer to the hollow of his shoulder and shut her eyes tight against the glare. She relaxed, she stopped shivering, she seemed to float on a comfortable sea of warmth and safety: the sense of coming happiness was strong.

Voices broke in, loud slams of a door, footsteps. Lights were on. She let one eye flutter open and saw two gray-coated policemen.

Her face was half-buried in his tweed overcoat; his arm across her shoulders held her snugly. She knew at once all that had happened, the storm, the refuge, the loss of light and heat—now restored, but the dream still occupied her whole being; she saw the white palace, the terraces and pools of blue ice, and she felt the emotion of overwhelming happiness like a rush of music. But her head ached sharply right above her eyes and her muscles had cramped themselves into angles.

For a few more seconds she pretended. No passion, she knew, not even affection—not very much, anyway. But she pretended. She had been in love once, during her last year in college: this

77

reminded her, the circling arm, the tweed against her face, the snug warmth of two bodies together; Harry Fitts, a melancholy jester, a charming cynic, doomed to fail in any serious endeavor —but she would have married him, she intended to, she loved him even though he always drank too much at parties, and redeemed himself later by writing funny apologetic verses which were sometimes published in his college magazine. But he threw her over. He escaped her. He could never marry a good woman, he told her; it would be too embarrassing. She knew she had been possessive—it was her inevitable mistake, but she couldn't help it. She took charge, she bossed. Weakness and failure offended her. She and Harry Fitts would have been miserable together. But she had loved and lost him. Some of the same emotions stirred now, the closeness of bodies, the merging, the escape from loneliness. It was like music.

He hadn't spoken. She knew he was awake—his hand had moved on her shoulder, had fitted her more comfortably against him. He was the man, of course, not like Harry a charming failure, not troubled about being bossed or saved from sin. She let the dream exist for another moment, then drew a long breath and began to move her stiff joints.

"It looks like the end of the war," he said. His arm released her.

She rubbed her eyes and face, pushed back her hair, and sat up. She saw that he was as rumpled as a scarecrow, but ruddy and alert; his eye on her was not critical or intimate, but in some way appreciative. "You look well this morning, Miss Eustace."

"I—probably am, Mr. Rossiter. It's nice to be reassured. The thing is to find out if I can move my joints."

She smiled with supreme happiness. These moments, she felt, were the best she had ever lived through.

He laughed, and she knew he shared it with her. They had it together, almost like old lovers.

"I doubt if I can stand up. Can you?"

"I very much doubt it. All I can feel are the needles and pins."

She studied him frankly, saying the words over and over to herself: needles and pins, needles and pins . . .

"Our friend Gus has offered us what he calls rest-room facilities —no, I'm the one who calls it that. He just sort of nods toward the back room there. They say the main roads are open and things are rolling again."

She could feel the energy in him, but she moved reluctantly. She said "needles and pins" half to herself again. He stood up, reached down and gave her a hand; she groaned and let herself be pulled up. "Are we off at once? In the dark?" The sense of closeness was still strong for her; she leaned a little against him and moved her arms and legs to help the circulation.

"Gus has some hot tea, too." He patted her as he might a faithful dog. "As you said—a little cynically, I fear—comes the dawn."

"Well—damn the dawn." But she straightened up and pulled at her clothes. "You and your energy. You'll be off to Worcester, I suppose, as soon as you can get rid of me. I tell you frankly I hate the dawn. Either I have to get up and go to work or I stay in bed and sleep—I just don't believe in dawns." But her tone intended to be more impudent than complaining. "Even here, I was just settling down into a wonderful dream of a palace made of ice and alabaster." She smiled; her strong-boned face resolved into a dazzle of warmth and pleasure. "It was a nice night. I can tell you now that I never slept with a man before."

She used it as an exit line, and walked off toward Gus's back room, but she saw that his answering smile was overlaid with surprise and embarrassment. There was even a flush of color in his weathered face.

When she came back she found that he had organized a collection plate for Gus and was making a speech of thanks: "And if it were not quite so early in the day, I would call upon our fellow orphan of the storm, Miss Mary Kyle Eustace, to recite a few verses of Whittier's *Snowbound* . . ."

The place was heavy with smoke and bad air and except for the clink of small coins in the plate there was little response. The policemen had gone out. Gus said, "Thank you very much." He had a face like a white squarish mask, with a small mouth and colorless lips, and his habit was one of silence and suspicion. But unexpectedly he tilted his chin upward a fraction of an inch and smiled. "Had to read it in the tenth grade," he said. "Old Miss Flaherty. She thought it was the greatest. Never expected I'd remember it again—specially in a joint like this." He shrugged and resettled his mask.

Mary Kyle quoted for him:

What matter how the night behaved?
What matter how the north-wind raved?
Blow high, blow low, not all its snow
Could quench our hearth-fire's ruddy glow.

"Takes you back, all right," Gus said by way of applause. "What they call the good old days. Old Flaherty thought it was terrific."

Mary Kyle felt a sharp little ache above her eyes. She sipped the warm tea and took a prophetic view of the makeshift store, the litter of magazines and comic books, the rack of paper-covered novels, the candies, cigarettes, the shelves and counters of cosmetics, bathroom supplies, pills, syrups, lotions, the displays and special offers: A four-way cold remedy. Complete vitamin protection. Relax with Super-Sleepers.

"Snowstorms," John Rossiter was saying, "are now measured in cost to the taxpayers."

Gus nodded at the plate of coins on the counter of the soda fountain. "First time I ever made any dough out of one. I appreciate it."

The aim would be, she thought, to put all remedies into one, to provide a one-a-day solution to the hazards of humanity including blizzards and cold and weariness of spirit . . .

"You needn't come with me," John was saying. "If I can get dug out, I'll come back and pick you up."

But she didn't bother to argue. "Ready? Let's go, then."

From the brightness and warmth they stepped knee-deep into dry snow. The first breath of cold pierced them like a blade too sharp to feel. They pushed out through a drifted sidewalk and stood for a moment in the once-plowed street.

"It's all clear up there," he said. "And no wind, and feels like below zero—" He spoke explosively, as though the facts were vital to them. He grinned at her. "Come on—we've got to keep moving."

It was like the silence of infinite space. Not even the mutter of a plow or the scour of the wind, though a northern pressure of air intensified the cold. The sky had begun to gray with the dawn, the stars faded.

"It's a fine morning," he said sharply, eagerly. "Don't freeze your ears!" He laughed aloud, and kept a pace ahead of her.

Her dream recurred. The whiteness, the pure splendor, the promise of revelation. They walked eastward toward a streak of rose along the horizon. A car passed them, crunching quietly under a high load of snow; lights appeared in houses; a steel shovel scraped. But the old litter of suburban streets was lost under drifts and carved shapes of snow.

She pushed along in the shifty footing and felt the air cut into her chest; she chafed her left ear and wiped the running tears from her eyes and nose. She nodded and laughed when he pointed to a parked car looking, as he said, like Mount McKinley forty miles away. Her head still ached and her shoes were filling with melted snow but the sense of coming happiness was still great in her.

His car on the highway had been pushed with others to one side and buried by the plows. The main lanes were already beaten smooth by the traffic. They stood at the edge, in danger from passing ten-wheelers, and tried to pick out his among the abandoned cars and mountains of plowed snow.

"No use getting sore," he explained to himself. "The police can't help it, the plows can't help it—the only thing I'm really annoyed about is that those Detroit builders could perfectly well make a car that would move in snow. Now I assume that bit of gray metal in there belongs to me—what do you think?"

"Even if it does, I don't see what you can do about it."

"Do? My dear girl, I can do my damnedest." He seized a chunk of snow in his hands and tossed it along the edge of the plowed lane. "You chuck 'em that way and I'll chuck 'em this way and if you work hard your fingers may not freeze." But the snow was a solid bank. He clawed it and kicked it, he climbed on the pile and pushed with his heels, he flung himself into it, he bored and churned and pounded like a snow-digging terrier. She tossed away the chunks, laughing and beating her hands together and rubbing her ears, and when all at once the sun blazed out across the white she felt again the stab of expectancy. Drift curves turned gold, the shadowy hollows were a deep greeny blue, above them the sky brightened to diamond-like blue.

He got at the cover of the rear compartment and forced it open, he dived in almost bodily and came out with a coal shovel which he brandished like a battle-ax. "Now! Now we'll see who's winning this war!"

He seemed to double his energy.

"You'll kill yourself," she said, but he failed to hear. She shouted it.

"Suits me," he answered, breathing hard and tossing a huge chunk to one side. But then he paused and grinned at her. "Nothing I like better than the morning after a blizzard: makes me want to get my old skis out of the cellar and head north—makes me feel about eighteen."

Her heart jumped, she felt the quick bump it made.

He went at his shoveling. "It's easy to be flippant about it—a short life and a merry one and all that, but after all why not?"

She said no more about death.

He started the car, backed out, and headed for East Compton. Her feet, she realized, were probably frozen. He was warm and flushed and happy. "I keep thinking I'll get back to the mountains again, but one thing and another seems to come up. You ever ski?"

"In college I did."

He shook his head a little. "I can see you're in a rut—both of us are, no doubt. What we need in the church is an outing club—some way of getting us off for a day or two—"

But the blaze of morning light on the great snow took on a pitiless look. Her head throbbed; her feet still froze. The car turned into her street, skidding and crunching on the loose powder; the slate-gray house looked dead.

"Will you come in for some breakfast?"

"No thank you—I'll be home in half a minute."

Home. She couldn't seem to move.

"You'll go to Worcester?"

"Oh, I expect so—after I do a lot more shoveling. The driving will be good on the main roads."

"You think I should go to work?"

"Well, with me it isn't merely work—I mean, if it was just going to the office I'd say the hell with it." He looked at her. "You'd better get a hot bath and some sleep."

Nothing seemed to count any more. She felt the choke of tears.

But she sat a moment longer.

"Thank you for taking care of me."

"I only got you into trouble—"

"Don't—don't say it that way. It was an adventure, wasn't it?"

"It was that, all right."

"It was—" She broke off. She opened the door and slid out and then looked back with a wide smile. Her strong and rather somber face grew beautiful. "It was a fine adventure. I think it is what I need—as you pointed out when you advised me to try sheep-farming in New Zealand. I'm grateful to you. If you can arrange other adventures—say shipwreck on a desert island—count me in."

"There's no one I'd rather count in."

For a moment she was transfixed. Then she reached out a hand and they shook with solemn recognition. Their eyes took a steady view of each other.

"Good," she said. "I won't forget."

✺§ CHAPTER 16 ੪✺

IN THE AFTERNOON of the blizzard, Patience Eustace called her mother to say that she was staying in for the dramatic club play and would spend the night with Edna Siegel. She often did—she made excuses to stay with Edna, who lived in a large and picturesque studio apartment with a widowed aunt. The place was full of artistic relics, easels, palettes, busts, bottles, jars, flamboyant oils on the walls and standing in corners, all a little dusty and quaint. The aunt kept it intact as a memorial to her husband, whom she admired with a sort of absolute finality, as though the major tradition of painting had culminated and ended with him. She referred to him by name, Albert Ryerson, as one to rank with Winslow Homer or John Singer Sargent, and any reference to modern painting or younger painters left her too angry for speech. Otherwise she lived in sentimental simplicity, devoted herself to children and grandchildren, provided lodging and board for Edna, and was available as a substitute teacher in the public elementary schools.

Among Edna's friends the studio was well known as a charming and rather secret gathering-place. The great north window, the high raftered ceiling, the long billowy India prints, all the decorative remains of what might have been a great artistic career, seemed almost operatic, like a setting for *La Bohème* or *Trilby*. The main entrance was on a balcony, and a flight of stairs slanted downward, so that goings and comings became inevitably spectacular. The sleeping and living arrangements were concealed by curtains, there were couches draped in darkly figured prints, and some baronial oak pieces and decorative items suitable for still-life.

Patience had got used to it, and was aware of its pretenses and lost hopes, but she made herself enjoy its charm. They had parties —Edna was a born party-giver: she drank and smoked expertly, she could sing, strum a banjo, act in plays, dance, handle men. Her Aunt Claire was always in favor of parties, more perhaps in theory than practice: she knew that the studio was ideally suited to parties, and she remembered brilliant gatherings of years before. She thought of Edna and her friends as somehow carrying on the traditions; she flattered herself that she knew all about them and shared their humors and tastes, though she could look down on them from the vantage point of a lifetime with Albert Ryerson. There were values and characteristics among true artists, she said, that never changed: only the poseurs and charlatans kept changing for the sake of novelty. It was easy at this point to goad her into a rage against all post-Ryerson art, and now and then a young worldling did so, but more often they were bored and hoped she would go away and leave them alone.

Edna was active in the Drama Club; she could direct or manage or paint a scene or act or do a solo dance—all with uninhibited ease. She simply carried on the little displays of talent she had been taught as a child, and though she talked of a possible "career," or let her friends talk, she had no strong intent about anything except the pleasure of being admired in her college and social world. There was something attractively easy about her— the way she literally plunged into any experience by the quickest and most obvious method: she could get good marks with the least work, she could win at games, she had no troubles with ethics or uncertainties of conscience, she was always right. She had no wit or brilliance but she seemed to be the essential member of the group: Patience followed her and did much routine work for the Drama Club on her account. "It would be good for me if I could act," Patience said. "But I can't—I just can't. The best I can do is to build sets."

Patience had become intensely self-analytical. She saw herself as a bundle of inhibitions; she referred to her puritan heritage; she assumed that she was doomed to hate her mother and resent her sister, that she had been deprived of what were called normal emotional outlets. She kept drawing up recommendations and programs for herself: she must take up music, she must join the

Drama Club, she must read modern French literature and find out about Existentialism, she must discover true sexual freedom, she must enter the new life of fulfillment. She had a vision of herself as wholly disillusioned, wholly honest, wholly ready to live in accord with the given realities of life; she looked off into a future beyond good and evil, beyond the foolish ethical entanglements superstitious humanity had invented for itself—it was almost a visible heaven in which intelligence and truth were in full control.

But meanwhile she lived a double life—at home the self-contained Patience, managing her affairs inconspicuously, almost secretly, at college known as Pat Eustace, one of a sophisticated set, a brain, a psychology major with advanced views. She was rather sharp and impatient, she made it her policy to be cynical with dullards and to shock the innocent; she called attention to her own emancipation and her acceptance of the realities rather than the illusions. Her whole appearance took on a fine urban polish, with no excesses, no frills, but with careful feminine style. What frightened her most deeply was sex. The university was inevitably a sort of hothouse where young men and women were subjected to every kind of relationship, where sex-consciousness was all-pervasive. Patience argued—with herself and some of her friends—that it was her duty to be perfectly realistic and rational; she allowed herself no inhibitions; she spoke precisely about the functions; she used all the words—she even made herself use them in class discussions, adopting an objective and experienced tone to indicate that it was no longer even a question of being emancipated. She spoke as though none of it had any connection with herself as an individual.

But in her candor she knew that she posed. She could not act successfully on the stage of a theatre but she could sustain a part in life: in a way she resented the rather glittery sophistication she had adopted, but there seemed to be no help for it. She even realized that it was vanity, that she enjoyed prestige and social admiration, that what she hoped for and lacked was a certain kind of sexual success. It bothered her that though the young men at first came to her naturally and even gladly, they grew uncertain and backed off and treated her with respect and a touch of fear. Her wit and worldliness dampened them, yet she could not seem to behave otherwise: in fact, she was goaded to mock and wound them. She saw their stupidities, their callow youth, their obvious inferiority to her vision of civilized behavior; she kept looking beyond them to find someone better—she even tried to magnetize one or two of the younger faculty members, without success. For a time she built up her attachment to Edna Siegel into a compensating affair, and as long as no one else interfered, the two complemented each other, but Edna had a succession of true lovers—or more aptly marriages of convenience, since she was capable of only the mildest of passions.

In this second half of her junior year Patience had been making better progress. She contributed a short poem to the literary magazine that gave her the kind of recognition she sought; she learned enough about music to be accepted among the serious listeners and critics; she found it possible to admire some of the young men who she thought were more learned and worldly than she. She even softened, grew charming, was aware of her prettiness; she almost felt that she had broken the barrier of her repressions and was entering at last into that heaven of intelligence and truth that she believed in. She settled finally, with outward poise and inward timidity, on Anton Kedjian—though it was hardly a free decision: she allowed herself to smile with unaffected warmth and he appropriated her. He was more beautiful and accomplished than anyone she had yet known: tall, fiercely dark with a hawklike nose, inscrutable Asiatic eyes, black crinkled hair, cleft chin, and a white and winning smile. He wrote one-act plays, he did most of the musical criticism for the university newspaper, he was a member of the fencing team: he was so conspicuous, in fact, that the girls called him Ozymandias, shortened to Oz, and assumed that he was dangerous and unscrupulous.

Early in their game Patience, whose habit was still to be candid, asked him. "Are you unscrupulous, Oz?"

He was alert—on guard, perhaps. "Un-scrupulous?"

"It's what they say about you."

"They say." His smile flashed and included her in a wondrous sense of awareness.

"Well you do look like the character in the movies who charges in on a white horse and captures the sacred city and all the maidens."

"Surely—not all alone?"

"Oh, there are others—there are cohorts gleaming in purple and gold. But you are the number one wolf—your name is in lights."

"Not if it's Kedjian." He always spoke softly and slowly, as though he were feeling his way toward the truth. "Anton Kedjian does sound suitably Assyrian, but for lights, for top billing, you have to have honest English or Scotch. Tony Gordon, or Hudson, or Curtis—"

"Well, that isn't the point. What I want to know is about how unscrupulous you are."

"Couldn't you put it more kindly? Couldn't you just omit the *un?* I mean, the principle of honest English law—under which we happily flourish—is that we are all presumed to be scrupulous. As a thoroughbred Anglo-Saxon named Patience Starrett Eustace—"

"How did you know about Starrett?"

"I know what I know, O infidel maid."

She was delighted. She played up to him, and he to her. They had lunch together and coffee together at all times of day and evening. They went steady. She decided that he was as scrupulous as anyone could be, even though he warned her against himself. He liked to speak speculatively, and as a student of philosophy he took a professionally detached view of behavior—he always did well in seminars and bull sessions, where he had learned to be modest and gentle in his talk.

"I don't believe any man can be trusted—or any woman—"

"That's what you learn sophomore year," she broke in.

"No—wait: I don't mean it as a sophomoric cliché; though perhaps—perhaps that's all it really is. But the basic truth of nature is conflict, or struggle for survival, or simply war. Every living cell fights for not only life, but for whatever it can gain—it is first, last, and always unscrupulous; it is made that way."

"You must be studying Darwin."

"Well—" his smile was charming. "You don't have to study Darwin, not these days. It's what everybody knows. To be good is to be unnatural—"

When he first said it, Patience was more excited than she admitted even to herself. She gave no sign, except for an appreciative glance at his interesting face, but the idea seemed to lead on into that realm of dangerous but essential truth that she had been imagining. She paid less attention to what he went on to say—

that it was man's fateful task to invent and build a workable system of virtue within a hostile environment. It was easier to believe that such a system would work when man regarded himself as allied with God rather than with brute nature, but now that all of us are brutes together, the task seems much harder—if not impossible. Even the idea of peace seems unnatural and unhuman, he said, but none the less, it was man's greatest duty to achieve at least a relative peace. One of Oz's notable habits, which entertained his friends at coffee tables and bars, was to draw a chart of good and evil: it began with a vertical line on a bare sheet of paper, with an arrowhead at each end. God existed infinitely high, evil infinitely low, and if time permitted he sketched in vistas of heaven and hell with appropriate harps, wings, sharp tridents, and infernal fires: man's range, he indicated, was at most about half an inch out of infinity. When we behaved well and nobly, like, say, Abraham Lincoln or Woodrow Wilson, we were at the top of our half-inch, and when we were Hitler, say, we were at the bottom: for most of us, our whole task was to gain a quarter of an inch against infinity—even an eighth of an inch might make the difference between savagery and non-savagery.

It was a source of endless argument. Where did the saints fit in the scale? Where did Jesus fit? Religious believers took issue and grew angry. Cynics applauded but felt that the half-inch was too generous. Oz remained reasonable and somehow sweetly serious, though he embellished his drawing with fanciful symbols and little caricatures of his friends and rivals up and down the scale.

Patience was convinced at first of his ruthless worldliness: she and others took him to be the character projected by novels and moving pictures as the irresistible male whose only concern was sexual satisfaction. Nothing made her angrier than the efforts at dominance on the part of young men who had learned about life from show business, whose sexual drives seemed to her more ugly and savage than anything she had read about in primitive cultures. But none the less she admitted to herself a profound unease, a longing for understanding, a need for the beginnings of marriage; she shared with all the others, savage or cultivated, the pervasive sexual consciousness of her surroundings. She saw Anton Kedjian as a challenge and a mystery: even his name and eastern aspect magnetized her, and she read Omar Khayyám and had glimpses

◄§ CHAPTER 17 §►

Buzz Eustace and his team played that same evening in Williams-town, and after the game drove back on the mountain road to Wyndham. It was one of their big games, and they were full of pleasure at winning. The storm, which dumped twenty inches of snow along the eastern coast, struck only a minor blow inland, though winds were strong and cold. About six inches of light powder had been swept and drifted by a northerly gale, and icy roads were unevenly coated. Buzz in the vanity of his youth and pride of victory drove too fast and went into a spin on a steep downgrade. The boys with him cheered and shouted advice and pretended they were on skis, but inexorably, like a slow-motion picture, the crash came against a stone parapet on a sharp curve.

There were cries of laughter, then curses, then silence. The wind rushed and boomed in the forest on the mountain steeps above them. Below the parapet on which the car still balanced a rocky gorge descended into a gulf of darkness.

"Anybody dead?" a voice said.

It turned out that one was. Cliff Wahn, sitting next to Buzz in front, had been thrown head-on against a sharp edge of metal.

The others were bruised. Buzz had broken one of his ribs against the wheel.

In time the forces of rescue came: the others of the team that followed them, then police and ambulance men and wreckers. Nothing could be done for Cliff Wahn. The car was condemned as junk. In silence and darkness they returned to Wyndham and Buzz entered the college hospital.

It happened that Cliff Wahn had been his roommate and

partner and had been, as he had gratefully realized, way ahead of him in nearly all accomplishments. It was Cliff who saw Buzz through his exams, who supervised his papers, who gave him little glimpses of what intellectual activity looked like. It was Cliff who had the polish, who knew what to do in New York, who directed him in social complications. It was Cliff, in short, who supplied the education he might never have got from Wyndham College. He couldn't have said it or even quite realized it, but he loved Cliff, whose rôle had been that of friend, brother, father, and wife all in one.

Up to that time he had been oblivious to most of the problems of existence. He ate and slept well and he played on the basketball team; all other affairs were merely contingent. The minimum grades, the fraternal duties, the summer jobs, the routines of living, were the prescribed functions of a happy-go-lucky basketball player: as for a future involving career and other responsibilities, he had assumed that it would take care of him in time. Everybody had a job of some sort; college men had good jobs—money, at least, was plentiful: look at the Chryslers and Buicks they drove. Cliff Wahn had been more serious, of course, and was going to law school.

For the two nights and a day in the infirmary he remained oblivious. His cousin Albert Livermore came, the dean came, even the president came, and each visit followed a funereal pattern in which he was soothed, comforted, and somehow warned: but he took it as ceremony. Even a lawyer visited him and mentioned possible consequences, at which he dumbly nodded. He was told of the profound shock to the college, and he acknowledged that it must be so. When his sister Mary Kyle called him he hardly took it in that his father had had a coronary stroke, but he agreed that he had better come home as soon as he could, though he had a couple of hour exams coming up: he started to mention the Saturday game with Trinity but broke off in uncertainty. Things would not, he began to see, be quite the same.

He came back to his room in the top floor of the fraternity house on a still winter morning when most of the boys were off to classes. A memorial service was to be at four o'clock in the Chapel and he had naturally intended to go. His rib still hurt intensely, specially when he coughed or sneezed, but it was bound up tightly and he could walk about well enough. He felt nothing but disdain for his own injuries.

Everything of Cliff's was gone, every scrap of his personal life had been wiped out; his desk and bed and bureau were bare, like items in an empty barracks. Even Buzz's own properties had been tidied and dusted into dismal impersonality. The room struck him abruptly: it was lifeless and airless—it was dead. He noted that even the window curtains were gone, the yellow ones Cliff's mother had hung there last September, and which he had simply taken for granted as an expected motherly gesture. Now he looked at the bare woodwork as though it were the framework of death itself. Had she come and taken them with all the other things, had she been there in person? He saw her in his mind. She had avoided him. She blamed him, of course. She had always regarded him with a sort of ironic patience, he half realized—he was unworthy of her son but harmless and even absurd.

He walked back and forth in the bare room, then stood by the window and stared at the skeleton of a snowy elm, then settled into a morris chair. He had no notion what to do or what to think. His ribs throbbed against the binding and he sat straighter in a temporary attitude. She would be at the service, he realized. They'd all be there, friends, family, dignitaries, team-mates, people, and they'd all be staring at him.

The whole inside of his stomach and chest and throat became a general ache, and seemed to press for release. His head buzzed, his eyes stung, the back of his throat hurt. He didn't know what to do or how to think: the wave of misery astonished him, and he sat a long time waiting for it to recede. He heard voices and idle whistlings in other parts of the house and was at first afraid someone would come in and see him—then he half hoped someone might come in and take care of him or divert him or make things right. His continuing notion was still that the routines would go on as before, the schedules, classes, games, the stream of college events that carried one along without the effort of decision. Nothing could be done now to alter what had happened: it was bad, of course, it was terrible . . . he began to cry in audible sobs and he stood up in an agony of shame, relishing the knife-stab in his ribs, and walked rapidly to the window and stared at the bare trees and roofs. He mopped his face, crossed the room and shut the door, sat down again, stood up and looked out of the window. His eyes still ran, but as long as he stared at the trees and roofs he could control the sobs: but everything out there looked like death.

In time he heard voices in the lower hall and purposeful steps coming up. He had been looking out of the window for a long time—it might have been an hour from the way he felt: his head still buzzed a little and the large ache still lurked underneath his chest, but his face was dry. He couldn't think what to do. It was lunchtime, and he had never in his life voluntarily missed a meal, but something kept him from going. His imagination tried to deal with the problem of the memorial service at four, but his only response to it was an inner shudder of fear. Now as the steps came to his door it seemed to him that it must be a rescue.

A knock and a voice. "Mort? Someone here asking for you."

"Come in."

A small untidy man entered with a little rush. He held an empty pipe in one hand, a crumpled hat in the other. "You're Buzz Eustace?" The smile showed gaps between his teeth. "Haven't seen you since you added the last foot and a half. Rossiter's my name—if you saw me on Myrtle Street back home you'd know it right off: we used to shoot baskets in front of Paul Mulhern's garage—before you went to Junior High—remember? I believe I taught you the hook shot with either hand—I'd probably got over expecting the miracle that would make me six-four instead of five-four, but I still practiced shots in Paul's yard. Maybe I can claim to have discovered you . . ."

They shook hands, and the talk rattled on. Buzz hardly took it in but once or twice he gave his ear-to-ear grin. He certainly remembered Paul Mulhern's yard and the basket over the garage door and Mister Ross, as they all called him, darting about like a terrier. Usually kids resented it when some old geezer came out and cavorted around with them, but they were all crazy about Mister Ross. He could still hear the shouts: "Hey, Mister—hey, Mister Ross—watch this, watch me hook one!"

He happened to be in Worcester, he said, and read about the accident in the paper—he thought he might as well run out to Wyndham and see if there was anything he could do. He had called up the family last evening—talked with Mary Kyle who said she'd have come on right away but her father was ill, too. So it was no trouble for him—the roads were all plowed, and there was less snow out this way anyhow. He thought of going home late that afternoon and would be glad to take Buzz along.

The effect of life going on, of the flow of events in time, was comforting, and Buzz began to think of his lunch: perhaps they could get off early, as soon as he packed up a few things.

"Saw some sort of assistant dean," John Rossiter was saying. "He told me they're having a service at four—"

"I don't have to go," Buzz said quickly.

"Well, it depends on how you feel, of course. A cracked rib can be mighty painful—"

"Oh—that—"

"But right now what I have on my mind is nourishment. I can do fifty miles on a half pint of coffee, but not much more; how do you feel about coming up the line with me—I noticed a couple of eating joints up near the center of town. Can you move that far?"

Buzz could and did. He felt that things were going fine. Being with John Rossiter gave him safety. He ate a large lunch.

"I don't think I feel up to that service," he said afterward. "If you are ready and all, why don't I pack up a few things—"

John Rossiter was smoking busily and diddling with his pipe and puffing and tamping the tobacco with the end of a stubby pencil.

"You mean your ribs don't feel up to it?"

"Oh, I guess I can stand that all right—I mean, a lot of guys get cracked ribs, specially in football. Last fall Norm Walsh played a whole half against Wesleyan with two busted ribs—never said a word."

"Heroic of him," John said.

"Oh, he's a good guy—he's all right."

"I'm glad to hear he's all right." John's smile was very bright. "I always say that a good deal of the important work of the world is done by people who feel like hell."

"I guess so—I guess that's true."

After a silence, in which the pipe sizzled audibly, Buzz went on: "They'll all be there—I mean everyone will. His folks—Cliff's folks will be there."

The silence continued.

"I figure they won't want to see me anyway. After all, I'm the one—I mean the whole thing was my fault. I expect his mother would feel like—like—I don't know what, but I know I'd better keep out of the way."

"Let's walk back," John said.

"Wouldn't it be better?" Buzz said as they went along. "I mean to say—well, I—I—" He swallowed. "I just hate to—that is, I hate to make them feel any worse. Don't you think so? I mean—don't you think it would be better . . . ?"

John Rossiter's expression silenced him. It was almost a smile but yet it wasn't really a smile. The little man had to cock his head to look up at him; the crumpled hat perched accidentally on the back of his head, the tweed coat flopped open to the winter air, the pipe in the left corner of his mouth had a sort of humorous curve to it.

"Anyway," Buzz said, "this church stuff—I mean, you go to church yourself so you're probably used to it." He flushed a little. "Maybe I hadn't ought to put it like that—I guess when anyone doesn't know what else to do he might as well pray. But I can't go for all the hocus-pocus they have in churches. It's worse than these fraternity goat sessions we have to go through—you know, altars and flames and mystic words and stuff."

When he saw John Rossiter's expression he grinned. "I probably talk like a goon of some kind. But it's no use trying to pretend—I just don't know how to say it . . ." He seemed to run out of ideas. His mouth stayed open to speak but nothing came. They walked for half a block.

"You think I ought to go, huh?"

"I think you'll have to."

"Kind of a duty, you mean?"

John shook ashes from his pipe, looked at it, and gave it a loud suck. He spoke out sharply and seriously. "Well, it's only my idea, of course. You'll have to decide. You ever read Conrad?"

"Who?"

"Conrad—the novels."

"Oh—him. We had to, I guess—back in Freshman year. I kind of forget: was it called *Victory?* We had a choice, and that had the fewest pages."

John did not sigh. He spoke hopefully, with a quick gesture of his pipe. "There are some things you either face or you are licked. It isn't a question of religion—in any church sense, I mean: whether you pray or not is beside the point. It isn't even a question of taking your medicine or doing penance or any of those things. It is simply a question of facing it. The whole thing is a fact—it has happened; the consequences are a fact too." He shook his head impatiently as though his words were not coming right. "If you run away from it, I can almost promise you that you'll never stop running. You'll be dodging and skipping the rest of your life. If your friend's family decide to hate you, that's part of their tragedy: what you need is compassion for them, not fear for yourself. I suppose you think the whole world is blaming you—all you really want is to get into a hole and hide. It's not a thing you can solve—there's no happy ending to it: but there's a best way to handle it and a worst way. The best way often seems to be the toughest."

Buzz had learned to control his body with grace and economy, but his face at this moment took on the bewildered sadness of adolescence; it looked like the almost tearful face of a young basset hound. "Yeah," he said in a half whisper. "Yeah, I suppose— I mean, I guess maybe you know more about it than I do. I just hate to—that is—"

"You hate to face it."

"Well, I—I guess that's it. I hate to face it."

John looked at the tower clock across the white village green, then pulled out his watch. "Best advice I can give is this," he said. "For the next three and a half hours don't think about yourself at all—just forget about Buzz Eustace. Think about those other folks if you want to; maybe you can see and feel the way they do—a little bit. I expect they need help. You got a checkerboard here?"

"Huh?"

"I never get time to play, but twenty years ago I thought I was getting good at it. I presume a well-built fraternity house like this has a checkerboard in it."

"Oh, sure—"

"Well, let's have a game. We've got a couple of hours now, and then you can get packed up."

ᴇᔕ CHAPTER 18 ᔓᴇ

Wʜᴇɴ Buzz came home, driven from Wyndham on a cold winter evening by John Rossiter, the household was mainly concerned about Edwin, who had been taken two days earlier by police ambulance to the Waltham Hospital. At the time they arrived, the house was dark and obviously empty, Buzz had no key, and they sat for some minutes wondering what to do. He had once had a method, he said, of climbing up to the roof of the bay window in the back and getting into his bedroom, but with all this snow and ice plus a fractured rib it would be crazy to try—and he had his good clothes on anyway. He said he could wait at the Callahans', whose lights were still on, and John argued that he might as well go on home with him—and was reaching to start his motor when an old Chevrolet sedan came along with a clink of chains and stopped in front of them near the middle of the empty street. "Chivers, for God's sake," Buzz mumbled.

Doors opened: out stepped Harold, with boots well buckled, black coat buttoned over white wool muffler, black hat, black ear-muffs held in place by a light steel clamp; he bustled round the rear of the car with an eager gesture of good manners and held doors for Josephine and Mary Kyle.

When they all stood together in the cold air, almost nothing was said. Josephine glared at Harold and then at John Rossiter with what looked like hatred, then took a sharp look at Buzz. "They told us you broke a rib," she said in a tone that implied she had been deceived.

"Cracked one, bent another—nothing serious, nothing to make a fuss about."

99

"Serious," she said with a slow emphasis. "Maybe a rib or so isn't serious, but it's about time you began to—"

"How's Pop?"

Mary Kyle began moving them toward the narrow path to the house. "Pop has started to cuss again—he sounds fine. Come on in. It's cold. We'll all freeze. Mother, a few appropriate lines, if you please: something about *a chill no coat, however stout, te tum te tum could quite shut out!*"

She herded them along. But at the steps Josephine turned and blocked them. She spoke out with a voice made strong and explicit by an inner passion:

> O Time and Change!—with hair as gray
> As was my sire's that winter day,
> How strange it seems, with so much gone
> Of life and love, to still live on!

Her face expressed a fierce pleasure in the words and for a moment was full of tragic beauty; then it fell back into the old lines of desperation.

"I'm afraid I'll have to be going," Harold Chivers said. "It is kind of you to ask me in—"

"Oh, come on, Harold. Be bold tonight! I'll see that you get nothing stronger than hot cocoa."

Harold bobbed his head and smiled his V-shaped smile, like a pen-and-ink cartoon. He couldn't, he said; tomorrow was a working day. But he'd be over again about seven.

Josephine kept on in a subdued mutter with Whittier while she climbed the steps:

> What threads the fatal sisters spun,
> Through what ancestral years has run
> The sorrow with the woman born,
> What forged her cruel chain of moods,
> What set her feet in solitudes,
> And held the love within her mute,
> What mingled madness in the blood . . .

"Well, thank you, Harold," Mary Kyle called back. She tried to express gratitude for his help, said she'd better call him about tomorrow, and dashed up to the porch with the door key in her hand.

"I ought to go along too," John Rossiter began to say, but she pushed him bodily into the hall. "Hot coffee? Cocoa? Old Swanee? Say which, but no back talk. After a hundred miles on a zero night in that jalopy—"

"My good woman, if you call my car a jalopy ever again, our friendship will end."

Her smile broke out like sunlight. It wrapped him up in a sudden radiance. "It'll be coffee unless otherwise ordered. Okay? We live on it here, we are all victims, addicts, fiends."

Josephine had already retreated; they heard the clink of pots and the rush of water from a tap. "I'd better wash a couple of cups," Mary Kyle said, hanging her coat in the dark closet. "Take your things off—I'll be right back. I want to hear about everything."

"I hope it isn't too serious—about your father," John said.

"Well, it's a case where he has to be perfectly quiet for about three months, and after that he has to be—quiet." She hesitated. "What's really serious is Mother. She can't stand much more."

John nodded. He was filling his pipe as an almost unconscious routine. "It seems to have hit her very hard."

"Everything has," she said. "Everything does."

"Hey," Buzz spoke suddenly, full of a new idea. "What's about the Chrysler? He can't drive it, can he? I guess we'll have to—we have to have a car, don't we?" In the silence, he looked at Mary Kyle's face, then at John Rossiter's. "Well, I mean—" His own face glowed red. His head fell. He looked like a young basset hound again. "Yeah, I—I forgot. I'm still in dutch. I better shut up about cars. Jeez, I—I'm sorry . . ."

"What we most need," Mary Kyle said, "is a useful boy round here. How about straightening out those ribs and doing a little snow-shoveling."

"Yeah, sure—I can do that. Tomorrow or next day I'll be okay. But even so—I mean somebody ought to use the thing— keep the battery charged at least . . ." He seemed to run down. He turned away and walked aimlessly about. "I better shut up about everything," he mumbled. But when his sister had gone to the kitchen he spoke again. "You know, I just can't see it—"

"See what?"

"Going back—going on there."

John nodded as though he expected just that. He puffed, looked at his pipe, gestured with it. "You'll have to go back. You can't not go back."

Buzz seemed not to take it in. The doglike look remained on his face, but it had closed itself to reason, even to communication.

"You made your choice when you went to Chapel this afternoon," John said. "You faced it. You stood up and were counted."

Buzz turned his back and opened the pages of a magazine on the table.

"The first step is the hard one," John went on with reasonable enthusiasm. "The next will be a little easier. It's the only way for you."

"I know all that," Buzz said, looking down at the magazine. "I can't argue about it. I can't even explain very well. But Cliff— I guess I told you. I couldn't have stayed in college if he hadn't kept me going."

"You couldn't give a better reason for keeping going, then."

But he knew Buzz hardly heard him.

"That room we had together—" Buzz idly tossed a pencil, over and over.

"Well, you'll see it clearer tomorrow," John said.

Mary Kyle came in with the tray of cups and an assortment of crackers and doughnuts and two pieces of raisin cake. "Odds and ends," she said, "but edible. The coffee will be along in a minute. Anybody besides Buzz want cream? All we have is milk anyway— but he never knows the difference."

She whirled and disappeared.

"Your sister," John said, "is quite a dynamo. I could use her in my business."

CHAPTER 19

"EVERY ONE of your basic pleasures is taken away one by one," Edwin Eustace said. "Eating, fornicating, drinking, sleeping— even going to the bathroom. You'd think there'd be something left a man could enjoy, but I'm damned if I can see any fun in breathing." He had grumbled all his life with a sort of technical relish, as a man who had perfected an art, but now the performance repeated itself mournfully. He sat in a brown oak rocker with a brown carriage-blanket over his legs—an old, old blanket with a fringe. They had given him lighter, softer, newer blankets, but he clung to the old one, a century old, he said; it had belonged to his great-grandmother and the wool was hard and matted and eaten by moths—he boasted of it to anyone who came to visit, and recalled the pleasures of driving long ago and the buffalo robes in winter and the charcoal foot-warmers they carried right into church with them.

He sat all day in sight of the television—sometimes watching, sometimes ignoring it, generally letting it go on and on, always cursing it. "If I could live with myself I'd turn the damn stuff off, but I need the racket. They won't let me drink, damn their hides, I'm too stupid to read—if I could use my fingers I might learn to knit. Opium might do the trick if I could get hold of any. Meanwhile I watch and listen to my fellow countrymen, and what they refer to as America the Beautiful, and if I haven't lost my mind in six weeks it means I don't have one to lose. If that machine gives us a reasonable facsimile of this nation, and I don't see why it doesn't, then I tell you we are doomed. What we fatuously refer to as the great American way of life is nothing but sex, salesmanship, and permanently arrested development; the whole damned racket is simply one aspect of juvenile delinquency, as they call it, which is several notches more sinister than old-fashioned cannibalism. You take what they call the Hit Parade, for example—there's the voice of a nation for you: did you ever stop and *listen* to it—did you ever think what it means?"

His face had sunk into hollows, more like a death's-head than ever. "We used to talk about wet dreams when I was young—that's what comes over the air *hour after hour*. Wet dreams set to music, purveyed by pimps and crooned by luscious little whores. There it is, the soul of a great nation made visible and audible."

For a week after they brought him back from the hospital he refused to shave or be shaved, and a white beard grew in tufts. At that time he stayed in bed upstairs. He'd be happy enough to have his throat cut on purpose, he said, but he'd be damned if he'd let any woman fumble round with one of his razors: he never knew a woman who could sharpen a pencil with a pocket-knife. As for spending money on a barber, there was no sense in it: his carcass wasn't worth a plugged nickel anyway and the next time they got an ambulance or a doctor or any other bloodsucker for him it would be over his dead body. The theory of life at any price, he said, was where your vision of hell came from: the tortured, the useless, the utterly worn-out, paralyzed, incontinent, insane, yet clinging to life, dragging on from minute to minute, destroying the happiness of others, wasting money and time. If you believed in the devil, you knew these were his works.

But when he saw himself in the bathroom mirror he shook his head in shame. "I just never believed it could be as bad. A man no matter how far gone feels that his whiskers are the sign of his potency, but Jesus! These are just scrofulous. They look like a couple of bottle brushes afflicted with leprosy." He took out a razor and made passes with it and looked down helplessly at his fumbling fingers. When Josephine said that Buzz seemed to get along fine with a safety razor he mumbled to himself.

"What?" she asked.

"I said damn all safety razors to hell."

"Well, they do the work."

"I have just two principles in life, as you ought to know by now. I'm a Republican and I hate safety razors. That's where I stand or fall, and any damn fool could tell you that I'm licked on both counts. You know what Republicans remind me of? Morticians at a funeral—the goons people pay to wear black suits and stand round looking like cabinet members. That's my party. And I'll wager you two bits to a one-legged clothespin that I'm the only fossil in East Compton who uses a straight razor." He looked at the instrument in his fingers. "Who did use one, I better say. From now on it will be in a class with flint ax-heads."

Josephine paid no attention. "You look like the dickens," she said.

When he came out to sit all day in the living room, both Mary Kyle and Patience attacked him. He wore pajamas, socks and carpet slippers, and the bathrobe he had had in college, a mustard plaid: he looked, Patience said, as though he had been made up for the rôle of Volpone in Jonson's play. Mary Kyle simply said he looked like a convalescent goat. She brought home various new articles for him—some fancy knitted slippers such as skiers might wear before an open fire, a tweedy robe designed for men of distinction to be photographed in (she said), and an electric razor guaranteed to handle whiskers of any length. He scolded her for her folly and extravagance, and she responded in kind; but he wore the clothes and utilized the razor as a basis for continued diatribes on the condition of modern man. The razor came in a pigskin bag in a box with a hinged lid and a chromium clasp; there was a booklet of directions and praise. The whole thing looked and smelled like something magical, and gave out a sense of happiness and success. For several days Edwin kept it in range of his hand and eye: he read and reread the booklet and he minutely studied the smooth little mechanism and fumbled with the controls. Eventually, in a mid-morning silence, with Josephine lost in *Lady Audley's Secret* (she had run out of Trollope), he moved slowly out of his chair and connected the cord to one of the complex of wires that lay about the edges of the room. He waited for a few minutes with fateful deliberation, as though he were culminating a lifetime of research, and at last pressed the switch—released it—pressed it—again and again, with a glittery little smile. He spoke to himself, almost audibly: "It is undoubtedly the goddamnedest slickest little hunk of gadget I ever did see, but I'll bet two bits against a used toothpick that it can't handle the job." He waited another day before trying it.

❧ CHAPTER 20 ❧

FOR THE FIRST few days after Buzz came home, it was assumed that he was convalescing and recuperating. He had a right to sleep and mope in silence. No one lectured him or probed his conscience. Whatever they said about him they said when he wasn't there: Edwin kept repeating that he had never had the slightest doubt that this sort of thing would happen—Buzz was exactly like all the other young show-offs with inflated egos and no sense. Josephine replied that it was an awful night and anybody might have had trouble—in fact hundreds did have trouble. Edwin said there'd probably be lawsuits and the devil only knew who'd be ruined—did they realize he was the legal owner of that jalopy? Every passenger would claim damages, and he supposed the dead boy's family had a right to set a price on his death. He knew of people who had lost every cent they had that way . . . Mary Kyle said he might at least do some studying—he wasn't so badly shocked he couldn't read economics. But they meant to be kind and left him alone.

On the second Monday morning he came downstairs about eleven and poured himself a cup of cold coffee.

"Don't you want it hot?" Josephine called from the kitchen.

"Doesn't matter," he mumbled.

"What? I can't hear you."

"I said it doesn't matter. I don't care if it's cold."

"You always used to want it hot."

"Well, I don't care."

"What?"

"I say I don't care. Never mind."

She came and peered at him with her worst expression. "Anything ailing you?"

"No—I'm all right."

"Your ribs all right?"

"Yes—I've told you they're all right."

"Well, it's mighty queer you want to drink cold coffee."

"Just—don't bother about me, will you?"

"You need breakfast, don't you? You want two eggs?"

"I don't know—it doesn't matter."

"Speak up, will you? I can't hear you when you mumble. Do you want two eggs?"

"All right—sure—anything—" he waved his hands.

She glared a moment and turned away.

"You two," Edwin said from the next room, "don't seem to have learned to talk the same language."

Later he tried to talk to Buzz himself. "You suffering any?" he began.

"Suffering?"

"Anything serious the matter?"

"Well—it's serious enough." Buzz's tone was severe.

"I mean," Edwin said impatiently, "is anything preventing you from getting back to work—or whatever it is you call your activities at college? I'm aware that you can't play games for a while, but I had a notion you were supposed to go to classes and do a little studying."

Buzz said nothing; a blank mask settled over his face.

"Work is undoubtedly too strong a word," Edwin went on. "I got myself through college too, don't forget, and I doubt—I very much doubt—if the basic operation has altered in thirty-five years. It is not something I can afford to be proud of. But at least, I made some motions, I got the credits whether I deserved them or not."

He waited, expecting Buzz to answer.

"Not," he went on, "that I'm worth a hoot in hell as an example to anyone—unless as a warning." He turned his gaunt face and glinting eyes full on Buzz. "Son, I'm not sore about anything—not yet, anyway. I'm sorry, of course—I regret—but what happened, happened. The thing for you to worry about is what to do next."

Buzz looked almost as though he had heard nothing. His only concern was for the cigarette he fiddled with. "All I'm asking," Edwin said strongly, "is what are you planning to do?"

The silence lasted for many seconds. Edwin's mouth twitched and his eyes glowed. "They tell me to keep calm," he said. "My only hope of survival is to keep calm. I asked you a question, son."

"Who—me?"

"Goddamit—who do you think I'm talking to?" the voice came out like a shout.

Buzz blinked and looked at his father's face almost for the first time. He was pale and his fingers shook a little on the cigarette. "Well, I—I don't know. What was it you—I mean—"

"All I asked you is what you intend to do. It is now Monday noon. You've had a nice twelve hours' sleep. You've been resting quietly for more than a week, as I calculate it. I understand that your bones are in fairly good shape. So it is natural to wonder what you figure on doing. Is there any good reason why you aren't back at college?"

Edwin sat with closed hands as though he had to hold himself together by force. But Buzz seemed to take little notice of anything. His face had a doglike set to it, or rather sheeplike, since it expressed nothing but a basic determination not to think. He muttered something.

"What?" Edwin called out.

"I said, I don't know."

Edwin held his breath a moment, then swore steadily for perhaps ten seconds. "Will you tell me what in hell ails you? Can't you talk like a human being, for God's sake?"

"I'm sorry," Buzz said in the false tones of a boy being polite. "I don't mean to make you mad. I just don't know what to say."

Edwin waited through a long silence.

"I can't seem to explain," Buzz said. Everything about him was subdued. He made gestures of helplessness with his hands. "I just don't feel able to—to—do any studying or go back to college or even—" His voice faded. "I guess I've lost my nerve." The words had a little effect of finality, as though they clarified everything. He straightened up. "That's what it is."

"Well, Jesus, boy—" Edwin broke off and took another breath. He considered the words respectfully. "Okay, so you've lost your nerve. There's only one thing to do—and that's to go right back. You know that—everybody knows that. Face it now—or never. Isn't that so?"

"Oh, sure. Mister Ross kept telling me the same thing."

"There you are, then. Pack up your bag and get going."

Buzz stood up abruptly and walked out to the stairs.

"Don't forget you're all paid for, too," Edwin called. "Tuition, room and all—you can't afford to chuck that down the drain."

When Josephine came in with his lunch on a tray he lectured to her. "You know that poor young sprout—he'd have moped round here till kingdom come if I hadn't got after him. He feels pretty bad about it, there's no doubt of that; he's in a kind of funk—he's acting like a puppy that's been kicked once too often. I told him the only thing was to get back to work—or whatever the motion is that he goes through out there."

Josephine said nothing. She almost never said anything to him.

"You have to be sorry for what happened," he went on. "We all act like damn fools sometimes—it's the human condition. I can't afford to be self-righteous—because I have at times been undoubtedly the biggest damned fool in Christendom: in fact, I used to be proud of it. But when something like this happens it isn't funny." He stared resentfully at his food. "None the less, I freely admit that the boy almost drives me nuts. There are times when you'd say he has no brain, no trace of a brain: he operates on some sort of zoological level, on the same principle as a scared sheep or a year-old puppy who's had the stuffing kicked out of him. He's nothing but a mass of instinctive cussedness. If you were to ask him"—Edwin held up an orator's warning finger—"if you were to ask him the time of day you wouldn't get a thing out of him: he'd think you were trying to trap him, he'd assume you were digging up his guilty secret."

During the afternoon no sound came from Buzz's room upstairs. Edwin snoozed off and on to the steady accompaniment of the television. He roused himself to watch a western from four to five, then thought of Buzz again. "Where's the kid?" he called. "He gone yet?"

Josephine spoke from the kitchen, but he couldn't hear her words, and called out again. She answered more loudly, but still he couldn't hear above the racket of the television. He muttered and waited. "Quiet, damn you," he muttered with a sort of rhythm. "Quiet, damn you, quiet. It's done, it's over, it's finished. You're through, Eustace; all you do now is sit and wait—you face the fact that from here on in all you are is a piece of potential humus. Food for worms, brave Eustace—like father, like grandfather, like Julius Caesar or Hotspur or whoever they were." He let his closed hands open and spoke to himself in a trance. "What in hell does it matter? What in hell did it ever matter? Eustace and Caesar and millions of great and small bastards—and the only single honest fact about the whole lot of them is that they are dirt." He stared unseeing at a girl pressing her painted lips against a piece of white tissue. "It never kisses and tells," she said.

"What were you calling about?" Josephine said, keeping her finger in *Lady Audley's Secret*. She looked at him over the top of her shell-rimmed glasses.

"I said what in hell is the kid up to? Has he gone back yet?"

"Haven't seen him. He could have gone."

"You mean to say the damn fool has cleared out without a word?"

She shrugged. "He never talks to me—any more than he does to you."

Edwin roused up. "Well, Jesus Christ—" Then he paused, sank back, let himself brood for a moment. "I don't know. I keep telling myself it doesn't make a knothole's worth of difference. But I do know this—when a man has to sit in a chair for the rest of his life he finds out things about himself he never knew before—"

"Poppycock," she said.

"What's poppycock?"

"Sitting in a chair. You don't have to—not after a while."

"Well, there's no real difference. I can walk around the back yard with a cane and a goddamned pair of rubbers on." He pointed a hostile finger at the TV screen where a girl was demonstrating a bottle of Love Mist. "Shut up, for Christ's sake! I'm not interested in aphrodisiacs, and as for you, you haven't brains enough inside that hairdo to realize that all you are is a spiritual prostitute." He nodded at Josephine. "I guess I can give 'em hell, eh?" His mouth had a bitter twist. "I brood too damned much, but what else can I do? My father fell off the hayrick and broke his neck like an honest man, my grandfather was elected to the state legislature at the age of seventy-six—what I mean is, they lived and died with honor, they had good consciences. But no one can say that about me. The fact is, to put it as simply as possible, my conscience is bad—and I might just as well come out and say so." He looked again at Josephine but she wasn't there. He heard her steps on the stairs. "I suppose nobody besides me gives much of a damn about it," he muttered. It angered him that the girl was still insisting on Love Mist. "*Shut up!*" he shouted.

Josephine came down and returned to the kitchen. He waited for what seemed a long time. Then he slowly arranged himself for a trip to the commode in his study. He teetered a bit, balanced himself with his rubber-ended cane, and shuffled into the hall, touching landmarks along the way. He peered into the kitchen. "You find him?"

Josephine nodded. "He's there."

"No fooling?"

"He says he feels terrible. He's gone to bed."

Edwin stood swaying a little. "Well, I'll be damned."

"I don't know what to do," she said very distinctly. "Except to let him alone."

He turned with extreme deliberation and started shuffling toward his study door. "No use to talk to him, I can see that. All I can say is that I feel terrible too; I think I'll go to bed."

৺ঠ৻ CHAPTER 21 ৡৼ

When Mary Kyle came out of her office building every afternoon at five she had to decide whether to walk straight to the
station or to go by way of John Rossiter's parking lot. She recognized it as a moral issue. Health, honor, and peace of mind commanded her to take the straight route, and often she did. On those
days she was full of certainty and self-control; the choice was so
obvious that her feet seemed to step along of their own volition.
Her dreams of love and companionship were the most foolish of
delusions. But on other days she hesitated, strayed, and without
conscious decision found herself turning the corner toward Haymarket. It might have been the quality of the air, she thought—
some touch of early spring balm, or a fragrance of sea; it might
have been hunger, or need of comfort, or the sight and sound of
Joe Bass, the man without a soul who infested her office. Sometimes she felt reluctant to go home at all and she loitered past
taverns and hardware stores and sea-food restaurants; she had little visions of herself leading another life far away from the bondage of home, office, and daily trains.

She seldom saw him, though she tried to keep track of his do-
ings. But the simple act of identifying his car gave a sort of
point to her day: it was there—or not there; the fact was the
most important event of her daily life. My big moment, she
called it—my epiphany: the recognition of a dented and dusty
Ford. She even encouraged a bit of talk with the shifty-eyed attendant, though she never betrayed herself by speaking John
Rossiter's name. Miserable poverty, she told herself—the un-
profitable existence of a commuting female with no spiritual re-

sources, no function, no purpose, nothing to do but to snoop round the edges of John Rossiter's life. "I must take stock," she said. "I must make friends, join the League of Women Voters, take up painting again, read history and philosophy." By temperament she was not one to feel sorry for herself.

But when she did see him she behaved without ordinary common sense; or so she accused herself. She made herself beguiling. She smiled. She flattered him. She played up to his whimsies and appreciated his wit. If he had proposed driving off to Florida or California she'd have agreed at once, but he never proposed anything except an occasional ride to or from East Compton. He always treated her with whole-hearted affection as though they had become the oldest and best of friends. Two or three times he called her at her office a few minutes before five and said he'd be driving home—would she like to join him? Once in early March she called him. She needed advice—they were at their wits' end about Buzz.

It was partly an excuse, of course. She had a new spring topcoat, a heathery green soft tweed, and a yellow silk scarf, and she had washed and set her hair so that it waved lightly and gave off glints of reddish gold. She walked with long free strides, thinking of spring and John Rossiter, though the damp cold blew through the new coat.

"What would life be," he said, "without women in it?"

"Brief and simple, at least." She made herself look sternly at him. "What are you being ironic about now?"

"I don't like that 'now,' " he said. "It implies disdain. What you take to be meretricious irony is actually delight. The day is dismal, the wind is cold, winter oppresses us, and here you come like something out of a Botticelli picture—"

"Ha! You can stop right there. It isn't even irony any more. Sinister nonsense, I'd call it." But she smiled, she grinned from ear to ear with something of the look her young brother had once had. It was preposterous, she thought, to be so swept by delight, as though the air were full of music and brightness. She felt herself bound to him by a palpable excitement that radiated round the two of them. He must feel it; he grinned also, his eyes and mouth were quick with responsive ideas.

"As the poet says, you take the winds of March with beauty."

But the words confused him. He got out his pipe, sucked it, tapped it, fumbled for an oilskin tobacco pouch. "So the boy's in trouble, you think. I supposed he was back at his college."

He was always the uncomplicated one, she said as they drove out of the city. He never bothered with troubles. Matters of conscience passed him by. Life consisted of food, sleep, and games.

"He's been going through college," John said. "You probably don't realize what has happened to him."

"You mean guilt and sin? Is that what college does?"

"It's a stage, I'm afraid. It destroys innocence. Knowledge can be terrible."

"Oh, stuff!" But she nodded. "It's so, of course. I just resent the notion that knowledge always implies guilt."

"Oh, but—"

"I mean guilt and frustration are like a plague of influenza. Everybody, who counts, *has* them. I do, you do, now here's poor Buzz with the worst sort of case. I don't see why we all have to be like that." She looked at him as though she expected an answer.

"The thing is," he said, "you have a vision of what is good and desirable—you fail to achieve it—you blame yourself."

"As simple as that, is it? Well, I don't believe it. I think sin was invented by the Christian religion mostly as a threat, a kind of ecclesiastical blackmail. All you miserable sinners, do what we say or we'll see that you spend eternity in hell."

"A girl," he said, "in a new spring outfit has no business talking like that. I refuse to take you seriously, even though you are perfectly right—at least, you are right up to a point. But let me remind you of Rossiter's Law, which I expounded at two in the morning while you were asleep not long ago. There is a point beyond which truth will not be pushed. The good you cling to a little too long becomes evil, like money or fresh eggs or innocence—like this whole idea of guilt, which is true and right and necessary to human success *up to a point*. The trouble is we don't stop, we don't use restraint, we push on into corruption. The eggs all go bad."

This was all part of it, Mary Kyle thought. The way his mind jumped from this to that, the energy and vibration, the quickness of his voice, the gesture of hand and pipe, the smile with the gaps between his teeth.

"A responsible college education," he said, riding the rapids of his thought, "has to take you through all that and come out the other side—I mean to say, it first destroys guilt—the old ecclesiastical blackmail and the new psychiatric kind which is equally vicious—"

"You think it does all that?"

"Well, it aims to—or should. Wisdom does exist, after all—let's not be cynical. We notice often enough the failure of the ones who should be wise, who have had every opportunity to be, but we don't see the inconspicuous victories: the fact of it is that a wise man doesn't advertise himself—he just tends to his own business. There are a lot of them, though—not all college graduates, either —I'd like to introduce you to a few: chap lives near me named Caskie, a financial man, buys and sells stock—is he corrupted by the filthy stuff? He is not. He's what I'd call not an average sensual man, in the condescending phrase of the intellectual, but an average *civilized* man. He's probably not very interesting, but I love him. And there's Tom Marcher, runs the hardware store down near the railroad overpass—you know him?"

"Looks like Winnie-The-Pooh?"

"That's the one. Soundest man I know. Large in the waist, I grant you—weak eyes—not much chin: next time you buy some carpet tacks, stop and visit a bit."

"Married?"

"Widower. You interested?"

"I certainly am. I've always wanted a hardware store. I love hardware stores."

"Perhaps we can arrange it." But he glanced at her and when their eyes met he smiled suddenly as though he knew all about her and was part of her consciousness. She trembled.

"How—how does all this relate to poor old Buzz," she said faintly.

He laughed, then turned solemn. "I would guess that Buzz has just discovered guilt and fear. You know that poem of Horace's about the boy who was so pure and innocent that the wolves let him alone? I believe Horace was just kidding—you can't take the idea seriously: you have to take it in reverse, actually. I mean—it is preposterous—"

He broke off and she laughed aloud, and instantly she regretted it. It was as though she had interrupted him midway along a tight-rope. She wondered if he talked that way at home, and if his wife listened or answered or simply let him keep going.

"I just thought you've forgotten Rossiter's Law," she said.

"Do I contradict myself? Then I contradict myself and be damned to you!" His good nature revived and he grinned. "What did I say? I talk so much I can't remember."

"Do you ever get mad?"

"Mad?"

"Angry, mean, irritable—"

"Me? Why, bless your heart, I can be the meanest and cussed-est—what are you getting at?"

"I'm just reacting like a female. They say women always make everything personal. I butted in to your theorizing and then when you were nice about it I wondered if there were ever times when you were not nice. But for heaven's sake don't try to answer —don't give it a second thought. I guess it all started because you seemed to be saying that purity and innocence were foolish and even dangerous, and I thought it all depends on how far you go with them. There must be a point where Rossiter's Law ap-plies. And then I got to thinking practically—about Buzz—and I'm sure he isn't the sort of boy Horace meant. He's not pure, though he may be innocent in too many ways—or at least dumb. I always thought his kind of innocence was nice—it was natural, at least."

"Probably you think of him as your kid brother still. What is he now—twenty-one? Twenty-two? He's on his own, you know. He had a girl, didn't he? What's happened to her?"

"Lollipop—she's off at a junior college in New Hampshire; she wouldn't be much help—"

"You sound a bit arrogant, Miss Eustace."

"Well—I am. My God—Lollipop! Have you ever seen her?"

"I've seen a good many females. Wonderful creatures, some of them."

"Arrogant," she muttered. "You sound pretty damn superior yourself."

They went on in silence and came into East Compton. "You want me to try to talk to him some more?" he said. His tone was impersonal and a little sharp.

"He won't listen to me. Father is mad because of all the tuition and board money he is wasting. Mother is mad because he won't graduate with his class. He's mad because he thinks we're all against him. Home life was bad enough anyway: I just hoped you might have some idea about it."

"You can take a little comfort that he hasn't started holding up filling-stations. I tell you, girl, there are about a thousand young men in the North End that feel the way he feels. Their fathers and mothers and big sisters are all mad at them, and they are mad at everybody, and all they can think of to do is to commit assault and battery and armed robbery."

"Comfort! I'd hardly call it that."

"Well, I'll talk to him, I'll speak my little piece. Why, damn it all, he isn't so badly off; all he needs is time. Can't you relax, let him be for a while? The army will have him anyway—that'll take care of two years."

"Is that good?"

"No, but it happens. It's what men have to do these days."

She turned on him. "You sound like a professional—you aren't *in* it. To you we're all just cases. What happens, happens—pretty soon it will stop happening and by then we'll be dead." She looked at him in anger, and her voice trembled. "It's as though you didn't have to live yourself or have any share in the mess we're in. You just run around like some sort of medicine man telling people to be patient, relax, let nature take its course—we're all in the same boat anyway so there's nothing we can do." Her voice choked itself off for a moment. "So far as I can see, life is nothing but a swindle anyway. It isn't your fault—I'm sorry I said all that. I keep getting my hopes up—and then something else happens: I mean, what it comes to is one damned thing after another."

For a minute or more she couldn't look at him.

"I'm ashamed to talk like that," she said.

He reached his right hand toward her and she took it in both of hers. She looked at the three hands. She began to say something, thought better of it, put his hand back on the wheel, and blinked the tears away from her eyes.

CHAPTER 22

"Why in hell," said Buzz, "do you all keep after me this way? Why don't you let me alone?"

"Keep after you about what?" she said. "Who's been after you?"

"Well, there's a general attitude round here that I'm a disgrace to the family."

"Vanity, my boy; you aren't as important as you think you are."

"Just because I decided to quit college—you wouldn't have gone back if you'd been me. I mean, what else could I do? I killed my best friend, didn't I?"

"It could have happened to anybody—"

"I admit I'm a coward. Probably some other guys would go back and face it—I mean guys like old Mister Ross there. But I guess I don't have that kind of guts. I admit it—I lost my nerve."

"Well, you keep saying it as though it took care of everything. Lost your nerve, lost your nerve—" She checked herself. "You can't go on that way, Buzz."

"There it is," he said. "You keep after me too."

"Oh, stuff! You act like a neurotic puppy. Naturally people are concerned about you—what do you expect a family to do when you are in trouble? Pay no attention? You toss away a thousand dollars' worth of education—naturally Father has fits. Why wouldn't he? You know what college degrees mean to Mother— how can she help being upset about it? Why don't you think how they feel instead of brooding about your precious nerve all the time?"

"I know how they feel, but what good does that do? It's how I feel that gets me down."

"So all you do is mope. You go upstairs and play juvenile records and read juvenile books and grumble about how nobody understands you. Tell me honestly, Buzz, what good does it do?"

"It's no good—I can tell you that."

"Well, look. You are as of now young and healthy. You have, say, fifty years coming to you to deal with. You can't just shut yourself up and play records and read westerns."

He bowed his head with a kind of stubborn vanity. "If a man doesn't care, if he doesn't give a damn, then he doesn't give a damn."

"Boloney," she said. "You act like a baby who won't drink its milk." But she checked her impatience. "We all act like babies often enough, but there's no sense in keeping on with it, or in being vain about it. This not-giving-a-damn attitude is simply false. The truth is that you do give a damn—otherwise you wouldn't be making all this fuss. What you really want is flattery and comfort." Then she smiled and her face took on beauty. "I'm sorry, Buzz. You know how I talk. I suppose I mean most of it, but I could say it less bluntly. I sound just like a big sister. What about Lollipop, speaking of flattery—have you heard from her?"

"Oh—sure." He hesitated. "She read about it."

"Well, she'd better come down for a week-end and cheer you up."

"She doesn't know I'm home."

"Why not tell her, for heaven's sake?"

"She—" He shrugged. "I haven't felt like telling her."

Mary Kyle was silent. She thought about it. "Are you off Lollipop?"

"Well—I don't know."

"Poor old Buzz—you're having a time, all right. Tell me, is it too late to go back to college?"

"Yeah. I wrote to the dean."

"Did he just let it stand that way?"

"Oh, he called up—he talked about five dollars' worth on the phone. Next day Prince Albert called—"

"Who?"

"Cousin Albert Livermore—the guys all call him Prince. He talked a couple of bucks' worth, too."

She shrugged. "All I can say is, you'd better join the army—that'll take care of everything."

He almost grinned his old grin. "Matter of fact, I saw the draft board. I'll be in by June or July or so—I'll have my physical in a couple of weeks."

"You don't seem to sound like a boy who's lost his nerve," she said.

"Oh—the army, all they want is deadheads. I mean, I'll do fine in the army, except I'll be bored stiff. March here, march there, stand in line, clean up the latrine, police the barracks, pick up cigarette butts—that's all it is. Two years out of a man's life right down the drain—no good to him, no good to the country, no good to anybody."

"You know all about it, huh?"

"Oh, sure. Plenty of guys talk about it and every damned one says the same thing. Just do what you're told, don't stick your neck out, don't volunteer, don't think, don't move unless you have to—that's all there is to it. The only thing you have to worry about is to keep on breathing."

"Well, you'll get away from your family, at least."

"That'll be something. I don't know why it is, but the family drives me nuts. They never used to, not all that, I mean. What bothers me is the next three or four months. If I had nerve enough—" He paused.

"Nerve enough," she prompted.

"Well, what I mean is I'd like to go off south somewhere—or west—and bum round for a while. Just get out of here, I mean . . ."

"What in? What do you do for money?"

"Yeah, that's it. It was just an idea anyway. Matter of fact, I've got a job."

"You? A job?"

"A sort of job, anyway." He looked self-conscious. "Starts Monday. Drugstore boy down at Carlson's—two to ten."

"Selling medicine, you mean?"

"Yeah, that's it: sodas, cones, floats, frappés. I figured I might as well start my career."

Mary Kyle studied him for a few seconds. "I believe you're a born soda-jerk, at that. You'll be a riot with the high-school crowd."

But he didn't respond to her grin. He dropped into the melancholy vein again. His expression reverted to that of the abandoned basset hound. "It's about what I'm cut out for."

"Stuff!" she said. "You're just being sorry for yourself."

He nodded. "I got good reason for it."

She lifted her head to answer more sharply. Irritation took hold of her. But it was as though he had shut himself off; his ears were not open to hear, his mind had ceased to be aware of her.

CHAPTER 23

WHEN PATIENCE came home for the spring vacation they spoke of how tired she was. They said she worked too hard. She seemed thinner, more nervous, much more critical of their failings. She snapped at them. Like Buzz, she withdrew; she read books behind her shut door—not westerns, but the latest from France: Céline, Sartre, Camus. She disdained her old record-player and allowed Buzz to use it—as long as he kept the noise down: she admitted jazz as one of the arts but rejected what she called the juvenile aphrodisiacs. Buzz had no taste, no insight, no sense, and she paid almost no attention to him except to engage in irritable surface bickerings. She called him Mortimer—and sometimes Mortimer Snerd; she even made the kind of comic noises Mortimer Snerd made on the radio, but with more wicked intent, and Buzz retaliated with looks of baleful disgust. "How come she has to be snooty like that?" he asked. "Is that what they learn in that bargain-basement school she goes to?"

As the week went on she grew more difficult, or at least more visibly nervous and drawn. She moved about like a conspirator, not speaking or explaining, going and coming on secret errands, sleeping by day and waking by night. She joined the others at dinner with an air of one doing a reluctant duty.

"There's a good deal more jollity," Edwin said from his chair in the living room, "at a funeral. I figure I'm lucky to be out of it—not very *far* out of it, but enough so that I can have a hilarious time watching the Happy Oats program." But he made no effort to talk directly to Patience. He was, he said to no one in particular, afraid of her. "She's graduated from this family," he announced. "She's advanced. She reads French novels in French. How the hell can a bum like me talk to her?"

On a Tuesday evening Patience and Mary Kyle had a row. It began after supper when Mary Kyle spoke of dishes. "Let's Patience and me have a go at the dishes," she said to Josephine.

"You keep out of my kitchen."

"My kitchen! You think we'll contaminate it?"

"I'll take care of it," Josephine's voice was a martyr's.

"My kitchen, my dishes, my mess—you've had it your way for thirty years, but what's the sense of it? Why don't we strike? How about it, Pat—do we take over? Do we do dishes by force of arms?"

"Go ahead if you feel like it." Patience shrugged. Her face was cold and white. "I'll do it if I have to—not otherwise."

The words seemed so deadly that a silence followed.

Afterward, upstairs, Mary Kyle opened the closed door without knocking and spoke fiercely to Patience on the subject of selfishness, snobbishness, and duty. In her anger she struck out cruelly. "As far as I can see," she said, "you have nothing in you that can be called a heart."

"I hope I don't," Patience said in a voice of restrained desperation. "I'd certainly kill it if I could."

"Oh, stuff! You talk like one of your French poseurs you love to read about. How bitter I am, how utterly disillusioned, how damned superior! My precious suffering is so great that no one else's counts! Jesus, Patience, what ails you, for heaven's sake? Are you just being an unbearable adolescent or is something really the matter?"

"Look, Kyle, if you don't get out of here and mind your own business I'll—I'll murder you." She spoke in a tight, half-choked voice and glanced into the corners of the room as though she looked for a weapon. "You and your damned family virtue—all you are is a frustrated virgin, you and dear Harold—both of you. Don't you come telling me what to do." The tight voice hardly got the words out clear.

Mary Kyle drew breath to fight back. She felt the blood rush to her head. But the tenseness of Patience's face, the white glitter of it, the stare of her eyes, the strain of her voice, almost frightened her. "What's the matter with you?" she whispered.

Patience stood up with a gesture of fury. Her hands groped for a book, a bottle of ink, the back of a chair. "I swear I'll start throwing things if you don't get out. What I do or don't do is none of your business, and I won't stand for this damned holier-than-thou attitude. You can mess up your life and I'll mess up mine, but I'll do it my own way. Now just please, please, *please* get out of here!"

The voice cracked. Mary Kyle stood a moment to discover whether she would fight back or go. Her anger rose up fiercely. "I'm sorry, Patience," she said.

She went out in a rush, shutting the door with a decisive click.

They spoke no words to each other for forty-eight hours. Patience had hardly been seen at all the next day; she went to town and stayed late, not giving out any information. On the day after, Thursday, she came into Mary Kyle's room about nine in the evening, without knocking.

"I'm in trouble," she said. She walked back and forth across the room. "I've been acting like a bitch." She glanced at her white face in the mirror and pressed her lips together in a look of pain. "I'm sorry—about what I said and all." She spoke not warmly or tearfully, but with self-control and a preoccupation with larger matters.

"Well, you're wearing out the floor," Mary Kyle said. "Why not sit down? What's the trouble?"

"Are you mad with me? I mean, you should be, after the way I acted."

"If you're in trouble, you're in trouble. I certainly thought something was wrong. What is it—are you pregnant?"

Patience sat on the bed and stared at her hands in her lap. "Is that what I look like?"

"You obviously look like hell. Something's certainly the matter with you."

"Why did you say pregnant?"

"Because that's what trouble is for a girl."

"Is it always that?"

"Oh, come on, Patience. I don't know—I'm just talking. Trouble is all kinds of things. Father has trouble, Buzz has trouble. You could be disappointed in love—or you could flunk out: I don't know."

"Well—" Patience stared fatefully at her sister for a second or two, then down at her tense hands. "I'm pregnant—nearly two months."

"I—thought it must be that: I mean I was afraid—" Mary Kyle looked at the cracks in the plaster ceiling. "I did hope you'd have some sense. My God, Patience, do you realize what this—"

"Of course I realize. What do you take me for?"

"I take you for a damned idiot, if you want the truth. You so smart, so wise, so know-it-all, so full of advanced psychology— what got into you, for heaven's sake?"

"Kyle—"

"As far as this branch of the Eustace family goes, it's the end. Oh, I know all the arguments about sexual freedom and it's-no-one's-business-but-ours, but Jesus, Patience, look at the family."

"Kyle, please—"

"I honestly think it would have been kinder if you had built a fire in the front hall and burned up the whole damned miserable lot of us."

"I know, I *know*."

"It will be the end of Mother, I can tell you that for sure—"

Patience's voice was a whisper. "Kyle, for heaven's sake—I'm not a monster. I know what it means—"

They sat on the bed in silence.

"If we were singled out for trouble," Mary Kyle said after a while, "like Job, say, it wouldn't be so hopeless because you always know that Job was a special case—his luck was bad for a while and by the law of averages would be better later. I mean, all it proves is that sometimes things can all go wrong for a man. But with us—we just seem to be part of a general hopeless mess. We don't have special afflictions, like bolts of lightning, we aren't singled out or put on the spot: we merely lead pointless and futile lives, without any faith or any purpose. God certainly isn't testing us or using us as an illustration for anything unless he's getting us ready for annihilation—"

"Kyle," Patience said. "What am I going to do?"

"Can you have an abortion?"

"I—I've been trying to find out—" Patience suddenly flung herself face down and cried.

Mary Kyle put a strong hand on her shoulder. "Females," she said. "Jesus."

"There's a man who'll do it for five hundred dollars."

"I could raise it—or borrow it—" Mary Kyle thought of John Rossiter and felt stronger. "It's a bad idea, what I know about it, anyway."

"You—you think it's bad?"

"Sure it's bad." She wished John were right there with them, sitting on the bed, talking. "I don't know, Patience. It's dangerous, I guess—but it's worse than that. The trouble is—"

"I couldn't," Patience whispered. "I intended to—I thought you'd help with the money, I knew you would—" She cried again. "I went to see the man." She waited, then spoke more carefully. "I'm not against abortions if they can be done decently—I mean, there are times when they might be good. But—well, I can't do it, not with a man like that. I just couldn't. And besides—"

"So—no abortion. We have a baby." Mary Kyle's mind jumped ahead. "October, is it? Do we have a father for it? What do we do about that?"

Patience gathered herself up with a return of dignity. "Look, Kyle, you may think I'm nothing but a damned female idiot— and I'll admit—"

"Hell's bells, we all are female idiots," Mary Kyle said fiercely. "God in his infinite wisdom made us that way."

Patience considered for a moment. "Maybe it sounds fatuous, but I've tried as hard as I can to be—well, honest is the only word I can think of. I fell in love, I'm still in love, as far as I can tell I'll always be in love. If I have a baby, I'll love it. Maybe it all sounds idiotic from a social point of view—"

"Well, who are you in love with, for Pete's sake? Why don't you marry him?"

"Marry him!"

"It's done, you know. Now and then."

"Oh, he—" She shrugged and moved her hands.

"He isn't the type, you mean?"

"Oh, I—I don't know—I don't think so."

"Maybe he has a wife already?"

"No—of course not."

"Look, Patience, let's try to talk sense. Who is he?"

"Why, Tony, of course."

"Of course—but who is Tony?"

"Why—you mean you don't know?"

Mary Kyle took a breath. "It could be," she patiently said, "that you have mentioned the name in the last three months. There used to be a Roy and a Dave, I think—"

Patience made a gesture of disgust.

"You haven't communicated, you know. You haven't told us the facts of your life."

"He's the one they all call Oz—the kids call him that, I mean . . ." She went on in fragments of recollection: how she got to know him, what he did, what he was like, what Edna said.

"But why not get married?"

"Well, marriage—" Patience spoke as though the arguments were too familiar to repeat. It was really another matter, she implied: it had its place in the social order, but it hardly pertained to students and—she groped for the right words: Tony, she said, was *different*. He belonged to no social or domestic system. For one thing, he had no money, no job, no nice little rut to fit into . . .

Mary Kyle made herself take a sober view of the case.

And of course, Patience went on, Tony had to go abroad: his music, his writing, all his wonderful talents, demanded that he live in Paris and study at the Sorbonne and visit Vienna and Salzburg. Marriage and babies would be a disaster for him. She overflowed in tears. "The thing is, Kyle," she said severely, taking control of herself, "you just don't understand my generation—"

"*Your* generation, for God's sake!"

"Well, I mean—my college generation. After all, you went to a nice girl's college and they all had money and families and social weddings—they were respectable and dull and their only idea was to settle down in the suburbs with two cars—"

"Well, fancy that," Mary Kyle muttered.

Tony, Patience rushed on, simply didn't belong to that system. He was on his own, he was free; if he belonged to anything it was to a sort of international underground of artists and intellectuals, the perfectly free spirits who lived without ritual or thought-control or bondage to any social tradition. That's why he had to go abroad—

"He'll need money, won't he?"

"Oh—money. Heavens, money is the last thing he worries about. Anyway, he was in Korea—he can get the GI tuition money at the

Sorbonne or somewhere. But that's what you socially-oriented people always think of—money: houses, cars, deep-freezers, TV sets. To Tony none of that *matters*. He can live on soup and bread—he can sleep in a bar or a park or a cellar. All he wants is freedom to think and create and—and be alive."

"Is that what you want too?"

Patience pulled herself up. She took thought. "Look, Kyle, I'm not as half-baked as you think I am. We argue all this stuff till we're dizzy with it—money, happiness, ethics, morality, marriage, religion—I don't know what all. You don't have to tell me that money is useful—and houses and cars and all that. But what *gets* us—the one thing we *agree* on—is the mess that society has made of itself. I mean, it isn't only this family—though God knows we're typical enough—but it's the *world*, the screaming mobs, the communists murdering people by the thousand, the lies people live by, the intolerance, the cruelty—a lot of it carried on in the name of civilization, in fact most of it." She spoke in low tones, but her face was tense and spotted with color. "The thing is, do we have to be like that too? Can't we let all those respectable hypocrites go fry in their own hell? Not that I wish evil on them, but the world they have made *is* evil—it's hopeless and pointless too—if it blows itself to smithereens, well and good. And I don't mean only Russians and Chinese and Arabs, I mean us too—" Her tenseness almost choked off her words. "There's nothing *new* about people like Tony and—and the others: I mean—it may sound wild, but it's what saints and prophets and hermits and crazy philosophers have always done. Look at Blake and Saint Francis and—and Thoreau: look at the millions of hypocrites calling themselves Christians who pay no attention to the way Christ actually lived—even the churches and the ministers dodge most of the issues—"

"Patience—"

"Huh?"

"You say you're in love with Tony?"

"Yes, of course. What do you take me for?"

"Don't be huffy. I'm just trying to get things clear. Is he in love with you?"

"Is he—?" The words broke off sharply.

"I'm sure he says he is, but is he *actually?*"

Patience waited several seconds. "Yes," she said. "He is."

"Does he know you are pregnant?"

"No."

Mary Kyle took a long, steadying breath. "I can't help saying it," she said evenly, "but in my judgment, soberly and rationally arrived at, you are a damned fool. I simply don't follow your reasoning at all—"

Patience was not angry: rather she spoke with sad knowledge. "Well, that's just it. You don't understand us. It isn't only me alone—it's a lot of us. It's what I was trying to tell you—"

"Will you please stop acting as though I were your grandmother: I *know* what you are trying to tell me—I even know how you feel—but the simple fact seems to be that you are going to have a baby, and babies have to be paid for, taken care of, brought up. You know perfectly well you're in a jam, and all this talk of yours is nothing but collegiate hot air—"

"It isn't!"

"You've been in a panic for days; you're sick with it—you were desperate enough to come in here even after we'd had a row: it's *real*, I tell you—you know it's real. The only thing you can possibly do is to put it up to your Tony and get married—nothing else makes any sense."

Patience looked right and left in anger and despair. "It's no good, Kyle—you just don't"—she began, but stopped. She held herself in suspension for several seconds, then bowed her head and cried.

"I meant to do everything honestly," she said. "Other people made a mess of things—not me: I thought if I did what I believed was good and right I'd somehow be safe. I thought I could be free—I still think so. I thought Tony could be—he *has* to be, Kyle; he wouldn't be Tony at all if he were tied to some stupid job, living in a stupid suburb, catching the eight-thirteen every morning and the five-something every night—I mean, he'd be better off dead. So would I . . ."

Mary Kyle glanced round at her walls and ceiling. It was after midnight. Her mother, she realized, was still downstairs—in the kitchen, half asleep in a chair. A car swished by in the road out-

side, a heavy airplane roared somewhere in the dark void overhead. "I know a good deal about that too," she said. "The eight-
something and the five-something." She thought of John again,
but decided not to try to expound Rossiter's Law: it applied, all
right—it always seemed to apply.

CHAPTER 24

"I SUPPOSE you admire Tennessee Williams," Harold Chivers said.

"You mean you think I should?"

"Oh, no—I meant that his plays seem to be very popular among the intelligentsia."

"Now Harold, do be careful—"

"Oh, I'm no judge myself—I know nothing about his plays, but of course I've read some articles. There was a piece about him in *Time*, I believe. Tell me, what contemporary dramatists *do* you admire?"

Mary Kyle took control of herself. "Let's not pretend we are intellectuals tonight—let's just be our natural dull selves, huh?"

Harold smiled at her wit, as he always did. "I could certainly hope for nothing better than your own natural self." He spoke the phrases as though he were reciting them from memory. "In my case the word 'dull' applies, I fear, but for you it should certainly be 'vivacious'—or perhaps 'sparkling,' or even—"

"No, no—hold it, be restrained. The evening is much too young still." But she laughed. There was something unavoidably good about Harold.

They were driving to town for dinner and theatre. The April night was cold enough but no longer wintry, and daylight lasted unexpectedly late. Harold alluded to the pleasures of spring and the release from the long winter.

He conducted the expedition with perfect mastery of all details: the progress through traffic was slow but unhesitating, the parking lot had been carefully selected for both convenience and an air of respectability—the attendant even wore a sort of uniform; the restaurant was celebrated for its antiquity and oysters—and it turned out that Harold had visited it earlier in the day to select and reserve a booth for two. With all her deliberate restraint, Mary Kyle found herself in a mood of childish giggling, and when Harold, having seated her in the booth at precisely the scheduled minute, proposed a cocktail and would she have a martini, or an old-fashioned, or perhaps something else—she burst suddenly into half-choked mirth and laid her head on her arms. "Please, please forgive me, Harold. I think you are wonderful—really I do. You ought to be in charge of royal progresses." She giggled in a brief helpless burst, then sat up and took herself to task. "Is the drink just for me, or are you really intending to have one too?"

"Oh, it's for you, of course—" But he realized at once that he was caught. He grew a little paler and his V-shaped smile took on a reckless glitter. "Is it—is it my duty, do you think?"

"It wouldn't do for me to have a drink alone."

"Well, in that case—certainly—I—" He had grown distinctly paler. "What do you suggest? An old-fashioned?" He said it in the brisk false tones of one who knew nothing about it.

But she looked at him respectfully. He had passed through a small moral crisis. With all his planning he hadn't been quite ready for it and he showed the effects in his paleness and in the tone of his voice as he spoke of the old-fashioned. "It's quite a responsibility," she said, "to be as virtuous as you are." But she restrained her irony. She was always impelled to be cruel to him, to attack with mockery and superior taste in worldly affairs. "No, no drink tonight. I abandon all efforts to corrupt you—though from what I've heard of this play we're going to a drink would be good preparation."

"Really? I thought the critics were taking it quite seriously." He spoke with such bright innocence that there seemed to be nothing else to say. He proposed lobster or filet mignon, and she persuaded him that what she craved this evening was broiled mackerel. He insisted on a preliminary dish of oysters on the half shell. It troubled her that the play as far as she had heard of it, dealt with the depravities of sex, and she tried to decide whether to warn him. It had been his choice, after all—a play that critics took seriously. Perhaps he wouldn't be aware, or wouldn't hear the audience snickering at what they thought were the dirty parts.

It might have been better if she had not got them into it: she could easily enough have diverted him to something safer.

But she wanted to see it. Patience knew all about it—she cited it as one of the significant reflections of the times. It might throw light on what ailed the Eustace family. The shock of it, if that's what it was, might even be good for Harold Chivers, though it was a consideration that owed something to malice.

He paid the dinner bill with dignity, left a tip of eighty-five cents, and escorted her along Tremont Street with the air of a gentleman on duty. He wore gloves. His face was white and eager in the glare of the lights. He remarked that the cold air was refreshing, that the lights were brighter than ever, the streets more crowded. Did she mind walking? It was only two or three blocks, and they had plenty of time . . .

The play turned out to be as fantastic and compelling as a nightmare. *The Pink House* was its name. The scene from first to last was the lobby of a hotel in Memphis, Tennessee, in fact a brothel with decorations in dirty pink and white, a place of filthy and symbolic ostentation, populated by an itinerant set of whores and pimps and customers. Comedy was provided by the innocent traveler seeking lodging, and the audience was kept in a state of half-hysterical giggling because there were presumed to be peepholes in one wall where customers could entertain themselves by spying on undescribed activities. But what might have been bawdiest comedy was suppressed and overlaid by the thesis of bondage and ruin. A father seeking a son he had quarreled with found him providing sexual entertainment for a paying public twice nightly, and taking pride in his work: in due course, the father joined the paying public, but in the end, while drunk, in a splendid dramatic scene began smashing the pink and white properties, was beaten senseless by the bouncer and lugged off by the police. A girl was murdered by a patron who was angry because he recognized her as part negro; he had paid for a white girl, he pointed out. A young man spent most of the play trying to find out why he was impotent, and ended in suicide. The major rôle was that of the madam, the owner and proprietor, whose simple intention was vengeance for the betrayals and rapes of her girlhood, though in the end, in a climactic final scene, she was overcome by the fiercer savagery of her own daughter. The curtain left her moaning and groveling on the floor.

There was applause, the cast came forward and bowed, the celebrated actress bowed alone with a look of dignified suffering; then the lights came on and people moved into the aisles. But hardly a whisper was spoken. Eyes for the most part were cast down. Faces had a drugged look; it seemed that ordinary emotions had ceased.

In the lobby, coming out into the air, Harold made an effort; he spoke as though someone had prodded him with a pin. "Well— that was certainly quite—er—quite—" He tried a jaunty smile. "I must say I hadn't realized—I mean to say, I'm afraid you found it pretty shocking; that is, it isn't quite the thing for a—er— lady—"

She smiled reassuringly. "There's one thing you ought to know, Harold, and that is that a lady, as you call her, is naturally tougher-minded than a gentleman. Did you notice who laughed at the bawdy jokes? and who first got the point about what went on? The ladies, by a big majority."

"Oh, but the kind of women who go to these plays—"

She laughed, not too scornfully. "You think a lady is a different species."

He answered with a sound of triumph. "I don't think I heard you laughing at any of the—er—bawdy jokes."

"Maybe it's because I wasn't candid enough. But humor is a different thing—what people laugh at. The fact is that funny or not funny, sex is much more important to women than it is to men—and by women I mean all women. I think women know more about it and think more about it and accept the realities of it more openly—"

"Surely," he broke in, "you don't think this play was an example of—of the *realities*." His tone expressed anxiety.

She said nothing.

"Don't you consider it merely sensational?" He waited and then spoke more sternly. "Surely you agree with me that it is intended to appeal to our—that is, to people's basest instinct. In fact it is—if you will pardon the word—pornographic. I really feel badly about it—I mean I shouldn't have chosen it—" He sputtered a little. He was whiter than usual, but little spots of color appeared on his cheeks.

"You don't seem to agree with the serious critics."

He had decided to be indignant. The authorities, he said, ought not allow such things. As for critics, he simply couldn't understand. He considered himself quite reasonably liberal, but this was something no responsible person could endorse . . .

His voice hovered over her. He seemed taller and more remote; he existed up above somewhere, in thinner air, as though he had nothing to do on the ground. But he insisted. "Don't you agree with me? Surely you feel, as I do . . ."

"Don't keep at me, Harold."

"Well, you must certainly agree with me that . . ."

"I don't know," she muttered.

"I'm surprised no one has written to the *Herald* about it. I mean in Boston of all places you'd think they wouldn't tolerate such a thing."

"I don't know," she said again. "I don't know." But then suddenly she flared out. "Do stop talking like an idiot, Harold. You just don't understand anything."

It hurt him, she saw—it was almost the first time he had let one of her insults hurt him. He receded even farther into the upper air. His thin profile took on a sharply angular look.

"I'm sorry, Harold. I have a mean disposition." She touched his arm. She smiled. "But I can't tell you what I feel about the play—I mean, I don't think I can discuss it as though it were a— a topic. Did you see the way people looked at the end? Did you see their faces? Something terrible had *happened* to them—to some, anyway. I don't know whether it's good or bad—I mean the thing that happened. I can't talk about it."

He responded like a gentleman. He pointed out that the air was really very refreshing, that theatres were always hot; he hoped she didn't mind the walk to the car—it was only two or three blocks . . .

They hardly mentioned the play again.

Harold, she thought, blamed the characters for being evil, and blamed the author for inventing and projecting them; he even blamed the audience for being fascinated. He was right too—up to a point: always up to a point. Rossiter's Law again. You had to fight evil—there was no other human choice: fight the good fight. But while you fought you had to condone and be compassionate and even love, like a parent or brother—again up to a point. *The Pink House*, she thought, went beyond the point—but she wasn't sure. In some obscure way it made her feel guilty, not because she took part in it but because it accused her of a failure to accept and condone. There was no love in it, only a sort of pride in the completeness of its evil.

But all these tragedies, she thought, dealt with palpable disasters such as enmity and murder and degeneracy and betrayal. The quiet failure of good intentions seemed hardly worth dramatizing.

"Shall we stop for a snack on the way home?" Harold was asking. "I'm sure you'd enjoy a cup of coffee and a doughnut."

"Coffee for you too, Harold?"

"Well, not at night, not as late as this."

"No—we'd better go home. We'd better brood quietly to ourselves about the play, don't you think?"

He looked as though he wanted to discuss it. But he didn't know how to begin.

·§ CHAPTER 25 ૨·

She had an image in her mind of Anton Kedjian as dark, neurotic, irresponsible, and wholly self-centered. She even saw him as she saw Joe Bass, the man in her office who had no scruples. She thought of him as a cultural tramp, a drifter, a shrewd pretender who talked about "writing," about ideas and art and personal emancipation. He would resent success, scoff at convention, yet expect to be taken care of and admired by the society he despised. She was prepared to be afraid of him.

The address was on the wrong side of Beacon Hill where the jungle of the west end began. Her movements were conspiratorial: she called a friend of her father's at the university, who in turn called a girl in the office who looked up his address. She knew no other way of finding him than to visit his room after five in the afternoon, which meant walking a mile and climbing four flights. The first two trips were fruitless. The third discovered someone there.

The door opened letting out fumes and waves of oil heat. "Come right in," the young man said. "Not many girls are strong enough to walk up here. I'm delighted. I hope you were looking for me."

"Are you—Tony?"

"Well, no—but come in, come in. We can't afford to heat the hall."

"I should think you'd die of asphyxiation."

"Oh, we do, we do—a thousand deaths, as the poet says. I'm the poet, at least I try to be, I work at it—I was working when you knocked, I had just written a phrase. Would you like to hear it? We haven't any money, by the way, if that's what you came for—

I mean if you are selling insurance or soliciting or anything like that—"

She couldn't help grinning. He looked like a too-well-fed satyr in T-shirt and chino pants tight round his cushiony waist and bottom. His dark eyes twinkled narrowly at her, his mouth quirked at the folly of what he was saying. "We need a woman's touch, as you see." He moved lazily to shut the door behind her.

Oz, he said, usually slept there—he'd surely be home by midnight, if she cared to come back then: or why not stay—there was a can of beef stew and a jug of wine . . .

A rat's-nest, just as she thought. Bohemian squalor of strewn books, papers, clothes, and general trash.

"I'm Mary Kyle Eustace," she said.

He nodded with almost expressionless understanding, as though he knew. "I'm Jack Lazarus." He always looked as though he knew.

"Can I leave a note for—Oz?"

He handed her a sheet of paper and a pencil.

"You may know my sister."

He nodded.

But after she wrote the note, using a pen from her bag, he began at once to read some of his poems to her. "I am compelled, you see," he said. He smiled with a sort of confiding charm. "Being a poet is the dreariest, lonesomest damned profession—"

"Do you publish any?"

He considered the question. "It is very nice—I mean the way you ask it. Do I publish—and *any* is such a kindly word there. As a matter of fact, at least six editors are giving my work serious consideration." He rummaged up a copy of *Harper's Magazine*, already open. "My works," he said, pointing. It was eight lines: "Night Song: Beacon Hill," by Jack Lazarus.

He had been at the university, she found, but had dropped out —because of "differences of opinion." They failed to appreciate him; he failed to appreciate them. "I withdrew my patronage," he said. "Since then I've been associated with the Old Colony Tallow Company as night watchman, with Ted's Lunch as counterman, with the Metropolitan Opera as spear-carrier, and with the Middlesex Lying-in Hospital as orderly. I might add that I made myself so obnoxious on the subject of the hospital's name that I was fired: how do you feel about it, by the way? Middlesex, I mean—"

It was what she expected. The self-appointed poet, the garret, the mess, the ironic defiance of all responsibility. She remembered how Patience flared up at the mention of money and property.

"I celebrated by writing an ode," he went on. "At least, I think it is an ode—a sort of epicene ode, if you know what I mean—it has both short and long lines in it and it is called 'To the Middlesex Lying-in Hospital'." He turned over the scattered papers. "Would you care to hear it? I tried to be funny and sort of blasphemous, but it's no good; in fact it's the worst thing I've done since I quit college—though it uses a lot of obstetrical language. 'Hermaphroditic conception,' for instance—don't you think that has possibilities? But I won't read it—I'm ashamed of some of it. Now here's one called 'Common or Garden'—any Bostonian would see the point, but I have to explain it a little bit for my larger public—people in San Francisco, for example. It is extremely symbolic, and is mostly about homosexuals—that's where they operate, of course; the Common specially, up near Tremont Street and the bandstand, but in warm weather they begin to migrate toward the Public Gardens—they go there for the summer."

"Look," she said, "I've got to make a train—"

"It's just that I have a deep sympathy for homosexuals—I guess I have compassion, though that's one of those serious words. I'm not one myself, but I can see how they might feel: they aren't all freaks—you see what I mean by common or garden; it's a damn clever idea, really—"

She laughed, and he looked at her appreciatively. "I don't have many intelligent callers—I mean simply that I hate to see you go. We have parties enough, Lord knows—you ought to see the hordes that come pounding up the stairs every night; they think we run a kind of floor show here. I'd urge you to come, but mostly we act like a bunch of goons. I enjoy it in a way—I feel flattered, I drink their liquor and I suppose I show off, but it's a foolish way to live. Half the time Oz can't stand it—he stays up in the library as late as he can . . ."

She had to walk out. She smiled, waved, let his voice follow her down the stairs. "Your sister is a fine girl," he said for all to hear. "She's very serious-minded—tell her to take life easier. You know that poem by Yeats about taking things easy—tell her to read it. She'd admire anything by Yeats." The last sounds she heard were the lines of a poem echoing down the tenement stairwell:

> . . . take life easy, as the grass grows on the weirs;
> But I was young and foolish, and now am full of tears.

Deceptive charm, she said to herself. But her smile lingered, and she walked down to Cambridge Street and waved at a taxi. On the other two occasions she had walked to Scollay Square and taken the subway. Her disposition was always for walking and subways; she hadn't been alone in a taxi for years, and she looked about her with amused surprise. Certainly Jack Lazarus had given her much pleasure, though it was still her considered opinion that she disapproved of his way of life. He was like a free and precocious child, she thought; he was very charming and perceptive, and his poetry was a genuine part of him: she couldn't accuse him of posing—not invidiously, at least. He did it spontaneously. But how, she wondered, could it be a life? What was Jack Lazarus at forty—or sixty? Did he go on sending sprightly verses to *Harper's*? Did he live forever on stew in a tenement room? Or did he close entirely the chapter of his emancipation and become—say, a taxidriver?

"You weren't a poet once, were you?" Her voice popped out of its own accord.

"Huh?"

"I just asked if you ever wrote poetry."

He considered. "You mean—me?"

"Well, it's a foolish question. But I was wondering what poets do when they have to earn a living—I thought maybe they sometimes drove taxis."

He seemed as nervous as a rabbit, and bloodless and hollow-cheeked; the fingers of his left hand were stained yellow. He didn't answer for some time, and she hoped he had forgotten about it; her impulsive question had come straight from Jack Lazarus.

"They don't pay much for it, huh?"

"Oh—poetry? I guess not, unless you're somebody like Ogden

Nash."

Another silence. "Who?" he asked.

"Ogden Nash."

"He write for the *Post?*"

"Yes, sometimes."

"He's good, is he?"

"Well, I think he is, but—"

"Yeah, I know—he's funny. As a matter of fact he's very funny." The tight nervous face relaxed long enough for a smile. "I guess most poets aren't that funny. I guess a lot of them have a tough time of it, like you said."

He twisted through the narrow streets with perfect competence, but she saw that his mind was absorbed in her problem. "Folks talk," he said. "Out-of-towners—want to know about Paul Revere and all that. Old North Church, one if by land, two if by sea— I tell 'em what I can. Matter of fact, I grew up right here on Hanover Street, me and about fifty thousand other Wops. We got Paul Revere practically in the first grade. But what I mean, nobody ever talked about how poets make a living—it's a subject that doesn't often come up: I doubt if many people ever think of it at all."

"Well, is running a taxi a good way to make a living?"

He shrugged. "It either drives you nuts or it doesn't." He got out a cigarette. "Mind if I smoke? Some folks can't stand it." He lighted it with a dexterity amounting to sleight-of-hand. "Matter of fact, it drives me nuts. But it's a living. You have a wife and five kids—"

"Five?"

"Pretty soon six." He made a face of despair. "I dunno—it's the racket, I guess—or the fumes. All I know is I can't sleep nights. I don't have the weight, is what it is."

"How long have you been doing it?"

"How long? Since I got married—ten years, maybe. I played the drums—you know, traps—" He rattled his fingers on the wheel. "I quit school—used to play in some of the clubs and local dances. Swingbands we had then—" He rocked his head from side to side and beat out a measure on the wheel. "Lot o' fun, all right —I mean to say, I enjoyed it. But we had the war—I was in for three years. It's when I got married, I was on leave, you know, and when I came out afterward there wasn't no sense trying to play a drum—I mean with a kid already born and another one coming. Things happen pretty damn quick, I can tell you."

Not for me they don't, she thought.

They parted at the station with good will. "Drink milk," she said. "Cut out the cigarettes." She smiled.

He nodded intently. His white face seemed to glitter—he had the look of a martyr in the act of suffering. "It's a rat-race whatever you do," he said.

When Tony Kedjian called her at the office next day she spoke kindly to him and listened curiously to his soft voice. She had planned it so long that she went ahead boldly: would he meet her at a place on Tremont Street, have supper—on her—she overcame his hesitations; a time was set.

But the human actuality astonished her, not because he differed from her vision—though of course he did—but simply because he was a reality. He breathed, smiled, moved about; he looked at her with critical interest, he judged her as keenly as she judged him, he reserved his thoughts. Even his clothes represented a reality, and it flashed across her mind that the desperate men pictured in journals, the thieves and murderers, wore white shirts and neckties and suits which they had chosen to wear with the same impulse toward vanity and respectability that all men had. Not that she judged him in those terms, but his brown tweed jacket and maroon wool tie implied calculated good taste, and reminded her that she really knew nothing about him. It was not an expensive jacket and was thin at cuffs and elbows but it still represented sound judgment.

What most startled her was his head. It seemed too statuesque —heroic enough, with stern, deep-cut features, but exaggerated. The fine hawk's nose jutted almost too far, the mouth and chin looked as though they had been shaped with a chisel.

He spoke first after they took opposite seats in a booth. "You look like Pat only more so."

His words and smile transformed him. He spoke so gently that she had to listen for the words to take shape after he had said them. And the smile seemed almost a weakness. The strong face gave itself away in an unspoken appeal for understanding.

She was too intent to speak lightly. She was preoccupied with her theme, driven partly by a feeling of guilt that she was there at all, and fear that she might do harm. Young people, she knew, took it upon themselves to manage each other's destinies: discretion could simply be defined as letting be.

A waitress bustled between them with place settings and menus. He raised a deceptively gentle dispute about whom the meal was "on," and she saw that he took it for granted that he would have his own way. But it did seem odd to her that they should be ordering food together: with an impulse toward modesty, she chose a salad and a cream-cheese sandwich; he muttered inaudibly to the waitress and pointed to items on the bill.

"I suppose you want to talk about Pat."

Mary Kyle had it in her to be angry and even mean. His words were an opening, but she resented them: I want to talk about you —what you think you are up to, what you intend; I want to tell you a few plain truths . . .

"I'd better say at the start that I'm in love with her."

It silenced her again, the strength of his face combined with the gentle sweetness of his voice. He smiled, and the mouth expressed almost a confiding weakness.

"Are you asking her to marry you?"

"Well, marriage—" She could see his mind begin to take charge. He lifted his chin with a little gesture that she recognized as a sign. The voice grew more brisk. "I think in most ways we are already married—we feel that we are, at least: I'm sure Pat would agree. I'm not proposing anything that she wouldn't go along with. But economically it is a different problem—socially too, I guess. I haven't any money, or any money-making job. My father was a fruit and vegetable peddler—he had a cart—" Again the lift of chin. "I know one's father is not supposed to be an issue any more, but backgrounds certainly count: Pat has a whole set of tastes and attitudes that represent an old New England tradition. In a way I haven't any background because my people used to be Moslems and very simple and almost illiterate. I see some of them now and then—my sister works in an Armenian restaurant and we have a lot of cousins and uncles: but here I am, a sort of existentialist—a student of philosophy and music, without much of any tradition at all."

"What will you do—in life, I mean?"

His smile came again, that confiding weakness. "You know, the adventure of being in the university has been—well, overwhelming. Specially since I came back from the army. Up to then I'd just been breezing along as what they called a good student—that is, I got the marks and scholarships and the teachers were all nice to me. But it wasn't till later that it got me—I mean, it was as though I suddenly found out I could fly. One day I was just stumbling along down in the bushes—then, bingo, I was up there swooping round with Plato and Hume and William James and all the rest." This time his grin was enormous. "And Bach and Stravinsky. And Shakespeare—and Proust—" He made gestures of despairing grandeur. "All I've wanted so far is just to *be*—I suppose I've been intoxicated: but considering my chances in life, perhaps you can understand."

"Pat says you write—plays and things."

"Shakespeare and me."

They tackled their food with better appetite than they had at first.

"I'm not against marriage," he said, "any more than I'm against law or taxes or government. It is a civic arrangement—"

"Partly," she put in.

"I always see marriage as an actual picture—or it might be a scene, a series of scenes: small house in suburb, garage, car being washed Saturday, grass being mowed, three kids—one toddling, one with red tricycle, one with red bicycle; inside, white stove with push-buttons, white washer-dryer with push-buttons, white refrigerator and freezer, white bathroom—"

"You've never seen our house," she murmured.

"And up and down the street, as far as the eye can see, the same thing." His voice had a note of intellectual scorn, but at once he suppressed it. "Civilization—law and order and peace. It would be unintelligent to deny it, dull and uncreative as it may be. But you can see that everything I've been doing and thinking is alien —different. Not only me, I mean Pat too—anyone who—" Again his gesture suggesting a grandeur too great to apprehend. "You spend a semester reading Dante, you put your mind and soul into it, there's hardly any other life left." He looked at her. "Didn't you? Am I specially susceptible?"

"It's a question of proportion," she said rather primly.

"Proportion! Wisdom and beauty in small doses?" His chin lifted, but his voice grew gentle. "In my view there's nothing more subversive than a liberal education. If there's one thing it teaches more than any other, it is the folly of worldly ways and means."

It occurred to her that he wasn't altogether serious. His eye seemed to be testing her. There was a sort of discrepancy between his words and the speculative tone of his voice.

"*Were* you specially susceptible?" She said it as she might give out a little more rope.

"I was a white page—or better, a new film."

"Are you still?"

"With most others the exposure is only partial—it certainly isn't as absolute as it was with me. Intoxicated, did I say? It wasn't a good word, but I don't know what one to use: transported, maybe."

He had turned out to be a more formidable person than she expected, but less fearsome. His intelligence seemed great. She thought better of Patience. But his gift of talk could be beguiling: what did it conceal? She had glimpses of strength and weakness at war in him. Idealism fought with what at moments looked like cynicism.

"The human being is not really intended for grandeur," he said. "We just look in that direction, we move toward it a fraction of an inch. I've been learning that lately—I think I have, at least. Perhaps that is the beginning of sanity—or at least safety."

With all this he might also be cruel or unscrupulous. She studied him for signs.

"One thing I like about Pat—she has a past, a continuing part to play."

"The main reason I wanted to see you—against her wish, by the way—is to tell you that she is pregnant."

"She—" He had begun a speech and was stopped as by a head-on collision. His mouth opened slightly, he looked from side to side as though more might come.

Mary Kyle watched him. His face settled back to its sculptured lines, rather stern.

"Why didn't she tell me?"

"For some of the same reasons you've been giving me. She doesn't think you ought to be bothered by matrimony."

"She—said that?"

"More or less."

"Do you mean it?" He seemed not to know he had spoken—he didn't look at her. An odd pattern of red showed on each side of his forehead. He put down his fork, glanced at his wristwatch, and gathered himself to make a move. "I'll have to see her. Is she home? Is she at the dorm?"

"Wait a minute, for heaven's sake—"

He was on his feet, wallet in hand. "Here's for the supper—that'll just take care of it." His voice had gone soft and gentle again, and somehow remote.

"Sit down!" It was a command.

"You were right to tell me—I guess I should have known, but I didn't." She could barely hear the words. "I'll have to see her, though."

"But I've got something I want to say."

He turned and walked out.

In her anger she almost shouted after him. But she was angry partly at herself. She hadn't done it right—as a matter of fact she didn't understand the man.

She finished her salad and paid the bill with the two dollars he had left.

CHAPTER 26

PATIENCE HAD KEPT ON with the college routines, but more and more it was remarked how ill she looked, how white and nervous, how distracted and bad-tempered. She had succumbed, her critics thought, to the arrogance they had always attributed to her. She avoided the groups and parties, and even stayed away from her room in the dormitory. She saw a good deal of Edna Siegel, partly because the studio where Edna lived with her aunt seemed to enclose her in silence and safety—specially after dark or in the dusky afternoon when she could be there alone.

It was her intention to manage herself with rational self-sufficiency. She would be serene and free of guilt; she would recognize the natural laws that controlled life and behavior; she would reject the illusions. Most of the anguish of life, she felt, stemmed from superstition and unintelligent emotionalism. People invented their codes the way children made up games, and what began as pretense ended as the only reality. But in spite of her clear reasoning she suffered; her bowels were tense with anxiety, and sharp darts of fear stabbed her vitals. It angered her—not that the world was contemptible or that she had done wrong, but that her will was inadequate. She hated her own white face in the glass. She lay at night in sleepless rage listening to the pound of her heart, on and on and on. She practiced serenity, took deep breaths, commanded her arms and legs to lie inert, fixed her mind on green meadows and twilit seas. In daylight she resolved to accept her existence, to deal candidly with each moment of time as it came. She abolished fear. But in spite of all, her heart pounded, she lay sleepless, she looked into the future with the clutch of doom in her breast.

"It's so *senseless*," she said to Edna Siegel. She spoke with a kind of helpless anger. "It's atavistic."

"What is? What are you talking about? What does 'atavistic' mean anyway?"

"If I could sleep decently," Patience muttered.

"Oh, I can get you some stuff for that—I mean some really useful stuff. The man down at Heilmann's has it—Aunt Maude gets it there; she had a prescription once, there's dope in it or something, and we can get all we need."

Patience had confessed to no one but Mary Kyle, but she now told Edna. She spoke with quiet logic, with calm control, as though the whole matter were part of her normal expectation. "But for some foolish reason I can't sleep decently—I can't eat—feel pretty much like hell."

"Better see a doctor," Edna said coolly. "Or have you?"

"Well, sort of—" She confessed further.

Edna expressed no surprise about any of it. "You'll need a doctor, of course. You'll have to make arrangements."

Patience looked at the bland face. The smooth features seemed to have been shaped in wax, with no blemish and little sign of vitality; they sloped downward, receding toward the chin—though the effect was produced partly because the head bowed itself forward and the shoulders seemed to droop. "Why don't you see Tom Hicks?" Edna went on. "He took care of Rowena a couple of years ago—and you remember Letty Axelrod, she swore by him; the family used to know him pretty well—in fact, he and my cousin Angie were engaged once, or practically engaged. She married that fellow from the Bronx, Zabilski—he wanted to be an announcer, you know, but he has this Bronx accent, it sounds just terrible, and he never could get a job, and they had a bad time—I guess they're divorced by now, it was coming up this month—"

"I haven't told Tony yet."

"You mean he doesn't know?"

"No."

Edna thought about it carefully. "You shouldn't put it off. I mean, as long as it's, say, six months, people don't talk too much. It takes a little while, you know—I mean, getting a license, and you have to have some sort of medical certificate these days. But you can't just let it slide."

"Well, Tony—"

"Oh, Oz—he won't run out on you. After all, there were witnesses—I mean practically. He'll have to make it legal."

"That isn't the point."

"Why isn't it the point? What other point is there? I mean, you can perfectly well get a divorce later. It's a sort of mess, all right; it's what happens when you get careless. But jeepers, Pat, you aren't the only one—I mean, you just have to go through with it. Look at Sue Tubman—Little Tubby, we used to call her—she's married again by now and they say the new one is a poorer bet than the first; and look at that Keller girl—remember her? She hooked the wrong man—everybody knew it but him."

"I wouldn't marry anyone with the idea of getting a divorce as soon as possible."

"Well, sure—no one would want to, certainly. But when you're in a mess, what can you do?"

"You can damn well get out of your own mess."

"That's all well and good, but what you don't seem to realize is that a baby is a baby. My advice to you frankly is to get an abortion. Tom Hicks won't do it—and he won't tell you who will, but he'll tell me, I mean I can wangle it out of him. And believe me, you haven't got much time—"

"I won't do it—"

"Look, Pat, be practical, for heaven's sake. How would you have a baby? Would you go home to your mother? What will you do with it? Do you realize you're stuck with it for life, practically? Do you have any idea what a stink there'd be?"

"Don't—don't talk like that, Edna."

"Don't talk? Okay, if you say so. I'm just giving you the facts."

"You act as though there was nothing decent or *human* about any of this. All you do is calculate how it will look, how to get away with it."

Edna shrugged. She drooped a little, she seemed tired, but her expression was one of bland certainty—it was, Patience knew, the only expression she ever had.

"You don't seem to have any *feeling* about it," Patience muttered, and suddenly anger seized her like a poison in her blood and brain. "Beasts!" she hissed out. "What do you live for—all of you? Appearances, surfaces, whatever you can get away with? Are we all nothing but filthy hypocrites?"

"I expect—we all—are."

"Well then, I'd rather be dead."

Silence followed.

"Will you tell me why not?" She snapped out the question as though Edna had disputed her. "Why can't a person—why *shouldn't* a person—have the right to decide? Why do they keep saying it's a sin or a crime—I mean, it's actually against the law, isn't it? All the religious people make such a fuss about it, but I can't see why it's any of their business. If a person wants to be dead, why can't he be? I wish you'd just tell me."

"We had all that in Prof Westervelt's course. Why ask me?"

"Well, it all seems so—so *senseless*."

"Maybe, but there's no point in worrying about it—I know I'd a good deal rather be alive than dead. I mean—after all—there's no need of agonizing the way you do. Even if you have your baby, and there's a big stink about it—well, you can survive; you might even have some fun, I mean you can get along—" Edna went through a characteristic routine of lighting a cigarette, inhaling, and blowing a long plume of smoke off toward the ceiling. "I just think you'll get on easier if you do it as legally as possible. You'll certainly forestall a lot of the stink. As for not wanting to involve Kedjian, that's utterly fantastic: it won't do him a precious bit of harm to marry you for a year or so—or less; in fact, the sooner he leaves you the sooner you get a divorce—in this state desertion is the surest grounds."

"Desertion? What are you talking about? If we ever did marry there'd be no deserting, either way."

"Look, Pat, I hate to talk like a Dutch aunt, or whatever it is, but you can't go on being as naive as this. Kedjian is probably a decent enough guy, goodness knows—I mean, a lot of guys are more decent than you might expect; he'll come up to the mark if we put a little pressure on him—a shotgun, for instance—" Edna hardly smiled at her own jest. "You can have fun with him for awhile—I certainly wouldn't mind going to bed with him for a month or so. But as a *husband*—well, don't be silly. He just isn't the type."

"Why isn't he?"

"A wolf like that?"

"Wolf, wolf—that's all you can say. You're as bad as all the other idiots."

Edna's shrug was indifferent. "I'm just telling you."

Patience stood up with both hands to her head as though she were holding it together. Her chalky face was splashed with red. "I'll have to go," she said in a voice of desperate restraint. "I won't be back. To me, you—all of you—are just *hateful*. I don't know what I'll do. I can't stand the dorm. I can't stand my room-mates or any of my so-called friends, including you. As far as I can see, you all live in a sort of moral sewer, and you like it there. From my point of view it would be a lot pleasanter to be dead."

She picked up her coat and bag and mounted the stairs to the balcony.

Edna watched quietly. "I think," she said at last, "you're acting like a fool."

But Patience went on without answering.

CHAPTER 27

MARY KYLE, reading in bed, heard the click and thump of the front door. Buzz, she thought, home from the drugstore—but a bit earlier than usual. No heavy footsteps, though; only a curiously hollow silence. Then after a while the sound of voices. The house transmitted all sounds, but specially the bass notes of radio or television, which seemed to shake the floors and walls; Mary Kyle did all her reading to a continuum of vibrations like a half-suppressed electrical storm underneath the floor. But these new voices were distinguishable as human, and after a bit she realized that Patience had come home. She got up, belted her woolen robe, put on slippers, and went down stairs.

She moved swiftly, with a sense of urgency, as though to a fire, but in the lower hall she paused, listened, then let herself materialize in the room with the others.

It was a moment of silence and immobility. The television had been turned down, but voices came out in a sort of rhythmic mutter; the bright pictures showed waves breaking, a cake of soap equipped with water-wings, a girl in a bathtub, a salesman smiling . . . only Edwin looked toward it. He was hunched over in his armchair, and turned partly away from the television so that his head had an unnatural rightward twist as he watched the flashing scenes. The light from above cast black shadows across his eyes and cheeks and mouth and underneath the line of his jaw. The high ridge of his cheek looked like polished bone. He didn't turn or look up as Mary Kyle came in.

Josephine sat on the edge of a wooden chair near the open double doors to the dining room. She too was oddly twisted, with feet side by side toward the dining room and body and head so far right as to be facing down the length of the room; her eyes had rolled round toward the fireplace so that the whites showed wildly, with a look of panic. She seemed rigid. Her mouth was open in the shape of a smile or shriek, slanting upward into her cheek like a deformity.

Patience sat carefully and neatly in the shabby stuffed chair by the fireplace, with her back to the door where Mary Kyle came in. She wore two gray sweaters, a gray flannel skirt, white socks and blue sneakers; she managed to look compact even in the half-dilapidated stuffed chair—her hair was severe, she wore no decorations or color, her white face seemed to be reduced to its plainest elements.

"I was telling them," she said, hearing Mary Kyle.

"He hasn't seen you?"

"He?" She spoke with no inflection.

The word *guaranteed* came out of the TV set, followed by *day and night protection* and a burst of music.

"I talked to him—early this evening," Mary Kyle said.

"You—*what?*"

"I butted in."

Patience gripped the arms of the chair and tightened her body like a spring. Her face and lips were white. "If I knew how, I'd kill you," she said.

The two similar faces set themselves in opposition.

"Well, go ahead," Mary Kyle said. "But I'd do it again—if I thought it would be any use. You don't seem to have any sense of your own."

Patience began to tremble. Her mouth opened slightly in a grimace. She stood up and walked out and up the stairs.

"There was someone called her about seven o'clock," Edwin said.

"Man's voice? Did he say who he was?"

Edwin glanced at Josephine and waited. She was not aware of him.

"He wants to find her," Mary Kyle tried to say, but the words hardly carried in the silence. "He—" Her mouth stayed open on the word. There were things she could say; there was information, news, a sort of comfort perhaps; but the air was like a curtain through which no words could pass. She saw that her father's face glistened and a drop hung underneath his unshaven chin.

"I don't know," he said repeatedly. "I don't know." The words were slurred, and blended in with the noises of the TV set. Mary Kyle moved across the room and turned it off. When she looked up again she saw that her mother had gone.

"This Tony," she said loudly in the silence, "he's in love with her—he'll—he'll . . ." She couldn't bring herself to say it literally.

Her father wiped his face with a handkerchief, then drew a gasping breath, turned his head away from her, and sobbed. His shoulders quivered. His voice broke out in falsetto cry.

She came close and stroked his head and back. After a while, when he quieted and dried his face again and looked round at the room, he spoke steadily. "You needn't pay a damn bit of attention to me. I'm old enough to know better—I mean, all this bawling is nothing but the baby coming out in me. I can't do anything about it, but I'm ashamed. I guess I'm astonished too—I thought I had more sense. The thing is, it isn't the girl, it isn't Patience I'm making all this goddam fuss about—it's *me*: all it is is lousy self-pity. It just comes over me that everything I've ever hoped for, or tried to do, or thought maybe I'd *like* to do—everything I've ever put my money on, every single solitary thing, has gone bad. I thought I could ride it out to the end, I thought I was a hardy sort of bastard—and by God I still think so in spite of this prime piece of soap opera, but what really got through to me was the picture I had of Patience—" He stopped abruptly and took several deep breaths. "God, the mind or the id or whatever the hell it is inside us is a fearsome thing. I remember like a picture—no, not a picture, but a whole reality, with a spotlight focused on it—I remember the naked female child. She was on a bed, I was changing her diapers—I suppose the light must have been on her because I see her the way you see a Christ child in a manger scene, I mean I have that kind of *image* of her in my head—the poor little white innocent lying there to be looked at. But what struck me— maybe I'd better say what scared me, because it did—was her sex. It came over me—I mean the doom of it. A time like that is when you pray, even a bastardy heathen like me; you *hope*, you have fears and premonitions—I'm not talking about the curse of Adam and all that religious hokum, I'm talking about the power of sex, the straight-out thermal power of it. That poor little embryo there, two weeks old—I conceived her, I was responsible, I changed her diapers, watched over her, hoped for the best, feared the worst —and now I guess it's come, and I guess I knew it all along." He looked up and pointed a finger at Mary Kyle. "No doubt you consider me guilty—"

She began to speak but he went on, thrusting his finger ahead of him. "Well, I'm not responsible for the female sex, nor for the male sex. Whatever is alive is doomed—I know that much. I guess I talk like one of the damned—and as a matter of fact I *am* damned; but the fact is that a lot of my life was full of hope—I hoped for Jo when I married her, I hoped for you and for Patience and the boys, I had a sort of dream about it all—I'm just trying to say why every now and then I—that is, why I—"

They heard Buzz thump across the porch and open the front door.

"Understand," Edwin went on, "I'm not in a position to give anyone hell—and I'm not even mad, not in the usual way. Shocked —I concede that; hurt—more so than I want to admit; defeated— if that is possible in my position. But let me tell you, I was brought up by a heavy father, an upright puritan—and I admit he was a good one: he was the sort of Vermont independent who never took much stock in the tribal superstitions of Calvinism, but morally he was about as tractable as an oak stump. I began to disappoint him when I was two years old, and for the next eighteen years he gave me steady hell. Doubtless I deserved it, but I don't know that any of it helped: matter of fact, it just made me cussed." He wadded his handkerchief and stuffed it in a hip pocket. "What do we do about the girl? Let her suffer, I suppose."

Buzz came in eating a doughnut. "Where's Ma? Gone to bed?"

Mary Kyle let herself out the back door and looked into the darkness of the yard. Then she went up to her room, dressed, took a coat from the dark hall closet, and slipped out again. No one noticed her: Patience was in the bathroom, the TV was on again downstairs.

She had no idea where her mother could have gone, but set off in a half-trot along the empty street, looking ahead at the misty glow of the lights. The air was heavy with moisture and cold, and she expected to feel a drizzle on her face, but she could see two or three faint stars—or thought she could. Nothing in any direction was clear. One of the stars moved and became an airplane; it sounded faint, then loud, then shook the sky as it passed overhead.

She seemed strong, and ran along with vigor, yet at the same time her eyes stung with tears and she felt the taste of grief in her throat. Is it always yourself, she wondered, that you cry for? The failure of hopes—the simplest hopes of peace and serenity, of a sort of ideal fulfillment where everyone lives without disappointment. Her father's cry was the last extremity of disappointment. Her mother's twisted grimace was like one of the old Hogarthian cartoons where agony is an elementary statement.

She made a circuit of blocks and came back to the house. Buzz was watching television, Patience seemed to be still in the bathroom upstairs, Edwin hadn't moved. She went out again. It occurred to her to fetch John Rossiter and she began imagining how it would be and what she would say—she could tell everything, conceal nothing, count on him wholly. Weakness, weakness, weakness—she half-muttered the word in the darkness of the back yard. In the crises of life some were strong and many were weak, and she, Mary Kyle Eustace, was one of the weak ones. She stood in the gloom and let the tears run over her cheeks. She turned first one way, then the other; she looked at the lighted windows above and below. Was it up to her to save them? Was she their present help and only hope? How could you save anyone from life itself? Her mother, for instance—out walking in the night, or plunging into a river or under a train, or reaching some pitch of desperation beyond all understanding.

Mary Kyle struck her own face with both hands; she kicked the concrete cellar wall hard enough to feel pain in her toes. Then she wiped her face with a paper tissue, rubbed it violently with her palms, and set off up and down the streets again.

A half-hour later, when she came back to the house, her mother was in the kitchen, standing under the naked light bulb as though she had never been anywhere else.

"I've decided what we had better do," she said with the resolute emphasis of one announcing a state policy. Her voice had taken on a professional enunciation. "Patience is going to have a baby in October. She will need a doctor's care, and I should prefer it if the actual delivery occurred in a hospital. There may be both emotional and physical difficulties and we must be prepared to do our best for her." She glared at Mary Kyle. "Don't forget that we must do our best for her!"

"Where in the world have you been, Mother? I've looked all over the neighborhood for you."

"Never mind me. I've been thinking, that's all. There's the question of disgrace. The family as such has failed. We had dignity and honor, and are brought low and almost destroyed— perhaps because of pride. I don't know, but it seems to me that my pride was too great. I can't account for the causes of failure; I do not understand the mystery of God; but I know that pride and hope have always been struck down, they were the tragic flaws that invited disaster."

"Well, don't brood about it now, Mother. It's late—"

"Oh, I don't brood. I accept. Disgrace, sin, catastrophe, have all come to us. But it isn't only that—it isn't only our personal failure; it is the end of an era, of six or eight generations of moral effort and hope. The end, you understand. For a long time I refused to accept it. I pretended. Even yesterday—even this morning; at least, I tried to pretend—" Her eyes showed white as she looked sideways at her rocking chair under the light bulb. She spoke more sharply. "I am not indulging in lamentations. You needn't commiserate—I mean, with me. What we can all do is to see to the future, whatever it is. We must take care of Patience and try to prevent public disgrace—we must if need be lie and deceive. Family honor, as such, no longer counts. But the child's future does, and even Patience has a whole life to live. Now if she stays on here, she and the child will be branded —they'll be notorious. The only thing to do is to go away some- where. I have decided that when the time comes I shall take furnished rooms in Portland—"

"Portland, *Maine?*"

"It is the right-sized city; we know no one there; it is not too far. I must find out more about the procedure and other details, but I am prepared to be as deceitful as the occasion demands—"

"You mean you'd be there for months?"

"Perhaps five—or more. We can work, of course. I suppose I could do cleaning—I believe the minimum wage is quite good now. For a while, at least, Patience could find work as a clerk or salesgirl."

Mary Kyle studied her mother's face. It had the stern set of a statesman's; it was rational, austere, wise.

"How do we take care of Father?"

"He can shift for himself. His future is no longer important—"

"Mother, for heaven's sake!"

"It is a question of reality, child. Your father is what he is." The words seemed to interrupt her thought and she said nothing for a few seconds. "He is not helpless. As long as I am here he pretends he is. To tell the truth, I have always oppressed him. He used to call me his parole officer. I had to be—he expected me to be; it was my duty. He admires discipline and austerity, you know, but only in theory—never in fact; he admires all the virtues but he doesn't love them—"

Mary Kyle interrupted. "He feels terrible."

Josephine turned her face as though she were brushing the words aside. "Yes, yes. But feeling terrible, as you call it, doesn't do us any good. We all feel terrible, I suppose. The thing to remember is that a child will be born. We can at least do our best for it—that's all I'm trying to tell you—"

An electric bell rang from the wall over the kitchen door. "Front door," Mary Kyle said with a start. She moved to the hall, then turned and spoke. "Here he is at last. Now be *decent* to him—"

He seemed large and fierce as she opened the door; he looked like a man preoccupied with his own destiny. His deep-set eyes caught the dim light from the hall and flashed darkly back at her. "Is she here? I've tried everywhere I can think of."

As it had before, the voice won her to him. She wondered if he could be as gentle as that.

"Come in. She's upstairs—she's gone to bed, probably. I'll see. Come in here, will you?" Her father's miserable little study, with sagging cot and Morris chair showing two coil springs dangling underneath—not, of course, that any of that mattered now. He loomed above things like some sort of remote and ancient nobleman. "I should explain that she has told the family—and we are all having various kinds of fits. I am not being flippant about the affair but it is hard to know what to say."

"At least we can be candid," he said steadily, as though he

knew what he wanted to say. "We have been wrong to conceal so much. We are brought up in fear—I think I've always had a sort of fear, and I suppose envy too, of the old families like yours, and I've acted with instinctive secrecy and even hostility: it's not deliberate—you would probably ascribe it to my sinister Asiatic heritage, though I think the whole semi-bohemian class I live with behaves the same way. We are a social underground, I guess. But Patience is worse—she assumes there's a *virtue* in secrecy and repression: she is like that boy who let the fox gnaw out his vitals rather than admitting the fact that it was there at all. Is that what you call the puritan heritage?"

"If so, it has its points," Mary Kyle said sharply. "The boy was Roman, I used to be told, but puritan is a word you can apply to any pig-headed martyr."

His smile was full of warmth and anxiety. "You know, you sound so much like her, like Patience. You both make me think of good steel. Please forgive me for saying so, but she has spoken of you so much that it seems natural: she always calls you Kyle— do you mind if I do too?"

She drew back a little from his warmth. Let's stick to the point, she almost said; let's not be beguiled . . . he watched her—like a hawk.

"It would be well," he went on, "if I could see her tonight. When I say she has been wrong, I mean it with love—with admiration too. How can I put it? I am *dedicated* to her. I desire only to be her slave, her husband—"

"Well!" She threw it in as a cushion against his eloquence. "The last thing she said was that she wanted to kill me—I told her I'd been to see you. I do agree with you that she is pig-headed—"

"You said it, not I."

"But I'll try again—I'll be patient and reasonable—"

"Oh, be more—be eloquent, be irresistible, be—"

"Never mind all that. I'll do what I can. I'll leave the rest to you—the irresistible part."

"Thank you, Kyle."

She went upstairs.

Patience was still in the bathroom, with the door locked, and when she made no answer or sound the truth exploded in Mary

Kyle; she flung her shoulder and weight against the door again and again until it burst. The others came running and they lifted the body from the blood-filled tub, laid it on a bed, bound the cut wrists, applied warmth, and called for an ambulance from the Waltham Hospital.

"Police would be quicker," Edwin said from the foot of the stairs.

"No—no police." Josephine's voice was more explicit than ever. "Police means newspapers. Let the hospital report it if they think they have to. They'll send a doctor anyway."

"Well, how *is* she, for God's sake. I can't get an answer out of anyone."

"She's—all right; she will be all right. She's alive."

CHAPTER 28

ABOUT FOUR O'CLOCK the next afternoon Mary Kyle answered the doorbell. She had stayed home from work, had driven her mother to the hospital in the Chrysler (with instructions, warnings, and prophecies from her father), and was to fetch her again between five and six.

"Is Mr. Eustace in? I wanted to ask how he is. My name's Heath—Tom Heath; I'm at the university—"

She knew at once. Her father liked him—lunched with him sometimes in the office; he taught government, Patience had had him for a semester, considered him competent rather than brilliant.

"Perhaps he isn't up to seeing me, but I thought I'd ask—"

"Oh, he's up to it—he'd love to see you. Come in."

But he stood looking at her. "You aren't the girl who was in my course—or are you?" A tall, rather stern man with a Roman nose and a brown mustache.

"My sister."

"Patience, yes." He smiled widely and studied her carefully. "Your father told me a good deal about you all; he is very proud of his family."

She drew back a little. "Come in, won't you?"

"I've hardly seen Patience since she was in my class. How is she getting on?"

Mary Kyle felt her eyes shift. She controlled her voice. "Oh— she isn't too well; she's in the hospital for a few days."

"I'm sorry to hear it. Operation?"

She almost glared at him. "Yes—a—a minor one. Leave your coat right here—I'll tell father." There was something grimly

insensitive about him, she thought. The mustache made him
look a bit like the bad man in a western—that and his dark, stern
features.

Her father had hunched himself into a sorrowful waking dream,
and stared at the empty TV screen. A baseball broadcast came
from a small radio.

"Heath?" The name worked its way into his dream. "Tom
Heath? Here?" His face seemed to her for an instant like a death
mask; then a quiver of life came over it. "Well, for God's sake
show him in." He called out: "Tom? What in hell you doing out
this way? Come in—tell me all the scandal: I hear they've hired
two new vice-presidents to take over my job . . ."

She slipped into the kitchen and stood listening to the ritual of
good cheer and insult. Her father's voice took on the up-country
nasal accent he affected in happier times; Tom Heath's deeper,
slower tones responded in kind: "Well, Ed, you aren't as much
of a wreck as I expected you'd be."

"Wreck, is it? Reminds me of Hez Applegate's new yellow-
wheeled buggy: he started down Bear Mountain in it with a bay
colt and two hundred yards above the hairpin turn what did they
meet but a genu-ine brown bear. For the rest of his life Hez
always said they shot the wrong critter: the colt had three good
legs left after it was all over, and Hez had less 'n one. The yellow
ash spokes made nice firewood in the Methodist meeting-house
at the foot of the hill, which is where they fetched up—all but
Hez: he got off at the hairpin turn—they found him on the far
side of the stone wall there. They never saw the bear. Hez used
to say if you figger on making a burnt offering, do it in advance:
it's no damn good afterward."

It was a long time, she thought—four months, perhaps—since
she had heard about Hez Applegate, who could be cited to
illustrate almost any event in life. On an impulse she thrust her
head in the dining room door. "Tell him about Hez and his
grandson."

Edwin almost chuckled. "Why Judas Priest, I could tell about
Hez all night. He stammered, you know. And he cussed pretty
near all the time. Whenever he started to say goddammit, for
instance, he'd get all tangled up and strangulated—it would take
him about two minutes just to get it out—and believe me the

effect was potent. We'd all wait while he got started on the g's, and he'd work up pressure—and by the time he got to the d's you'd expect him to explode—and then damned if he didn't begin all over again—"

Tom Heath grinned widely. His eyes twinkled and for a moment he reminded her of Mr. Punch. She had thought of him at first as of professorial age, but suddenly it appeared that he was young. It occurred to her to consult the university catalogue to find out his rank. "What about Hez and his grandson?" he said with honest eagerness.

Edwin pointed a finger at her. "You, girl—get a glass, get two glasses, fill 'em up with ice and bring in that fifth of Swanee River. If we intend to talk about Hez Applegate, *somebody* has to have an honest drink."

She didn't move for a moment; he eyed her with grim appreciation. "It's for you two," he said. "I don't guarantee to keep on, but up to now I'm in the hands of doctors and womenfolks."

She fetched one glass and the bottle. "I have to stay sober enough to drive Father's Chrysler," she said. "If it were just any old car it wouldn't matter." She poured out a drink for Tom Heath.

"I guess mine is what you'd describe as any old car," he said. It was odd how his wide smile alternated with the dour set of his features.

She stayed. It was the first time in ages, it seemed, that ordinary life and warmth had stirred in the house. Only an hour earlier the place was like an emblem of death. She noted that Tom Heath had a sardonic humor very like her father's; he talked about the university as though it were a bureaucratic madhouse, but he did it without personal involvement: the spectacle of scholars, publicists, advertising men, educationalists, and financiers all trying to direct the same operations at the same time was one that interested any student of government—

"Don't forget Grogan," Edwin said.

"How do you rate him? Ward boss? Gestapo?"

"I rate him as plain, ornery, primitive, unwashed bastard."

"That'll do as a start. Lucky you aren't working for him any more, huh?"

"Damn right." Edwin's face almost glittered. "And that reminds me, by God: I was going to write a letter—I was going to cut loose and tell 'em a few things—"

Mary Kyle saw Tom Heath's quick smile; he seemed almost to be winking at her. "How come you two got acquainted?" she said to change the subject. "I thought professors didn't speak to ordinary folk."

"Oh, we don't," he said. "Usually we're too timid. But my classroom is on the top floor and when the wind blows east it is so hot they all fall asleep and when it blows west—"

"He complained," Edwin interrupted. "Every damn day for a month, there he'd be in my office raising hell about the heat or the cold or the draught—no matter what I did, he complained. He spent so much time down in my office I told him he'd better bring his lunch and rest in comfort."

She jumped up at last with a sudden cry that it was nearly six—she had to start the supper and get her mother. She bustled off to the kitchen.

"Let me drive you," Tom Heath called. "I'm a very reliable one-drink driver." He followed her with tinkling glass and she had the impulse to bar his way: the house was dreadful enough, but the kitchen was worse than anything. But his visit had changed the whole climate of the place. They had laughed and spoken out freely and her father had talked about Hez Applegate, and Tom Heath seemed to be as relaxed and unselfconscious as a great Dane. She had to take the glass from his hand to find a cleared spot to put it on, but he hardly seemed to notice. "Maybe I could say hello to Patience—unless you think the sight of a professor will give her a turn for the worse."

It was a Volkswagen, and she climbed into it with a childlike curiosity to see how it worked and how it reflected its owner: it seemed like a big toy, but he took his seat and drove with perfect efficiency as though it were the only desirable car for a big man to have. He bought it, he said, because there was a little niche in the alley behind his apartment in Cambridge just big enough for it. And did the story go from scorn to love, like any good romance, she asked. He smiled and nodded, but said he was pretty much of a utilitarian: the thing worked fine for urban driving, but if he had a family to transport or long trips to take he'd get something bigger. "I do most of my real traveling by air," he added.

She took it in for a moment. In these days everybody traveled—

everybody but her, or so it seemed. "Where do you go?" she said suddenly.

"Where?" He expressed a deliberate uncertainty.

"Well, you said traveling—real traveling. I'm just being a little envious. Where do professors *go*?"

"Meetings. We take in each other's lectures, as it were. If we're lucky we get grants to investigate something or other—we go to Cambodia or Pakistan or Turkey—"

"Do you?"

"Well, I spent a year in Turkey."

"Investigating?"

"Oh, yes."

"Did you write a book?"

"Yes."

The thought made her sober. She had a vision of mosques and minarets.

"Where else have you been?"

"Oh—Germany: I was in Military Government after the war. London—I studied at the University, quite a while ago. Japan. South Africa once."

"Adventure," she said.

"Work," he shrugged.

"Don't you *like* it?"

He considered. "I like my field. I like to travel with a purpose, I suppose. But actually one place is much like another—or perhaps I should say every place wants to be like every other place. Turkey wants to be just like East Compton here—and eventually it will be."

"My God," she muttered. "So all my dreams are futile."

"Oh, tourists have fun—some, at least. But mostly they are just trying to escape themselves."

"That's something, I should think. Right now I'd like nothing better."

"Oh, come—I don't believe it." His smile was full of innocent kindness. "Maybe you'd better begin counting your blessings. I can promise you you'd find fewer and poorer ones in Turkey or almost anywhere else."

"Well, that isn't the point," she began warmly, then paused. She felt suddenly that she couldn't talk to him. He was somehow impervious. He knew all about the world, but nothing about the human soul—or even the human id, as her father called it. It was easy to call people uncomplicated or obvious. It was more often than not a sort of arrogance, and she knew she could be arrogant. What Tom Heath really was, she told herself, was normal, he was in fact *adjusted*—which meant rational, realistic, objective, and unpretentious. You admire virtue, she thought; you admire the good citizen, the good professor, the good sensible useful *man*, and when you get him in the flesh, as it were, you condemn him for his very virtues—you say he lacks soul, and perhaps you mean he lacks folly or misery. He had implied that he had no family and she tried to think of some way of asking, but they came to the hospital.

Her mother was standing in the lobby like a statue, but she looked at Tom Heath with malevolence, made no acknowledgement of the introduction, and walked to the door as though she were alone.

"Well, hello Tony," she heard Tom Heath say. "How do you happen to be here? I hope nothing's wrong."

"I wanted to see Patience." That strangely gentle voice—like cellos playing, like the sound of all human longing. "Mrs. Eustace thought I'd better not." He looked at Mary Kyle.

"You know Tony too?" Tom Heath said. "When I lecture on the Ottoman Empire I use him as my exhibit—my Visual Aid. What I hope is that he will appear in costume as Suleiman the Magnificent—"

"Go on up anyway," Mary Kyle was saying intensely. "I can explain to her." She felt Tom Heath's sharp eyes watching them. "Just don't be—try not to be—too emotional about it: you know what I mean—" She floundered and then turned and spoke sharply to Tom Heath. "They're in love. Mother—" She broke off. "She takes it hard; she's been under a strain anyway—she may not even speak to you on the way home." Mary Kyle indulged in the dramatic gesture of pushing her hair back from her temples. "As a matter of fact, we're all a little crazy—all but me, anyway. Whether I'm really as competent and able-bodied as I think I am is a question. Where's Tony?"

"He headed for the elevators."

"Love conquers all—I devoutly hope."

"Well, he's a very brilliant chap."

"So I hear." She smiled with sudden warmth. "Let's find Mother. She acts as though she is walking in her sleep."

On the way home Josephine turned and said to Tom Heath, "Was there ever such a man as Tamburlaine?"

"Oh, yes—certainly."

"Did he do what they say he did?"

"He didn't talk in blank verse, I expect. He looted towns and killed people; he ran a big empire. Timur the Tartar. The modern totalitarian government copies the one he and his predecessors set up—the first principle of which is to murder the opposition."

"What for?" Josephine explicitly asked. "I mean, what did they really want? What did they live for?"

"Power and wealth, I suppose. Palaces and slaves and harems."

"Were they happy?"

He took the question as a joke, but she asked it again. Were they successful people?

"I have no idea," he said. "I never considered the question." But then he began to consider it. "The conquerors were happy, I think. Fighting was their sport, and they did it with pride and zest—they must have been happy in their victories, and I'm sure they enjoyed the loot."

"No consciences, I suppose. No sense of sin or wrong."

"I suppose not—at least from our point of view. Life was certainly cheap—and expendable. The weak and helpless were doomed."

She said nothing until they almost reached the house.

"Christianity was intended for the weak and helpless, wasn't it?"

"I suppose it was."

"But it hasn't been adequate."

He shrugged, smiling a little.

She started up the walk, then turned and bowed her head stiffly. "I am grateful to you for bringing me home."

ᦥ **CHAPTER 29** ᦰ

"You'll have to make up your mind," Mary Kyle said, "whether you are miserable or happy. You can't go on having it both ways."

"Don't keep at me, Kyle."

"If you mean don't talk, the answer is no. You ought to know me better than that. As long as you're here and I'm here, I'll say my say. You're too damned touchy, Patience. If anybody in the family tells you there's a smudge on your nose or your slip is showing you think we're interfering with your precious freedom."

Patience lay back on her pillow and said nothing for almost a minute. Her face had a thin and colorless look to it as though it had been made of white stone. "All right," she said very quietly, "I'm too damned touchy; in other words, I act like a bitch. But after all, Kyle, you've been pretty bossy, haven't you? Ever since I can remember anything, you've been telling me what to do and what not to do. I've probably got a kid-sister neurosis. Even when everything you do and say is good for me I get sore. I make a disastrous mess of my life just to show you how independent I can be. Why not try leaving me alone a while and seeing if maybe I can learn to be less of a damned fool."

She spoke with so much restraint that Mary Kyle studied her clinically. It came over her vividly that Patience had been through torture more intense than anything she herself had ever felt. She had loved, conceived a child, lost it in a critical miscarriage; she had tried to die by cutting her wrists with her father's razor. Yet she had never been a passionate girl, or large-hearted, or generous in her emotions: it would have been better if she had. It was the holding-in, the secret tension, that made the trouble.

"I can live all of it down," Patience went on in the same level voice, "except for what it did to them." Her glance implied the family downstairs. "To you too, a little—but when I told them, when they understood—" Her voice stopped abruptly. Her face took on a fierce intensity as she struggled to control it. Tears flowed, and then ceased. "You saw their faces," she said faintly but distinctly. "Up to then I hadn't really thought—about them. Except with the usual feeling that they wouldn't approve of anything I did, and wouldn't understand; but mostly it was just my own predicament—I was in trouble and I couldn't really go on pretending that I wasn't. But now when I think about it all the only thing that I—that I can't bear—" She stopped again for a long minute. "There's nothing to *do* about it—I mean the worst has happened, for them; there's no way for them to get over it."

"Well," Mary Kyle said, "it wouldn't have helped if you had finished yourself off."

"No—probably not; but it wouldn't have made it any worse either."

"Oh, nonsense!"

Patience waited a long time and then spoke remotely as if she didn't expect to be heard. "You know, Kyle, I don't think you really understand. You live in a too—a too obvious world. You talk about being either miserable or happy, as though it were a choice. You think I can solve my problems by keeping my chin up and using common sense and all that—"

"Well, sister, there's no harm in trying."

"No, no harm in trying; but you saw their faces as well as I did—better, I suppose. Do you expect me to go off and be happy after that? Do you think I can just forget what I did to them?"

Mary Kyle opened her mouth to speak in anger, then clamped it shut for two or three seconds. "All I think is that there's no point in making the worst of it. You want to be more guilty than you deserve to be—you want to build it up into a drama—"

"You mean I'm just showing off."

"No, no, no—unless you're showing off to yourself. Damn it, Patience, can't you get it through your head that I'm not *against* you? I'm not jumping on you, except to say that you are making too much of a production of all this. You didn't destroy their lives all by your little self: they've been living in misery for years

—they've been *inviting* the worst—"

"A lot of good it does to say that!"

"In a way they expected you to do exactly what you did—be seduced and corrupted by a foreigner of no visible background."

"Kyle, for God's sake—"

"No, listen a minute—let big sister talk. I'm no prophet or psychology major, and doubtless I'm simple-minded, as you say, but as far as I can see there's only one thing you can decently do and that's to marry your honest man and produce an honest child—"

"Decency," Patience muttered. "Is that the point now?"

"Oh, stop quibbling! Don't be so obsessed with your own precious guilt. Here's a good man who loves you, is crazy about you, talks about you like Solomon: more than a good man, he's a prodigy, full of brains and talents and everything. I'm not kidding—I think he's wonderful, I wish I had someone like him. I assume you are equally crazy about him—you were the other day, at least, even though you had some sort of intellectual theory about why you shouldn't marry him—and please don't interrupt for a minute. You say you are mostly worried about the parents and feel you have destroyed their last hope—but why not give it a try? Remember, they know nothing about Tony and naturally assume he's an unprincipled barbarian with an outlandish name, but once they find out what he is really like they'll begin taking the credit for discovering him, and as for a grandchild—they'll worship him, or even her."

Patience relaxed. She seemed to brood for a moment. "You certainly are simple-minded, Kyle." But she said it mildly, almost affectionately. "It sounds fine. At the moment, though, Mother won't even listen to his name. Whenever she *thinks* of him she takes on that wild glassy look—it's really frightening."

"I'll work on her," Mary Kyle said. "I'll appeal to her reason—she's always proud of being rational."

"Don't let's kid ourselves: you know quite well what her idea of being rational is. If it were only a plain one-track mind you might somehow deal with it, but honestly—when I say frightening I mean it. I only began to realize it lately—I used to get sore because we were always bickering about this and that, but now, just since the other night, I've felt that something is really *wrong*.

Don't you? I mean—don't you feel it?"

Mary Kyle stood up, looked in the mirror, looked out of the window at the brown-painted clapboards of the Callahans' house. She tried to remember Rossiter's Law—what they had said about it. Too much truth, too much reason, too much principle—she tossed back her head as though she could shake the notion off. But she felt something move deep inside of her. His words and laugh rang in her ears.

"What you ought to do is to go back and finish up your college year. You could do it—you've only missed a week: Tony can get books and assignments for you—or Edna can, or someone."

"Not Edna. We're finished."

"Had a row, have you?"

"The thing is, I really feel *ashamed*—I mean, to have made such a mess of everything. I always thought I wouldn't—I prided myself."

"Well, be humble for a change." But Mary Kyle said it gently, smiling. "I know what the vanities of college life are—even I, in my spinsterish way—"

"I'm *sorry*, Kyle. I'm a bitch, really; I know I am."

Color came into Patience's cheeks.

Mary Kyle paced round the small room with a sense of freedom. "Don't give it another thought. Our motto from now on is humility, but not too much: *ma non troppo,* as they say on programs. Tell me about Tom Heath. Is he a nice guy?"

"Heath? Why? What about him?"

"He's a friend of Father's."

"Well, I knew that—they used to have lunch, down in that cell Father called his office."

"Is he married?"

"No."

"Why not?"

"I don't know—he's afraid, or cagey maybe. He does look after his father, they say: the old man is helpless, I guess—has to have a day nurse. Heath never can have anybody in—I mean like friends or any of his students." Patience lifted her head. "My God, Kyle, when you think what people have to *stand* in this life! Doesn't it scare you—I mean just to realize what goes on?"

"How can he travel so much? Spend a year in Turkey, for instance."

"I don't know—except I guess he has a sister out in Saugus with a lot of kids; he may have more family—I'm not sure. Why? What about him?"

"Oh, he cheers up Father. He came out one afternoon and before you knew it they were telling funny stories to each other. I thought maybe we could get him out again. It improves the atmosphere, I can tell you. Even Mother started asking him about Tamburlaine the Great."

"Why Tamburlaine?"

"His field, I gather. Mongols and Tartars and Ottomans. He's a friend of Tony's."

"I know." Patience reflected. "Well, it would be nice to have someone here that everyone approves of—for a change."

"You know what they keep saying about a good athlete: he has to be *loose*. I can see you aren't loose enough."

"Can you learn to be loose?"

"Oh, sure—you can. Some people can't, but they haven't ability."

"It sounds degenerate." Her smile made the remark seem idle. She stretched. "I feel loose enough now, but not athletic at all—not even adequate." But she straightened and gathered herself with deliberate effort. "It makes me realize what a cloistered life I live."

Nothing, apparently, bothered him: noise, crowds, drunks, brawls, lost children, even defeat for the home team. He controlled his charges by a kind of mesmerism; they called his name constantly—Mr. Ross, Mr. Ross, all afternoon—and they could be as wild as hoodlums, but they kept an eye on him with a little glint of love and pleasure, and they called out questions as though he were their private oracle: what was Ted Williams batting now? How many r.b.i.'s for Jensen? Why did they have that fence in left field? What was Sullivan's won-and-lost record? Why didn't Ted just bunt it down the third-base line every time? Why didn't they build the right-field stands so he could hit more homers? As for Mary Kyle, they hardly seemed to notice her except as part of the social scenery, like the subway guards, ticket collectors, and ushers. Two of the girls called her teacher, one called her Miss Kyle, and the fourth paid no attention to her at all. All four were in love with Jackie Jensen, and two—the two who called her teacher—screamed it out each time he came past them to right field.

"The truth is," she said, "I kept thinking how pleasant it would be to choke the life out of those two maniacs. That isn't the professional attitude, is it? You seemed to be fond of them—or at least to be willing to let them live." She remembered how once when they were screaming through megaphoned hands John had turned and looked at them with a smile, and they glanced at each other in a flash of self-consciousness and even blushed, and she remembered how suddenly polite they were at the end when they recited little speeches of thanks. "Girls," she said, "are deadly creatures." But it wasn't what she meant; she couldn't think how to say it. "At least you can see what boys want and fight for."

"What boys want is a free baseball—and they will fight for it unto death."

One of them had got one. He and three others had dived into the next section of seats like a dog-pack after a chunk of meat, snarling and snapping among the slow-moving adults, and when he got the prize and returned clutching it, new, white, official, stamped and signed, he rushed back over the barrier, stumbling, shouting, holding it out: "Hey, Mr. Ross—hey, you want it? You can have it. No kidding, I'll give it to you."

Cassandra, he said, was the girl who took care of the office—and she was going to Texas; there was another girl who did typing and kept records but wasn't bright; there was an office boy aged sixty-three, a retired light-heavyweight now weighing two hundred and thirty—not what you'd call bright either, but the most valuable man in the whole organization: he did whatever had to be done; his name was Jake . . .

"I'll bet he loves you," she said.

"A Saint Bernard: all he needs is a keg round his neck."

There was a board of trustees that met twice a year. There were more or less itinerant field workers, migratory sociologists from the colleges in the neighborhood, volunteers, strong-minded Bostonians, mostly female, determined to work for the common good . . .

"What are you?"

"I'm the Executive Secretary." He looked at her with a gleam of pleasure at having said the words. "That means I'm the Admirable Crichton of the outfit. I do everything from licking postage stamps to trying to persuade the governor to pardon murderers."

She knew by then what he had in mind, but when he actually said it—asked her if she would take over Cassandra's job—she felt an almost physical sense of crisis and doom. He didn't press it, of course: he went at it, in fact, obliquely. The pay was inevitably poor. The office, as she could see, looked like the sort of place Uriah Heep might be found in. The work—well, you couldn't define it, but at least she wouldn't feel cloistered. He grinned at her. It was like being stabbed.

She had to believe that he had no inkling of it. He paced the floor, gestured with his pipe, spoke out joyously about the long hours, the crises, the catastrophes, the hopeless war against human savagery, but whether he knew anything at all about her feelings could not be told. Like most honest men he seemed to have no realistic understanding of women.

"You'll undoubtedly get more money out of that advertising outfit," he was saying. "For all I know, they may be intending to make you a first vice-president and partner. But I gather you sometimes find it hard to breathe over there, air-conditioning not-withstanding. As for us—we've been in business eighty-six years and haven't prospered yet, but I believe we are spiritually sound. We breathe bad air but we breathe it freely—"

"You better talk facts," she said, pretending to take a practical view. "Wages, hours, duties. Omit the drama for a while. I'm a working girl, remember."

He snatched out his watch and studied it. "Be practical, she says. After a hard day at the ball game, with no supper—no, no, I was carried away by the sight of you brightening up the old office here. If you insist on bargaining we'll do it later—preferably at nine or ten in the morning when our wits are really sharp."

"Why do you offer me the job?" she persisted. "Why pick me?"

"Well—"

"And don't tell me it's because I have muscles." She almost held her breath; she listened with all her senses. This would be the time and the place, she thought; this would be the moment for the overwhelming question—

He was blowing into his pipe. "I know girls hate the idea of muscles," he said. "But I'll make a confession to you—I'll give myself away: what I have longed for ever since I was sixteen is a genuine acrobatic dancing girl. I fall in love every time I see one do the splits or a couple of aerial somersaults—"

"I'm the wrong girl for that," she said sharply.

"Oh, there are other talents—and as far as this office goes the somersaults wouldn't be much help. What we need here is really more of an acrobatic brain—" He looked at her with unexpected seriousness. "What I mean is the free brain, the uncramped brain. Most people live in grooves. They have principles and pieties. They believe in technique or method. They follow law. They go through motions. They aim to be sound. They think there are right ways and wrong ways—and even good people and bad people." He waved his pipe. "I don't deny their world—it exists mostly as a dream or a hope; we have to have it just as we have to have a heaven. But the fact of the matter is that people like that are no good at the kind of work we have to do here. That's why I shudder whenever I see a nice Junior Leaguer coming in the door hoping to do good, or a lady with a Beacon Hill hat, or even a young master of arts from a school of sociology."

"How much of this do you mean?"

"More than most people want to admit."

"And you think I can operate without benefit of principles—"

"I *hope* you can."

She felt tired and scared, as though she were out on thin ice. It would be well, she thought, not to make a move or even to speak aloud. If she could stay perfectly still nothing would happen, no engulfment, no plunge into the dark unknown.

"Any man," he said, pacing round the room, "who denies ideals is in the classic sense a lost soul; he is defeated—there is no health in him. The one requirement of life is that it be lived as well as possible—that's the only rule, and applies to insects and men and elephants—"

"Are you," she interrupted in hardly more than a whisper, "addressing me personally, or the ladies with Beacon Hill hats?"

"Oh, they know that much; you may not, but they do. No, no, I'm defending myself against the charge of irresponsible blasphemy."

"Whose charge?"

He grinned. "Okay, lady—you're welcome to that trick. If you think my conscience is gnawing at me, you may be right: but I had a notion I ought to try to put our operations here in a better light: I didn't want you to think we had no aims at all."

"Sales talk?"

"Not very good, is it? I was afraid it wasn't. Actually, you didn't give me a chance to get going. But never mind—it's too late in the day; you'll be wanting to get home."

She stared at the oak desks, the oak filing-cabinets, the framed photograph of a prophet in a frock coat. "Who is he?" she asked.

"Our founder, William Bolles Redfern."

"Looks as though he had principles."

"Whatever he had was good. I'm proud to be his humble disciple, the frock coat notwithstanding."

She waited as though something held her. She waited for a sign or a word. The room, the building, seemed deserted; an eight-day pendulum clock ticked on an inner wall. In the corner near it stood a varnished hatrack, a pole on tripod legs with angled wooden pegs near the top. Bad air, he had said. Closed-in, almost musty.

"Why do you want me here?" she said in a low, half-choked voice.

But he merely smiled like a kindly friend and companion. He opened the door. "Come along," he said.

CHAPTER 31

A BLUE STATION-WAGON was standing in front of the house and Mary Kyle felt a little pressure of concern. Doctor? Lawyer? Bad news? Callers seldom came, except ones they knew like Harold Chivers with his old Chevrolet. This car looked new and worldly. She passed round the blind side of the house and slipped in the back door. She listened, wondering whether to attack or make a secret retreat to the stairs.

Voices—a man's, her mother's brisk and strongly articulate. "Payson Livermore," she said, "settled in Amesbury in sixteen thirty-two. His first wife was Ann Weste—spelt with an *e* on the end—and was killed by Indians. The Essex Historical Society published his journal, you know: he gave thanks that God in his mercy had spared *him*; he felt that God had done the *right thing*."

The voice sounded urgent, as if the matter of Ann Weste Livermore were pressing hard on her. Mary Kyle had always admired the precision and competence of her mother's speech; it would go well, she used to say, on radio—unlike most women's. But lately a note of strained intensity had sounded in it, and now listening from the kitchen Mary Kyle heard it more clearly.

"All Payson Livermore really cared about was *his own salvation*." The last phrase was almost frantic in its emphasis. "Of course, you must take into consideration the Calvinistic belief, which is hard for us to do. We should make the effort to see things *from his point of view*."

"I really ought to learn more about the family history," the man's voice said. "You're the one to teach me, I can see that. Not that I'm too fond of those old puritans: they always struck me as an unhappy lot of people." It was a confident voice, easy and cultivated and accented with conscious refinement. Whoever he was, Mary Kyle thought, he played the part of a gentleman of the world. He was obviously a cousin of some sort.

Josephine at once took him to task for his typical modern ignorance of the true nature of the puritans: they lived, she said, a thrilling melodrama whose outcome was eternal glory or eternal hellfire; life to them was an exciting battle between God and the devil, and every daily event was charged with cosmic meaning.

Edwin's voice broke in, more nasal and up-country than usual: "Damnedest mixture of sense and nonsense in all history. I take it they were the most virtuous and competent people who ever lived—I mean, as a society. They had guts and common sense and decency beyond any people I ever heard of. They admired reason and learning and brains. But the whole business, all their piety and virtue and learning, was based on the crudest, the stupidest, the most asinine religious dogma that ever hypnotized the mind of so-called civilized man—"

The smooth laugh of the unknown cousin made light of it. "You sound just like yourself, Edwin."

"Well, I am myself, I presume. It can't be helped, not at this age."

"Oh, I'm delighted. I'd heard you were having trouble last winter—"

Edwin interrupted. "Yeah, you can say trouble: it's what I had then, have now, and will have tomorrow. If this house had only been half a mile further from the station, my trouble would be over—completely. I doubtless deserve hellfire—say a small dose at least—but what I count on getting is simple oblivion. I believe it will be a relief."

"Oh, come now, Edwin—"

"He just wants to get a *rise* out of you, Albert," Josephine said, and Mary Kyle smiled slightly and walked into the room.

"Hello, Albert—is that you?"

"Why Mary, how nice—you look exactly the same as you did in college." His smile came warmly; he shook hands with a strong clasp. "It must be five years at least."

"Nine," she said.

"Oh, no—impossible."

She remembered when he came to Wyndham College as an instructor. "You look the same too." Her smile was touched with a small irony. "In training, I'll bet. Do you still ski?"

"Oh—well, yes. I've had to give up racing—most of it, at least."

"Tennis, too?"

"Well, I've been coaching off and on. It takes too much time, but I can't seem to keep away—"

"Sailing in summer, of course."

"Oh, of course." His bland smile seemed to welcome her teasing. He represented the very pattern of the college athlete; in his speech, deportment, and clothes he could have passed as a senior at Wyndham; only the fine etchings round his mouth and eyes hinted at the added fifteen years. "You may not believe it, though —but my job really interferes with many of my old habits; I even have to be in Wyndham a good part of the summer." Abruptly, as though he had pushed a button within himself, he turned serious. "The admissions problem grows more complicated every year. Most people have no idea what it involves—they assume that a college can readily pick out the men it wants to admit and reject the rest. But the pressures and calculations are really terrific—"

"I'd hate to think," Edwin said, "where I'd be—why, I wouldn't stand the chance of a pig-tailed chinaman of getting into your place."

"Oh, we all feel that," Albert said. "My old chief always told the boys he interviewed that *he* couldn't qualify—"

"Do you tell them that too?" Mary Kyle asked.

"Well, of course, it is probably true, but I don't know that it is quite tactful to say it—quite professional, I mean."

"Spoils their young illusions?"

He smiled quickly. "That wouldn't do, would it?"

Before he married, she had asked him to a dance—it was just after Harry Fitts had abandoned her, and she was determined to show Harry and everybody else that she was a woman of great resource. The event turned out splendidly: Albert looked like an Ivy League divinity disguised as an Air Force lieutenant, and Mary Kyle had a social triumph. But something about his perfections brought out the worst in her; she dealt with him perversely and ironically, made fun of the bland manners and the complacence. Everything's under control, he used to say with ritualistic satisfaction as though nothing else needed to be said, and of course she mimicked it. He regarded her with patience and kept a little distance between them. "You aren't really sure," she said, "if I'm under control. I think I make you nervous—not that you'd admit it. But I'm afraid you think Cousin Mary isn't quite *quite* . . ." He married Edith Warburton of New York and Greenwich, a girl of wondrous beauty and wealth who once rated ninth among the nation's tennis players.

"Bring us up to date on your family," she said. "It's three, isn't it? Boy, girl, boy?"

He nodded, then caught the look on her face and smiled. "That's keeping things under control, isn't it?" The lines round his eyes and mouth seemed very reliable as he smiled—very sincere, she had to admit. He was such a perfect pattern of the collegiate ideal that it was hard to believe in him, yet there he was in actuality.

"They must be beautiful," she was saying. "Do they combine the best features of their parents?"

"Oh, better than that!" But he spoke with a conventionality that seemed to put an end to the matter. Was it part of his code to be reticent about his family? or about himself?

"Do you like being Director of Admissions?" she asked. "Or do you wish you were still teaching?"

"Oh, of course—I do reget that. I think the most rewarding thing a man can do is to teach—"

Edwin made a growling noise. "I beg to say that I am unimpressed and unconvinced—in fact it all sounds like a weak solution of unsalted eyewash." His smile glittered in appreciation of his own words. "Forgive my tactlessness—I've come to be what Hez Applegate used to call a dry-throated bastard—but the fact is that for five years I've been listening to these high-minded directors of this, that, and the other explaining how they'd just love to get back to a life of simple teaching and pure scholarship: they sound like the politicians who never admit that they might want to be governor or president, whose honest desire is merely to be a humble lawyer or a simple corporation executive with a salary of, say, two hundred thousand—"

Albert laughed. No color tinged his face, no frowns or compressions. "Right you are, Cousin Edwin. But in my case it isn't entirely eyewash. I used to dream of going on into scholarship, and I still see it as a good life—perhaps the best, but maybe I'm better at this sort of thing. My regrets aren't really very acute."

"Why, you'll be a dean some day," Josephine said. "Or a president. I haven't any doubt of it."

He laughed blithely. All his gestures were done with the right style, as if he had rehearsed them to a point of perfection. He should, Mary Kyle thought, be seen by an audience.

"As of now," he said, "I'm not a candidate for anything."

It was sociology, she suddenly remembered, that he had gone into—as far as a master's degree, at least. He had intended to go on for the Ph.D. but the war set him back; so did the skiing and tennis and sailing. She tried to imagine him doing John Rossiter's job, and she felt a tremor of resentment or jealousy because of his accent and his clothes and his assurance of being one of a happy few. Ivy League sociology, she thought: the sincere smile, the understatement, the bland certainty, the perfect control, the code of the gentleman-sportsman.

"This is almost our busiest time," he was saying. "The acceptances all go out at once, the annual sweepstakes reaches a sort of climax, thousands of boys and girls are made happy or miserable, and for the next four months colleges try to figure out just where they are." Again the button of sobriety was suddenly pushed. "We've been quite concerned about young Mort, you know. I had to come on for some meetings in Cambridge, and I thought I'd better have a talk with him. Dean Bridges urged him very strongly to finish out his year—I did too, of course; now there seems to be some question about his coming back at all."

A moment of silence, then Edwin said as though he were quoting something, "No use to talk to him."

"You must talk to him," Josephine said. "He won't listen to us."

"He listens," Edwin said, "just like a wooden Indian: you couldn't get an idea into him with a brace and bit."

In the pause Mary Kyle could feel the deep concern in her mother's mind over whether to urge him to stay for supper. It was after six. Buzz wouldn't be home until ten-fifteen or so. It might even be a question of asking Albert to stay all night, and the third-floor room was full of junk and dust and bad air. Josephine's face expressed a terrible anxiety, as though she were physically suffering.

"You must certainly have dinner with us, Albert," she faintly said.

"Dinner," Edwin began, "is a misleading term—"

"I'll show you where to wash your hands," Mary Kyle said briskly. "Follow me."

But Albert became a man of affairs. He had just time for a chat with Mort—and he hoped they could manage it at the drug store. After that he had to be on his way—he gave the impression that he operated on a strict schedule, like a visiting statesman.

Then he resumed his rôle as a warm-hearted cousin, and left his best wishes for Patience, whom he had never met. "And we want you to know that we think very highly of Mort at Wyndham. He is a genius with a basketball, of course, but he is really coming along well in other ways. It would be a great pity if he didn't finish out."

"Exactly," Josephine said.

After he had gone, with directions from Mary Kyle, she telephoned Buzz. He seemed, as she expected, hostile. "Didn't you tell him I'm busy?" She tried to be earnest with him. "He's a good man, Buzz, even if he is your cousin. You'd better listen to him."

"Yeah, I know—the place is crawling with good men. You know what they call him up there: Prince Albert—either that or Little Lord Livermore. Oh, he's a nice guy, all right, and a terrific man at tennis—he could still win the Intercollegiate Singles—but he's strictly from Brooks Brothers and Yale."

"Well, don't be a snob about it, for heaven's sake. Just because he wears decent clothes and has good manners you needn't scorn him."

"Don't worry, I won't embarrass the family—I'll try not to, anyway. But I already know everything he'll say." His voice deepened a note. "Mort, old man, we think very highly of you at Wyndham. We just want you to realize that we're all behind you—and so forth."

"Very funny, brother—but a trifle adolescent, don't you think? If you had any sense, you'd be damned glad they were all behind you."

"Yeah, you can say that again. But the fact seems to be that I haven't any sense. What do I do about it?"

Afterward Edwin made a sort of grimace of sympathy. "You might as well whistle jigs to a milestone, as old Hez used to say."

"I thought it was your grandmother who said it."

"Well, the truth prevails, whoever said it first."

✎§ CHAPTER 32 ᵹ❧

THE NEXT MORNING turned sunny and very warm for mid-May. Windows and doors stood open for the first time, and Buzz was driven to bring up screens from the cellar and remove the storm sashes from the north side. Right after breakfast Mary Kyle in jeans and T-shirt hosed and brushed and wiped whatever seemed to need it. The birds sang and chirped in the young leaves and the air was rich with fragrance.

"A lovely morning," Harold Chivers said, coming round the corner of the house. "It is delightful to be alive on such a morning." His V smile expressed such an eager innocence that she looked away almost with embarrassment. In all details he was dressed for church, even to a pair of gray suede gloves. He carried a gray, rather stiff hat with a white satin lining. He inquired as to the health of each member of the family, was gratified to hear that Patience was doing well after her operation, and noted that Buzz was able to be quite active again.

"I suppose you've got your windows and screens all tended to," she said, feeling the sweat trickling here and there.

"Oh, we always do those in Father's April vacation." He responded to her smile. "We are very methodical, of course—we do everything with mathematical precision."

She let her smile envelop him. "I know." The best thing about Harold was his little appreciative humor about himself. "I do admire it—specially in contrast to the mess we usually make of everything. Look at that busted screen—and all this paint cracking off—"

"If you would wait till this afternoon I could come over and help out—I could fix that one, and the others: we could scrape them down and put on a coat of paint."

She made light of it, but he went on intently. "I'll make a bargain with you. If you will get ready and come along to church, I'll agree to devote the afternoon to working on the screens."

"Oh, nonsense—"

"I'm quite serious!" He said it with the eagerness of a boy wanting to be believed.

She rubbed the back of her hand across her forehead, thinking that something would have to be done about Harold. Against all her own disorder he seemed as changeless and invulnerable as a monument; he existed as a complete fact, from the precision of his costumes to his mastery of the problem of window-screens. He represented both private and public virtue; he did his duties with innocent pleasure—even the unending commuting, the five-day-a-week journey in and out of the city, seemed to be a natural function to him and as enjoyable as eating and sleeping and going to church. His one mistake, his aberration, was to have fallen for her, though it was exactly the sort of joke nature played on the innocent. He could have found any number of suitable suburban maidens.

"The thing is, Harold," she said with a sudden rush of severity, "I don't give a damn about your church. It's a way of doing something—you put on good clothes and advertise your good conduct—you go there and come home again—you use up a couple of hours of life—you make pious noises—" She stopped. What was the sense of talking like that? "I'm sorry, Harold. I sound like the campus atheist. But I mean it, too. You won't ever believe me, you think I'm just trying to shock you for the hell of it, but I wish you'd get it through your virtuous head that mine is a blasphemous disposition."

He adopted an attitude of stubborn respect. "Yet for years you have been going to your own church. I hardly consider that evidence of blasphemy."

"Oh—that. It's merely that I'm fond of Mr. Rossiter." She almost said the word love—I'm in love—and shook her head ruefully. "I have to sing in his ridiculous little choir—if I didn't it would collapse." She looked at her wrist watch. "That's in half an hour too—I've got to run."

"I'll drive you," he said.

"Oh, don't bother—I mean, it's only a five-minute walk, thanks just the same: unless of course you want to abandon your principles and come to our church—you can even join the choir, we always need male volume."

"Well—thank you, I believe I will: if you really mean it, that is?"

"Holy smoke! I had no idea you would even consider it." She noted the reckless glitter of his little smile. "I'm—I'm stunned. What about your parents? Don't you always take them? What about ushering and passing the plate and all that?"

His father, he said, had a cold—his mother preferred to stay and watch over him—he only passed the plate on alternate Sundays—

"I was really only kidding," she said. "It serves me right for it— I mean for talking foolishly. But come on anyway, you can see how we amateurs do it. Give me ten minutes to clean up."

In twenty-five minutes they were off in the old Chevrolet, and for the occasion Mary Kyle felt herself to be charming and even beautiful. She wore chartreuse green silk with a very full skirt that swung airily about her long legs, and she wore Patience's year-old spring hat, a bit of white basketry cocked on the side of her shining hair. The May morning grew warmer, more fragrant, more benevolent. Even the plain painted church was full of air and sweetness, with lilacs and tulips and a branch of budded apple blossoms. The windows and doors stood open. People chatted in normal voices and stood about socially as they might at a club meeting. "We aren't very ecclesiastical here," she said. "Our patron saint is Emerson, or sometimes even William James. We are told that the good life is a nice mixture of idealism, nature, and common sense."

He glanced at everything with the bright alertness of a bird. The lenses of his spectacles seemed to sparkle as they took in the scene, and his mouth made an angle not so much of humor as of relish, as though he were savoring strange flavors. The sermon, she told him, would be on John Dewey: what they'd been having all year was a course in the history of philosophy; next week, Existentialism.

She led him up the stairs to the small balcony where organ and choir performed.

"Re-enforcements?" John Rossiter said. His hair stood up like a bush and he had the grin of an eight-year-old.

She introduced Harold all round as a professional tenor and then, as she saw the color suffuse his white face, regretted it. She kept forgetting how sensitive he was; she used him cruelly as a target for irony.

"Oh—I—I—Miss Eustace is really just joking—"

John's bright glance took them in. "Miss Eustace," he said, "can't always be trusted."

"I'm afraid I can't even carry a tune." Harold spoke out firmly, as one who had no intention of deceiving. "I have never been musical in any respect."

"Oh, you can make some tenor noises, I'm sure," John said.

"As long as you're a *man*," Letty Hirsch put in, and then suppressed a giggle. "I mean—goodness, just a man is all we need. That's what they keep saying down below—why don't you get more men?"

"That's the big question, all right," Mary Kyle said. She smiled brightly at Paul Schindler, the only other tenor; the two baritones had not arrived yet. "But where would we be without the ones we have?"

"We'd be—down below," John said. She noted that one point of his soft collar was already askew and the tie had pulled an inch sidewise. He wore a rough-textured brown suit, much too hot for the day. "This is one enterprise where we can all feel indispensable. The rest of the week we are humble underlings, but not here: no indeed! For the next hour we are the Lord's chosen." He winked at Harold and turned to the organ to begin the prelude. The baritones slipped in, nodding.

Harold sat apart, stiffly and correctly, watching everything with glittering spectacles

"It's all very friendly," he said to her afterward as they drove back. "Delightfully informal too."

"A little heathenish, you think?"

"It is different, certainly." When she laughed he produced his thin twinkly smile. "You doubtless think I'm a conservative Baptist: hard-shelled is the term they use, I believe. But I consider myself quite liberal—in fact I admire John Dewey very much. I thought the sermon—or talk, as I suppose it should be called, was quite stimulating. I do miss the old rituals, though—mostly be-

cause I was brought up with them, I realize. But worship is really
a nonrational activity, isn't it?"

She was silent for a time. His simple and literal honesty always
touched her with surprise: she thought she knew him well—much
too well; she was arrogant toward him and treated him like a
somewhat absurd piece of human mechanism; but he did have a
mind of his own, and he used it with dignity. He should have
been rescued from his virtuous parents and thrown out into the
world, though even that notion was an arrogant one, she realized.
She affected the sort of worldliness that mocked virtue and was
jealous of innocence.

"Are you a happy man, Harold?" The words popped out, but
she instantly regretted them. "I mean, do you like what you are
doing in the world?"

The moment grew serious. Instead of smiling and speculating
on the nature of human happiness he drew up under a maple
tree at the curb of the suburban street. He turned off the motor.
The sweet air and quiet Sunday benevolence poured through the
open windows of the Chevrolet.

"I could very easily be a happy man," he said. "I have quite
good health. My work is interesting and fairly lucrative—that is, my
salary is regularly about seventy-five hundred, but I can quite
often earn more on special jobs: more and more people want to
use our calculating machines and of course we are glad to have
the extra fees—"

"You run the machines?" She put it in hopefully to distract him.

"Well, I'm a statistician. I try to explain what the results mean."

"You don't just push the buttons and oil the wheels and all
that?"

He allowed a small smile and shook his head. "I've built up
some investments too," he went on, "and I may say that so far I've
been quite fortunate."

"You mean you speculate?"

"Oh, we statisticians don't call it that. We calculate. Of course
the men in at the office are very sharp about business affairs and I
get the benefit of their experience—they don't realize how much
because I think it is wise to keep pretty quiet about those things."

"Why, Harold, who'd ever suspect that you were a secret specu-
lator!"

"Oh, I assure you there's very little risk. I buy only the best—"
But nothing, she knew, could turn him from his course. He
noted that he was an only son, and would eventually inherit a
small property along with some quaint old heirlooms he was very
fond of—though all that would be a matter of the very remote
future: his parents were still in excellent health.

She sat silent in almost agonized helplessness while he went on
with it. He had first admired, then loved her. All other girls in
comparison seemed the merest shadows—they were, in fact, in-
sipid. But she—so vital, so beautiful, so intelligent, so genuine . . .

Mary Kyle felt the tears sting her eyes. Her throat ached. An
anger welled up in her—not at him but at the predicament.

"I have never let myself hope too much," he said, "because I
know I am not really worthy of you."

In her frustration she nearly giggled. She choked the hurt back
into her throat.

"You asked if I were happy," he went on. "The answer is wholly
up to you. I'd say that ordinarily I'd be happy enough: my life is
certainly a pleasant one. But I can't conceive of being happy without you; the thought of it is—well, like a perpetual prison sentence. With you as my wife—" His voice trembled and he ceased.

She said nothing.

"Of course," he went on more briskly, "I realize you'd want to
have a place of our own. Mother has been urging me to marry
for at least ten years—and naturally she knows how I feel about
you: she has even asked once or twice if there is any hope, and
warns me not to be faint-hearted—"

"You mean," she said hoarsely, "they *approve* of me?"

"Oh, certainly. They share many of my own views. You don't
really know Father very well; he is quite shy, but he loves to
joke—and he refers to you as Boadicea—"

"What?"

"Oh, he means it kindly; he thinks you look like an early Brit-
ish queen—he really admires you very much."

Outside the car, all was serene. She glanced helplessly at the
grass and trees and sunlight. The pressure in her throat and chest
almost stopped her breathing. Once as a child of nine she watched
her cousin Herbert Bellows put four kittens and a stone in a burlap bag and toss it into a pond. He did it as he did other farm

chores, without any special emphasis, and at the time she took it as part of the routine of country life: Herbert at eighteen seemed to her a competent adult and she never doubted that he did his duty. But the image of the kittens recurred often; it existed in the back of her consciousness—the soft, furry, helpless trustfulness, the mewings and nuzzlings, the loving innocence. Sometimes the cruelty of it seemed unbearable, but how were things to be done otherwise? Every good farmer like Herbert Bellows presided like a god over his stock and properties, doing right as best he could: he created life and destroyed it as ruthlessly and professionally as a deity. The fact of innocence, helplessness, personal appeal, was irrelevant. But cruelty persisted.

"I am taking Mother's advice, you see," he was saying. "I am being brave. You are not at all surprised, I am sure—they say women always know about these things—not surprised that I am being brave, of course, which you surely didn't expect, but that I am devoted to you so—so deeply and am asking you to be my wife." His voice had grown husky, but he kept at it. "I want you to take time—I mean you should certainly feel free to—to think about it."

The hopefulness of his face kept her from speaking. She loved him, and his father and mother, and the honest plain geometry of his face—she even loved his Sunday clothes and the correct gray hat: she felt a surge of tears at the sight of him. But she shrank, she pulled herself tight together in fear that he might even touch her with one of his clean ungloved hands. The closed car was a trap out of which she saw herself bursting with a sudden push at the door and a leap into the free air.

She said his name in a choking voice and stammered out some meaningless syllables.

"Oh, you needn't answer now," he said, as though she were debating with herself. "I want you to be quite certain—"

Again she almost giggled. It was all pathetic and preposterous. It was perfectly senseless.

The irritation of it made her suddenly resolute. "I cannot marry you, Harold."

"Oh, I'm not at all surprised to hear you say it—I know I am not really worthy of you, but I want you to think about it much longer. Even if you don't consider me as a—as a romantic ideal, as

it were, I can really offer you a fine married life, with a home and
a secure future: not that I mean to sound boastful, specially about
material things—and I am aware that it is unwise even to talk
about security, but I am a practical man and naturally I try to
consider all the possibilities. It has always seemed to me that I
shouldn't think seriously about matrimony until I could properly
afford it."

"I'd better be getting home," she said. Her arms were locked
across her breasts. Women, she thought, are supposed to know
how to deal with proposals just as they are supposed to be able
to lie and deceive: women take delight in the skirmishes and duels
of sex, even in the proposals of such a man as Harold Chivers.
The impulse to giggle took hold again and she inwardly cursed
herself. Of all the damned idiots, you, Kyle Eustace, are the
damnedest . . . the intensity of her frustration astonished her.
Why not simply discuss it with him? Why not tell him in so many
words? Why not act like a reasonable adult?

She almost cried out in relief when he started the motor.

"I've been thinking and planning—and hoping—about this
almost since the day I first met you," he said with a tremor.

"I practically bit you," she said.

"Oh, you did—I remember it vividly. You thought I was selling
magazine subscriptions."

"Well, even when you convinced me you were simply a good
citizen collecting for the Community Fund I wasn't very nice to
you."

He laughed with delight. "You asked me why I didn't mind my
own business."

They came to her house and she whisked out of the car the
instant it stopped. "Harold, I hate to do this so brutally, but really
it's no use. Please try to believe that I mean it—"

"No," he said. "I'm not listening. I want you to *think*—"

"Oh, nonsense," she cried with a sudden release of feeling. "I
have thought—"

"Besides, I'll be over this afternoon. We have a date to do the
screens, you know."

"No, we don't have a date. You won't be over."

"Oh, surely—"

"Damn it all, can't you get it through your head that I *mean* it? I won't marry you. I couldn't—no matter what you say, I *couldn't*. And that means we can't go on—you can't come over and fix screens—it won't *do*." She glanced fearfully to be sure no one overheard her. "And it's no good to keep telling me to think it over—"

His face looked as pale as paper. His thin mouth expressed **fear**. "I won't believe it—yet." The voice essayed to be jaunty.

She shrugged. "You'll have to believe it. I'm sorry, but that's it— that's the end of it."

He saw the cruelty in her face and was silent. She turned **and** walked up to the house.

In her room she shut the door, walked about, then lay on **the** bed and stared at the cracked ceiling. She felt weary, almost **empty** of life except for a clutch of misery in her stomach.

৩৪ CHAPTER 33 ৯৯

IN THE AFTERNOON Patience dressed and came down, and when Tony Kedjian arrived they sat on canvas chairs in the back yard. The day continued mild and serene. Mary Kyle in jeans and T-shirt worked on the screens, and rejected Tony's offers of help. Buzz had gone back to the drugstore. Harold Chivers did not appear.

Inside the house Edwin watched a double-header on TV and Josephine read a novel by André Gide called *The Immoralist* that she had found in Patience's room. The windows had all been closed, but as Mary Kyle got the screens up she left them open. She also kept track of the ball games and felt a strong personal attachment to the whole Red Sox team; now and then she called out items of good news to Patience and Tony—Malzone started a double play, Jensen drove in two . . .

But they, Patience and Tony, existed in a little space apart. Their heads were close together, they murmured on and on—at times they seemed almost angrily intense: Tony's dark face frowned and threatened and he gestured strongly: Patience made few gestures but she had the pale stubborn look the family knew well. Yet they seemed to hold on to each other. Their hands touched, she pushed at his thick hair with a wifely gesture, and now and then their voices broke out in gusts of vitality and even laughter.

When at last the downstairs screens were all on and Mary Kyle sat on one of the back steps, Tony seemed to take notice of her. He brushed aside the invisible curtain, smiled across with the sudden warmth she was never quite ready for, and asked how the game was going. It was evident that he hadn't taken any of it in. She explained that the first game had gone badly and added that it seemed ridiculous to condemn a good big-league team to go through the season with minor-league pitching. "Look at the records," she said warmly: "more runs scored against us than any team in the league; that's pitching—bad pitching, I mean."

"Well, I never suspected you were an expert!" His tone was genial, though touched with a small masculine irony.

"Oh, she went to a game," Patience said. "She really knows her stuff."

But Mary Kyle relaxed in the dapple of shade that a clump of straggly locusts threw across the yard. "I'm available whenever they need a new manager. I'd build a fire under 'em, believe me." She smiled widely at Tony. "There's a story for a low-browed writer: 'The Girl Who Won The Pennant'—not in your line, I suppose, but if you happen to be going to commit matrimony the royalties would be handy: can't you see it in Technicolor, with somebody like Ethel Merman?"

Her chatter seemed to fall on empty air. Nothing was said for a few seconds.

"We want to consult you," Tony said with his soft and reasonable voice. "We need advice. I think Patience is a little reluctant to ask, but I don't need to tell you that she is for independence at all costs—"

"It was my idea, for heaven's sake," Patience said.

"You can see how things are going with us. Man proposes, woman takes the credit." But his look carried such affection for Patience that she flushed and even tried a small answering smile. She would be difficult to live with, Mary Kyle thought; she had a fierce pride that made her touchy and prickly, but she could be fanatically loyal—she would bind herself to Tony with bands of steel, she could squeeze him to death if he were not himself resistant.

"As soon as it can be arranged," he said, "we want to be married."

Mary Kyle opened her mouth, closed it, and nodded as though she had expected him to say exactly that.

"We can see about the legalities all right, but we want to do the best we can about—our families."

"He means mine," Patience said.

"My family," he said, "would expect very little. If I introduced my beautiful bride they would be proud—my sister would like to be included in any arrangements, but she wouldn't really expect it. My father died about six years ago, my mother has no knowledge of the world—she is oblivious of it." He shrugged. "From your point of view, I am not a desirable match—"

"Will you *please*—" Patience began tensely, but he reached a big hand and covered her face.

"Just smile a little," he said. "Relax. Let me make my foolish jokes."

She struggled, seized his hand in anger, then caressed it. "Talking about desirable matches isn't funny," she said.

"It had better be." He glanced at Mary Kyle. "But it does depend on the point of view."

Patience made an effort to speak calmly. "Tony, it isn't a question of the match, as you call it, being desirable or undesirable—"

"It may not be a question for us, but what we started to discuss was your family: your mother, for instance, considers me undesirable."

"Well, it's not a social matter, for heaven's sake; it's not because your people were Syrian immigrants. It's because she thinks you are—personally, that is—are—"

"All right—it's a fine distinction: the main point is, she doesn't approve. What do we do about marrying?" He looked at Mary Kyle, expecting an answer.

"You want me to intercede, I suppose."

"We want to do the best we can, with your help."

"Right now, you mean?"

Tony and Patience each waited for the other to speak. "I think so," he said after a bit. "Patience thinks so too, but she hates to say it."

"I don't know," she said. "I don't know what to say—or do—"

"You know perfectly well. We've had it out."

Patience looked up at the slate-colored clapboards of the house. "I said I wanted to go away—anywhere, as long as it's with Tony. That's how I *feel*, at least. It's terrible to hate your own home, but I do—just the *place*, somehow. It seems so wicked of me—I must be a monster of some sort. But I'm so sorry for *them*—if I could only do something for them I would, but I don't know how. There's only one thing I can really do, anyway—and the question is simply how to do it with as little misery as possible."

Tony stroked her hair and neck as he might stroke an angora cat, with slow sensuous motions. She stirred and leaned against his hand. The sleeves of her jacket lifted slightly and showed the bandages on her wrists. "I certainly feel like a human mess," she said, but there was a quieter sound to her voice. She smiled slightly.

"So I'm it, am I?" Mary Kyle stood up. "Is it just parental blessing you want?"

"We want to inflict the least misery. She might even come round to the idea of a wedding—I mean, something besides a hasty trip to a justice of the peace."

"Well, I'll see. I warn you I won't argue—but I'll broach it. But it may not be a good time—don't count on anything."

When she went in, voices sounded in the hall and she realized that Tom Heath had come to pay a Sunday visit. No chance now to talk to her mother, of course. Her impulse was to slip up to her room and change, but then with deliberate intent she washed her hands and face in the piled-up kitchen sink and went in to the sitting room. She liked Tom Heath, but decided to let herself be homely in his presence.

ক্ষু CHAPTER 34 হ্ব

Buzz Eustace, making no plans for his future, waited to hear from the draft board. He argued that the next two years of his life would be in charge of the army anyway—there was nothing he could do about it. He became a skillful soda-counter boy at the drugstore, not so much devoting himself to perfect frappés or cheese sandwiches as to showing off the speed and ease of his operations. He tossed oranges or bananas or glassware from hand to hand; he whipped up two or three orders at the same time, sold toothpaste or photographic films or magazines, made change, and chatted with the young customers. After a few weeks he had built up a sort of social life in and out of the store. There were girls in the afternoon, in groups of two or three, on their way from school, all clean and outwardly pretty but indulging themselves in chewing or eating too much, reading theatrical scandals, listening to sex music, screaming the argot of their special underworld. To them Buzz was the right man for the job. His big hands did their work with a flourish. When he grinned he seemed miraculously ugly and endearing: it was the sort of face they saw on screens, not the romantic lead but the trusty and humorous pal, the athlete and the good guy.

But in the evening another group came, boys with their girls attached, or boys or young men on the prowl, scouting parties forever searching for the adventures they had heard of or seen projected. Buzz, they took for granted, was one of them. A few had known him in school, when he was locally famous. They lived as profanely as they dared; they yearned for speed and gratification and heroic freedom from any social restraint, and they moved every evening from one joint to another, from juke box to juke box, drugstore to tavern, hoping for the pleasures they dreamed about. It was a way and a state of mind that Buzz took to: after all, he said, two years were going to hell anyway—what can you do but horse around?

He came home late, then later. He let it be known that it was none of their business, though he moved very silently, shut doors without a click, mounted stairs in his socks, let no water run in the pipes. In the morning nothing was heard of him until noon.

Josephine hardly spoke with him at all, though she made an effort. At his combined breakfast and lunch, when she brought in the warmed-up coffee and beef stew, she sometimes sat with him in the dining room as though she expected to carry on a conversation; she looked at him intently and her face twisted into lines of anguish—she mentioned the dangers of inflation, the growing wastefulness of government on all levels, the miseries of the American Indian, but after the first statement nothing more was said. If a nod was called for, Buzz nodded. Once he remarked that the Wyndham tuition would probably go up next year; he said one of their football men, Harvey Lindholm, was part Indian though mostly Swede. But he said little else. What he did in the night, whom he was with, what he thought or hoped, were matters not spoken of. The sense of constraint was very strong in both of them.

Edwin spoke a good deal, a kind of theatrical monologue addressed to the surrounding air. The worst part of the whole thing, he said aloud, was that the kid seemed to be taking after him. It was enough to make a man shudder to see his own folly repeating itself. No wonder all primitive religions were founded on the idea of the fatal cycle; what happened once happened again and no man could alter it. But he went on to note that in a way both he and Buzz were victims of the world's savagery—he in the first war, Buzz now: once you start teaching the ways and means of professional slaughter, the rest follows inevitably. The nice little domestic habits, the manners, the good taste, the consideration, all begin to seem pointless; there's no use even pretending to be civilized. "I understand the kid," he said. "I went through it myself. But even so he makes me so damned mad I could bust a chandelier over his head. I ought to talk to him—it's my duty as a father—but I'm afraid to, I'm a coward, not because I'd have a thrombosis myself, which undoubtedly I would, but because I don't want to hurt his tender feelings. I might upset him emotionally or something. Furthermore, I know damned well I'd be taking out my own miserable failure on him and we'd just have a hell of a fight."

On a Friday night in mid-May Buzz came in late as usual, but there were noises both outside and inside the house. Car doors slammed like explosions. Voices called, laughed, whooped a little, and one sang. Feet clomped up the steps, the door banged open. "Quiet, everyone," a voice called. "Don't wake 'em up—cut out that singing, for God's sake." There were whispers and breathings and shufflings of feet—and someone called "in here" in a loud voice. A chair upset. Music sounded from a radio.

Upstairs Patience made the first move. She slipped into Mary Kyle's room. "We'll have to do something," she said.

"Throw them out, you mean?"

"If we don't, Father will."

"We?"

"Come to, for heaven's sake, Kyle. If Father gets going on this there's no telling what will happen to him. And Mother—my God, can't you realize?"

Mary Kyle put on slippers and a woolen robe. The house quietly reverberated from the voices and music below. "How do I do it? Just politely tell them to get the hell out?"

"Well, they may. I'll—I'll back you up."

"That's my sister—but you'd better get one of those bats in the hall closet."

She fluffed and patted her hair and went downstairs. "Look, boys, my father has been ill, he's had a heart attack—could you be very quiet? It's after two, you know."

There were three besides Buzz, and the room seemed filled with them. She hardly took them in, except that one was standing in the middle with a bottle in hand and she spoke directly to him. He seemed bulky; he had black curly hair and a black stubble on his white skin. "We ain't makin' noise, sister. We aim to be quiet —I told 'em to be quiet. Did'n I, boys?"

"S'my sister," Buzz said. "S'not your sister." He lay in a stuffed chair, flushed and slack.

"Okay, okay—you can have her. S'your sister if you want it that way."

"She the bride?" a voice cut in. "Wedding day, huh?" It was a

youth with the clear-cut features and darkly flashing eyes of a
fallen angel. He looked up from the television set he had been
fiddling with and smiled at Mary Kyle as though there was a
secret between them.

"Hold it now, Barney," Buzz said. "Cut out the funny stuff—"

"Yeah, cut out the funny stuff," the bulky one said. "I keep
tellin' you—be quiet, let 'em sleep up there."

"Sure, let 'em sleep." Barney eyed Mary Kyle again. "We got to
be ready for the big day, don't we? Bride better get all the sleep
she can tonight—"

"I said cut it out!" Buzz stood up, swaying a little.

"She ain't the one anyway," the bulky one said. "S'her sister you
mean—s' Patience you mean. Jees, I knew her back in school."

Barney struck an attitude and sang: "Oh, the girls of Timbuctu,
They are warm, they are hot, Oh, the girls—" He jigged a few
steps, and when Mary Kyle went to turn off the radio on the
table he made as if he would dance with her. She gave him a hard
right-hand slap and sent him crunching into a floor lamp.

"Jesus," the bulky one said, "we better get out of here."

Barney struggled to his feet just as Buzz swung a clenched fist
which caught him on the side of the head and sent him crunching
into the lamp again. "S'my sister, damn it," Buzz called out with
a kind of anguish in his voice. "What the hell you want to make
all this trouble for?"

Barney came up with a look of murder in his dark face. "You'll
get plenty of trouble for this—"

"Mother is calling the police," Patience said from the doorway.
"My advice to you boys is to get going quick."

The bulky one turned and grabbed at the third youth, who had
been sitting motionless and unfocused: "Come on, you bastard.
Out—get moving." He threw a strong arm across Barney's shoulders. "See you later, folks. Nice to meet you. Sorry about all this
noise—I tried to keep 'em quiet. Keep going, you!"

In the hall they looked up and saw Josephine standing at the
foot of the stairs. Her sparse hair had straggled out of its braid.
Her mouth had opened in the desperate upward slant that looked
as though it were uttering shriek after shriek. The dim overhead
light darkened and deepened the lines of her face. "You are part
of the curse that has come on this house," she said. "You are piti-

ful creatures, all of you—you are miserable, insignificant, mindless fools, but you are the world's evil." She spoke the last word with a strong accent on both syllables; it hung for a moment in the air.

After they had shuffled off she stood glaring at the door. Buzz slipped into the living room to pick up the lamp and keep out of the way; he tucked an empty bottle under his jacket, looked quickly round the room and slid it behind and under a pile of newspapers.

"What's this about police?" Mary Kyle asked.

"I just thought it would get them out quicker," Patience said. "It did."

"No one called them?"

"No."

"I shall fight," Josephine said, "to the end. It is the only thing I can do, or that I believe is worth doing, but I am now convinced that there is no hope. I believe nature hates reason. I see that life is a disease that perpetuates itself. It devours and consumes and destroys—it is nothing more nor less than a raging fire of self-gratification. Our hopes and ideals are too weak. In the old days our fathers recognized moral evil and fought against it and thought they could win—I thought so—we all thought so—but they knew too little about nature itself, they were innocent, they seem to us like trusting children. Now, today, we know what reality is." Her eyes turned with a glare toward Mary Kyle and then Patience. "Survival—that's the word you learned in your schools. Oh, I have thought about it, I can tell you. The philosophy of bugs. The real fact in the world is not civilization but lice and rats—and you simply assume that people are the same. Nothing counts with you now but your pleasure and your survival—"

"Mother!" Mary Kyle spoke sharply, as she would to a sleepwalker. "Don't say these things—"

"I will say them. I will say what is true."

"Well, they aren't true."

"Ask your sister—she knows."

"Oh, stuff! Let's go to bed and sleep it off. Nothing's busted but that old lamp—which should have been thrown out years ago. Everybody's all right. Buzz just had a couple too many, but I'll bet he's as sober as the rest of us by now." She looked into the living room. "What about it, Buster? Apologies and all?"

"Yeah—I guess." He stayed out of range of his mother. "Acted like damn fools, all right." His voice was sullen, a bit blurred. "I'll get you a decent lamp," he mumbled.

"Upstairs, Mother," Mary Kyle ordered. "We all need sleep. No use arguing now."

Josephine stood for a moment in anger, her mouth ready for speech, her eyes flashing, like a figure in a ballad: then she looked at the floor and turned with a gesture of helplessness. Patience took her arm and they started up the stairs.

Mary Kyle had a few words with Buzz. "Do you mean to say you talked to these goons about Patience?"

"I don't know—I guess I just told them she's getting married tomorrow; I mean, after all, that's okay, isn't it? She is, isn't she? I mean—is it supposed to be a secret? They know her, anyway— she was in school with some of them."

"For heaven's sakes, Buzz, don't you know that guys like that are nothing but poison? They haven't any more scruples than a flock of vultures: there's no telling what they'll spread round about Patience—that Barney, he's out for whatever trouble he can make."

"Yeah, Barney—he's smart, all right."

"Smart! He looks to me like a born juvenile delinquent. What's the matter with you, Buzz? Can't you get it through your head that these pals of yours are just *goons*?"

"Oh, sure—most guys are goons, I guess. I mean—hell—that's the way they are. You wouldn't know, you don't hang around the way I do: matter of fact, I'm mostly what you'd call a goon my-self." His face expressed weariness and bewilderment, but he spoke out more sharply to forestall her. "I know, I know—you needn't say it. I feel enough like a damn fool already. But there isn't too much I can do about it. Just for God's sake leave me alone, will you?"

Her anger flared up, but weakly. It was after two, she noted. She felt sick with weariness. "There's plenty you can do, but never mind tonight. Just tell your friend Barney if he wants to come again I'll hit him with one of your old bats. I'm not kidding, either."

⋟ CHAPTER 35 ⟩⟩

"Champagne?" Patience spoke the word impatiently. "No, of course not."

"Well, cheer up a little, anyway," Mary Kyle said. She shook the iron and thumped it on the board. "The darned thing goes off and not on again."

"Try re-plugging it."

"We can do without rice and old shoes, but we need *something*."

Patience hardly listened. She paced about her room and in and out of the bathroom. She carried clothes from one place to another. She stared at blank walls. She came in and sat on Mary Kyle's bed, then abruptly got up and went off.

"You look awfully scared," Mary Kyle said after awhile. "What ails you?"

"I don't know, but I'm scared all right—I'm petrified." She sat on the bed again. "Talk about a raw recruit going into battle—" She caught the look on Mary Kyle's face and managed a pale smile. "Oh, it isn't that, it isn't sex I'm afraid of. I guess it's simply the unknown future. Or maybe it's the idea of leaving a home I've never really been happy in. I know—it's weak and silly of me. In a way I feel as though the whole thing was a play of some sort—it isn't really happening—I'm not actually packing up to go off God knows where." She lighted another cigarette, and the hand holding the match trembled. "I'm being a coward, but I can't help it. It's the whole thing, I guess, the whole damned foolishness of Patience Eustace."

"Well, for heaven's sake, I had the notion you were in love.

204

Aren't you?"

"Yes, of course."

After a pause Mary Kyle went on. "My notion of being in love may not be like yours—"

Patience broke in: "Yes—yes—all right. It's what I tell myself every half-minute." She tried a smile as though it were a duty, then her face began to light up and grow pretty. "You don't really know Tony, Kyle. He may look like Ozymandias, but he's almost too sweet and gentle for this world; he lives in a Platonic dream, I think. His mind is wonderful but it isn't very practical—I mean it isn't interested in the minor essentials of life. I'm the one who'll have to do all the practical things. Tony is really like a sort of holy man, though it sounds absurd to say it: he is dedicated to great thoughts and visions." Patience brooded over her cigarette. "Not that he is inhuman, the way holy men usually are—and maybe I shouldn't have called him that at all because it sounds religious and dogmatic; in fact, even to talk about ideals is deadening. Professional idealists are so damned complacent, as though they had a license for practicing righteousness—and then I suppose ideals are more often than not false or anyway pretentious. I guess what Tony mostly is, is an artist, and even if he never creates great art himself, it is what he lives for—I mean the whole *idea* of art."

Patience sat more quietly while she talked. She watched the smoke eddies. She went on almost as if Mary Kyle were not there at all. So many young people, she said, were clearly seeing the ugliness and hypocrisy of society that a kind of crusade for candor was building up among them. She and Tony wanted to live without pretense, so that their inner and outer lives were all one. You went to college to learn the truth about human nature—you took anthropology and biology and psychology and all the rest, and then you were supposed to behave outwardly as though all such truth had no social relevance. What resulted was hypocrisy, which was simply another word for respectability.

Mary Kyle glanced at the tense, repressed face. In some ways Patience seemed like herself on another track, fated to go her own way. It hurt her to be so cut off from Patience, to be left out, abandoned, but at the same time she felt the taste of grief in her throat as she listened to the confessions and hopes of a young idealist: it was as if Patience were her own child doomed to a disillusionment she could not prevent or interfere with. Every youth worthy to be called human, she thought, has a time when he—or she—resolves to live so that inner and outer truth become one. It brought tears up to her eyes, but there was nothing she could do: she couldn't share the hope, because Patience wanted to be alone in it—or alone with Tony; she couldn't embrace or even touch her with an affectionate hand because they were sisters of fixed habits; in a way she couldn't talk because Patience was in no mind to listen.

"I'm so afraid I'll be a *drag* on him," Patience was saying. "He has to be *free*, specially these next few years. I do think I can help him—be free, I mean: I can earn money—I can make things possible for him . . ."

After a time Mary Kyle said, "Are you going to change before you go?"

"Change?" The strain came into Patience's face again. "Oh, God—I suppose so. I better not go off in that baby-blue nylon—goodness knows where we'll end up: in a hotel somewhere in Boston, probably. But don't talk about going-away clothes—it makes it sound like something in a country newspaper with a full account of costumes, scenery, and someone rendering 'O Promise Me'; it sounds like a *wedding* and I've always hated the idea of *weddings*."

She paced the room two or three times, then took a deep breath. "I don't know why I make such a fuss about life. I feel that I have to struggle *against* it—as though I were fighting all the time like a fly on a window screen. It's all so damned silly, this everlasting straining for something you can't ever have—in fact, you don't even *know* what you want, you just go on banging your head."

Mary Kyle disconnected the iron. "It's too hot all of a sudden. Haven't you got any stuff you want me to do?"

"Stuff? I don't know—I guess not. I can't seem to think." Patience put both hands to her head. "Here I'm supposed to be the practical one, and I don't know if I'm coming or going." Then she straightened, took a deeper breath, lifted her chin. "At least I can let off steam to you, Kyle. Before the next chapter begins I want to say I'm grateful, even though I do sound like a neurotic bitch. From now on I'm going to do better—I know I am. I'm going to be calm and wise and practical and everything a good wife should be—" She paused abruptly. "There's Mother, though —she doesn't say anything to me. I mean, she doesn't talk to me. I don't know how she feels."

Josephine said almost nothing to anyone. When the minister came at three, she remained in the kitchen with the hall door closed and Mary Kyle welcomed him with a hostess smile and introduced him to her father in the living room—who was watching the Saturday game on TV.

When Tony came, with his sister and Jack Lazarus, Josephine was not even in the kitchen. Mary Kyle found her upstairs sitting on her bed. "I don't know what I can wear," she said. "All my things are very old."

"It doesn't matter, Mother. No one is thinking about clothes. You've got a couple of decent silk things anyway—that dark gray one is fine."

"It's old," Josephine said. "I got it ten years ago. Maybe more—maybe twenty."

"Well, it isn't that kind of a wedding. This thing is old too—Patience's blue nylon is old! The main thing is to be decent. Come on, I'll give you a hand—do you want your black pumps? And your hair—let me do a job on it, I can whisk it up in a minute. They're all here, you know—even Dr. Engels: you'll like him, I'm sure, though he's terribly serious-minded—he always introduces himself as Doctor Engels, and if you give him half a chance he explains that he is a Ph.D., not a D.D., but he really isn't as stuffy as he sounds. He's the one who lectures us on the history of philosophy—he just got his degree a year ago, and is proud of his knowledge—"

Josephine allowed herself to be combed and brushed and dressed in the gray silk and the pumps. When she came downstairs she looked neater than anyone had seen her for many years, but she said almost nothing; her expression had become a fixed glare, and even the voluble Doctor Engels seemed for a moment taken aback.

"He tells me you can combine philosophy and religion," Edwin said loudly, with an edge of satire in his tone. "It's like saying that whatever is, is right—"

"No, no," interrupted Dr. Engels with the light of debate in his eye. "*Right* must be regarded as a moral term—"

"Do wait a while," Mary Kyle cried out. "For goodness' sake, we've got a show to do here!"

But Edwin roused himself, and pointed a finger. "Philosophy, I take it, is what is—whether you like it or not. Religion is what you hope."

"That's true of a great many, of course, but—"

"Religion is what you personally want it to be."

"Oh, come," Dr. Engels cried, "that isn't fair, you know. You can be as intellectually honest about religion as you can be about anything."

"Hah! Can a mother bitch be intellectually honest about her puppies? Can a hen—?"

"Father! Cut it out, now!" She leaped between them like a referee at a boxing match. "Dr. Engels, you come into the dining room here. Don't you have to confer with the bride and groom before the event?" She pushed Tony into the dining room after him. She bustled about. She introduced Rose Kedjian to Josephine, but neither of them said a word.

"You've killed off a good debate," Jack Lazarus said, looking slightly like a clothes-dummy in a blue serge suit and white shirt and crimson tie. "I'm for the doctor, myself. I'm a poet, you know —a published poet: I showed you my works, didn't I? It is my theory that a poet is a religious philosopher—it's a theory I've just this minute arrived at: you might even say I've been converted, because when I came in, half an hour ago, I thought I scorned religion—I was full of the vanity of atheism—but now I see—"

She rushed upstairs to find Patience staring at herself in a mirror. Her face seemed perfectly white, both in and out of the glass. "I can still say I won't do it," she said to her reflection. She was dressed in the pale blue nylon, with a dark belt. "I can still decide, can't I?"

"No—you can not still decide." Mary Kyle picked up a lipstick and applied it lightly. "Don't talk—don't move—you need just a touch: easy now! There, come on—you look fine."

"I can't, Kyle."

"Oh, Pat, for heaven's sake don't be an idiot. Come along, now."

"I—really—"

"*You can't do anything else.* This is your part. It is written, as the prophet says." She pushed her to the stairs and down.

When she walked into the living room Patience smiled with serene self-possession. She kissed her mother's cheek. She greeted Rose Kedjian like a loving sister. She patted her father's sparse hair.

Afterward Buzz brought in a tray of wine glasses and two bottles of champagne from the refrigerator. Up to then he had lurked on the edges of the affair, keeping well away from Tony and his screwball friend, paying no attention to Tony's silent sister. He wore his basset-hound look, Mary Kyle told him, but he hardly noticed her irony. "This Lazarus," he muttered, "what kind of a clown is he? He talks like a goddam jack-in-the-box." But the bottles and glasses restored his confidence and humor. "We got to toast the bride," he announced, and popped out a cork with a flourish. "*And* the groom." He poured and passed glasses and gave out a sense of innocent celebration. Mary Kyle handed round a plate of sliced fruitcake.

"One of the biggest hoaxes of modern times," Edwin was saying, "is that champagne is to be considered a high-class liquor. As a drink, it rates about with a ten-cent soda, except that you can get a bang out of it if you try hard: but it ain't in the same league with well-seasoned hard cider—"

"Pipe down, Pop," Mary Kyle cried, and they raised their glasses and called out good wishes—all but Rose, who had taken none, and Josephine, who sat in a straight chair with the glass clutched in her hand and resting on her knee. They paid no attention to her, or pretended not to, except that Mary Kyle came and put a hand on her shoulder and whispered something.

"I have a poem," Jack Lazarus was saying. "It is called 'Epithalamium.' I'm not sure what that means *exactly*, but it has something to do with marriage; it isn't finished yet, I'm sorry to say, but it begins quite well." He held up a pencilled note, made a modest declamatory gesture, and read: "*Two rivers are arcs in space.* You see, there's another poem called 'Epithalamium' about one river, but I am beginning with two. I think my idea is more symbolic, really. Please notice the *arcs*—that's my key word, so to speak, because I have just come to realize that all reality is circular, and naturally every *part* must be an arc—"

"Thank you very much, Jack," Tony said more loudly than necessary. "And thank you all for your kindness and good wishes."

"I should have said *spherical*," Jack muttered. He looked for a responsive eye and smiled at Rose Kedjian who made a timid little quirk in reply and then blushed.

The group made motions of departure. Dr. Engels shook hands all round and promised to return in order to thrash out, as he put it, the great question of religion and philosophy—though Edwin answered with no enthusiasm and remarked that thrashing-out great questions was about as useful as trying to weed a cowpasture. "But come in any time and give me a chance to blaspheme a little," he said. "It's the only pleasure I have left."

Patience came downstairs looking flushed and elegant, with a light tan topcoat over one arm and a tan traveling bag in her other hand. She behaved decisively and it seemed evident that she had rehearsed a part in her mind. Without hesitation she kissed everybody, said goodby once, smiled with an effect of radiance, and ran out to the Chrysler. Tony followed with the bag. Mary Kyle drove them off.

Rose quietly wiped the corners of her dark eyes. Jack looked at her warmly and tenderly as though she were something good to eat. He took her arm and went off with her toward the station.

Edwin, who had been at the door, walked back and switched on the TV, but the game was over.

"I don't see any need," he said, "of taking it so hard. I can see why you might take things in general hard—I mean, when you think about all the infirmities and all the futilities and all the whole damn shooting-match—but as far as this particular event goes, we could have done a lot worse. I grant you our son-in-law doesn't have the fine local name we might have expected—something reliable like Hoggins, say—but I kind of take to him. I admit his friend reminds me of an overripe banana, but after all he stayed sober—in fact, the party was almost too damn sober: what's a wedding for if not for a little whoop-de-do? What that philosophical stuffed-shirt Engels needs is some stimulating alcohol. No, no—there's no need of taking it so hard. Cheer up, Jo; the worst is still a long way off."

But Josephine walked out and upstairs without speaking.

In the kitchen Buzz finished the second bottle of champagne and then very tenderly washed and dried the glasses. He broke only one.

✑§ CHAPTER 36 ೪⌣

Tom Heath called the next afternoon. It was another warm Sunday, and Edwin had walked round the yard inspecting shrubs and the clump of iris flowering at the corner near the front steps. He intended to go in to watch the ball game, but sat for a while in a canvas chair in the direct sunlight in back. "It's not bad," he said, "not bad at all: earth and sun, I mean. What I ought to be doing is some old-fashioned spading out there—and by God I believe I could. I feel damn near human again."

Tom Heath had rung at the front door and Mary Kyle opened it.

"Father's out in the back yard." She said it gaily, as a fact of special interest.

"Good," he said. "Why aren't you out too?"

"Me? Well, I do housework, for one thing. Mother—" She glanced back and up the stairs and lowered her voice. "She isn't—very well."

He didn't move.

"Would you walk round to the back? He'll be delighted to see you."

Tom Heath did not hesitate or affect shyness. "Yes, I'll certainly walk round—but I have a project in mind. I'm on my way over to Saugus, where my sister Bonnie lives, and I'd like to take you along. I think you might enjoy meeting them all, and it's a lovely day." He looked at her with direct challenge. His teeth gleamed white under the dark mustache; his strong features expressed the reliability of a portrait sculpture. "She has very nice children, and they live in a pretty sort of place with a pond."

She drew back a little and studied him. It was clearly an overture, and it took her by surprise. She saw the challenge in his face. He looked like a man making a bet; his eye was steady and his smile waited for her next move.

"Yes, it sounds very—pleasant," she said rather slowly. "But I couldn't go right off—it will take me twenty or thirty minutes to finish—"

"Very good."

"And I ought to be back by six or so."

"Very good. Come out when you're ready." He turned, smiling, and went off around the house.

Since yesterday Josephine had stayed in her room upstairs. She said almost nothing, except to announce that she wanted no doctor. She looked more and more like someone who had undergone torture. Mary Kyle brought in some familiar Trollope and a recent Joyce Cary and a light-hearted murder story, but they lay untouched. She found books on manners and morals in Patience's room, but Josephine paid no attention. "I don't want to read any more," she said. She lay on her pillows staring at the opposite wall.

Mary Kyle attacked the kitchen, and by now, early on Sunday afternoon, had got most of the dishes and pots washed and put away. She ran upstairs to change, and told her mother she was going for a ride with Professor Heath.

"Who?"

"Father's friend, Tom Heath."

"Do I know him?"

"Why, of course. He's been here several times—he's the one you talked to about Tamburlaine."

After a while Josephine said with finality, "I don't know him."

"Well," Mary Kyle said, "he's a splendid character and an authority on Mongolians and Ottomans. He has invited me to meet his sister and her family. If they all approve, he might ask me to marry him."

Josephine, staring across at the opposite wall, said nothing. Her face had a look of agony, but whether or not she realized what Mary Kyle had said could not be told.

"I'll be back about six," she said. "But I promise you I won't do anything rash." She leaned and kissed her mother's cheek, remembering that she was once a celebrated beauty. "It would be good if you could sleep a little, Mother. You've been much too— tired lately." Her voice suddenly choked. Guilt cut into her like a stab. More love could have prevented all this, she thought; now it was too late, too late. "Do try to sleep," she said. "It's what you most need." She stroked her mother's hair.

She went slowly downstairs, took her heathery green spring coat from the dark closet, and stood for a few seconds in the kitchen looking at the clean table and counter and the stacked shelves. She heard the voices through the open back door, and sensed the fragrant air that came in; the world outside on a spring afternoon was full of bloom and growth. Tom Heath's laugh floated pleasantly in the benevolent quiet, and her father's profane accents. Beyond the meager yard the land reached away to boundless distance, through all the cities and suburbs to the green hills and woods and flowing rivers and far blue mountains in the north and west, to regions of air and space where the soul could expand and merge with infinity. She had a flashing vision of hills golden with buds and young leaves and valleys of blossoms, apple and plum and pear and cherry, and lilacs massed round old farmyards.

She hung a saucepan on a nail above and behind the stove, turned the hot-water faucet hard to stop the drip, and shut and latched a cupboard door. The kitchen seemed like a relic of a long-dead institution; a faint smell of death and decay came up out of the sink and the dark corners and pipe-holes were the haunts of mice.

Outside, voices again. She stepped out, facing the sun, and saw John Rossiter standing there—she saw his grin and the wide-spaced teeth and the gesturing arm and hand. "No law of physiology or alchemy," he was saying, "has yet been adduced to explain why a Don Larsen gets himself knocked out of the box one day and throws a perfect no-hitter another—and it is my contention that as long as man's behavior remains in part mysterious and adventurous, so long is life endurable; but once the mind can wholly control behavior—then good night to all of us! I was once a professional psychologist myself, and I can tell you frankly I have the deepest suspicion of all professional psychologists. Fortunately, they so far seem to be largely impotent—though even that may be a forlorn hope: when the Russians take up baseball, they'll undoubtedly produce a race of no-hit pitchers. It is frightening."

Mary Kyle felt herself smiling from ear to ear. The sun dazzled her, the air filled her with balm, she walked across the yard with a buoyant stride.

"Now, behold," he said, grinning wider, "we have the mysterious and adventurous Spirit of Spring herself—"

"Ha! No spirit, brother—look at that grass flatten down?" But she did feel that she walked without bending a blade.

Tom Heath glanced sharply at each of them, not with any suspicion but with intense interest. He was a careful observer, she thought.

A small figure carrying a blue ball cut around the corner of the house, moving rather stockily, like an animated hydrant—a boy, stout, red-faced, about four and a half, the one Mary Kyle had seen many times in church confined and controlled by his mother. Now he stamped along with an air of freedom, though his face remained impassive.

"Hugh," John Rossiter said. "Say howdy-do to Mr. Eustace—and Miss Eustace—and Mr.—er—"

"Heath."

"Mr. Heath."

The boy set his ball securely on the ground, marched up to each and thrust out a hand and muttered "howdja-do" very quickly: he went through the ritual as though he had been wound up, and then walked to a patch of smooth grass, put his head on it, and lifted up one leg and then the other as a demonstration of his head-standing method. His face grew redder, but did not change its expression.

"He is stronger on persistence than headwork," John Rossiter said. "If I can only put the weight on him I intend to train him to be a lineman on a professional football team: it is an almost ideal career—you go through college free, you work only half the year, you get big pay, and you retire at thirty—I think they even replace your lost teeth for you."

Hugh stood up on spread-apart legs and looked hard at his father. Mary Kyle at first made no advances, spoke no word to him, but studied the expressionless little face for a sign of some sort. John Rossiter's chemistry must be in him somewhere, and she tried to project him into a life of his own. If he liked me, she thought, he might spontaneously smile, his eyes might sparkle, he might speak the magic words of trust and love.

Tom Heath picked up the blue ball and made as if to toss it, but Hugh regarded him with contempt and edged away until he was behind his father. "He thinks all men over five feet six are dangerous," John said. "Specially with a mustache."

Tom shrugged his acceptance of the fact and rolled the ball out on the grass. Mary Kyle found herself walking to pick it up. She held it out like bait and smiled and nodded and tossed it up and down. Hugh watched her with one eye, round his father's leg, and when she bounced it toward him he let it go by. She had a sense of failure, she felt the ineptitude of her little gesture, the foolish spinsterish advance that no child can tolerate, but suddenly he pounced on the ball and gave a yell and threw it at her with all his energy. It went off to one side and he rushed and threw it again and shouted and at the third try got it near enough so she could pick it up. "Throw it! Throw it!" He turned into a demon of excitement and rushed after the bounces and flung the ball wildly. Presently they were all after it, tossing it back and forth and letting Hugh run for it like a puppy, and he kept on and on. "Throw it here! Throw it to me!" His voice split the air and echoed from house and tree. Mary Kyle saw his father in him and found herself laughing and laughing: all that energy, intensity, joy, spent on chasing a ball, the devotion and abandon—even the shape of the smile and the wide-apart baby teeth were like his.

"The problem is to know how to turn him off," John said. "You'd think he might run down, but he'll outlast all of us in relays." He held the ball and held the squirming boy and talked him into acquiescence. The game was ended. Hugh looked about with perfect stolidity, red-faced, grim, disapproving but silent. He went off by himself and practiced standing on his head.

"What I want to know," John Rossiter said, "is whether Miss Eustace intends to accept my offer of a job."

They all looked at her. He was grinning as if he enjoyed putting her on the spot, but he spoke before she could gather her wits. "Don't answer, Miss Eustace. I've taken unfair advantage on a nice Sunday afternoon."

"Any money in it?" Edwin asked. "If so, we'll take it."

"I can say categorically that there's no money in it," he said. "That's why it can be mentioned on Sunday."

"Sounds damned suspicious to me. When a man tries to sell you a horse with a good *character*—watch out."

"Oh, I've warned her," John said. "She mistrusts me already. But some people can't resist the high-minded appeal—they think character in a horse is more desirable than sound wind and legs."

It brought a twitch to Edwin's thin lips and he tipped his head to scrutinize John Rossiter. Then he addressed Tom Heath: "You might not realize that this here horse-trader is an organ-player, choirmaster, and elder of a church."

"There's a saying in the East," Tom answered, "that men are measured from the heart upward and camels from the heart downward." He smiled at Mary Kyle with direct and candid purpose. "Shall we go?"

She responded with perfect grace, kissed the top of her father's head, looked at John Rossiter cordially, almost confidingly, waved and smiled at Hugh, tossed her green coat on her arm, whirled her skirt very slightly as she turned to step away. "We'll be back soon—I hope mother will sleep a while. You two can indulge yourselves in a little baseball." Then she smiled directly and warmly at John. "I'm not really trying to evade you. We—I'll just have to talk about it a bit more. So much has happened lately I haven't been able to think."

They were off, stooping into the Volkswagen, becoming aware of each other in the small space, almost touching elbows. Yet her mind was full of the last scene, of John's face, his eyes on her, his knowing little smile that seemed to appraise her motives and enjoy her folly. He had looked smaller than usual—he wore no jacket and no hat or tie; his shirt had been buttoned crooked, and her fingers had wanted to rebutton it. Tom Heath had towered over him, tall and broad, neat in worsted suit and brown tie, an obviously successful professional man.

"What's this job?" he was asking.

"Job? Oh—nothing much. Just some crazy idea of Mr. Rossiter's. I haven't thought much about it." She paused long enough to sneer at herself: what in hell, she thought, do you have to talk like that for? She felt trapped in the Volkswagen and looked out sourly at the suburban streets.

"I gather you have a very fine job with the Allston people."

"Do you know them?"

"Oh, just in general. Aren't they one of the big advertising firms?"

"Public relations, if you please. We never use plain English if we can help it."

He kept at her, and she noted to herself again that he was a man of direct purpose. Her work, her pleasures, her interests: he almost forced her to confide in him, even to admire him, by his freedom from the vanities and pretensions that overlay most human ventures. He talked of himself with no apparent concealment: college teaching, he said, is often a refuge from the main battle of life; as Shaw or someone said, those who can, do; those who can't, teach. The neurotic and the fearful take cover in the academic preserves. But so also do the brave—so do all sorts of people, most of them well above any sort of human average you might imagine. What he was arriving at was gratitude that he was able to work so freely and fairly. His father had been a salesman for a paint and varnish company, and eventually managed one of their branch offices in Albany, a career of respectable bondage. He retired with an inscribed Paul Revere bowl and no real sense of achievement or adventure: all his grown-up life had been controlled by the company for its own ends. Some business could be very adventurous, of course; his sister's husband, for example, had got in with a group of electronic experts who were making a new device for testing the strength of any material, and they were like a band of dedicated mountain-climbers assaulting an unclimbed peak. But he took some pride in thinking that such people were university products who used their skills and brains to create something valuable. As for the advertisers—the public relations people, he should say—he had his doubts, though he was willing to hear her views on them. There was a chap in Dickens who was always full of train oil: he wasn't very sure what train oil was, but he had a notion that its modern equivalent was what public relations chiefly dealt in.

Though he spoke gently, letting his ironies seem more tentative than final, she felt herself turning perverse. Oil, she said, was necessary to modern life, perhaps even more so than books about Turks. If he had the idea that she was selling herself to the Allston people as a sort of eight-hour-a-day kept women, he was perfectly right, but there was good money in it and right now she needed money. As for John Rossiter and his projects, she shrugged them off as though she had no interest in them.

After a silence, after he remarked that it was a fine afternoon, she sat up a little straighter in the bucket seat, took a breath, and said it was lovely; she was delighted to be there—she had been cooped up for weeks, she hardly remembered what it was like to be human, she thanked him for making her come. Her expression and smile conveyed friendliness.

But for a long time they spoke only of the events of the trip, and the visit and the children and the dog and cat and the pond. A sort of truce existed between them as they drove back.

At the end, as he said goodby, she looked at him with a warmth that surprised her. He could, she knew, be a friend, a brother, a husband—anything except a true lover. She liked his suit and brown tie and button-down collar; she liked his ready smile and white teeth and even his mustache, and his face reminded her a little of those craggy stone faces of Easter Island, with large and decisive brow and nose and chin. There didn't seem to be anything wrong with him—except perhaps for a lack of interest in what she regarded as the arts: he was essentially a practical man, though not an insensitive one.

"May I come again? I mean—to see you?"

"Oh—well, yes, of course." She almost stammered. "Yes—I—I —I mean, just call up. I may be involved—with mother, that is." Mary Kyle gave herself a sharp inner nudge. "And thanks for the outing. I had a lovely time." Her face, she felt, was pink. She ran lightly up the steps, tripped on the top one and caught herself with a heavy thump and stumble.

❧ CHAPTER 37 ❧

"I wondered," John Rossiter said on the telephone, "if you could do some rescue work for me on Saturday. I'm the one who needs rescuing, of course—" It was a trip to various places in New Hampshire to deliver three boys for summer farm jobs and to leave a year-and-a-half-old girl at an agency in Concord—a long day's drive, he said, with nothing to recommend it except country scenery. He could handle the outfit alone, probably, but it was a policy of the Association to provide chaperones for girls of one and a half. They didn't care, he added, about girls of twenty-five and a half.

She made herself speak slowly. Yes—yes, she thought she could go—

"How's your mother?"

"I—don't know. No worse, I guess. But Father's getting very active—he spends half his time in the kitchen: I never realized that all his life he's been a frustrated cook, and with Mother upstairs and me gone there's nothing to stop him. He has a passion for baking-powder biscuits—"

When she hung up she felt almost dizzy. She sat in the dark hall letting the feeling surge inside her. Five days to Saturday. It meant nothing, she said to herself. After all, her mother was ill, her father was an invalid, Buzz was in a stew, the house needed cleaning, food had to be bought, meals planned, laundry done, dishes washed, and beyond the daily chores all sorts of problems lay in wait—taxes, bills—Patience's hospital bill was enormous: the furnace needed overhauling, the toaster and a radio wouldn't work, a gutter drainpipe was clogged, the bottom front step had begun to sag, and Edwin complained every day that his Waltham watch was erratic and needed cleaning. And now the railroad was taking off trains and she couldn't get home till nearly six-thirty, and they were threatening to take off more. If the House of Eustace would only crack open and tumble into a dark tarn all at once, she brooded, their troubles would be well ended. And if the thought of Saturday was like the felicity of heaven, what then? Nothing followed, except Sunday, and the clogged pipe and sagging step, and the bills and taxes, and her mother upstairs staring with glassy eyes at the cracked ceiling; and then the seven-forty-nine on Monday, and the office and Joe Bass. But the blood ran dizzily in her veins: five days, she counted—five times twenty-four times sixty—times sixty again; she was conscious of the ticking seconds, and of the need to be alive, and well, and wholly ready for the day. She could buy a blouse and skirt, a fine tan cotton she knew of in Jordan's, with unpressed pleats and a wonderful flair that would blow in the breeze and be free and joyous. Her hair—she might have it done in the noon hour Friday, be late getting back to the office but to hell with them: it would be all waving and shiny for Saturday . . .

All week she worked like a fury, without fatigue. In the evening she dusted and vacuumed. She drove Buzz up a ladder to clear the gutter. She made him prop up the step with three well-based bricks. She nagged Edwin into studying the accounts and bills. She argued her mother into seeing a doctor. She lugged home bags of groceries from the store near the station. She got up early and washed and hung everything out. "The place ain't safe," Edwin said, "for a lazy bastard. I been living like an old mouse in a nest all winter—I grant you it's been a mess, but a mighty cozy one if I do say so. I mean, I knew where everything lay. But now you got it so damn neat, I feel like I'm just visting here."

Patience came out to get clothes and books and housekeeping articles and they drove back in the Chrysler at night and carried the stuff up four flights to the cold-water flat. Tony had a night switchboard job in an apartment hotel. Jack Lazarus had gone— more or less gone, she added; he might be back, he moved about as easily as a stray cat. She herself had begun to look pretty again, and said she was happy, though her eyes were anxious and she kept a little barrier between herself and Mary Kyle. She had to drop two courses at college, but she was trying to finish three others and was way behind. She ought to be working, earning money. Tony had too much to do—he hardly slept at all, except catnaps at the switchboard between twelve and two at night. They were lucky to have the flat but the sun on the roof made an oven of it and no air came in the windows. She wasn't used to the cockroaches either, though everyone else seemed to take them for granted. But those things didn't really matter: they were temporary, and as long as you had hope and love you could endure anything. Tony, she added, never complained; she herself did—at least she always had, but she was learning not to; she was learning a whole new attitude about life, a mental and spiritual discipline, a kind of oriental self-control, perhaps: she didn't want to use fancy names for it because it wasn't a cult or anything like that; it was just common—or uncommon—intelligence.

All this came out at intervals, not as a candid sharing of experience, but as a series of announcements and conclusions. She spoke evenly. She dealt in truth. The whole of life, she implied, could be controlled by rational adults like herself and Tony.

Mary Kyle, driving home in the night, thought of John Rossiter's voice, his laugh, his teeth, his bushy hair, his rumpled shirt and baggy suit, the energy of his walk, the gesturing pipe, the flow of speculative and metaphorical rhetoric that never ceased. His presence was palpable to her senses, not as though it were sitting next to her on the empty seat but more as though it pervaded her being; he was all about her, active and amused and alert, full of the adventure of being alive.

Saturday, day after tomorrow—almost tomorrow. The day she lived for. Her only aim and point. She took a contemptuous view of herself. A coward soul, afraid to tamper with the little pattern of their suburban lives, afraid to seize the life she desired, afraid to upset custom. Afraid. She loved, and her love was as splendid as a legend. Helen and Dido and Isolde—what were they but herself, Mary Kyle Eustace, in other times and lives? They were faithful to their love through all dangers and barriers to death itself, while she clutched her little secret as though it were a shameful social error. What of the respectable dull wife and the well-trained little girl and boy and the drab suburban house? What of all the Eustaces and Starretts looking down on her? In the face of grand passion, what did they amount to? Even little Mr. Chivers called her Boadicea, a pagan queen, a woman who doubtless followed her destiny with unhesitating audacity. Or what of John Rossiter himself? If he truly loved, would he not have the courage of his passion? He was no victim of suburban conventions; he did what he did, he had a hero's heart and blood.

She feared in truth that he didn't love—not yet, at least; probably not ever. When she put the car away in the wooden garage, and switched off the lights, she felt the small black space close over her like a vault. Dreams of love, delusions and yearnings—she tried to smile knowingly: all the females of the world drugged themselves to the extreme of folly and death, specially the virgins like herself, the virtuous ones, the good puritans, all full of erotic sentimentality. Her cheek touched the cold rim of the wheel and she began to cry. In another instant she was on her feet slamming the car door like a gunshot; she yanked the rickety wooden doors, flung them together knowing they wouldn't shut, gave them a parting kick that stung her toes, and walked fast to the back steps. The unlighted house loomed above her like a black box on end.

In the morning her resolution was to tell him she couldn't go. She ought to stay with her mother anyway: the doctor had said she was partly in shock and should do nothing but rest, and he gave her drugs. And Saturday was a bad day for Buzz, who seemed to make a habit of staying out most of Friday night and drinking too much. But she didn't call him. She took up the telephone after breakfast and put it down again. She decided not to have her hair done that noon, nor did she get the blouse and pleated skirt. She walked to a telephone booth but passed it by. It was clear that she was going on Saturday, regardless. On Friday evening she washed her hair. On Saturday she put on a faded sea-blue denim dress she had had since college days, one she had mended, shortened, lengthened, washed and rewashed; she thought of it as a natural part of her and imagined it to be becoming, even to the mends and frays. It occurred to her, standing for a last look in the mirror, that no fact in all human history was so strange as the fact of clothes.

It was to be a day of no expectations, she told herself; no delusions, no folly. When he came at eight she was ready, but rather stern, almost grouchy. When would they be back? Did she need a light or a warm coat? Did it look like rain? She wasn't used to year-and-a-half-old babies—she hoped this one was docile.

But the ride into town almost beguiled her. He had all the look of a man on an outing: a plaid shirt, unmatched jacket and trousers, no hat, pipe in action; and he gave off such an air of delight that she felt it all through her like a current. The fog was burning off, he said, sky blue, sun shining, wind west—no better day for going to New Hampshire had ever been devised. One of the farms they were going to was up on a shoulder of Mount Kearsage—oh, a beautiful spot, a place to dream about, and there'd still be lilacs up there: if he had life to live again he'd spend it in a place like that, milking cows and raising apples.

Dreams and visions. She shrugged them off with a palpable twitch of her shoulders. "I doubt it," she said. "No ball games up there." No people, she thought; no boys and girls to rescue, no choir to struggle with Bach, no philosophical arguments. But she saw herself as his farm wife, getting in hay, picking apples, digging out after a snowstorm. They'd be full of life and strength and hunger . . .

"Where else do we go?" she asked abruptly.

He explained fully. The best thing in the world for a city orphan was a farm; he wished he could send a thousand boys out to work on farms every summer, but he was lucky if he could arrange it for a dozen. And even with those it didn't always turn out right. If they liked each other, fine; if they didn't, everything went bad. It was always a gamble. But one of his boys was now first selectman of Brown's Mills—a Mike Da Prato he'd sent up there years ago. There were others who stayed, or went back, or married local girls.

As for the little girl, he was simply acting for an adoption agency; he didn't know much about her, but had agreed to deliver her in Concord under suitable chaperonage. When they started off from the city at last, with three boys in back, sullen and speechless and somehow furtive, and the child between them in front, Mary Kyle knew she shouldn't have come. She thought John Rossiter might have known better—she thought he was blind, even insensitive. She herself was a damned idiot. She had no business to be there. The child sobbed vaguely and kept a thumb in her malformed mouth: a swarthy, soft little blob of lost humanity, going from nowhere to nowhere, an embryo of all the instincts and atavistic desires that female life was cursed with.

"You may not think it is possible," John said, "but someone wants her, someone will love her, someone will see her as beautiful."

Mary Kyle felt a choke of tears. She was tight inside, angry with herself, inarticulate, despairing.

But the long ride continued. She looked at green fields and rivers. June—and leaves were out in full, blossoms mostly gone by, grass deep in meadows. Northern hills, far mountains pale in haze, evergreens—then the first farm near Contocook, a sort of suburban truck garden with geometrical spaces of celery and cabbage and lettuce and a network of sprinkler pipes. No charm to that, no dream: a house almost as ugly as hers in East Compton. She busied herself changing diapers on the unhappy child.

Then on to Concord and the orphanage—called the Lucy Hancock Child Center—where the new parents were waiting, full of hope.

The last stop was the farm on the slopes of Mount Kearsage, beautiful enough, no doubt, and remote and high, but she made herself see the harshness of it, the weathered sheds and leaning silo and rusty machines; she saw that the farmer walked with a halting limp, and greeted them somberly, though gently. He said his mother hoped they'd come in for some coffee—and as he said it she came out on the kitchen porch and called, a woman who seemed almost as young as her middle-aged son, and more animated. "Come in, come in and visit before you go back. I don't get to see many folks up here." She welcomed the city boy—she was glad to have another man on the place: all her own grandchildren seemed to be girls.

"How about it?" John Rossiter asked later, as they drove down the narrow road. "How would it do for a lifetime—the farm, I mean?"

He looked relaxed and at ease. The windows were open, a breeze blew through, he smoked the pipe and drove slowly over the bumps.

"You need more than a farm," she said.

Here it was at last, what had filled her head all week: the two of them alone, the long road home, the end. The Last Ride Together —she tried to say the verses: then, dear, since 'tis so—something,

something. Passionate nonsense, she told herself. Victorian hokum. Trying to glorify hopeless love, as if it could ever be anything but misery. Self-torture. Frustration. And Browning's notion of love was mostly romantic illusion, suitable for flattering complacent ladies and gentlemen.

"It's just a sentimental notion," she said sharply. "You look at the view and say how lovely."

"Well, I grant you it's a notion, but—"

"You don't see the toil and trouble—all the barns falling down, all the machinery rusting away, all the grief. They were lonely, those two—and probably as full of misery as—as the rest of us."

She sounded so angry that he glanced at her.

"You keep riding along on your own little wave," she said. "You have a fine time being enthusiastic and busy—it's almost a sport for you; but you have no idea how—how other people feel."

He tapped his pipe out the window and put it in his left jacket pocket. He swung the car into a main road and drove along fast. "Let me know if it's too windy," he said.

They kept silent for a long time.

"I can't take your job," she said. "I—I've decided. I can't work for you."

"Well—I'm sorry. You'd be good at it, and I think—I thought —you'd like it. The pay isn't good, I realize. I can talk it over with the Board—they might do better."

"It isn't that."

He said nothing.

"I'm—I'm giving up the choir too."

"That's a real disaster—for the choir."

He knew now—he ought to know. But he drove on without speaking.

The last ride together, she said to herself again.

"You must have other plans," he said after a while.

"No—nothing to mention." Tom Heath might be a plan of course—she could make it so if she tried. Then she spoke briskly, with false good cheer. "No—I've decided. This is our last outing —our last ride—" She didn't say "together."

For a long time she sat tensely, waiting for him to speak. He knew—he must know. If he stopped the car, if he turned to her, if he queried, pressed, talked—did something, her world might all at once be transformed.

"I'm sorry to hear all this," he said very evenly, a little sooth-ingly. "I don't know that I understand—I mean you must have reasons—perhaps something has happened—" After a minute he went on. "I know you've had a difficult time of it at home— you've had very great problems and burdens—I don't know any-one who could have faced all that as wonderfully and—and com-petently as you have."

She said nothing.

"I was wondering about your brother," he said. "If he really wants to be drafted, I think I can help him out. I know the Draft Board pretty well—they have to pick out the names arbitrarily, and they'd be perfectly willing to pick his. If he asked them him-self, they'd do it."

When they got home to East Compton about six, Edwin was in the kitchen mixing biscuits. He glanced at her, at first with a defensive little smile, then very sharply. "For God's sake, girl, what ails you?"

"Me? Nothing. Tired, maybe."

"Tired! You look like a ghost. You must have been run over by a truck or something."

"No, I'm fine."

"Fine, she says. Okay, I hope you are—but Jesus, girl, don't for-get you're the only able body left in this outfit. Without you we'd be licked for keeps."

"Never mind me," she said. "I'm all right. What's for supper? Besides biscuits, I mean."

CHAPTER 38

ON MONDAY Mary Kyle's classmate Sandy Farr called her up and they met for lunch at Filene's. Reunion was next week, she said, and she was driving out with Greta Holmberg and maybe Judy Casby, and why didn't Mary Kyle come too—it was only Friday afternoon to Sunday, and they'd have fun. It wasn't actually a scheduled reunion—that would be their tenth, in two years, but some of their crowd would be there and a lot of their friends from other classes.

It wasn't possible, of course. Mary Kyle spoke of her mother—and her father. Sandy looked at her closely. "Why don't you get married?" she asked.

"Well, get me a man."

But Sandy kept at it. Any competent woman could find a man—that wasn't the problem . . .

"Of course it's a problem," Mary Kyle said. "I simply can't stand most men."

"Oh, baloney. You always were snooty about men, and there's no sense in it. They aren't any less human than you are. Do you realize we're practically thirty?"

"We!" Mary Kyle laughed. "You certainly can't complain. With three kids and two cars and a house and an acre of land in Wellesley you've done quite well—not to mention the fact that you still look nearer twenty than thirty."

But Sandy stuck to her point. Marriage, she said, was simply *life*. It was the whole works, as it were. It might not be a pleasure—it could be full of trouble and anguish—but at least it was where life had to be lived. "I know I look and act like a complacent suburban matron," Sandy said, "and I guess that's what I really am. I'm lucky so far—don't think I don't realize what can happen in life: I read the books too. But I'm telling you, Kyle, almost any marriage is better than the trap you're getting yourself caught in."

"Trap! You don't know the half of it."

"What don't I know, Kyle?"

"It can't be told—not at lunch, anyway." Mary Kyle shrugged.

It was all very well to be devoted and loyal to one's parents, Sandy went on, but there was no sense in sacrificing one's own happiness and future—and certainly most parents wouldn't want one to.

Sandy had always been perfectly practical in assessing her desires and going after them. "I'm all for idealism," she said. "I'm for love and romance. But first of all I'm for an actual husband and an income and a house and a child or two or three—and don't tell me I'm just a materialist. I'm simply taking an honest look at what life really is."

When Mary Kyle told about Tom Heath, Sandy sat up as though a pin had stuck into her. "For God's sake, take him, grab him, don't put it off another minute! Are you crazy, Kyle? Really, I think you need a guardian." She speculated rapidly. "Look—bring him out, will you? Make him drive you out some evening—how about Wednesday? We'll ply him with our best scotch and be nice to him—Rog can be terribly nice when he's primed for it."

Mary Kyle looked at her friend coldly. "Just go slow, Sandy. This is my show, after all." Then she smiled; her strained face relaxed and grew charming. "I appreciate it, though. I probably need rescuing. When it comes to the point we'll buzz out to Wellesley and sample your scotch. Incidentally, he lives with an aged father too. I really don't think things are as simple to arrange as you suppose."

But she walked back to her office more buoyantly than she had come. Sandy had fulfilled all the prophecies they used to make: her husband and children and house were exactly what Sandy had trained herself for and earned. Socially they were the best people, culturally they represented a conservative elite, and of course financially; and their success was perfectly honorable, without pretense. Roger Farr was already known as an able surgeon. Sandy was being mentioned as a candidate for School Committee. If anyone had described her as a textbook model of suburban American culture, she would have been the first to agree. She knew clearly what she was.

Mary Kyle smiled as she walked along, remembering Sandy's address book which began as an annotated file of eligible men; in her senior year she had eliminated all but three, and by graduation had selected Roger Farr and announced the engagement. There were no hesitations. News and photographs appeared prominently in New York and Boston papers. To Mary Kyle it was a success to be admired rather than envied, and even now it seemed to her like a book or a play, unrelated to her own actualities. She herself had no such certainty. Her heart was beguiled by John Rossiter, whose world Sandy had almost no inkling of. She could not see herself as a Sandy.

But the question of Tom Heath pressed down on her. Sandy was as right as could be: any woman in her position would be a fool not to go after him, family or no family. The thought spoiled her little pleasure; she came back to the office with a pale, tense face.

"The truth is," Joe Bass said quietly, leaning on her big desk, "you get a little paler and a little wan-er every day. I mean, for a girl as beautiful as you are, it's a crime." He spoke with tones of kindness that startled her, and she glanced quickly to read his face. It had been an axiom never to trust Joe Bass; she saw him as the tempter, had laughed at him as a sort of sideshow that she had no trouble passing by. The only word for him was suave—he seemed to be made up to act his part, even to a trimmed pointed mustache. "You see, Mary, life pours out like water from a pitcher —and there's only so much of it and when it's gone it's gone. Now my policy—"

"I know: be merry, tomorrow we die."

His smile was confiding. "You can't really find anything wrong with that—if you are willing to be honest, that is."

"Oh, I can find a lot wrong with it—"

"No—listen. You think the worst of me, I know. But I'm really not a sex fiend or a drunkard or a betrayer of innocence." He made his smile appealing. "I mean, I have standards—so have you, of course. In my book, any man who has to go out and hire a woman for a half hour—or even a night—is a miserable failure, and either

I'm sorry for him or I despise him. Love is a lot of fun, but only half the fun—or less than half—is in the body: the best part is —spiritual." He watched her with gleaming dark eyes. He had managed to speak casually, unheard by the surrounding office. "Isn't that so, Mary?"

"Oh, you're the expert—not me."

"Well, I think—I honestly think we could have a lot of fun—just being together. I don't mean New York and all that—but just going to a show or dancing or something. No fooling, Mary, you need fun—I hate to see you miserable like this. It's none of my business—I know you have family troubles, of course: but what about a real date some night? We'll do it up big—dinner at Locke-Ober's to start, then a theatre, then whatever you like. I promise you—no strings, no snares."

She wavered, glanced from side to side.

"Tell me, Joe: why me? You must have all kinds of girls. Surely you aren't doing it just because you think I need cheering up."

"Well, to be honest, I—like you. That's all there is to it."

"Not very plausible," she said.

His smile was appealing. "The fact is, you give me the brush-off so hard that I'm intrigued. You've got what I'd call character —you aren't like the other girls: I mean, there's something real in you. And you haven't found out yet how pretty you are, though it isn't quite the right word: let's say—beautiful. But you need to have more fun in life; that's my main argument."

"More fun, he says." She made marks on a paper on the desk. "All right, Joe. I'll give it a try. Flattery may get you some-where after all—not very far, I hope." She studied him. "How do we start?"

On her way to the station she walked past John Rossiter's office in Haymarket—she walked rapidly, not glancing at it, but she saw the dusty car in the parking lot. He never locked it, she knew. She projected herself into it—she could do it in a flash, unseen, and wait until he came: here I am, your slave and follower forever, asking nothing—except to be allowed to ride in your Ford. Ignore me, or treat me like one of your children, be fatherly, brotherly, anything as long as you let me ride in your Ford.

She walked on fast, taking strides, looking like a woman in

command of her destiny.

At home she found her father standing at the top of the stairs. "There's trouble," he said. "Doctor's just gone." He spoke from above with conscious theatrical effect. His face was lined and set in a mold of doom. His voice carried the accent of back-country finality he had practiced over the years. What he was announcing at last was the worst, and he intended to do it exactly right. I knew things were bad all along, though the rest of you paid no attention: now you'll see: this is it. The worst. You should have known. "She's in bad shape," he said. "She's mighty close to the end."

He had gone up with tea and soda crackers right after the game —four-thirty, about. She liked plain dry soda crackers—always had; didn't like tea as much as coffee, but tea was supposed to be better for her. She wasn't there. She'd gone up-attic, had moved trunks in the storeroom, lifted boxes, had papers and letters and stuff all over the floor—enough to stock a library. She had keeled over in the middle of it: hot as hell up there anyway. He called a doctor—had to call three before he got one; called Buzz—who was in with her now, sitting in her room. He'd have called Mary Kyle, but she was already on her way. He didn't know how to get hold of Patience.

"Shouldn't she be in a hospital?"

"Doc said he'd see tonight—he's coming back round eight."

But nothing, then or later, could be done for her.

At her death, Josephine seemed serene and even beautiful in her final austerity. Her face had a patrician look, with good cheekbones and chin and severe, down-turning mouth; her aquiline nose alone gave her a quality of ancient breeding—she could have modeled for a saint or a queen in effigy. The strains and distortions no longer marked her, though her face showed no touch of happiness.

The papers in the attic, Mary Kyle found, embodied a century of family history. Letters, mostly—boxes of them. Many photographs and daguerreotypes. Even some family account books kept by her great-grandfather Charles Lawrence Starrett. Hundreds of letters from Nigeria, from Henry Cowles to his daughter Mary Starrett—the ones Josephine always intended to do something about. But many of the items were unlabeled—picture after picture, babies on silk cushions, little girls with ringlets, ladies and gentlemen in black silk, black broadcloth, as stiff as iron. No one could remember them, no voice could speak their names, cry out in affection and recognition, recall the loves and hopes of their lives. A more recent album was full of photographs—Josephine in college, scenes from a play (with no men), graduation, cap and gown—a tall, straight young woman full of stern idealism; then blurred views of parades, canteens, embarkations, and officers—and one of Josephine in long khaki skirt and a military sort of jacket, still very stern.

At least, Mary Kyle thought, she could write down one name, Josephine Starrett Eustace, before it was forgotten and lost with all the others: but a conviction of futility came over her. In the face of eternity, what did it matter? These loves and hopes had all been sustained by faith in the Christian promises that death meant immortal life in a magical spiritual heaven. Even her mother kept an unspoken hope that the struggle would not be in vain; she expected somehow to be reunited with her people. She would need no labels or written names.

The hot attic was a miserable suffocating spot. But Mary Kyle's own room seemed no different. She lay on her bed, not crying, not thinking, feeling the weight of time and oblivion crushing her.

After a time she began to think of what had to be done. There were a few cousins to write to—the Livermores in Wyndham, the Ted Harveys in Pittsburgh, the Whitesides and Bellowses in Vermont, and old Aunt Josephine Cowles in Santa Barbara—she'd take the news very hard. There'd have to be a service too, but where and what was a question: probably the philosophical Dr. Engels was the man to do it. As for burial and all the rest, she had no idea what to do. There was a Starrett lot in the Cambridge Cemetery. The professional undertakers would take over—for a price. She began making a list of people to write to. There'd doubtless be items in the papers too—after all, the Starrett connections were still remembered. A little gust of laughter came over her as she thought of something else: she'd have to call Joe Bass and tell him their date was off.

But then for a while she couldn't move or act. The letters and pictures in the attic, specially the pictures, filled her mind with the drama of her people. They were very good, very virtuous, she believed, but proud of their virtue; they lived as honorably as any people on earth; they were hopeful; they looked ahead to a better and more godly society with innocent idealism; they worked and loved and suffered. And they were all dead. Nearly all forgotten. The human condition, she told herself; why brood over it? Every philosopher and poet and fireside pundit reiterates it: queens have died young and fair, golden lads and girls all come to dust. Her mother, she had always known, was a noble character, exceptional in mind and integrity, who began life with faith and the best possible intentions, who was very slowly and inexorably thwarted and destroyed.

Death, Mary Kyle told herself, was the only possible release, but a long-ago little scene flashed in her mind like a projected picture: her mother holding her in her lap and rocking in the Boston rocker still in her bedroom, and Charlie, two years older, leaning against her knee and letting himself be rocked while she sang to them: *And we'll rally round the flag, boys, we'll rally once again, shouting the battle cry of free-dom!*

◄§ CHAPTER 39 ͡▸

"I wish to announce," Edwin said at breakfast, "that as of now I am resuming as much manhood as I can muster."

Mary Kyle, in her morning rush, hardly paused to listen. "Use up the hamburger for lunch, Father. In the meat tray—just a little hunk."

"I reserve the right," he said, "to recite 'The Cremations of Sam McGee' entire when the spirit moves me, and if you give me the smallest encouragement, I will continue with 'The Shooting of Dan McGrew.'" He lifted an oratorial hand and tried a few lines.

> There are strange things done in the midnight sun
> By the men who moil for gold:
> The Arctic trails have their secret tales
> That would make your blood run cold.

"Manhood, is it?" She hovered at the door, with bag and gloves, ready for flight. "You mean no more baking-powder biscuits?"

"Oh, that. Matter of fact, I thought it would be a damn nice career. I always hankered to wear a white hat. If I start in at a short-order joint I can work up—" As she went out he shouted after her: "Don't forget—one box of good berries: get 'em cheap in the North End! I'll show you a shortcake my grandmother'd be proud of." As she closed the door she heard him mutter, "And anyone who believes that is a ring-tailed idiot."

She walked along through the bright morning air, in and out of shade, feeling the waxing power of the sun, hearing robins and an oriole in the tall maples, letting the cool breeze of her walking blow against her skin. June twenty-first, longest day of the year, the high point of the cycle, the great divide. She made an effort to respond to it. The roadside grasses and yards were greener than they would be all year. Young tomato plants were strong and full of promise. A bush of red roses bloomed at the full. Old sheds and fences were sunk among leaves and vines. She acknowledged to herself that all these things were a solace, at least in the fresh-ness of early morning. Mind and heart were beguiled by hope and general benevolence; unfolding day gave promises of such purity and natural truth as had never been seen before. Just the sunlight pouring on weathered shingles was a sign of beauty beyond man's knowledge: the texture of old wood in the brightness, the rising silvery stream, the lines and pools of dark shadow, all made a mystic experience for the senses.

Then came the stores, filling-stations, the flow of eight o'clock traffic, the commuters like patient cattle along the platform, the whistle and rush of the train, the dust, the feel of the day's heat. Summer stretched out ahead, hotter and hotter. Then winter again.

Mary Kyle took out her Proust. The damned stuff went on and on and on like an etherized dream, but she plugged along from page to page hypnotically. She had given it up for several months, but once again it seemed appropriate. Her life had leveled off, and the Proust carried her across an endless plain where life existed sim-ply as an awareness, without activity or outward body, yet with a curious importance. It seemed to her that Europeans always took life hard: their ambitions were fierce, their jealousies and vanities acute; they were terribly intelligent and perceptive, but at bottom were like spoiled babies, demanding, demanding, always discon-tented, always jealous. She was intensely curious about Proust's world, but never for a moment part of it: the magnification of vanity and self-seeking seemed like a preposterous nightmare with no end and no sane purpose. But it went peculiarly well with a train, specially a commuting train, five days a week for ever.

"A lovely morning," Harold Chivers said over her left shoulder. "It will be hot, I fear; Mr. Rideout said it would be in the upper eighties. But the morning is very temperate."

He spoke a little more respectfully than he used to—or perhaps less expectantly, but he still kept it up. He raised his hat, he walked now and then along the platform at her side, and though he made no efforts to sit with her he managed to pause in the aisle over her shoulder, as now, and issue little statements on the weather. He had of course come to the service for her mother— as had John Rossiter and Tom Heath also, and even cousin Albert and his lovely wife Edith. Harold had composed and recited a short speech of condolence, which Mary Kyle had to remind herself to receive very gravely: she remembered reading a curious little book of eighteenth-century etiquette in which such a speech appeared with a note that it was recommended for use on the occasion of the decease of a member of a family or any other melancholy event of a similar nature.

"I see," he went on, "that your brother has been called up for military service. I hope he is not—er—unhappy at the prospect. It seems to me that taking two years from a young man's life is a pretty serious matter."

"You say you saw this somewhere?"

"Oh, in the Compton *Sentinel*; they always publish the names of the local boys. There was only one other this month, a boy named Faberman, I believe—"

Mary Kyle tried not to betray the fact that Buzz had not said a word about it. "Oh, it will be a relief," she said. "He's just been waiting and wasting time." It was John Rossiter who had done it, of course.

"I thought," Harold went on, "he might be exempted. He surely has a claim—I mean on family grounds. I understand they are being very liberal in granting exemptions."

"Well," she half muttered, "don't suggest it." But as they walked up the platform she asked him what he thought about the army and the draft. He had been an officer during the great war, she knew, at a supply depot in Jersey City—in charge, he had once explained, of boots and shoes.

"Oh, I'm told it can be quite demoralizing. Not, of course, that I *know*—it is what I hear. An army in peacetime has no sense of significant purpose and many of the young men simply resent being there. Their chief aim, I am told, is to evade their duty."

The worst sort of prospect, she thought, for Buzz. Whatever happened was all wrong. Could she talk to him, give him sisterly advice? It seemed unlikely: he never discussed his affairs or took anyone's advice—certainly not hers.

She glanced respectfully at Harold's thin profile. Self-command like that—it forestalled the heartaches and natural shocks. Did he ever really love? did he passionately hope? grieve? despair? If he loved her, as he had said, could he go on making respectful speeches about weather and the state of the world? But except for age and death, he was as safe as a man could be. He made his daily rounds, summer and winter for a lifetime, with no wastes of emotion, no growing sense of disappointment and disillusion. A safe man—except for death. She could still marry him, perhaps —though she knew for a certainty that if she didn't very soon someone else would. Once he had decided on marriage he would see it through.

He lifted his hat with an angular motion, as though he operated by hinges and wires, and walked away toward the elevated train he took as far as Scollay Square. If commuting could ever be bearable, she thought, it was now, early in a June morning before the heat and dust when the crowd stepped out briskly with scrubbed bodies and clean clothes and the girls were all as pretty as they could make themselves, in crisp flowered dresses. But outside along Portland Street the sun poured and shimmered on the pavement and the air tasted of dust. She reminded herself to be grateful for an air-conditioned office. She glanced down toward the Haymarket building where John Rossiter worked and remembered that it smelled of old plaster and something that could have been rats.

Her own building provided a marble, gold-trimmed lobby and six elevators, all crowded. In the crush she felt two hands on her waist and turned her head to look almost level into the face of Joe Bass. "Not the best spot for a date," he said, "but better than nothing."

"Oh—good morning. I didn't recognize you by the touch."

"It's high time you did." His smile seemed to expect a great deal from her. She couldn't move, but she made herself unyielding and he felt it and looked at her sardonically—at least it seemed so to her. "After all," he said, "this is very like some of the best night clubs."

"I wouldn't know," she said.

"Well!" They pushed out toward the corridor. "It's high time you did a number of things."

For ten days he had behaved with a sort of modest watchfulness, and even now he seemed to be waiting. But something in his eye made her very wary. She said aloud, "Don't think I've changed my original notion: you do a very slick job of tempting. And I guess I'm far from immune to expert tempting—but I do wish you wouldn't look at me with that amused satisfaction. It isn't like a cat watching a bird's nest—cats aren't really amused at their own technique—but that's the nearest I can come to it."

He let himself chuckle as though she were flattering him. "All this temptation stuff—don't you realize it's just a fairy tale, a way of keeping good little Christians in line? You've taken over the myths about sin and soul and the devil as though they were true—instead of bedtime stories to scare kids with."

When he left her at her desk he reminded her that they still had a date—whenever she said the word. But he seemed just then to mean nothing to her; she could watch him as she might watch an actor reading a part. Expert—she gave him credit for that. In another mood she might take to him, but now she felt detached from almost everything—a watcher as it were in a dream, unable to act or take any part in outward events. It was ten days since the service in memory of her mother. A few people had come and kind and solemn words were said, but one little event remained very vividly in her mind. Her mother's only real friend in the world was Irene Kinglake, a high-school Latin teacher in Springfield, who after the service looked at Mary Kyle very carefully. "You are so like your mother," she said, "it is uncanny." There was nothing sentimental about Miss Kinglake: she made it clear that she had stern self-control and rational intelligence. "You are probably taller and naturally heavier than she ever was, but your features and coloring are exactly the same and you move your head the way she did. I can see it in your sister too, but not nearly as much. I can remember *her* mother too—I used to come for visits when we were in college—and there's quite a marked resemblance. Josephine used to say it was the Cowles look."

Miss Kinglake spoke of these things so briskly, with such an attitude of reasonable interest, that they seemed to have no emotional significance, but Mary Kyle found herself brooding over them with grief and even guilt. Josephine's life came over her as

tragedy. Great purpose, great hope and promise, strong character
—what might have once been called a high and noble estate—
all frustrated, brought low, destroyed. But slowly: there were few
crises and catastrophes before the end. No one, until the last, was
aware of any moment of destruction.

She herself, Mary Kyle, had never entered her mother's inner
life; she had kept out, held herself away, permitted no emotional
involvement. It was her feeling, never clearly acknowledged, that
they were divided by nature and time. She made a habit of not
taking her mother seriously enough, of reacting ironically and sardonically: in her adolescence there had been conflicts and quar-
rels and passionate anger, and she had learned the techniques of
irony. She felt herself to be emancipated from the moral solemnity
of her mother's world, the tiresome concern for family and duty,
the visible worry that nothing seemed to be going right. She understood well enough—or thought she did; she recognized that
her father was in some major ways an impossible man to live
with and that many of their troubles were real ones, but she kept
herself separate and retained a critical attitude.

"It is extraordinary," Miss Kinglake said with sharp certainty,
"how you resemble her."

More than in looks, she had meant. Thinking about it ten
days later she had a sense of her own superficiality and cold-
heartedness; perhaps nothing could have changed their destinies,
but more love and loyalty might have done miracles. Too late,
too late—the anguish had run its course. Love, she thought, ought
to be taught and practiced, not just taken for granted. It was what
they all lacked, like the necessary red corpuscles: Patience with
her tensions, Buzz suddenly all alone with his inadequate self,
Edwin going back to his whisky, Josephine most of all . . . too
late, of course.

No one, Mary Kyle believed, could ever take honest stock of
himself. One could try, and pretend, and resolve to be wise—
perhaps something could be done. Some consulted doctors and
analysts, usually in desperation. She hardly considered herself
desperate, not yet, but she went through her daily rounds with
no sense of purpose and no satisfaction with herself or her life.
She even doubted that she had the ability to love: was her one
great passion merely a girl's delusion? If she had the character

she used to think she had she could do more with herself than pine for John Rossiter: at least she might save Buzz from himself—or make some effort to; she might see that life meant something more to Edwin than successive bottles of Old Swanee—she might even find new affection, or trust, or love. She had grown up with the assumption that her father was not quite adequate, or quite worthy of loving admiration: he was to be humored as far as possible for his weaknesses but not honored as the head man of the family. In her memory, Josephine had never spoken a word of spontaneous affection to him. But now that they were partners in the household, as it were, now that he puttered about doing chores, making biscuits, fixing faucets, and now that they watched Buzz and talked candidly, a pleasant sort of dependence might grow between them. He had resumed his afternoon and evening whisky, but moderately: "I've found out what I'm really cut out for," he said. "I believe I'm a talented loafer. I wake up every morning and say to myself there isn't a damn thing I have to do." When she came home in the late afternoon he had drinks ready, with ice tinkling in her glass, and they felt comfortable together. "Here's to oblivion," he still said, with sardonic voice, and she took off her shoes and stretched her legs and smiled at him.

When Buzz went off to Camp Dix for his basic training they felt that life had grown simpler. The days moved past very quietly. But Tom Heath dropped in quite often, almost like a member of the family.

CHAPTER 40

HE WAS TEACHING in a summer session that ended in early July, and he planned to go to Seattle afterward to attend a conference on Asiatic politics.

"What do you do at a conference—give a paper?"

"Oh, we all give papers. That's why we go."

"What's yours on?"

"Mongol invasions."

"Old ones—or new ones?"

"Well, new—at least, that's the question. They know about the old ones."

It was the last Saturday in June; they were sailing in a boat in Marblehead Harbor, a rented dinghy shaped like a big bathtub. He sprawled in the stern, holding tiller and sheet, stretching his legs diagonally across to the lee side. A hazy hot sun made a dazzle of air and water and a cool southerly breeze fanned the boat along with almost no sound. Mary Kyle sat on the floor forward beside the centerboard box and watched the dazzling scene—squinting, wishing she had a hat or dark glasses, aware of the strange elements of sea and space, but alert to every detail of a wondrous adventure. The crowded harbor was all in motion, a circus of color and speed: outboards like waterbugs, cruisers, racing craft, sight-seeing parties, work boats, launches, everything in motion—even the moored boats dancing and bobbing. Motors hummed, sails flapped, horns blew, voices called. Great glittery yachts moved as though their progress was part of a cosmic plan; a gentleman with white whiskers and a white canvas hat rowed past in a varnished skiff within arm's length and neither nodded nor glanced; a group of city revelers in the scantiest bathing suits rushed about the harbor in a red plastic speedboat.

"Honestly," she said. "Honestly—I—" She gestured at a passing launch, all brass and mahogany, piloted by a uniformed sea-captain, with a lady in a high-collared dress sitting in a wicker chair holding a parasol.

Tom Heath grinned appreciatively. "Biggest nautical show on earth—except for the Golden Horn at Istanbul."

"Oh, it beats any circus that ever was," she said. "It—it's just—why don't they all run into each other, why don't they *crash?*"

"Hold on," he said, turning to meet the wash from a cruiser. Their dinghy bobbed violently.

"Do you mean to say all this goes on all the time—or is today some kind of special yachting fiesta? Look at that!" A skiff dashed past with four children in red life-preserver jackets—one of them, a girl with blonde pigtails, at the controls.

"Any day in summer," he said. "Race days are busiest."

Outside the harbor fleets of sails grouped and moved in patterns and diminished into the seaward infinity.

"Well," she said, "I am transported. It is like going through a magic door."

She led the life of a prisoner, almost; she was confined to her room, her train, her office.

"I learned to sail at a boys' camp," he said. "Had a job teaching it for a couple of summers."

A freshening southerly took them out into open waters; they felt the sea roll and saw where it broke and creamed on outer ledges. Eastward sky and sea merged in hazy brightness.

"Looking at ocean from land," she said, "is different from being in it. Just the idea of space seems suddenly important—and being part of it, as though you had the power of flight. Think of how much world is out there—strange lands and perilous seas. The Golden Horn. Do they have ladies with parasols there?"

"The only gold is commercial. The water looks like bean soup. As for ladies in yachts, or children in red life jackets—no. I mentioned it because it is as busy as a beehive—day and night."

"You refuse to let me even dream," she said. "Bean soup, for heaven's sake! What's the good of sailing off Marblehead if you can't have visions of the wonders of the sea?"

He didn't argue. His smile beamed at her.

"I think of the insignificance of my life," she said with unexpected severity. "What I am is a mouse in a cage with a few little doors to go through. Push this and you get the cheese. And suddenly for one Saturday afternoon I escape into a whole new world." She looked at the boats and gestured. "Who are all these free people?"

A tall blue-hulled racing sloop slipped past, steered by a bronze girl with gold hair.

"You probably sit with some of them on the train every day," he said.

"Well, they aren't mice. Don't tell me they are just like me, or even that they live on Myrtle Street, East Compton. Anyone sailing a boat like that has the soul of a god."

"Goddess, you mean. I'm sure they look at you and think the same thing."

"Well, they couldn't be wronger."

He hardly took her seriously, she felt. It amused him, but doubts and yearnings seemed to play no real part in his life, he was not beguiled by dreams. Yet he lived with a good deal of vigor.

"You like to sail," she said, "but why? There's no sense to it, is there?"

"Sense? Well, no, probably not. But don't make me be too utilitarian. I suppose any recreation is good: you feel better and happier if you do something useless now and then. But—there are lots of things I like about it. Maybe it is elemental—maybe it reminds you that you are part of the same chemistry of sea and air. Anyway, I'd like to have a boat I could live in—just for a week-end or a few days: I think to myself that when things settle down more regularly, maybe I can get one."

He meant that he took care of his father, she supposed. She surprised herself by the calculations that went on under the surface of her mind. She saw herself off with him in his boat, for a week-end, a few days—or weeks—free and clear of all the past. Mary Kyle Heath—it had a plausible sound to it. He called her Mary: that sounded all right too. Mary Heath.

She shook herself and looked hard at the nearest boat, a big yawl that seemed to have come from a toy-store window. Made of glass, he said. Price, thirty thousand.

They were both involved—he with his father, she with hers.
Was she responsible for hers for life? Yes—of course: if he was,
she was. But Edwin was hardly a problem—not yet, anyway. He
pretended to be useless, but he'd be out looking for a job again
—she saw him as a clerk in a store, perhaps, or a watchman; he
wouldn't care how humble—he no longer had that kind of vanity.
He could still live on his own too—make biscuits for himself, and
pancakes: he'd been experimenting with pancakes lately.

"How's your father?" she asked.

"Well, no different." He looked very serious—not, she realized, because of his father but because of her. "I was going to suggest that you come in and see him on the way home this evening." His anxiety made him look boyish, and he smiled confidingly. The white quick smile under the dark mustache always
surprised and then attracted and pleased her; it seemed to have
no overtones of calculation. "He can't remember much of anything," he said. "For a long time he remembered his boyhood,
and talked about it: I learned all sorts of things I never knew—
I mean for example, that he had an older brother, my uncle, of
course, who went out west and disappeared, but they think he
became a bandit."

"I knew it," she laughed. "I always said you looked like a bandit.
I'll bet he had a black mustache just like yours."

"Oh, longer, I'm sure, with drooping ends." He watched her.
"I wish they'd told me thirty years ago. I'd have been proud, I
can tell you. But it's all gone now—there's no one left to remember, unless of course he had children we never heard of. Poor Pop
can't remember anything at all now—his brain has just about
given up. He knows he had a brother Darius but that's as far as
he knows."

She felt that he wanted to confide in her—that he was involving her in his life. His father, he said, was a very kindly man—
and that was really all that was left of him: a gentle sweetness
of nature—and nothing else. He didn't read any more, or pay attention to what he heard or saw; he could still walk a little bit, and
at times he shuffled from room to room aimlessly, stopping at windows to see movement in the street below or to follow the flight
of pigeons over the roofs. He had to be watched—or at least someone had to be there most of the time, and Mrs. Jefferson was won-

derfully reliable about coming. And his sister Bonnie was good too—she took him for long periods, but with her kids and all it was a burden for her.

For a few moments, looking down into the boat, listening to him, she felt again the pathos of age and loss. No one left to remember—no one left. Then spray flashed in her eyes, cold drops tingled on her face, the boat swashed and bobbed over the dazzling summer sea, and round about the yachts raced, white sails slanted and curved like wings. Sun poured down through the white sea air, wind blew in from the Atlantic, the boom and thump of surf sounded in low reverberations from the ledges.

"Do you know," she said, "that this is all new to me? I mean it's a new element—or maybe a new cosmos. It isn't where I've lived all my life."

"You like it?"

"If you found yourself on Mars, would you like it? You'd be astonished, excited—"

"Scared, probably."

She reflected. "I hadn't thought—I mean about being scared. Maybe I am a little. Look at this enormous water. But mostly I'm living a new life—almost in a new body. It is a miracle—I mean, to me. Probably it seems simple and normal to you and all these sailor people, but not to me."

She tried to remember how the allegory of the cave went: something about shadows; people living in darkness, looking out toward light and truth, seeing only shadows. She lived in a sort of cave and now found herself out in the white radiance.

"Well," he said, "it's probably good for one's ego to put to sea now and then, even in a cat-rigged bathtub like this, but most of the time people have to go on making like people." He smiled. "I would say, for example, that it's time we headed for shore and a good restaurant. Aren't you hungry?"

"I'm always hungry, damn it." She saw John Rossiter bringing the sandwiches on the night of the blizzard, heard his quick and eager tones: our special midnight collation, he said. They came out into the icy radiance of that winter morning and his voice still rang in her memory: ". . . Mount McKinley forty miles away. . . . Do? My dear girl, I can do my damnedest."

"You must be a good sailor, then," Tom Heath was saying.

"This tub certainly rolls." He seemed far away; she hardly heard his voice.

But when she walked on land again, feeling the solid planks, the earth, the pavement, their little sea venture was like a bright dream. She told him she liked it and loved it, and after they had supper and were driving back it seemed that she had known him a long time and depended on him for companionship.

He took her up the self-service elevator to the third-floor apartment, introduced her to Mrs. Jefferson, a massive negro woman, and to his father, who sat motionless in the warm room in a thick gray sweater and a shawl over his knees: he said how-do-you-do twice, with elaborate courtesy, and smiled cordially, but she knew that he was hardly aware of her at all. The apartment, she noted, was furnished at random, without plan: no curtains, no pictures, a few magnificent oriental rugs, a lot of brass scattered about on tables and shelves, books piled along the floor, odd chairs that might have been assembled for an auction, and a fragment of marble bas-relief propped on the mantelpiece showing arms and legs in violent action and a tangle of spears and swords. "Supposed to be the battle of Issa," he said, seeing her glance. "Original—and not stolen; a present from the Turkish government. More than twenty-two hundred years old."

A pleasant mess, she told herself. It seemed to be waiting for order. He smiled a sort of self-conscious apology: "I always plan to fix things up better but I never do."

"The rugs are wonderful," she said.

At last, on the way home, he came to the point. In a way he seemed bashful about it: she could feel him putting it off, waiting for the moment; she saw that it was hard for him to break through his habit of perfect self-command. It was a long time since he had spoken of love. He had been engaged once, he told her— entangled was a better word because he found that the girl was just using him as a sort of decoy, and he was too naïve to realize it. He'd been wary ever since. He almost married a Turkish girl —until he met her family: they frightened him so much he ran away. Another time, after the war, he spent several months in Japan and fell in love with the Japanese way of life and thought of marrying and settling down there but nothing came of it.

Now, he said, he had no doubts whatever. Even at first sight, he had had no doubt, but he waited to make sure. He tried to be wary.

The crises of life, she thought, the declarations and overtures of love, occur in cars. He steered, shifted gears, watched the road ahead; she was conscious of the small space they were in, almost like a trap for the occasion, but too small for the activities of love. The Detroit models were better for that. He had to do a lot of shifting of gears, and the motor hummed and buzzed. She steeled herself against him, and realized she was both foolish and stupid. Thirty in November, in four months—she reviewed in a flash all of Sandy Farr's arguments, and all her own. She remembered the girls in the office, the daily and hourly hunt for men, the appraisals and calculations, the pretense of humor, the desperation. And here he was, Tom Heath, Doctor Heath, scholar, gentleman, and sailor, with honorable intentions.

"I wasn't going to speak of it," he said, "as long as I had Pop to take care of—at least that's what I told myself. But Bonnie keeps after me. Don't wait, she says; life won't wait, she says. Marriage is best, come hell or high water, she says. She's been working on me for years—that's why I had to take you out to see her."

"Inspection, was it?"

"Certainly. She called me up that night and told me not to waste a minute. Get the ring, she said. Don't dally. Get after her."

"Did you?"

"No." His smile came quickly and innocently, as it always did. "Bonnie makes me stubborn—at least for a while. I decided to go very slow, to think it out carefully—you know how the academic mind works. In the end I concluded that she was right all the time."

He drew up to the house and stopped the motor. He spoke so seriously that his voice was uneven. "I don't want to lose you, Mary—or lose whatever chance I might have. But you see how it is with Pop: he may be like this for a long time, or he may get more helpless—he may die."

She made ready to speak, but he went on sternly. "I don't want any final answer—I mean yes or no. If you have it in mind to say no I'd rather not hear it tonight. This means—everything—to me. I love you and want to live with you for life. But I'm sure, in spite of Bonnie, it is better to go slow with it. I wanted you to meet Pop, at least. I want you to see how it really is." He looked up at the looming gray house. "It isn't simple—on your end as well as mine. Of course, if you are at all interested—if that's the word for it—I'd like to know, but I'd much rather be slow and sure. We had a pretty good time out there, didn't we? I think we always have a good time."

When he opened the door for her she had the impulse to reach out a hand, to make the first gesture of consent. But she saw a busy little dog trotting and sniffing and then the silhouette of a man in the road. He stepped along and hailed them cheerily. His sharp voice rang out. "Here you see a conscientious suburban athlete doing his nightly roadwork. Pete and I are in training—"

"What for?" Tom Heath asked.

"Oh, for old age." John Rossiter's face in the street-light looked like a boy's. "That's the next big event. Whether it is the best, as the poet says, I don't know, but I'm getting ready for it. Once round the block every night."

Mary Kyle said he'd better come in with them for a drink, but he waved and trotted along after Pete.

CHAPTER 41

THE NEXT EVENING about ten o'clock she found him sitting on the back steps. She heard Pete whining and plaintively barking, and looked out. "Back for the drink?" she said.

"Come out here." He motioned. "Sit down a minute."

Summer night, crickets and locusts sounding on and on. Enough light to make his face visible.

"We've got to straighten this out." He spoke angrily.

"Straighten what out?"

"Don't be perverse. We can't afford to play games."

"Perversity," she mumbled, "thy name is woman."

"What?"

"I claim the right to be as perverse as I damn well please."

"And there's no need to talk nonsense, either." He kept his voice low, but there was more edge and tension in it than usual. "I concede you every female advantage if you insist on taking it. It used to be my hope that I wouldn't make too much of a fool of myself, but I've given that up—at least for the time being."

"What's bothering you?"

He got up, paced a circle, sat down on the step again. "You know damned well what's bothering me. All that talk of yours about not taking my job, not singing in the choir: are you trying to tell me you—" He stopped abruptly.

She said nothing.

"Look here, Mary Kyle: I lead the life of a bird dog—you know that. Coming and going and running in circles. I don't read, I don't think, I don't stop and wonder who I am—and it's all okay, it's dandy, I thrive on it: or—I did before you came along.

249

Are you in love with me?"

She didn't move or breathe.

"I know, I know! No man in his right mind would ask it like that. But I haven't been in my right mind for some time. I told you I wasn't playing games, Mary Kyle. I just don't know what to do."

She said nothing.

"You are the woman I want to be with," he said. "Work, play, life—I loved them all, I thought everything was going fine, I had a wife and family, I had got safely into middle age: then you climbed into my car in a blizzard. Look here: I love you! I am damned forever for saying it, but I say it. It came over me after you left the other day—up to then I hadn't had the wits to see or know it: and you said you weren't coming back. I didn't believe it—or understand: I was as stupid as a man could be. And then the fact began to filter through. I saw what it was. No you any more at all—ever—and I began to think what you meant by it."

"You sound angry," she said.

"Angry! What can I be? Happy? Complacent?" He stood up and kicked a stone on the ground. "Let me tell you something, if you don't know it already: I am a man of inordinate vanity, I am a damned little peacock. Call it pride if you want to flatter me, but—what the hell are you grinning for?"

"Nothing—go on. I'm not grinning anyway."

"No? I tell you—I can't stand being laughed at. When I don't want to be, that is. Oh, I know all about what it is to grow up as a runt. In college I weighed a hundred and twenty-seven pounds and every fall I went out for football. I thought I was Jack the Giant Killer. I thought I could do anything if I tried hard enough. In the end I learned a few things—I even thought I learned discretion. You probably don't believe me, but I admire moderation, the golden mean, even compromise. I've tried hard not to be the fool I naturally tend to be. I thought instead of muscle and weight I might do something with brain and even character or whatever you want to call responsible behavior. I decided not to be Napoleon. I invented Rossiter's Law. I married, I settled down with a good wife and a family, I thought I had everything fixed. Then you walked in—you climbed in—you and your big long legs: do you realize you are bigger than I am? What do you weigh—one fifty, I bet."

"I do not!"

"But let me tell you I can lick you any time you want to try it: one hand tied behind my back too."

"Yes, sir."

He looked at her for a moment and then spoke quietly. "When I was twenty-eight I fell in love. I was grown up, I thought, and very serious about it—just finishing graduate work, ready to settle down: she was a senior in the School of Nursing in town and the prettiest girl you ever saw, tall, with light brown hair and blue eyes. When we went out together she wore low heels. She was quiet and steady and rather naïve—she came from a farm up near Ashby. Well, we went to a big dance, a university ball of some kind—she asked me to go—and she was chosen as the beauty queen and given a gold crown and a bunch of orchids. After that she was selected as the press-photographers' dreamgirl, and in the spring became Miss Apple Blossom of Nashoba Valley. She was still a wonderful girl and she did her best to stay faithful, but there were just too many tall and handsome men. I don't blame her— I am sorry for her, in fact, because I think her life was spoiled. But I took it very hard. I thought she abandoned me because I was small—I was humiliated. I was mad, too—oh, I broke out in all sorts of complexes and neuroses and topped it off with a case of mononucleosis. Most of it was hurt vanity, I suppose."

He sat on one of the steps, took out his pipe, blew through it, and began to fill it without being aware of what he was doing.

"It must be a curse of some sort: I am fated to fall in love with big women." He leveled the pipe at her like a gun. "Did you hear? I said *in love*. Do you know that love is nothing but a virus? It's a physical fact in the blood."

"Yes, I know it."

"Perhaps you know how to cure it. There must be a special medicine."

She said nothing.

"A few months later I married. She's a nurse too, of course— doubtless it was part of my complex. And let me tell you frankly that I love my wife." He looked at his pipe as though he hadn't seen it before, and put it in his jacket pocket. "It is idiotic to say these things. What do they mean? She rescued me when I was ill and crazy. She takes care of everything. She is faithful and honorable. I love her. I could no more desert her than I could cut off my right arm. But—I am not in love with her, or whatever the name of the physical disease may be. And I even know that I am quite capable of cutting off my arm." He held it up like a club. "Are you? Could you?" He gestured theatrically. "Don't answer, don't commit yourself. It's all insanity anyway. My profession is to give advice. I tell people how to live, I tell them to be loyal and sensible and moderate—" He stopped and studied her intently. "Tell me once and for all, do you love me?"

"You know it."

"I don't at all. If you do you're a damn fool—but do you?"

"Yes, but—"

"No buts. Do you?"

"I told you—yes."

"Will you marry me?"

"How?"

"Does it matter how?" He gripped her shoulders and leaned to kiss her. He smiled with a sudden wildness and pulled her close. She touched his bushy hair and ran a hand down over his temple and cheek and nose. "Will you?"

"Yes," she said.

"Now? Tonight?" He watched her with a kind of glitter. His hand held her breast.

"You mean—tonight, or for life?"

"I mean—everything. I mean just us two, now and tomorrow."

"Leave your family? Desert them?"

"Yes!" His hands were rough and demanding. "I mean—"

"You'll cut off your arm?"

"Yes! Yes!" His passion enveloped her. She couldn't draw back or even stir. He pressed with all his strength. "I tell you, this is all there is for me. I love you entirely, more than life itself, or the world, or anything."

"No," she said abruptly. "No."

He didn't hear.

"You've gone mad." She struggled against him. "John," she called. "Listen!"

"What is it?"

"I say you're crazy." His hands were against her flesh.

"John!"

"What?"

"I will not let you rape me on the back steps."

"Why, Mary Kyle, I love you—I love you for ever and ever. I think we are meant for each other—I know we are."

In a fit of anger she used all her strength against him. She fought, and for a few seconds they were at each other brutally. Her clothes tore. "Well, damn you for a female wrestler," he muttered, "I'll show you who's boss of this outfit."

"Stop acting like a sex-starved runt," she said.

He let go, looked at her as though he had just seen that she was there. His face went slack; he rubbed his forehead with the back of his hand. "What gets into me?" he whispered. "I told you—I've spent most of my life trying not to—" He sat down a little distance from her on the bottom step and for a few seconds said nothing. "That hurt badly," he said after a while, speaking so low she could hardly hear. "What you called me. Like being stabbed. I think I deserved it." He looked up and went on more buoyantly. "But I tell you, Mary Kyle, I saw you—I see you—as my woman. I may be sex-starved, and I'm ashamed—not of the appetite, which is a good one if I do say so—but of losing control. It's what I have to fear most. Temper too. I confess to you— I betray myself. I'm struggling to be a responsible citizen, but don't be surprised if I am convicted of assault with intent to kill— or rape. I have it in me. I'm compelled to tell you this partly because I acted insanely—till you stabbed me with that word: and I believe if a man said that to me I'd try to kill him—at least I would have then; but mostly what I mean is that I have the highest opinion of you—in every sort of way. I grant you it would give me great pleasure to seduce you—and if a man really loves a woman he always wants to get at her as fast as he can—but in my judgment, you are what a man needs for a lifetime, I mean as a guide, philosopher, and friend—as well as woman. And damn it all, when I put it on that level, when I become reasonable and responsible and adult, I don't know what to do—I'm frustrated— I'm stuck—"

"Oh, we know what to do," she said. She let her hand touch him on the step below, and rest on his shoulder.

"But you don't—?"

"No—of course I don't."

"Even after I betray myself like that?"

She smoothed his hair.

"Don't start getting maternal," he said sharply. "I won't stand for it."

"All right," she said, but her smile above him was partly maternal. "How many other women have you raped?"

"It's none of your damned business! And I tell you, Mary Kyle Eustace, you better not get too sassy. You may think you're safe because you're bigger than I am, but I warn you you haven't seen anything yet."

"Yes, sir," she said.

He turned and laid his head against her knee. "Mary, for God's sake—don't be like that."

"Like what?"

"Like the woman I've wanted all my life." His voice trembled and choked. He made it sound angry. "Be something else for once. Be nasty or shrewish—or just stupid."

"Give me a minute or two—nothing could be easier—"

He jumped up and paced back and forth. "You know, this is all the old familiar human stuff. It goes on in newspapers and books. What do you mean we know what to do? That's what you said. Who ever knows what to do? Since they invented marriage, I don't know who—Hittites or Sumerians or old stone savages—this has been happening—and what do they do? On the stage they drink poison. In life they deceive and cheat and make a miserable mess of it. What do we do? You said you knew."

"You'd better say it yourself."

He glared at her. "What you mean is, we'd better be cowards, is that it? Forget the whole thing? Pretend it's all wickedness? Is that what you want?"

She said nothing.

"Well, you are right, of course." He paced in a small circle. "If I abandon wife and children—what am I? A hero of love? A betrayer of trust? I know what I'd be." He looked at her, came close, took her face and kissed it at first gently, then hard.

She stirred. "You can't, John. You know you can't."

His hands were rough on her, and she stood up.

"Yes," he whispered. "I know—I know—but damn it all—"

He held her more lightly, studying her face, memorizing it. "Women are supposed to be practical—about love, at least. Good women have charge of virtue. Now you tell me candidly, without faking, what is going to happen: here we are in this suburban beehive, two blocks apart, going to town and back five or six days a week in our appointed rounds like a couple of wind-up toys— this year, next year; we meet on the street corner, in a store, we say it is warm or cold, we hope the family is well—I tell you man's nature won't stand it. I don't know about woman's—it is said to be very tough. But I doubt if any toughness can stand up to a situation like that. Every night, every day, every turn we take— and no end to it except weariness and death. What do we do? The right thing, I suppose—as the man said to himself when he met a grizzly bear on a trail with a cliff on one side and a precipice on the other."

She didn't answer.

CHAPTER 42

"You LOOK as though you'd been barbecued," Patience said. "And freckles! You'll ruin your skin for life, you know. Where in the world have you been?"

"Sailing," Mary Kyle said shortly. "My boy-friend takes me."

"Who, for heaven's sake?"

"Why, Heath, of course."

"You mean *Prof* Heath?"

"Yup."

"Well!" Patience expressed eagerness. "Boy-friend! How long's this been going on?"

"Oh—since May."

"Is it—serious?"

"That's one word for it."

"Kyle, for heaven's sake! I'm your sister, you know. Loosen up a little. You act like the sphinx."

Mary Kyle shrugged.

"What's wrong, anyway?" Patience asked. "I mean, you seem sort of grim. Don't you have any fun sailing? Maybe you think he's too old or too—" She waved vaguely. "You know how you get in college—you don't think of faculty people as quite human. But actually Heath seems like a nice guy."

"He is."

"Well, you certainly don't act as though you cared two cents' worth. What about this sailing? What do you do? I went once on the Charles with a fellow named Fish, of all things, and he got into such a mess we had to be rescued—and poor Fish was so embarrassed about it he never asked me again. That's all I know about sailing."

Mary Kyle roused herself to talk of Marblehead. They laughed and chattered for a while. It was after dinner on a summer Sunday; they were up in Mary Kyle's room. Tony and Edwin were downstairs looking at the ball game.

"I can't see what's holding you back," Patience said. "You surely won't find anyone—"

"Anyone else?"

"Anyone more eligible—at least, there's no one in sight, is there?"

"Well—there's Joe Bass."

"Look, Kyle, I think this is serious—I mean, it's a big chance for you."

"You sound just like Sandy Farr."

"What's wrong with Sandy Farr?"

"My Lord—do you know what you said? Six months ago you had nothing but contempt for Sandy and all her kind. As a matter of fact, you had contempt for all respectable matrimony. The station-wagon set, you called them—or am I mistaken? Now you seem to think it's every woman's goal."

"Don't exaggerate so, Kyle. I do think your Sandy Farrs are a pretty smug lot. But marriage—well, I admit I'm for it. I suppose I did talk a lot of nonsense—you know how we talk in college; it seems ages ago. I can't imagine any other kind of life now—I mean with the two of us there's so much to live for, so much point to everything. And I keep learning from Tony—things like self-control and intellectual honesty: I admit it sounds silly to say it, but it really means something."

"I'm sure I could learn plenty from Tom Heath," Mary Kyle muttered. "All about the Ottoman Empire, for instance."

"Well, sure—why not? I don't know what makes you so snooty. Think of all you could do—trips to Bagdad or Istanbul—"

"Where the water's like bean soup."

"What of it, for heaven's sake? Something's biting you, Kyle. Do you know anything *bad* about him?"

"Not a thing—though you might say he hasn't much imagination."

"You surely aren't hesitating because of his father. It would be a problem, of course, but after all—"

"Hesitate! Who says I'm hesitating? I haven't any intention—"

"Don't say it, Kyle. Don't make it sound that way. You're just being stubborn—I mean, it's a family habit: look at all of us. But you've always had this notion that men are to be scorned—"

"I certainly haven't!"

"Well, you ought to hear yourself talk: what you used to say about poor old Harold Chivers—"

"Oh—Harold!"

"A perfectly good man—but a little dull, I grant you that. And all the men in the office—"

"You haven't seen Joe Bass."

"You've never said a good word about any of them. According to you, your bosses are perfect goons."

"Well—they are."

"And you think the girls are all imbeciles because their one idea in life is to get a man."

Mary Kyle drew breath for a sharp answer, then took thought. "I'm sorry for them, anyway. We've all been conditioned for sex by the books and shows. The idea that sex conquers all has made more money for people than anything else—" John Rossiter's voice came to her clearly from the night of the blizzard. *If I had to pick the ten all-round best women I ever knew, six would be virgins.* Was he just sounding off? What did he know about virgins anyway?

"I'm talking about marriage," Patience said firmly. "It isn't the same as sex."

"Neither does it solve everything. In the ordinary way of things, life can be hell—I mean, here we are, tramping along like a chain gang on the road to death—"

"Kyle! Stop it!"

"Oh, I can be cheerful enough about it—but the fact is the fact. And, it strikes me that a miserable marriage just doubles the hell, or multiplies it, maybe. My God, Patience, I'm not playing at misery just for the fun of it. If I was in love with Tom Heath I'd marry him as fast as I could, and I'd make the most of it. I'm not really a morbid character—at least, I don't try to be. I like Tom, he's a fine citizen, but I just don't feel like getting into bed with him."

"Well, I think you've got a block about it. Did you ever feel like that about any man?"

Mary Kyle waited a few seconds. "Yes, I have."

"Who?"

She shook her head. "Never mind."

"But—"

"Cut it out, Pat! It's not worth talking about—and besides, I—I *can't*—" The words choked in her throat. Tears ran suddenly in an overflowing flood. She turned away, groping to the bureau, the window, and then to the closet door where she buried her face in the cotton pajamas hanging inside.

"Kyle—I didn't know—I mean, you'd better get it off your chest, hadn't you? I never dreamed you felt this way about anyone. Who is it, anyway?"

Mary Kyle straightened her shoulders. "It makes me so damned *mad*—all this blubbering. I thought I had guts enough to be a grown-up woman." She went and stared out of the window.

"It helps sometimes if you just talk—"

"No! I won't—and don't keep prying. I'll survive it, I hope. People usually do. They can survive practically anything if they have to. The thing is not to want too much, of course. Keep your expectations small. Look at poor Mother—she always hoped for wonderful things and was always disappointed. No, I intend to get down into my little rut and stay there. Other people can hope and dream and weep—not me." She turned from the window with a sudden toss of her head. "I talk so theatrically, as though any of it *mattered*. I sound so sorry for myself. Maybe that's another Eustace habit; even Buzz acts as though he were a kitten about to be drowned. But I won't be that way—I promise." She paced back and forth. "You think I'd better marry Tom Heath, is that it?"

"Yes, I do!"

"Love or no love?"

"Kyle, I think the biggest thing in love is friendship. I know it sounds naïve to say it, but getting into bed is the easiest and most obvious part of it: I mean, look at all the people who do it for money—or just do it anyway. But living with someone day after day, talking and eating and planning and going places and just passing time—that's the part that counts. If you like being with a man, and really give it a thorough *try*, you can probably marry him."

"No love?"

"Yes—what I mean *is* love. You certainly love a friend and partner and companion: in the long run that's the best love possible."

Mary Kyle smiled at her sister's wisdom. "You take life earnestly, Pat! But thanks for the advice anyway. I'll think it over."

CHAPTER 43

FROM WHAT he had seen of the army so far, Buzz wrote, there was a good chance that he could get to be a general—either that or the camp he was in was where they dumped all the morons and creeps. He had never had a very high opinion of his own abilities, but compared with the rest of his outfit he felt like an Eagle Scout at least. "If there's a stupid way of doing anything, that's the way they do it. The day we got here we had to line up and wait, which is what we do most of the time. We had on the stuff we came in, and a big storm hit us, a hurricane practically, and it rained like hell, and we got soaked, and then it got cold and blew, and we stood out there three hours and about fifty men got pneumonia. That's just a sample."

Edwin swirled the liquor in his glass, took a swallow, and nodded at Tom Heath. "That's military tradition," he said. "Teach 'em stupidity; teach 'em to do as they're told regardless of how dumb or asinine it is. Better let half the company die of pneumonia than use ordinary common sense. But he'll learn: in a week he'll be as much of a moron as all the rest—maybe more; I believe he has a talent for it."

Tom glanced at his watch and stirred restlessly. Mary Kyle had gone to town to meet Sandy Farr for a Saturday matinee, and he tried to calculate her return trip. There were two trains—one in ten minutes: he stood up and said he'd see if she were there—it would save her a hot walk.

"Tell her never mind the milk and stuff—I bought 'em myself," Edwin said. "I haven't got that chef's job yet, but I'm getting in condition for it. You stay for supper—I'll show you how hamburger and onions ought to be done."

Tom nodded. "Is that what you're thriving on—your own cooking? You look like a new man since I went west."

"I do? You mean I've got to go to work again?" Edwin's grin made his hollow face look like a satyr's. "Anyway, I don't have to go back to Grogan's hell-hole. Matter of fact, I've got a nice old-man's job all lined up for September. I been doing some scouting, boy—she doesn't know it yet. No—can't tell you, not till I'm sure."

She was not on the earlier train. Tom moved his car to some shade and read the evening paper. At six twenty she arrived and he stepped out to meet her on the sun-baked platform. She gave a strange, half-frightened smile—not for him but for someone beyond: he could see an intense emotion and calculation in her face and he stopped abruptly and waited for her to notice him.

"Right time, right place," a voice behind him said. "The car is waiting."

"Oh, here's Mr. Heath," she said with perfect self-possession. "You know each other, don't you? Mr. Rossiter?"

"Two cars seem to be waiting," Tom Heath said. "You'll have to choose." He watched her. "I might add that I've been asked for supper."

She took it in at once and smiled her regret at John Rossiter, but for an instant her eyes held him. "I don't deserve this attention. And you'll weaken my morale too. But thank you anyway."

"Your morale," John said, "is in no danger—as far as walking goes, at least. This was merely a Saturday special; on working days we sternly do our duty." He turned with a wave. "I just happened to be coming along and thought I'd take the chance." He trotted off.

"Nice chap," Tom said, and wondered how he knew she'd be on the train.

"How was Seattle?" she briskly asked.

"A good deal cooler than this. Summer is wonderful in the northwest. Winter—well, it isn't wonderful—except up in the mountains."

He spoke of the place with so much interest that she took note. His best friend was in the history department in the University, he said—and as a matter of fact, they were offering him a job. He had to decide right away: it had been pending for a month, and time for changing jobs this year was running out. Bonnie was all for his doing it, even though she'd have to take full charge of their father—who had had another very slight stroke and was in bad shape.

"Seattle!" she exclaimed.

"I know. You New Englanders can't conceive of anyone going there to live—thirty-some hundred miles from Boston. But people out there are people—"

"Just like Turkey!"

"Certainly." His smile flashed at her. "Two-legged ones, of course." He had been there for two years as an instructor fifteen years ago—his first full-time job—and he knew the place well. The salary, he added, would be very good.

After the hamburgers and onions they did the dishes—Tom washed them with swift competence, as though he had done it professionally. Edwin left them, remarking that it was a primary mistake for a man ever to learn to wash a dish or make a bed. If you don't know how, he said, you're all right. He turned on the television.

They stood uncertainly in the bare and tidy kitchen. "Mother never learned to wash a dish either," she said. "Not really. Her idea was that someone would do them later. Not us, though—she never expected us to do them. I can't get used to the old dump all neat like this. It really looks more dismal than ever."

It was clear to her that he wanted to talk, but there was no place for them to be—except that he wandered out to the back steps, admired the misty moonlight and the warmth, and she found herself there with him, sitting on the top step, looking toward the garage and the tomato plants and the gray board fence at the back of the lot. The insects buzzed and sang in pulsing hot-weather rhythm. Life, she thought, reaches its emotional peaks on the back steps in summer. In cold weather, cars were the only refuge.

"Tell me about Rossiter," he unexpectedly said. "What does he do?"

She spoke carefully. He rescued the perishing, she said. He played the organ, went to ballgames—

Tom waited for her to go on.

Married, she said. Two children. Lived two blocks in that direction.

"He still wants me to work for his outfit," she suddenly said.

"Do you want to?"

She evaded the question, but kept on talking more candidly than she had intended to. He sat solidly beside her like an embodiment of honest good sense; he nodded a little, smiled a little, took in what she said, let her go on. She had worked up to a pretty good salary at the Allston Associates, she said, and the money had seen them through some bad times—in fact for the last six months it had been nothing but bad times. If Buzz had been sued for damages after his accident they might have lost everything, but the college took the responsibility—at least she gathered that their insurance covered it. But even so, the expenses had been fearful and her savings were gone. Her father had disability insurance— not much, but it helped. In a couple of years or so he would be eligible for social security—

Tom interrupted. "He has a job—beginning in the autumn."

"Job? Why—he *couldn't!*"

"He looks like a new man," Tom said.

She said nothing for a few seconds. "You get so used to things," she said. "You think he—?"

"I think he's quite a character."

He was a failure, of course—she had always realized it. Nothing he did had ever turned out right: jobs lost, opportunities missed, nothing left but drink and cynicism and profanity. He was the burden they had carried, the destroyer of her mother's hopes, the blight on all of them.

Tom said, "I like to hear him cut loose with 'The Cremation of Sam McGee.' Actually this attack he's had has done him good— and I've seen it happen that way with others: they seem to get a different attitude about life."

What had done him good, she suddenly understood, was Josephine's death. She was aware of the drab yard, the house beside her, the gray walls above in the dark. Why couldn't they sell it at last, be free of it forever—her mind took in everything at once, the years of defeat and disappointment, her father coming out of the bathroom buttoning the gold collar-button of his shirtband, his face like a mask of tragedy, and her mother downstairs peering from the kitchen door with her mouth twisted as though she were about to scream. "Eggs? You want eggs this morning?" They had never begun to live; they had put it off and put it off, waiting for the worst to be over.

"Poor father," she said. "I hope—I think you must be right. He does seem better. I wish we could get away from this dismal old house—it's such a miserable dump, really. Do you think we could sell it?"

"Certainly—you can sell any house these days, for a good price."

"You said father has a job? I can't think what—unless it's a short-order cook in a lunch wagon. He surely couldn't survive the racket and all. There really isn't much he can do—except if he wants to he can do anything: but usually he doesn't want to."

She thought about it broodingly. "How many people do you know who do what they want to? Do you?"

"Oh, mostly—yes."

"Well, let me tell you: every day I ride to town, walk through the station and along Portland Street past Haymarket—or sometimes I go on the subway—and about fifty thousand people do the same every day. I can see their faces, hear the shuffle and click of their shoes—they go like herds of sheep to offices and stores and warehouses, they sell themselves for eight hours—"

"What would they do otherwise?"

"Is that the realist's notion? You wouldn't do it, would you?" Her voice sharpened its tone. "It keeps all of us wage slaves out of mischief, but it's not for the chosen few—"

"The lucky ones, you mean."

"There's no *sense* in it," she flared out. "What's life good for if you spend the best time of it being bored and tired?"

He smiled patiently.

"And don't think this is just self-pity—there are a billion or so others who feel the same way."

He waited solidly on the step, nodding slightly to show that he saw her point but not sharing her emotion. Mankind, his look suggested, was too large a problem to deal with on a summer evening —though doubtless its plight was, as she pointed out, miserable.

"Lucky!" she said. "You certainly are. Who else is—round here, I mean? Not Father, certainly—"

"No, perhaps not—but your friend Rossiter seems to have a fine time."

"Oh—John!" She said it involuntarily, and paused to reflect.

"Well, he's a special case. You can't generalize."

But he felt her change of mood. She stirred, stood up, said they might as well take a walk—there was no point in simply sitting on the steps. When they set off she spoke of Seattle—was he going? Would she go too?

He took her arm and walked in step, slowly strolling, shoulder against shoulder. His hand was large, his shoulder broad and high; he looked down at her with a kindly pleasure, watching and relishing the animation in her face. "I like you very much," he said. "It strikes me often that I am rather a dull man. I try not to be—that is, I try not to exchange platitudes with my acquaintances and companions, but if I think candidly about myself I realize that I plug along much too predictably. When I'm with you, though, I feel—less dull. I feel almost—I won't say brilliant, but at least adventurous. To be truthful, I should tell you that I used to enjoy seeing your father for the same reason—I liked his originality or his Yankee seasoning or whatever it is, and then I met you and you seemed quite a lot like him—"

"Me? Like Father?"

"Except that you were beautiful and female and, I thought, just the right age to be my wife."

"Well! I was always supposed to be a Cowles—"

"Oh, undoubtedly you are all kinds of things—your variety seems to me infinite. It does strike me as strange that you haven't married—I should think the pressure would have been heavy—"

"Not at all," she broke in. "Nothing was easier. And if you are interested, I can tell you why—or rather I can give you one explanation."

"Well, couldn't you call it simply good judgment?"

"Call it cussedness. Or, to use the term more frequent in our office, bitchiness. You'd better be warned, Tom Heath. I'm not one of your docile dream girls."

He laughed aloud and squeezed her arm close to him.

"But I must say," she went on, "I never heard of a girl getting proposed to because she was like her father. I wouldn't call that predictable at all."

"Never mind that—what we want now is a good answer." His voice deepened with feeling. "It would mean a new life, new world, new future, and we'd be doing it together." His strong face was full of the vision.

She turned her head away. "This feeling you have about Father," she said, "it makes me think—I mean it comes as a sort of surprise."

"Well, he's my friend."

She looked at him carefully, and he tried to read her eyes.

"What about it, Mary? Are we friends too—and lovers? Will you marry me?"

"Yes," she said.

CHAPTER 44

BUT SHE lay awake half the night. They were supposed to be lovers now; she was his girl. He put a proprietary arm round her. He kissed her. It was pleasant—more than that, it was safe. He at once took her into protective custody; he made no demands, expected no demonstrations or declarations, assumed that their bargain was sealed with good faith and common sense. His first move would be to accept the Seattle offer, but everything else could be worked out—and of course, much depended on Edwin: they could even urge him to go west with them. At any rate, they could be married by the end of August, or sooner; he didn't suppose she'd want any elaborations, though it would be nice if his sister Bonnie and her family could be on hand for it.

She perceived that he was a solid man. From her place inside his arm, within sound of his quiet voice, everything worked out easily. It was only common sanity to renounce the foolish and hopeless passion—for a few moments she hardly believed she had ever actually had it. All the yearnings and frustrations of her life seemed to grow distant and small; she perceived herself at once entering a new life in a far picturesque country, in a new house with great clear windows looking to Mount Rainier, with clean-lined furniture, with miraculous equipment, with beauty and simplicity— with intelligent and charming children becoming inevitably wiser and happier and more successful than their parents ever were. Professor Heath—a very solid man. Mrs. Heath—

In the night she wept. Anguish gripped her stomach and chest like a vise.

At least, she told herself, she could be fair to him. Tell him everything, she said, tell him, tell him—maybe if nothing else he'll be sorry for you. She wept again. The sobs tore at her. She sat on the edge of the bed, put on the light, walked about, looked at her unlovely face in the mirror, lay back on the bed again with the light still on. How could you be "fair" to him, or anyone? Can you domesticate desire? What could you tell him? What good would it do? He'd say at once—she heard his voice—that the only reasonable solution was for them to marry quickly and go west. Of course. You get over passion in time, like pneumonia—what counted in the long run, through the deserts of old age, was wifely and motherly love—or loyalty—or friendship—or whatever you called it.

She wept at the sight of her room in the yellow light, the shoddy stuff it was made of, the iron bed and the cracked walls, the unfinished Proust on the table, the unframed water-color propped above her desk—she had done it with hope and delight eight years earlier, expecting to do more, to be a brilliant amateur, perhaps to have a show, sell a few. She looked back at the Picasso print above the bed and felt a moment of hatred for it, an ugly jumble of shapes, a pretentiousness, an accusation of folly.

I don't know what to do, she mumbled inside herself, I don't know what to do. The night dragged slowly on and she slept for weariness.

"Tom wants to marry me," she told her father at breakfast.

"Well, don't hesitate," he sharply said. Then he smiled at her with a kind of respect. "He does, does he? I suspicioned it. Poor bastard, he doesn't know when he's well off. Did you take him—I hope? You'd be a star-spangled idiot if you didn't."

"I took him."

Edwin looked at her as though he were just understanding it. "Well, by Jesus—is that a fact? You've got him, have you?"

"I—I guess so, I said so, anyway."

"Well! Son-in-law, no less. You look pretty damn peaked about it, I must say. You scared, or what?"

"I'm scared."

" 'T'aint worth it—being scared. Hell, just take what comes and be glad of it." But his tone carried good cheer. "I tell you, girl, I'm in favor of this. I mean, there's no sense in the kind of life you live. I'm damned sure I don't do you any good—there are times, in fact, when I wonder how you women have been able to stand me as long as you have—" He stopped abruptly and stared at the floor. "It doesn't do to think about it."

"He wants to go to Seattle," she said.

Edwin's face settled into its lines. He brooded. "By rights I ought to hold you here—at any cost. I read that in books." He shook himself. "It sounds dandy to me. Are you hesitating?"

"Well—why not come with us?" She smiled. "He's all for marrying you too—he only wants me because he thinks I'm like you."

"Eyewash, I should say." But Edwin contrived a quick skeletal grin. "Go west, old man—huh?" He shook his head. "I made my big mistake when I left the farm the first time: everything since then has been just temporary, and here I am at the end. I think, to be fair and candid about it, I'd have made a pretty good dairy farmer—that is, I'd have grubbed along at it, I'd have had a useful function, as they say. I might have lived like a free man."

When she started to speak he leveled a long forefinger at her. "The truth is, your mother never had any respect for me."

"Oh, nonsense."

"It was mighty hard on her. She needed to have respect." He gestured. "I know what it's been. I understand. I am aware. But now, at this point in the treadmill, I refuse to let myself get potted on self-pity. A dose of guilt—sure. Bourbon whisky—okay. I've done wrong and I can do wrong. But I'll be goddamned if I sink back into a wallow of chronic misery. Maybe I'm nothing but a bastardly hunk of old wreckage, but by God I'm alive, my bowels move, I can chew steak, drink liquor, drive a Chrysler, I can still utter free speech as profanely and foolishly as I damn well please. No, ma'am, I don't intend to go west nohow—not yet awhile, anyway. You can go—if you've got any sense you will go—but not me. I stay."

His face seemed to gleam.

"You sound cocky," she said.

"I do?"

"Pleased with yourself."

"I wouldn't want to overdo it. Matter of fact, I can tell you now: that young philosopher of yours—"

"Who?"

"Feller from the church, Engels, Ph.D.—he's offered me a job as

of September fifteen. I heard about it from Rossiter and figured
right off it was what I wanted—"

"What kind of job?"

"Why, janitor. Over at the egg-head church there. Custodian is
the word—"

"Father, you can't!"

"Nothing to it. Oil furnace—runs itself. Vacuum-cleaner—no
trouble. If there ever was an old man's job, that's it—and they
have a hell of a time finding anyone to do it. Low pay, of course—"

"You can't shovel snow."

"Oh, Rossiter—he said he'd have a gang of boys there any time
we needed 'em. We'll work it out."

"Cocky is the word," she said. "But watch out, you may be in-
fected with religion."

She started off for her train. The pressure of worry and uncertainty came back to clutch her vitals; she remembered the black
hours she had lain awake, and the choke of useless tears. She tried
to walk briskly and take deep breaths, but her motions were slow.
Cars rushed past her along the street and she found herself listening for the rattle of his old Ford and the slowing down behind her
and the chirp of his voice summoning her. Decisions and com-
mitments would brush away like cobwebs if he called her—she
could feel it already in her body, the response to him, the sur-
render. Her walk through the morning air seemed strangely la-
borious, as if she were swimming in a dream, straining and making
no progress: if he came behind her and called, as he might—he
knew she was there at that minute—she would be instantly free,
she would break out of the dark dream and go with him. They two
together would be life itself.

The station appeared and came closer; the morning passengers
clustered in the shade and the rails were lines of white light south-
eastward toward the city. She nodded palely. Mr. Buehler, broker
or investments or something about stocks and bonds. Mrs. Kar-
vonen, Filene's Crystal Salon. Francis O'Leary, politician and custodian of something-or-other in the State House. Naomi Kaplan,
secretary. Faces she saw every day, every week, most of them name-
less to her—all masklike, closed, expressing nothing but patient
acceptance of the day. Westward, away from the sun, the rails
hummed, the deep diesel roar rose louder through the quiet air.

Few glanced that way; they read folded papers or stood back from the rush and dust waiting for the right moment to move. With the patient expectation of sleepwalkers they grouped at the car steps and boarded one by one.

"I don't mean to be tactless," Joe Bass said at noon, "but you know, youth doesn't last forever. That's what they say, at least, and I believe it. Don't you?"

"Youth," she muttered. "My slogan from now on is the hell with it."

He made light of her. "What you most need is a good dose of me. How about that date you promised? For your own good—and mine too."

She looked at him almost as though she hadn't heard.

"Just a preliminary date," he said. "An introductory special. Money back if not entirely satisfied."

"Joe—I'm going to be married."

He cocked his head and studied her.

"I'm going to Seattle to live." She said it clearly.

He leaned closer. "You know, I've made a special study of girls. They are my avocation, you might say. Any man who thinks he understands girls is a damn fool, I grant you that, but right now my advice to you is—don't. Or at least, wait a while. I guess marriage is fine at the right time. I've even advised and encouraged it. But for you—now—this August sixth—tell me, Mary, what are you doing for a vacation?"

"I told you, I'm quitting."

"Hm." He studied her. "You need about a week on a beach somewhere. Never mind, though—I'm serious about a date—I mean just for the fun of it—just—oh, hell, we all take everything so damned *hard*. Why don't we have a good drink, a good dinner, go to a show? Why not?"

"I told you—"

"Oh, nuts." But he smiled warmly. "I'm telling *you*. This is something you need—I mean my introductory special, no strings, no fine print. How about Friday evening? We'll do the town."

"Well—"

"Okay, it's a date."

"No, wait—"

He smiled, made a gesture of all's well, and walked away.

The hell with it anyway, she muttered to herself. It didn't matter, really. They could go to Locke-Ober's maybe—she'd never been there. High-class restaurants always seemed preposterous to her. A theater would be fine. No night club, though—they were worse than preposterous . . .

She caught herself sharply. Joe Bass was nothing but a professional tempter. She liked him in a way—he did it with a sort of elegance.

But—it didn't matter. At least, he didn't matter. She could eat no lunch, though. The hours dragged. On her desk were the dummy pages of a brochure to be issued by the Citizens' Credit Union, designed to persuade its readers to borrow money. *Worried? Bills to pay? House need repairs? Time for a new car? Let us show you how you can safely and easily* BANK ON YOUR OWN FUTURE. Her idea, too. They all admired it, bosses and clients both: BANK ON YOUR OWN FUTURE. Very good, Miss Eustace.

She sat staring at it. Some aspirin might subdue the ache inside her, she thought. It was foolish not to sleep at night. It was senseless to make all this fuss about being alive—it was nothing but atavistic emotion, the basic female libido trying to assert itself, yearning and pressing and clutching at her bowels. Her mind perceived clearly. Undoubtedly Tom Heath was the best all-round man she had ever met: she admired and understood him, she liked him, she *liked* him. It was inevitable that she should marry him. Anything else would be stupid.

At five she walked past the Haymarket parking lot and saw John. He was leaning back against the front left fender of his Ford, no hat on, jacket crumpled under one arm, shirt collar askew, sleeves partly rolled up—she noted the bunchy muscles of his arms. Four boys were close in front of him, pressing and talking with such insistence and emotion that though she passed within five yards of him he didn't see her. "Hold your horses, now," she heard him say. "One at a time. Mike, you tell it. What's the story?"

She listened.

"Well, jees Mister Ross, I told you, these guys, some of 'em come from over across, from Charlestown somewhere, they're big guys, they ain't kids like us—well, they got Benny—that's my brother Benny: they got him in a cellar down there in Salt Lane, it's just a dump—"

"How do you know?"

"How? Because they told Al here—"

Al broke in suddenly with a squeak: "I seen 'em. I heard 'em too. 'You tell his kid brother we'll cut him up good': that's what they said."

"Jeez, Mister Ross, we got to do something!"

"You speak to the police?"

"Aw, hell—they say it's kid stuff. They don't pay no attention to a little jerk like Al here."

She passed on, then suddenly turned and waved. He saw the motion and smiled and came to her.

"It sounds dangerous and desperate," she said.

"Mostly threat." His glance enveloped her and he slipped a hand under her arm. "I thought I could drive you home, but I'd better see what this is all about."

"You aren't supposed to drive me home."

"No." He grinned.

She stepped back, looked away with a little gesture of anger. "Listen, John—I'm going to marry Tom Heath. I've decided—"

"You've told him?"

"Yes. I'm going to Seattle with him."

He seemed to hunch a little, with a flushed and glowering look on his face. "You can't do it," he said. His hand squeezed her arm.

She stepped back. She said nothing. They stared at each other.

"Hey, Mister Ross!" a voice shrilled.

"You can't," he whispered.

"I have to."

He turned his head. "Well—wait. Just wait a while, will you? Mary Kyle—my God, you *can't.*"

The boys moved toward them. He turned. "All right, boys. I'm with you. We'll see what we can do."

He waved and walked back to his car. Her eyes flooded and ran down her cheeks. She turned toward a brick wall and mopped and wiped herself.

✎§ CHAPTER 45 ?✑

EDWIN'S HABIT was to read the paper after breakfast, after Mary Kyle had left: he had been remarking all summer that what he most enjoyed was the realization which came over him every morning that there wasn't a thing in the world he was obliged to do. His big talent, he said, was a talent for doing nothing—or at least nothing useful.

She sometimes bought a *Traveler* on her way home, but usually she waited and read the morning paper—or glanced through it—after supper. So in the train this Tuesday she had no inkling of what Harold Chivers was about to say when he touched his hat and leaned close enough for a voiced whisper.

"This must come as quite a shock to you."

"What?"

"I mean about Mr. Rossiter—" He stopped, seeing the look on her face. "You don't know?"

"No."

"He was injured in some sort of rioting in the North End." He unfolded the *Herald*. "Here it is, but they only say he is on the danger list."

She held the paper in both hands, but for a few seconds it whirled and blurred. Harold's voice sounded remotely above her. Then the headline: Social Worker Stabbed in Teen Gang Fight. She read, and turned to an inner page.

"It is certainly a shock to us all," Harold said. "He was apparently trying to persuade them to—"

"Where is it?"

"Where is—what?"

"City Hospital."

"Oh—well, it may be somewhere out on Harrison Avenue. I think it is, or at least it is in that area."

"I can ask, they'll know in the station."

He looked at her white face. "It must be a—a very severe—" He made an effort not to say "shock" again, but said it. She sat without moving. After a while he moistened his lips. "I should assume from the report that it would not be possible to visit him at the hospital—I mean if he is on the danger list; and of course visitors are not usually permitted in the morning hours. It would be advisable to telephone—"

She seemed not to hear. He leaned closer. If she was determined to go, perhaps she would allow him to go along too. He was deeply concerned, and would like to do anything he could. At least at the hospital they might have reliable news about his condition.

He couldn't tell whether she took it in, but after several seconds had passed she said "Thank you."

She said nothing more until they were in the station and asked where City Hospital was.

"I can find it," she told him. "You don't need to come."

"Oh, I insist."

"No—it—I—" She ran for the elevated station and he followed. There were crowds. She hardly seemed to know he was there, though he hovered beside her, guided her on and off the train and along the streets. Her face was white and set. But at last she spoke. People always believed in premonitions, she said; they knew, somehow, that disaster would occur. She didn't. She had had no inner warning. "I said it sounded dangerous, but I thought no one would hurt him, I thought they all liked him too much, I thought he could get through any sort of trouble."

She thought evil wouldn't touch him. Even now, coming up the steps and into the dreary lobby, she knew he would pull through, that nothing could keep him down. The image flashed in her mind of the morning after the blizzard of last winter when he flung himself like a terrier against the piles and chunks of snow that buried his car. "Do? I can do my damndest!" The joyous voice as clear and sharp as winter air.

Harold Chivers had been inquiring at the desk, and there was delay. She came and stood beside him, full of confidence.

The woman at the desk told them Mr. John Rossiter had died early that morning, about four-thirty. After a moment she asked if they would care to see one of the resident doctors.

Mary Kyle stood without moving, until Harold glanced questioningly. "No," she said distinctly. "Thank you."

She turned and walked—not to the main door, but along a corridor. Harold touched her. "Come and sit down a while, there's a waiting room here."

She looked round. "No, I'd better—" She saw the door and headed for it.

He kept a hand on her arm. At intervals, back to the elevated station, he spoke to her. He offered his sympathy. It was a shocking tragedy. Mr. Rossiter meant a great deal to her, he could see; he must have been a very fine person.

She made no answer.

At Washington Street, underground, she took note of the station. "You'll be very late at the office, Harold."

"Oh, don't be concerned about that. I'd like to be sure you can get along all right."

"Me? Get along? Don't be ridiculous."

He made for the first time his little V smile. "Well, I'm only trying to keep an eye on you. This has been a pretty serious shock."

"Yes," she said. She seemed to see him. "You are very good, Harold. You took care of me. Thank you. But I'm really all right now. Your stop is next, isn't it? You needn't—I mean, please don't bother about me."

"Well, if you are sure. I'm really deeply sorry, Mary—"

"Oh, I'm sure," she almost snapped at him. She took a quick breath. "I'm grateful, Harold; really I am. Next time we meet I can tell you better."

He squirmed slightly; his little smile came back with a foolish twist, as though she had caught him at something. "I must tell you, Mary—I mean, it will be announced very soon anyway—" He drew erect and spoke his piece seriously. "I am engaged to be married." He waited a moment, and it seemed that she might not have heard. "I am going to marry a—a young lady from our church—in fact, she is our parish assistant, Miss Erica Gronberg. Possibly you know her? I should certainly want you to know each other."

The train slowed. He looked at her with some anxiety and began to stand up.

"That's fine, Harold," she said.

He lifted his hat. "Don't hesitate to count on me if I can be of use."

She said nothing and he went off.

She got off at Haymarket and walked slowly to the old building where his offices were. It was where she had turned and wept—only a few hours before; she looked at the same sooty bricks. But inside were many people, some simply standing, as though they expected something to happen. Many young ones; groups of boys. Others came and went in the office rooms. Two or three policemen, and men with the look and manner of politicians. A few reporters and cameras. She found herself standing among them. She felt no impulse to move or change for a long time—nor did others. They stood together in silence with solemn waiting faces; it seemed as though they expected John Rossiter to walk in and speak. They seemed to be listening for him.

Some drifted away, others came. Above the human smells she got whiffs of old plaster, old woodwork, dampness—rats, perhaps. There was an effect of quietness and dimness in the hall where they clustered; they spoke little, with whispers or murmurs, and even those who went officially in and out of the inner rooms moved slowly and kept their heels from striking the wooden floor.

She felt a touch on her arm. "Did they get the ones that done it?" It was a fierce whisper and she turned to see two faded eyes and a ramlike chin pointed up at her.

"I don't know."

"They'd ought to be put in the electric chair. They're wild beasts, that's all they are." The eyes turned toward a uniform in one of the offices. "Them cops—" he shrugged and muttered to himself. "What I say is shoot 'em." He looked sharply at Mary Kyle again. "He did everything he could for us. I never heard of a better man than he was, not since the Bible, anyhow. It ain't right."

"No," she said.

"I mean to say, I don't know what we're coming to—why, some of those boys carry knives and guns; why, they act like wild hyenas. You got kids?"

"No."

The watery eyes appraised her. "Social worker, huh?"

"No."

"Well, it's a bad thing, I can tell you. A man like that—my grandson would be in prison today if it wasn't for him, instead of making ninety a week. And they go and kill him like that, murder him. I wouldn't want kids either, not now, not the way things are in the city here." The voice went on, half to itself.

Mary Kyle walked aimlessly for two hours. She looked at the summer-blue water of the harbor, and the workboats and tugs and rust-patched freighters at anchor—she thought how massive and immobile they were out on the opaque water, just waiting and waiting as though they had eternity ahead of them. She lingered past chandleries, machine-shops, markets, and had glimpses of baskets of gutted fish and hanging carcasses of animals. She looked up at the brick and stone blocks of warehouses and saw that the upper floors seemed all empty and abandoned—was it there, she wondered, generations ago, that the Starretts and Lawrences made fortunes? It was a dead world now, though here on the streets the traffic came and went. Dark birds lived up there in niches on the walls and their droppings made bright stains against the time-blackened stone.

～ CHAPTER 46 ～

RATTLE OF SLEET on the east-facing window woke her before the alarm and she roused and studied the luminous hands of the clock in the darkness. Quarter of seven. Darkest morning of the year, and the east wind blowing straight in. The mill whistle sounded its two notes of doom. She reached for the button on the clock, then flung herself out of bed, slammed the window, stared a moment at where the lone yellow light shone on the frozen street, turned on her radiator, and taking a stand in the middle of the cold floor bent to touch her toes eighteen times. *Ein, zwei, drei—nicky, nocky, nye; nicky, nocky, nuss—duss, bis, druss. Ein, zwei, drei* . . .

House dark and chill. She darted in slippered feet downstairs, set the furnace going, put coffee-water on the stove to heat, and darted up to the bathroom. No other sounds in the house. Father's door closed. Patience's open. Buzz's open, but he was due home tomorrow night: five-day Christmas leave—from Georgia. Pretty damned dismal, she thought—nothing he could do at home but sleep and eat: too bad he couldn't enjoy some warm southern hospitality down there. But Patience and Tony would be out for the night—sleeping in Patience's narrow bed. She'd have to order a turkey and get a tree—the old ornaments were up-attic somewhere. And presents—my God, *presents*. She had no time. The Children's Aid office was still a mess of confused files and itinerant helpers and anxious trustees wandering in and out—and tomorrow was the neighborhood Christmas party and it seemed to be up to her to do everything, except that she had Jake, the ex-light-heavyweight, like a jinni who performed miracles at her behest.

She washed, brushed, dressed, and ran down to make the coffee.

The thought of Jake gave great comfort. With him she had the strength of ten. For some reason he called her Miss U—and because of that everyone else did, and in a way something of the old faith everyone had had in Mister Ross seemed to be transferred to Miss U. From the first Jake took charge of her and was her powerful slave. But even so there had been weeks of chaos. Just getting herself hired as an office secretary had involved days of anxious indecision and a general feeling that it would be better to wait for things to "straighten out"; and when she finally got herself installed with a secretary's weekly wage, no one knew what work was to be done—no one but Jake. A new Executive Secretary was eventually appointed, an M.A. from Columbia who had never been in Boston before, and the general chaos at the upper level was not diminished. But in a few practical ways she felt that she and Jake were doing pretty well: they'd have a party, at least, and Jake was a great one for getting coffee and cider and doughnuts and wonderful spumoni ice-cream for almost nothing. He could even perform on the harmonica whenever the need arose.

Orange juice, toast, coffee—and no daylight in the windows. She washed the few dishes, left the coffee-pot on the stove, made herself a sandwich of lettuce and a slice of potroast and a bit of mayonnaise, wrapped it up and slipped it and two apples into her handbag, and then bundled herself against the day: overshoes, coat, head-scarf, mittens. Once more upstairs, as quiet as possible, to fetch change purse and train ticket and the volume of Proust and throw the bed together—to pick up Tom Heath's letter to read on the train (slipping it into the Proust): he'd be at his sister's tonight, he'd call up, he had much he wanted to tell her— about Seattle and other things. She made downstairs, thumping a little, checked the time, and pushed on out into the cold and the wind, leaning leftward against the sleet as she slithered along the dusky street. In some inner part of her mind she heard the mutter of her father's elocutionary voice: "Talk of your cold! through the parka's fold it stabbed like a driven nail." He hadn't been saying it lately—and come to think of it she intended to get him to do it at one of the church parties. Bach in the morning, under the direction of Miss Eustace, Robert W. Service in the evening, as rendered by . . . being janitor was the job for him, all right— at least in that church, where he could act like a sort of cracker-barrel oracle and exchange wisecracks with the young philosophers. Except for the snow, of course—and so far there hadn't been much: this sleet might pile up—a degree or two colder and it would. She could do the shoveling on her way home. Ti-tum ti-tum titi-tum. "And she started on at the streak of dawn; but God! she looked ghastly pale." There was a line about sooner living in hell —she skidded on a hidden slick of ice, recovered, trotted ahead quickly. She could really take pleasure in a cold clean winter with dry snow—though even the sleet and slush weren't so bad. The rhythm kept on with her quick steps: "Strange things done in the midnight sun by the men who moil for gold."

They huddled in the lee as they always did and the train came late through the storm and patiently, patiently, they all got aboard. Day had whitened the sky but in the car, lights were on and moisture covered the windows and it seemed like night again. She re-read Tom's letter and remembered she had her choir-rehearsal tonight and the Children's Aid party tomorrow and by then Buzz would be home and she had to see about a turkey and get a tree— she knew where she could buy one for seventy-five cents, but she'd have to fetch it in the Chrysler which meant getting her father to drive it which meant that she'd have to prevent him from buying a great big two-dollar tree that would fill up half the room and have to be cut off at the top. Tom said he would call her as soon as he arrived, but with all this going on there'd hardly be time. He'd want to see Father, of course, and it might be easier if she could simply stay out of the way.

She noted to herself that she would really be very busy: there were a number of North End families that she and Jake planned to visit before Christmas. It wasn't a question of deliberately avoiding Tom—or was it? What she had done was a fact of her destiny, and on this darkest morning she accepted it, but the recollection of her last meeting with Tom Heath still troubled her. It wasn't quite clear in her memory after four months: a sort of dramatic arrogance had flared up when it shouldn't have, she knew, and she had told her love almost with pride—or even vanity, perhaps—and had dismissed Tom Heath as one unaware of the reality of passion. She had been beside herself. Yet he had taken it with quiet deliberation, like a faithful physician listening to an account of pain; he had been patient, even soothing, careful to note details, a little bit detached like one who listens with steepled fingers. He muttered that he understood—at least he would try to understand; of course he had had not the slightest inkling about how she felt —and suddenly she cried out that she hadn't been *fair*, that she had been dishonest and selfish. They were out on the back steps again—she remembered that very clearly—and he got up and put a hand on her hair: it seemed almost fatherly. "Never mind that," he said. "It isn't over, you know. Let it be—just let it be." He gestured. "I'll be back—I'll be back—"

"Oh, but it *is* over," she said, but by then he had gone.

She looked at the Proust faint-heartedly, and then opened to her mark and read: "I should have smiled pityingly had a philosopher then expressed the idea that some day, even some distant day, I should have to die, that the external forces of nature would survive me, the forces of that nature beneath whose godlike feet I was no more than a grain of dust." Once you started this kind of thing, she thought, you had to go on and on: you couldn't give up.

"Well, it's a rather dismal morning, all right," Harold Chivers said, bending over her seat. Then he sat across the aisle and looked at her with his small V-shaped smile. "I expect we'll have rain much of the day." He nodded with proprietary satisfaction. "Tell me, do you enjoy your new work? It must be quite—different."

"Enjoy?" She began a quick reply, then paused. "Why—I hadn't thought. It's a mess, of course; you can't imagine—" She saw his orderly face and figure and laughed. "What we need is a reliable statistician, though it would actually drive you nuts." She almost laughed again. "Yes, I enjoy it, now that you ask. It's worth going to town for—that's something, isn't it? And I feel virtuously poor, but honest. Not that I should boast at this stage of the game, but it's the kind of thing that has a good deal to look forward to. I don't believe we'll ever really get straightened out, but at least—at least—"

Someone passed between them in the aisle.

"And how are things with you, Harold?"

They were very satisfactory, he said; very rewarding. Of course, Erica was anxious to have a place of her own, and they were keeping an eye out for just the right thing, but meanwhile it was very pleasant for him to be in what he naturally regarded as his home, and his parents had welcomed Erica with affection—they were wholly devoted to her. Mary Kyle nodded gravely. "I'm glad it is satisfactory, Harold," she said.

They came to the station.

Then the long morning march up the platform, the steady shuffle of booted and rubbered feet, the grim facing forward to the city, the queer silence of separate people moving shoulder to shoulder in a kind of daily oblivion. It seemed like night still under the platform roof, and yellow lights made whirls in the misty air. Sprays of rain blew in from the side. Diesels hummed or roared aloud. No one seemed to speak or show human feeling. They marched intently with closed faces.